The
Orphan
List

BOOKS BY ANN BENNETT

ANN BENNETT

The Orphan List

bookouture

Published by Bookouture in 2024

An imprint of Storyfire Ltd.
Carmelite House
50 Victoria Embankment
London EC4Y 0DZ

www.bookouture.com

ISBN: 978-1-83525-672-5
eBook ISBN: 978-1-83525-671-8

For Lizzie

PROLOGUE

HEDDA

Munich, 1943

Hedda hurried under the red and black Nazi banners that fluttered above the station entrance, between the pillars of the great portico, and emerged onto the echoing concourse of Munich Hauptbahnhof. Her head bowed, her eyes on the ground, she carried her leather suitcase in one hand and clutched her handbag tightly with the other.

The station was busy, and in amongst the thronging passengers, soldiers in uniform, swastikas emblazoned on their shoulders, patrolled the concourse. Alsatians on chains strained at the leash. Shivers went through Hedda at the sight of those dogs drooling and panting, barking and growling at people in the crowd. She knew the soldiers weren't interested in her, with her long blonde plaits and blue eyes. As long as she kept her head down, she was safe, free to come and go as she pleased, but her heart went out to those who weren't.

She couldn't help her eyes from straying to one of the far platforms, where crowds of miserable, hunched people dressed in ragged clothes waited to board a train. Despite her resolve,

Hedda stopped and stared for a moment, horrified. Men, women, children, huddled together for comfort, guarded by lines of uniformed SS soldiers, smoking and chatting, guns over their shoulders, more dogs on chains snapping at their heels. Fresh chills went through Hedda. She knew who these people were, from the constant propaganda on the radio and in the newspapers. Jews, gypsies – all of them enemies of the state. They were being systematically removed from the cities for the safety of the population. They were being taken to concentration camps to work, everyone said, but Hedda couldn't help wondering, what had they actually done that meant they had to be taken away, and why did these people have no luggage?

Anger rose inside her chest and she felt her fists clenching around her bags. Then her father's voice echoed in her head: '*Don't look. Don't ask questions. Keep your head down.*' It had been his mantra. Poor Papa. Would he have said that now, if he'd still been here?

'Move on, Fräulein,' a guard tapped her shoulder, he must have seen her staring. 'These people are no concern of yours.'

She looked up into his stony face, no emotion in his pale grey eyes.

'But—'

'Move on, I said!'

Helplessly, she turned away and pushed on through the milling throng to join the queue at the ticket office, not meeting anyone's gaze. She shuffled forward and when she reached the front, she asked haltingly for a ticket to Füssen.

The female clerk behind the counter peered at her, narrowing her eyes.

'*Where* did you say?' the woman asked with a frown.

Hedda repeated her destination. It wasn't far away, around three or four hours south of Munich. The clerk must have heard of it!

'One-way, was it?' the woman enquired loudly, accusation in her voice.

Hedda glanced around to see if anyone had noticed, then turned back to the ticket clerk and nodded. That's what Sebastian had said in his letter, wasn't it? *Buy a one-way ticket to Füssen Station. There will be a car waiting for you there. Just tell the driver you are going up to the castle, Schloss Schwanburg. They will be expecting you.*

She felt her cheeks heat up as the clerk pushed the ticket under the glass screen, lips pursed, narrowed eyes still on Hedda's face. Hedda's scalp tingled with fear and shame. Did this woman know? Could she tell Hedda's secret just by looking at her face and the fact that she was buying a one-way ticket? But the woman's eyes flicked casually away from her, alighting on the man behind her in the queue.

'Next...'

Hedda pushed the ticket into her coat pocket, picked up her suitcase and sidled away from the window. She didn't dare ask which platform the train went from or what time it would leave. Looking up at the announcement board, she saw that it was going from Platform 9 and that it would depart in ten minutes. She hurried towards the platform.

The train was already in, billowing steam forming clouds on the platform. Hedda walked almost the whole length of the train, found a half-empty carriage near the front and stepped on board.

A man in a smart grey suit stood up. 'Can I help you, Fräulein?'

He took her case from her and swung it onto the luggage rack. She thanked him but took care to sit a few seats away from him. She didn't want to be drawn into conversation on this journey. Not with anyone.

The shrill blast of the stationmaster's whistle meant that the train was about to depart. Orders were shouted, doors were being slammed. Suddenly, three girls, who looked to Hedda to be about her own age, or even a little younger, scrambled on board the carriage, chatting and giggling with excitement. They found seats a few rows down from Hedda and collapsed onto them. There was a blast of the horn, the stationmaster blew his whistle again and the train began to move out of the station. It was soon gathering speed and travelling through the city.

Hedda stared out at the government buildings where red flags bearing swastikas streamed from every façade. Then they were leaving the centre behind and moving on through the blackened shells of bombed-out buildings, still smoking from last night's air raids, where children played and packs of stray dogs roamed. On through the outer suburbs of the city, past neat houses and their immaculate gardens, each flying the swastika from a flagpole as required by law. Finally, they were heading south towards the mountains, through rolling farmland, bare and featureless in the depths of winter, ravaged by war and poverty.

Looking out at the bleak countryside and mulling over her situation, Hedda leaned back against the seat and breathed a long sigh. But her mind soon went back to the crowds of desperate people on the platform. What would become of them? How could she be sitting here in the relative luxury of this train, travelling freely as if everything was all right? Surely it wasn't all right. Nothing made sense anymore.

Lulled by the motion of the train, she began to relax a little, as far as it was possible to relax. She closed her eyes and started to doze, but soon she was awakened by conversation floating over to her from the group of girls.

'I can't wait to get to the castle,' said one. Between the seats, Hedda could see the girl's plump face. Her eyes were alight with excitement.

'Me neither,' said the girl opposite her. All Hedda could see of that one was the top of her head. A flaxen plait wound

around it, secured by red ribbon. 'I can't wait to meet the officers. It will be so—'

'Oh, do stop it, Brigitte,' hissed the third girl, the one sitting
in the corner. Like the others, she was fair-haired, but unlike
them, her expression was serious, and her zealous eyes were
charged with passion. Hedda had seen that look too many times
before. 'It's not like that,' the sour-faced girl said. 'It's not meant
to be fun. It's an honour to be chosen. To do your duty for the
Fatherland and for the Führer. To be able to offer him something so precious. You should be proud.'

The hairs stood up on the back of Hedda's neck as she
instantly understood what they were talking about. It was what
Sebastian had hinted at in his letter. These girls were going to
the castle just as she was, but unlike her, they were not embarrassed or ashamed about making the journey.

Hedda looked down at the almost indiscernible but growing
bump under her coat. She stroked it gently, her eyes growing
misty as she thought of Sebastian. Then, surreptitiously, she
glanced back at the three girls, at their innocent faces. She
realised she felt pity for them. She wasn't like them at all, she
decided. She wasn't going to meet some stranger, some random
member of the SS. She was going to meet the man she knew and
loved and who had promised to take care of her. Her baby
would be born from love.

ONE

MARGARETE

Trento, Italy, 2005

The rambling old villa perched on the mountainside overlooking the town of Trento and the Adige river valley had once been the winter residence of a wealthy Italian family. Now, decaying slightly, it was the Our Lady of Mercy Home for the Elderly. The residents there couldn't afford to spend their declining years in a more modern care home, and most had no family to care for them.

Margarete was one of those. That Wednesday evening, in November 2005, she was sitting in her wing-backed armchair in the big bay window, upstairs in the old villa. She was watching the sun go down over the Dolomites. She did this every evening without fail, and every evening she wondered if she would still be around when the sun came up again the next morning. The care home faced due east, but if she moved her chair a little to the left and leaned forward, she could just about glimpse the higher mountains that lay to the north of the town, with their rocky, granite peaks. They separated Italy from Austria, and beyond that Germany. Margarete shivered, straining her eyes to look towards the north as the light faded from the sky. She knew those mountains well, and she knew what lay beyond them too.

So many memories, so many secrets that lay deep in the past beyond those hills. She would never go back to Germany again, not now; she was far too old and feeble. Her health was failing, her legs would hardly support her. After all, she needed a Zimmer frame just to get to the bathroom.

She gripped the arms of the chair with her bony fists in anger and frustration and drew in a deep breath. She had failed. Failed to tell her story despite all her efforts. She turned away from the sunset and closed her eyes, feeling the tears ooze out between the lids. She would die alone and unfulfilled.

She allowed herself to sob quietly for a second or two but then drew herself up. This wasn't about *her*, she reminded herself, wiping away her tears with the back of her hand. It was about all those she'd failed to help. She could hardly bear to think of them, living out their lives in pain and sadness, or simply in ignorance – never having known the truth about their families.

Turning stiffly in her chair, Margarete rummaged in the battered raffia shopping bag she always kept with her and pulled out her little blue leather-bound notebook. The one she had kept by her side for more than six decades. She opened it and peered down at her own handwriting. It was in blue ink, faded now on the brittle, yellowing pages, but still legible. She ran her hand down the pages of lists she had scribbled in there all those years ago. They represented names and addresses, written in a code that she'd devised herself. Looking at them now took her back to that terrible time. She could still feel the fear of discovery that had almost paralysed her as she wrote.

The door clicked open behind her and Margarete looked up sharply. There was no time to shove the notebook back in her bag. She relaxed, seeing who had entered the room. It didn't matter; Ginetta, the nurse on duty this evening, had seen the notebook many times before.

Margarete looked up into the younger woman's dark eyes as she approached. Ginetta was smiling as she always did, but the lines around her eyes betrayed her tiredness.

'How are you this evening, Margharita, my dear?' Ginetta asked, pronouncing Margarete's name the Italian way.

'I'm fine, thank you, Ginetta. It was a beautiful sunset again.'

'It was. You have such a wonderful vantage point from this room. Oh... you're looking at your old notebook again,' Ginetta smiled and Margarete caught the amusement in her voice and the indulgent look in her smile.

Margarete was sure that Ginetta thought the lists in the notebook were simply the ramblings of a confused mind. All the nurses here did; they probably laughed about it in the staffroom over their morning coffee. Let them think that. They also thought she was a native Italian. Margarete smiled. Let them think that too.

'Would you like anything to drink? Hot chocolate? Herbal tea?'

Margarete shook her head. 'Just a glass of water, please.'

'Do you want to watch TV?' Ginetta asked, pulling the heavy velvet curtain across the window. It was dark outside now, but the street lamps of Trento twinkled in the valley below and pinpricks of light picked out farms and houses high in the hills opposite.

'Yes, I would. There's a new current affairs programme on *Nachricht 24*. If you could find it for me?'

'*Nachricht 24?* That's a German channel, isn't it?' Ginetta paused and looked round, confused.

'I think so.' Margarete was deliberately vague. 'I've watched it before. It's very good.'

'All right... but... I'm not sure how you will understand,' said

Ginetta. 'Well, I'll put the subtitles on for you... if I can find them.'

Ginetta fumbled with the remote control, flicking through the satellite channels until she found the right one. Once it was on the screen and she'd activated the Italian subtitles, she manoeuvred Margarete's armchair so she was facing the screen.

'Is that all right?' Ginetta spread a blanket over Margarete's knees.

'Thank you, my dear. You're so good to me... you all are,' Margarete said, smiling gently at Ginetta.

'Not at all. You're a delight to care for, Margharita,' Ginetta replied, patting her arm. 'If only everyone in Our Lady of Mercy was so easy.'

When she'd gone, Margarete turned her attention to the television. She'd no need of the Italian subtitles, but although she pressed a few random buttons on the remote control, they remained on the screen. She shrugged. Satellite television had been a godsend to her these past few years since she'd been in the care home. Even if she couldn't go back to her native Germany, these German television programmes brought it closer, gave her a taste of her homeland.

The programme credits came up, the familiar theme tune played, then the presenter, Michel Altmann, started speaking, relaying the main news stories in Germany. They were the usual fare, politics and current events, the sort of stories Margarete was used to watching, but which had little real signif- icance for her.

'Today we have a report from our junior home affairs reporter, Kristel Meyer, about little-known stories from the war era that have been gradually emerging over the past few years and are only just beginning to be told. The victims are finally finding their voices, and discovering the truth about their past, sixty years after the fall of the Third Reich. I'll hand you straight over to Kristel, who will tell you more...'

Margarete sat up in her chair and leaned forward, her eyes peeled as Kristel Meyer, a young reporter with a photogenic face, long blonde hair and earnest, intelligent blue eyes began to speak. Margarete blinked. That face brought back so many memories. Memories of so many other young girls with blonde hair and blue eyes.

'A lot has been written about the Third Reich,' Kristel Meyer began, 'and yet, it is sometimes difficult for my generation of Germans to understand the enormity of what happened during the Nazi regime, especially during the war years. We have learned about the unspeakable persecution of the Jews, about the concentration camps, the death camps, and we are truly horrified by what we hear. We struggle to comprehend why it could have happened, and how it could have been allowed to happen. We have been taught about the Nazi theories of racial purity, of their desire to create a Master Race which led to the expulsion and killing of so many.

'But there was another side to this policy; a side that's less well-known than the Holocaust. As well as trying to purify and ethnically cleanse the German population, the Nazis also wanted to replenish and increase it... to breed a "master Race" of Aryans, as they termed it. To do so, they established the Lebensborn programme. Lebensborn means "spring of life". The programme was conceived by Himmler, the head of the SS, firstly to encourage officers under his command to father as many children as they could, but it developed from there into much, much more. Only now, sixty years after the end of the war, the victims of that programme, many of whom grew up as outcasts themselves, are finally emerging and speaking out, forming support groups and helping each other to research their past and try to make sense of it...'

Margarete's mouth had dropped open. She was transfixed by Kristel Meyer, by her face, by her voice, but most of all by everything she was saying. Margarete realised her hands were shaking, her heart was racing, her breath was shallow and fast. She watched the TV, hardly moving a muscle, as several people in succession were interviewed by Kristel. All were in their sixties, all were children of the Lebensborn programme, all had lived their lives in ignorance of who at least one of their parents had been. Some had tried fruitlessly to find out; others had found out and been horrified to discover they were the descendants of people who had committed atrocities. All spoke movingly about how the circumstances of their birth had affected their lives.

Finally, the report was drawing to a close and Kristel Meyer spoke directly to the camera.

'Today's moving stories are just the tip of the iceberg,' she said. 'There are thousands of people out there affected in many different ways by the Lebensborn programme. And they are not just in Germany – they are also in Norway, in Poland, Ukraine, the Czech Republic, and in many other countries occupied and subjugated by the Nazi regime. This has been my first report on this subject, but it won't be the last. If you'd like to tell your story, or if you or your family have been affected in some way by the Lebensborn programme, we would like to hear from you. Please do either email, write in or give us a call on this number...'

A telephone number was being displayed on the screen. Margarete stared at it numbly, her mind sluggish from the shock of what she'd just watched. She sat there for a few moments recovering, allowing her heartbeat to slow down, her jumbled emotions to settle. And as she became calmer and her mind stopped racing, she realised that this could be her chance. At last, after all these years of watching and waiting, praying for some way of healing the past, perhaps now was the time.

She needed to write down that number! She grabbed her basket and fumbled for a pen, but by the time she'd found it and a scrap of paper to write on – even in that moment of panic, she didn't want to write in her treasured notebook – the number had disappeared from the screen and the presenter was introducing the next report. Kristel Meyer's face had gone.

Margarete grabbed at the bell that would ring in the staffroom. She didn't often press it, only if she really needed something. She didn't normally like to bother the staff but now was an emergency, if ever there was one.

Within seconds, Ginetta was bursting through the door, her face a picture of concern.

'What has happened, Margharita? Are you ill?'

Margerete shook her head. 'Not ill. I'm sorry to alarm you, but I would like you to do something for me.'

'Of course. Just tell me what it is.'

'I would like you to telephone the programme for me,' she said, waving her hand towards the screen.

'What, that programme? The German programme?'

'Yes. Could you find out their number and phone them for me, please?'

'Well, I could... but—' Ginetta frowned, confused again.

'They did a report on the Lebensborn programme in Nazi Germany.'

'Lebensborn?' Ginetta frowned.

'Yes... it means spring of life.' Margarete looked up into Ginetta's puzzled face. How could she even begin to tell her about it? 'It was a sort of... a sort of breeding programme.'

Ginetta's face fell. 'Why did you want me to phone them about it?'

'They want people to call in if they have a story to tell about Lebensborn,' Margarete said, hating to see the expression on Ginetta's face turn from one of confusion to suspicion. 'Please could you tell them that I need to speak to them urgently. I have a story to tell. A story that I'm sure they will want to hear.'

TWO

KRISTEL

Munich, 2005

Kristel clambered up the wooden stairs to the top-floor apartment in Maximillianstrasse. Even though she prided herself on being fairly fit, tonight it was quite a struggle to get to the top. Her whole body ached; it had been a long and exhausting day. In contrast, though, her mind was buzzing with exhilaration.

She was late home – even later than usual. There had been a lot to do in the studio after the programme had finally aired. She'd texted Joachim to let him know she'd be back later than planned, but he hadn't replied. He would have been watching the programme, surely? After all, it was the first time she'd presented a full report on her own. Perhaps he'd given up waiting for her and was already in bed?

Once inside the apartment, she took off her boots. The place was in darkness, so she crept around, trying not to wake Joachim, but her stomach rumbled with hunger. She realised she hadn't eaten anything since lunchtime when she'd grabbed a baguette from the network canteen. She'd been so wound up about presenting her slot on the programme, she hadn't given a thought to food all afternoon.

Now, she pulled open the fridge and sighed. Neither she nor Joachim had had the time to go to the supermarket that week and there were just a few slices of pink ham, curling at the edges, some stale rye bread and a block of smoked cheese going hard with age. On the top shelf, though, she noticed the remains of a takeaway pizza. It must have been left over from Joachim's meal that evening. That was better than nothing. She took it out of the fridge and switched on the oven. She couldn't bear to eat it cold. Closing the fridge, she noticed half a bottle of Pinot Grigio in the door. It was a few days old, probably past its best, but she took it out and poured herself a generous glass. Pulling a stool up to the breakfast bar, she took a welcome sip.

Sitting alone in the half-darkness, she regretted not having gone along with the production team to the nearby bar for a debrief on the programme. She'd wanted to get home to Joachim, to hear what he'd thought about her piece, to feel his arms around her. But now, she was wondering why. She took another sip of wine.

'Hello... I didn't hear you come in.' Joachim stood in the kitchen doorway, framed by the light from the street lamps outside. He was wearing his grey towelling dressing-gown and his face was unshaven, his dark hair tousled, his eyes bleary.

'I'm sorry I was late,' Kristel said. 'I texted to let you know. I thought you might still be up. Did you watch the programme?'

'Of course.' He came towards her, slipped his arms around her and kissed her on the lips. 'You were very good. Very impressive. It was a moving piece.'

She put her wine down and kissed him back, relaxing a little.

'I'm glad you thought so,' she said, 'It was a huge moment for me. I was very nervous.'

'Well, you didn't look it. You looked the epitome of calm.'

He sat down on the stool beside her. There was something in his eyes that told her he had more to say on the subject of her report but was holding back.

The timer on the oven pinged. She took the pizza out, found a chopping board and began to cut it into triangular slices. 'Do you want any?'

Joachim shook his head. 'I'm still full from the half I ate earlier.'

Kristel sat back down and bit into her first slice.

'I'm glad you watched it. I was really hoping that you were,' she said. 'It helped me focus.'

'I wouldn't *not* have watched you. You know that,' he replied, but there was still that question mark in his tone.

'So, what's the problem, then?' Kristel asked between mouthfuls. 'You've got something to say about it. Something critical, I can tell. Tell me what it is.'

Even as she spoke, she knew she sounded aggressive, and she was already regretting her outburst. But she was tired, and the stress and emotion of the day were threatening to overwhelm her.

Joachim cleared his throat and ran his hand through his mop of dark hair, pushing it back from his face. 'I was a bit surprised about some of what you said, to tell you the truth.'

Kristel frowned, 'Surprised? But I've told you all about it. There was virtually nothing in my piece that we haven't talked about.'

'It's just when you announced that you wanted people to come forward with their stories. You hadn't told me that. I thought you were just doing *one* report on the Lebensborn programme. Not a whole series of them... that's all.'

Kristel's heart sank. This wasn't entirely unexpected, but all the same she was taken aback that he was commenting on her work decisions. It wasn't like him – he was normally supportive about her journalism and her career choices, respectful of her decisions.

'We've talked about this before,' Joachim went on. 'You know how I feel about raking over the past.'

'Yes, I know,' Kristel said, not wanting to have that conversation again now. Not while she was as tired as she was and as emotionally charged.

They had discussed this many times before and in many different ways, but it always came back to the same thing: they could never agree on how to respond to their country's shameful past. They had both learned history at school, been taught about the Nazis and the crimes they committed, the dark shadows that hung over their history. But now, their attitudes towards how it should be dealt with were fundamentally opposed.

Looking into Joachim's eyes, Kristel knew exactly what he would say if they discussed it again now. He'd said it so many times before: '*It is truly, truly terrible but how can we, in our generation, bear any blame at all for what happened back then? We weren't even born. Even our parents were either babies or very young children. We need to move on, Kristel. Not keep digging up the past and dwelling on it. We need to get on and live our own lives in a positive way, and make sure that such a dreadful thing could never happen again.*'

Kristel herself had a far more complicated, more emotional and nuanced response, one that she didn't even fully understand herself. She knew what Joachim said was logical, but her heart told her something different. There was something invisible drawing her back to examine that terrible time again and again. Not to rake over it, but to try to make sense of it, perhaps to try to atone for it in some strange way. Besides, she had another reason for wanting to find out more about the Lebensborn programme in particular, one she wasn't ready to share with Joachim quite yet. This was the one thing she'd held back from telling him and she still wasn't ready to.

'Look, why don't we talk about this another time?' Kristel said. 'We're both tired now.'

'All right,' he said. 'Oh, by the way, the wedding venue called today. They want to finalise numbers. We need to firm up the guest list this week if possible. Did you think any more about inviting your mother?'

Kristel blinked at him, at the sharp shift in subject matter. This one was hardly less controversial than the last.

'I haven't had a chance to think about that today,' she replied. 'I need a bit more time. I'm really not sure whether it's a good idea, Joachim.'

'I know it's difficult for you,' he said. 'But you *are* her only daughter. She'd surely want to be at your wedding.'

Kristel shrugged, wishing he wasn't pursuing this matter now either. 'I'm not so sure, Joachim. She's never been there for me before. Poor Dad had to be mother and father to me after she left.'

'I know... look, I'm sorry. Let's talk about that another time too, shall we? I'll get back to them and say we need a bit more time to work out the final numbers.'

'OK,' Kristel said, biting her nail, her emotions crashing down to earth as she thought of her mother, Greta, with her high-flying academic career in America, her lecture tours, her publications, her TV interviews. They barely spoke from one year to the next. And the conversation they'd had the last time they had spoken on the phone, Kristel would prefer to forget. There was such a gulf between them now, why pretend that everything was normal by inviting her mother to the wedding? Why not just acknowledge that they were now effectively strangers and move on?

But still... her mind went back to the discovery she'd made when she'd been going through her father's papers after his death the previous year. If Greta did come to the wedding, perhaps she would be prepared to discuss it then?

'Do you mind if I go back to bed now?' Joachim's voice broke into her thoughts. 'I've got an early meeting in the morning. It's the board, so quite important. I need to get some sleep.'

'Of course. I'll just finish this pizza and I'll be there too.'

'Goodnight then... Hey, why don't we meet up for lunch tomorrow? We've hardly spent any time together lately.'

'Yes... that would be lovely,' Kristel replied instantly, not wanting to let him down. He was right, they'd hardly even sat down to eat a meal together these past few weeks. But, at the same time, she was wondering how she would fit a lunchtime in with everything she'd have to do tomorrow in the aftermath of her report. There would be so many calls into the studio she would want to follow up...

'And well done this evening. I'm so proud of you, Kristel...' He kissed her on the forehead and she watched him wander off to bed.

Sighing, Kristel poured herself a splash more wine and, swallowing it quickly, finished the last piece of pizza. The exchange with Joachim had niggled her. Why hadn't he given her more support? Why did he have to raise difficulties when she was so obviously exhausted? She thought about their impending wedding and closed her eyes, pushing the questions away, not wanting to examine them too deeply. She wasn't sure whether it was the never-ending complications and expense of organising the ceremony and the reception that was getting to her, or something much deeper, something much more worrying and important. She was far too tired to think about that now. She would think about it when her head was clearer.

She washed the wine glass and the chopping board and stacked them in the plate rack. She was drying her hands when her phone rang. She rushed to grab it from the counter, not wanting to disturb Joachim.

It was Nicole, one of the researchers from the studio.

'Kristel? Thank goodness! I'm so glad I've got hold of you. I thought you might have gone to bed.'

'I was about to. What is it?'

'I thought you'd want to know straight away. A few people have called in. Most of them have discovered or suspected they were Lebensborn babies and have been trying to research their past with little success. We've taken down all their details and will follow them up. But there was one that stood out as a bit different. Michel's still here in the studio and he thought you'd like to be the one to follow it up.'

Kristel was instantly awake, her reporter's instinct piqued. 'Carry on?'

'Well, we got a call from a care home in Trento, in Italy. The lady who phoned, Ginetta Spinetti, is a carer there. She could barely speak any German, and I don't speak Italian, but she could speak a bit of English, so that's how we communicated. Ginetta said that there's an old lady in the home there who watched the programme. This old lady absolutely insisted that Ginetta called us tonight. It took Ginetta a long time to find the number and at first, she couldn't get through, that's why she called so late.

'The old lady, whose name is Margharita Bianchi, is ninety. She says she has a lot to tell us about the Lebensborn programme and that she is ready to tell her story. Ginetta wasn't sure of Margharita's exact involvement, but she said that Margharita has a notebook from that time that she thinks we will be very interested in. Margharita is German apparently, but until this evening, Ginetta had always thought she was Italian. She's been in the care home for several years and until this evening, no one had even suspected she was German.'

'That sounds absolutely fascinating,' Kristel said, her mind doing some quick calculations. If Margharita was ninety, she would have been born around 1915, which would have made her about twenty-five in 1940. The right age for someone who might have information about the programme. Perhaps she was even a Lebensborn mother.

'Michel wondered if you could go to Trento tomorrow morning and interview her.'

'Of course! I'd be glad to,' Kristel said straight away.

'I'll check out travel arrangements now and send you an email, together with all the details about Ginetta's call.'

'Fabulous. I'll log on from home first thing in the morning in case I need to go straight to the airport from here. Thanks, Nicole. That's brilliant news.'

Kristel ended the call, flushed with renewed excitement. This could be it! This could be the story she'd been hoping to uncover. She couldn't wait to travel to Trento and meet Margharita. She went through to the dark bedroom, where she undressed as quietly as she could. As she slipped into bed beside Joachim, he turned over.

'Straight to the airport in the morning?' he asked, sounding annoyed. 'Where are you off to?'

'Oh, I'm sorry. I didn't mean to disturb you.'

'I couldn't help overhearing. Don't they ever leave you alone?'

'It's my fault. I should have switched my phone off,' she said, but even as she said that, she was grateful that she hadn't. She wouldn't have wanted to miss this opportunity. 'An old lady who lives in Italy has come forward with some information about the Lebensborn programme. She's ninety years old, so it must be first-hand information. She was actually *there* at the time... it's so exciting. So, I'm off to Trento in the morning to interview her. It's too good an opportunity to miss.'

Joachim was silent for a few moments, then he said, 'I guess we'll have to have lunch another time.'

Guilt washed through Kristel. She hadn't even given it a second thought, Nicole's news had pushed it completely out of her mind. 'I'm sorry, Joachim,' she said, moving closer to him. 'You don't mind, do you? I'll make it up to you, I promise.'

She slipped her arms around him and kissed him on the shoulder, but he tensed and moved away from her.

'I'm tired, Kristel. I need to get some sleep. I've got that board meeting in the morning and I need to be able to think straight.'

She took her arms from him and turned over to face the other way. Soon, his steady breathing told her that Joachim was asleep. But Kristel lay awake into the small hours, her mind going over and over the events of the day, the excitement mixed with nervous tension of presenting her report, the conversation with Nicole, the unsatisfactory situation with Joachim. But, in due course, tiredness overwhelmed her and as she drifted off to sleep, she kept imagining a white-haired old lady, sitting there in her care home deep in the South Tyrol mountains, poring over her memories of what happened more than six decades before.

THREE

HEDDA

Munich, 2005

The downstairs neighbours were making a noise as usual. Hedda couldn't hear their words, but she could tell from the rise and fall of their voices that they were arguing – yelling at each other, in fact. She sighed in dismay. It never stopped. If they weren't arguing, the baby was screaming, or they were playing their dreadful music too loud. Thump, thump, thump, it would go on for hours at a time. Sometimes it carried on into the small hours and Hedda had to wear earplugs just to get some sleep. She'd thought about going down to ask them to be quiet, but was worried how they might react. It might actually cause more problems.

Now she turned up her television to try to drown it out, but the angry voices went on and on. Then came the sound of doors slamming, feet running down the communal stairs. She shook her head, tutting. If it wasn't the neighbours underneath her, it was the ones next door – the ones with the teenage son who was always in trouble with the police. When the parents were out at work, he would have his friends round to drink and take drugs. She could smell the marijuana smoke drifting along the balcony.

Even her poor cat was unsettled. Poor old Max. He was sitting upright on the floor in front of the electric fire, his ears pricked, his tail flicking from side to side, poised for fight or flight. Hedda bent down and rubbed his head. It must be terrifying for him.

She heaved herself out of her chair and went to fetch a packet of biscuits from the cupboard. While she was there, she poured herself a small glass of schnapps. It was a habit she'd only developed in the past few years since she'd been living alone here in the flat.

She'd given up her work as a secretary in a big pharmaceutical company more than fifteen years before and her pension didn't stretch very far. After her husband, Hari, had died, Hedda had sold their house in Nuremberg to pay off his debts. Not that they'd been living together by then – Hedda's pain and depression had driven a wedge between them, and he'd moved into an apartment on the edge of town, but they'd remained friends to the end. When he died, she'd decided to move back to Munich where she'd grown up, to find somewhere in the city to rent. The flat in the tenement block was very cheap, but shortly after Hedda had moved in, she'd realised why. She'd been so naive! If she'd have checked the place out properly, she would have discovered that there were many problem families living here.

She'd been here for five years now, lacking the funds or the will to move away. She was lonely and often miserable. A couple of shots of schnapps helped to blot it all out, or at least to blur the edges a little.

As she sat back down and sipped the fiery liquid, she realised that the noise from downstairs had stopped. Hedda heaved a sigh and turned her attention to the news programme on the TV. A young reporter, Kristel Meyer, was presenting and Hedda watched her with interest. Kristel had been on TV before and Hedda loved to see her. So fresh-faced, so full of energy and youthful enthusiasm. Just looking at Kristel made Hedda nostalgic for how she'd once been herself. Before her world came crashing down.

Her heart missed a beat, though, when she heard the subject matter of Kristel's report.

'Lebensborn!' Hedda breathed, repeating the word out loud, and she leaned forward and peered at the screen, anxious not to miss a word. She watched the deep emotion on the faces of the people interviewed, those who had found out they had been Lebensborn babies, their struggle to find the truth and their often heartbreaking discoveries. Her chest tightened with empathy for them, her eyes blurred with tears.

When the report had finished, she poured herself another drink and let it course through her. She needed it, just to steady herself after what she'd just seen. Her hands were shaking and her heart racing. Examining her own reaction, though, she realised that beyond the shock, she was actually relieved. It gave her a glimmer of hope to know that people were now talking openly about Lebensborn and that mothers and their estranged children were trying to make contact with each other.

Stiffly, Hedda got up from her chair and crossed the room to the mantelpiece above the electric fire. Max stood up and rubbed himself against her legs, but she barely noticed him. She picked up a framed photograph that had sat on her mantelpiece since a few days after Hari had died. She'd kept it for all these years, but now she looked at it closely with fresh eyes. It was the only connection she had to that time.

The photograph was fading with age, but the figures could still be seen quite clearly. A young, sweet-faced Hedda, her luxuriant blonde hair braided into a single long plait. She was standing beside another young woman, a little older than herself. The other girl's hair was slightly darker, but their features were so alike, they could have been sisters. The other girl was cradling a baby in her arms. It was swaddled in a white blanket, a shock of fuzzy, white hair just visible. Both girls were looking down at the baby and smiling, their eyes full of emotion. Behind them was a regimented flower bed and a neatly clipped hedge, and behind that, in the distance, loomed the towers and spires of a medieval castle. It looked like something from a Grimm's fairy tale.

With shaking hands, Hedda turned the picture over and fumbled with the clips on the back, realising as she did so that she hadn't looked inside it for many years. The cardboard came away from the frame and she saw that it was still there, nestling between the card and the back of the photograph, a lock of pale blonde hair, tied with a scrap of faded red ribbon. A lump rose in her throat and tears formed in her eyes as, with trembling fingers, she picked it up and held it to her face. She drew in a deep breath. Even now, all these years later, she could still catch a faint trace of it. That unmistakeable scent of a new-born baby that spoke straight to her heart.

Sinking back down on her chair, still holding the lock of hair between shaking fingers, she took another gulp of schnapps and let the memories come flooding back.

She was seventeen again and back there in the city of Munich as it was then, that early autumn of 1942, the day it all began. She was walking into college arm in arm with her best friends, Beate and Elsa, one on either side of her. It was the first day of a new term.

There were crowds of young people descending on the building in Marienplatz that morning. The girls were separated from the boys, of course. The laws of the Third Reich decreed that they weren't allowed to attend the same classes. That rankled with Hedda. She knew she deserved an education equal to any boy. She'd been a bright student and had yearned to continue her academic studies. She'd dreamed of becoming a doctor or a lawyer, but now she was compelled to attend classes on domestic skills alongside all the other girls she'd grown up and attended school with. Cookery, childcare, and household accounts were their main subjects, alongside the compulsory study of the geography of Germany, the history and philosophy of Naziism and the science of racial purity. Those who showed most intelligence and promise, the lucky ones, got to learn secretarial skills – shorthand and typing. Hedda was one of those, so in the afternoons she attended secretarial classes too, although that was hardly stimulating

It was that morning in September 1942 when she first noticed *him*. He was walking with a group of other boys. They were laughing and talking amongst themselves, moving towards the building just ahead of Hedda and her two friends. The paths of the two groups were about to converge. Walking at the rear of his group, he dropped back, and stood aside to let the girls pass, while the other boys barged ahead in front of them. He was well-built and good-looking, with dark hair and blue eyes, but it was the look in those eyes that Hedda noticed above everything. It was a look of intelligence, with the promise of something different from all the others. It was that which attracted her. In that split second, Hedda caught his eye and felt herself flushing at the way he was looking back at her.

The girls went on up the steps and into the building in silence, but once they were inside their classroom, Beate said, 'Whoever was that? I've never seen *him* before.'

'Me neither,' said Elsa. 'He must be new. I think we might have noticed him if we'd seen him before!' and they both giggled, nudging each other and rolling their eyes.

Hedda didn't join in. Much as she loved her friends, she'd

never liked their shameless attention-seeking behaviour with young men; she'd always thought it crass and undignified. Besides, she had no need to gossip or speculate about the newcomer. She knew it was her he'd been looking at, from the way he'd caught her eye and the look they'd exchanged. She knew in her bones that their paths would cross again soon.

Not that she would be interested in him once she got to know him, she thought grimly as she settled behind her desk and took her domestic science textbooks out of her bag. He was probably just like all the other young men around her, pumped up with Nazi ideas, full of their own superiority and self-importance. He would most likely be someone she would have no point of contact with, someone who terrified her with his fanaticism for the Nazi regime and everything it stood for.

After that first encounter, she'd almost forgotten about him, until a few days later she spotted him across the aisle on the tram on the way home to where she lived with her family in the southern suburbs of the city. She'd been reading a book to pass the time on the journey and sensed that someone was looking at her. When she looked up, it was straight into those slate-blue eyes. He held her gaze and smiled quizzically at her. She wanted to look away, but something compelled her to keep looking straight at him until the bell clanged, the tram ground to a halt and passengers surged through the aisle between them to disembark.

The next tram stop was Hedda's. She got up from her seat and hoisted her leather satchel onto her shoulder. To her surprise, the young man got to his feet too.

'I'm Sebastian,' he said, holding out his hand.

Hedda shook his hand and told him her name just as the tram screeched to a jerky stop and she was thrown against his shoulder. She moved quickly away and climbed down from the tram with a group of other passengers. Sebastian climbed down behind her and they stood on the pavement awkwardly.

'Do you live near here?' Hedda asked.

'A few blocks away. We've only just moved to Munich.'

'Oh, really?'

'Yes. My father is an engineer and a businessman. His company has posted him here to run their Bavaria factory.'

'Oh,' Hedda said, trying to keep her voice from betraying any reaction. She was relieved that at least Sebastian's father wasn't a member of the SS or working for the Nazis in the Brown House – their party headquarters in the centre of Munich. But if he was a businessman running a factory, that raised all sorts of uncomfortable questions in her mind too. It was common knowledge that most businessmen who hadn't been drafted into the Wehrmacht had either profited from the confiscation of businesses from Jewish proprietors or were using Jews and other enemies of the state as unpaid labour in their factories.

'Would you like me to walk you home?' Sebastian said. 'It's getting dark.'

'No, it's fine, thank you,' she replied, trying not to betray her disappointment. Despite her attraction to Sebastian, she was almost sure now that his family would have strong connections with the Nazi Party. She must have been mistaken about that look in his eye when she'd first seen him. He wasn't going to be a kindred spirit at all; he was just like all the others. 'It's only just round the corner and I'm used to walking by myself, thank you,' she said.

'Of course...' He sounded a little disappointed. 'But do take care. See you tomorrow.'

'Perhaps,' she said, turning and walking away without looking back.

The next day, he was on the same tram home again and the day after that too. He always seemed so genuine and earnest when they spoke and sounded so disappointed when she refused his offer to accompany her home each time.

On the fourth day, she relented. 'All right then,' she said. 'But, as I said, it's only just round the corner.'

'I'll carry your bag, it looks heavy,' he said, taking her satchel loaded with books. As they turned into Hedda's street, it began to rain. They speeded up and Sebastian held her satchel over her head. By the time her house came into view at the end of the road, they were running quite quickly and Hedda couldn't help laughing at how ridiculous they must look. Nearing her house, she saw her mother standing in the front window, and her little sister standing beside her. Her mother waved and rushed to the front door.

'Clara and I were just about to come and meet you with an umbrella, but I see you have company!' her mother called down the front path. 'Introduce us to your friend, Hedda. Won't you come in and get dry, young man?'

'I'd love to, , as long as it's all right with Hedda.'

'Of course. It's fine,' muttered Hedda, knowing she had no choice in the matter, and within minutes they were all sitting round the kitchen stove cradling warm drinks in their hands and Sebastian was telling them all about life in Berlin, about his family – he had two older brothers, both serving in the Wehrmacht – how glad he was to be now living in Munich and how much he was enjoying his classes at the technical college. Hedda watched her mother and younger sister's faces as he spoke, their eyes glued to Sebastian's face, smiling and laughing, clearly charmed by his every word, just as she was.

After that, without really thinking about it, they slipped into a regular routine. Sebastian would sit beside her on the tram after college and walk her back to her house. He would come inside and have a hot drink and a pastry that her mother would have made that afternoon, eking out the rations skilfully, as she always did. They would all chat amiably for half an hour or so before Sebastian gathered up his bag to leave.

'Oh well, my studies call, and Mutti will worry if I'm late home. Thank you for the tea, Frau Jenner.'

'Not at all. Such a pleasure. Please come again.'

In none of those discussions did Sebastian betray any hint that he believed in Nazi propaganda or approved of their policies. But, on the other hand, neither did he reveal that he disapproved of the regime. He was far too clever, Hedda thought, to let his guard drop in that way. They hardly knew each other and you couldn't be too careful. Anyone could be a spy or an informer nowadays. They lurked in the most unlikely of places and often hid in plain sight.

On the Wednesday of the second week, she saw him in the corridor at school. She told him that in the evening she would be attending a Bund Deutscher Mädel, Association of German Girls meeting after college, so she wouldn't be on the usual tram home.

'Oh,' he said, sounding surprised. 'I didn't think you would have joined that particular organisation.'

She looked at him. Was this her opportunity to come clean, to tell him the truth about her views?

'It's compulsory for all girls who want to study on the secretarial course to be in the BDM,' she replied. 'There isn't any choice about it...' She looked into his eyes, hoping for some sign from him that she could safely speak her mind.

'But, of course, if it *hadn't* been compulsory, you would have joined up anyway, wouldn't you? For the sake of the Führer and the Fatherland?'

Was he testing her? Was he mocking her? Her heart beat a little faster. She had no way of knowing. Despite the hint of a smile playing on his lips, there was no glint of humour in his eyes.

'Of course,' she said, keeping a completely straight face, 'that goes without saying.'

'You know, I'm a member of the Hitler Youth myself. That

organisation is compulsory too. There are *some* benefits, though...'

She looked at him with steady eyes. What he was saying was still not betraying any confidences.

'I'll perhaps see you on Thursday then,' he said, and Hedda went off to her classes, wondering what to make of his comments.

But, that evening, Hedda's world changed for ever.

The BDM meeting was much like any other. After roll call, the girls went through their rigorous exercise drills, then sat cross-legged on the wooden floor of the hall to watch a propaganda film about the important role of women in the Fatherland. Hedda had seen this particular film several times before. It extolled the virtues of demure beauty, domesticity, staying at home to look after the family, bearing many beautiful blonde children and supporting the community by voluntary work for the Party. It was all she could do to keep her eyes open until the end and not to roll them in disapproval when they were open.

She glanced at the faces of the girls around her and wondered how many of them felt the same as she did about the message of the film. She was aware that Beate and Elsa did; they had often spoken about how unfair it was that they were unable to study or have careers or even jobs like their male counterparts, but such views could not be expressed or even hinted at in this environment. The local BDM leader, Elke Schultz, sat at the front beside the screen, facing the audience, her jaw set, her hard eyes scanning the rows of girls for any hint of dissent.

By eight o'clock, it was over. Relieved, the girls pulled their coats on over their BDM uniforms – white blouses with a kerchief displaying the swastika, neat black skirts and ankle socks. They spilled out of the hall onto the dark street and said their goodbyes, going off to catch their trams separately.

The tram was less busy at that hour than on Hedda's usual journey home. There were only a few workers travelling to and from late shifts huddled in their seats, most of them asleep. It trundled through the night at speed, the blinds pulled down in compliance with blackout regulations.

Hedda thought about Sebastian and how he normally sat beside her on the journey now. How much longer it seemed to take without him. The swaying of the tram made her feel dozy and she was just closing her eyes when the shrill sound of an air-raid warning startled her awake. Within seconds, the tram ground to a halt.

'Everybody off!' The guard ushered the passengers off the tram quickly, telling them to go straight to a nearby air-raid shelter – a pillbox, just visible at the end of the street.

Hedda got down from the tram and began to run, following the other passengers, in the direction of the shelter. Before they could reach it, though, beams of spotlights were scanning the sky above the buildings and the first enemy aircraft were visible, flying low towards the city centre.

Hedda ran on, her heart hammering, ducking her head automatically as more aircraft screamed overhead. She'd experienced air raids before, but nothing so close. She could hear the rattle of anti-aircraft fire, followed by the crash of explosions, as she ducked inside the shelter and huddled amongst the strangers already inside, shivering with the cold, as well as naked fear.

They stayed there for an hour or so, nobody speaking, until the sound of explosions had ceased, and the drone of the last aircraft had finally subsided. Wearily, Hedda unwound her stiff limbs and climbed out of the shelter along with everyone else. She was still a couple of kilometres from home, but the tram had been abandoned by the guard and driver. The only option was to walk.

It was a clear, cold evening. The sky was filled with stars and her way was lit by the light from the huge fires blazing in the aftermath of the bombing. Even though the fires were some distance away, in the centre of the city, the light from them spread as far as her southern suburb. But drawing closer to home, she realised that something wasn't right here too. Then she noticed as she walked on that there were fires here – right here in the streets in front of her. People were running to and fro, shouting and screaming in panic; others were lying in the road, dead or injured. Hedda tried not to look at them, panic rising in her own chest. And as she neared home, the dreadful thought entered her mind that her own house might have been hit.

Passing her usual tram stop, she pushed on, hoping against hope she was wrong, but rounding the corner, her worst fears were confirmed. She stopped walking and sank to her knees. There was her house up ahead, there was no mistaking it, a pile of bricks and dust amongst the flames. The whole street had been hit, every house obliterated, reduced to rubble.

Hedda knelt there on the road, the gritty surface grazing her bare knees. She was sobbing, oblivious to people moving around her, screaming, shouting, throwing buckets of water onto the flames. With the clanging of bells, a fire engine arrived and firemen doused the flames with a huge hose, but with little effect. Still the street kept burning.

Hedda knew without a shadow of a doubt that her whole family would have been inside the house when the bomb had hit. Clara would have been in bed, Mother in the kitchen washing up, Father, home from the office, reading the newspaper in front of the fire. Their habits never changed.

She turned away, overcome with despair. She couldn't bear to stay here any longer. Hedda had no idea where she could go, but she had no care anyway for her own comfort or safety. Blinded by tears, she stumbled back along the road. As she reached the tram stop, she heard footsteps coming towards her. She looked up and there he was, walking towards her – Sebastian.

'Hedda!' He took her in his arms and drew her close to him, wrapping her in his warm embrace. 'I came as soon as I saw where the bombs had hit. I'm so, so sorry.'

She collapsed against him, sobbing uncontrollably. He drew her closer and held her tight for a long time. She realised, looking back all these years later, that that was the start of it.

FOUR

MARGARETE

Trento, 2005

When Margarete awoke the next morning, it all came back to her in a rush: the television programme on the German news network, the shock of watching Kristel Meyer's report, Ginetta's incredulous face as Margarete revealed enough about her past to get the other woman to take things seriously enough to make that phone call.

Ginetta had appeared back in Margarete's room several times that evening to report on her progress in contacting *Nachricht* 24. At first, she'd had trouble finding the telephone number, then she'd had great difficulty getting through to the network. From Ginetta's exhausted, despairing expression, her drooping shoulders each time they spoke, Margarete had known that Ginetta would far rather have given up and gone home to her husband than keep on trying to get through to the TV network an hour or more after her shift had ended. But Ginetta had a heart of gold and she always put the residents' needs before her own. Although Margarete felt a little guilty about preying on Ginetta's good nature, she knew that Ginetta wouldn't stop trying.

It was half-past eleven when Ginetta had come through to Margarete's room, looking relieved.

'I finally got through to the network,' she had said. 'I spoke to someone on the research team and told them all about you.'

'What did they say?' Margarete had asked.

'They sounded very interested. They took down all your details. They're going to discuss it with the producer and call back in the morning.'

'Thank goodness!' Margarete had breathed, but then, even before she'd taken her next breath, doubts had instantly besieged her. 'Do you think they really will call back?'

'I think so... The young woman I spoke to, Nicole, sounded very professional. She thought that one of the reporters might come and visit you here in Trento, to interview you.'

Margarete had been silent for a few moments, digesting the information. Then she had turned to Ginetta and said, 'You are a dear, kind soul, Ginetta. I can't thank you enough for your help this evening.'

'It was no trouble,' Ginetta said, sitting down heavily in the chair beside Margarete's and reaching for Margarete's hand.

'I wish I could understand, though, Margharita,' Ginetta said in a gentle voice, her eyes searching Margarete's own, 'why you never told anyone here that you were actually German.'

Margarete didn't answer immediately. How could she begin to explain the pain and fear of a lifetime to someone who hadn't lived through those terrible times, someone who hadn't had to make the choices she had made and been forced to live with the consequences?

'I'm not sure,' she said haltingly. The truth was so painful, so complicated that she didn't know where to start. 'It's difficult to explain,' she said at last. 'I was afraid, I suppose...'

'Afraid?' Ginetta repeated gently. 'But what is there to be afraid of now?'

What was there to be afraid of? For someone who'd lived in fear for their entire adult life, that was a difficult question to answer.

'I'm not sure where to begin.'

After another pause, Ginetta patted Margarete's hand and stood up.

'Don't worry. I'm sure you have very good reasons, Margharita. Perhaps you'll be able to tell the reporter when they come.'

'But what if they don't call back?' Margarete said, her anxieties descending again.

'Oh, I'm sure they will. I'll leave a note for Lorenzo. He'll be working in the office in the morning. I'll ask him to call them if by any chance they haven't called back by lunchtime. Now, let's get you to bed, shall we? It's way past your normal bedtime.'

Now, in the first light of the chilly winter morning, Margerete listened to the sounds of the care home gradually awakening – the clatter of pots and pans in the kitchen, the music from various radios and televisions, the nurses knocking on doors to wake residents, the creak of floorboards in the room above her.

Would they all be talking about her now? she wondered. Would they be gossiping about the fact that she was really German and had hidden it from them the whole time? Would they feel betrayed, and think that they couldn't trust her anymore? She sincerely hoped not. Everyone here in Our Lady of Mercy had been unfailingly kind and welcoming to her. She hadn't really wanted to hide her past from them, but by the time she'd entered the home, aged eighty-five, her Italian identity was so deeply entrenched, it was almost second nature to her. After all, she'd lived in Italy far longer than she'd lived in Germany. So, when she'd first arrived at the care home, she hadn't thought to tell anyone anything different. There was no need, and besides, there was always that fear lurking in the back of her mind, the fear she'd lived with from the war years, that people simply wouldn't understand if they knew the truth.

There was a knock on the door and Lorenzo put his head round. Despite her inner turmoil, Margarete's heart lifted just to see his face. He was always smiling, and she knew from their frequent chats that his contentment was more than skin deep. He'd recently returned to live with his ageing parents in the town after several years' globetrotting, finding casual work wherever he could. Over the past few months, he'd entertained Margarete with his traveller's tales for hours on end. He seemed equally content to be working with the residents of Our Lady of Mercy as he did trekking in the Himalayas or toiling in a vineyard in Argentina or surfing off Kuta Beach in Bali.

'It's just past eight o'clock, Margharita. Would you like coffee or tea in bed?' he asked and there was nothing in the tone of his voice that had changed from the last time they'd spoken, although Ginetta must have told him something of Margarete's news in her note.

'Coffee would be lovely. Thank you, Lorenzo.'

She heard him pour coffee from the flask on the trolley in the corridor, then he appeared with a cup and saucer, crossed the room and placed it on her bedside table.

'Shall I help you sit up?'

'No, thank you. I can manage.'

He walked to the window and pulled the curtains aside.

'It snowed in the night,' Lorenzo reported. 'Just look at the mountains!'

Margarete propped herself up on her elbows and looked out of the window. Snow glistening on the rooftops of the town and on the mountains across the valley on a sunny winter morning never failed to lift her spirits.

Lorenzo paused, admiring the view himself, then turned back to Margarete.

'I had a phone call this morning,' he said. 'From someone at *Nachricht 24*. One of their reporters is coming to talk to you later today.'

'Oh!' Margarete's mouth dropped open. 'Today...?' That seemed very soon and now that the chance she'd waited half a lifetime for was within her grasp, she wasn't sure she was ready. Her nerves seemed to be spiralling out of control.

'Yes. A lady called Kristel Meyer. She'll be here at some point this afternoon.'

'Kristel Meyer!' Margarete repeated, taken aback that the lead reporter would be coming to see her. They must be taking her seriously. She searched Lorenzo's face for clues as to what he was thinking about her momentous news, but he smiled back at her, his open, genuine smile.

'Please don't look so worried, Margarete,' he soothed. 'Ginetta's note said that you have something really important to tell them from the war years. It will be good for you to get it off your chest, won't it, after such a long time?'

She relaxed. How typical of Lorenzo, with his sunny, uncomplicated nature, not to judge her harshly, but to accept things at face value. She should have had more faith in him. She nodded, smiling into his dark brown eyes, overcome with emotion, unable to find the words to respond.

'Well, then... When you've finished your coffee, ring the bell and Matilde will be along to help you get dressed. I'll see you down at breakfast.'

When he'd gone, Margarete gulped her coffee as quickly as she could, then pressed the bell beside her bed. There was no time to waste. She needed to get up and prepare herself for the interview. Waiting for Matilde to arrive, she picked up her blue notebook once again and ran her finger down the columns of code. Perhaps the end of her struggle was finally in sight.

. . .

In the middle of the afternoon, a tiny red Fiat pulled upon the drive beneath Margarete's window. Margarete leaned forward in her chair and held her breath. Could this be her? Various vehicles had been and gone since lunchtime and Margarete had watched each one, eagle-eyed. But each time she'd been disappointed. She hadn't realised until today how many deliveries arrived at the care home, how many staff came and went, not to mention visitors. These were families and friends visiting the other residents. Margarete had no one to visit her.

The car parked in a space directly beneath her window, the driver's door opened and a tall woman with blonde hair topped with a floppy red beret got out. Margarete couldn't see her face, but she knew immediately that this was Kristel Meyer. She watched as Kristel lifted a bag from the car, locked up, wound a red scarf around her neck and walked towards the front door. She was wearing an elegant navy-blue coat reaching almost to her ankles and high-heeled boots.

Margarete sat back in her chair and took deep breaths, holding her notebook tightly to her, as fresh doubts entered her mind. Could she really trust Kristel Meyer with her story? Would Kristel understand, or would she misconstrue Margarete's actions? She was a reporter after all. News was her bread and butter. It would be far too easy to misrepresent Margarete's role in everything that had happened. Indeed, to do so would grab more attention than simply telling the truth about what she'd done.

She heard footsteps coming along the corridor. Her nerves failing her, Margarete shoved the notebook back into her bag and sat back and watched the door.

There were two short knocks and Lorenzo entered. Kristel Meyer was standing behind him in the corridor.

'Margarete,' he said, 'this is Kristel. She's driven all the way from Munich this morning to talk to you.'

Margarete stared at Kristel as she walked into the room behind Lorenzo. She no longer wore her coat or her red beret or scarf. She was dressed simply in tight jeans and a dark blue knitted jumper, her long hair tumbling around her shoulders. She walked forward, smiling, holding her hand out.

'Delighted to meet you, *signora*,' she said in halting Italian.

Margarete took her hand and looked into Kristel's eyes. 'You can speak German to me, Miss Meyer. I speak German too. It is in fact my first language – although I've hardly spoken it for many years now.'

'That's very good news!' Kristel said in German. 'My Italian isn't up to much, I'm afraid.' She smiled ruefully.

In the background, Lorenzo cleared his throat. 'I'll leave you to it then. Would either of you like a drink?'

'Tea would be lovely,' Kristel said. 'It's a long drive from Munich and it was snowing on the Brenner Pass. But it was more direct than taking a flight.'

Margarete shuddered, her own memories of the Brenner Pass surfacing suddenly. That road, snaking its way through the Alpine peaks, linking Germany with Austria, and finally Italy.

'I'll bring a pot of tea for two,' Lorenzo said and left the room.

Kristel settled herself in the chair beside Margarete's and took a reporter's notebook from her bag, together with a mini-tape recorder, which she placed on the coffee table between them.

Margarete watched her in silence. To her surprise, the young woman looked a little distracted, less sure of herself than Margarete would have imagined, especially having seen her confidence in presenting her report on television the previous evening. There was sadness in the young woman's eyes too, as if there was something troubling her. Margarete knew that look only too well. How many young women had she known in the past with deep troubles of their own?

Then Kristel smiled and looked into Margarete's eyes. Seeing those bright blue eyes so close sent a bolt of recognition right through Margarete. There was something about the tilt of Kristel's head, the angle of her cheekbones, the light in her irises that took Margarete straight back to those terrible times.

'Thank you for contacting the network, Miss Bianchi,' Kristel began. 'We've had an incredible response to last night's report. It's amazing how many people's lives were dramatically affected by the Lebensborn programme. My news report only really scratched the surface though... Nicole told me that you have some important information about Lebensborn. She mentioned a notebook?'

Margarete drew herself up stiffly. Now that Kristel was here, although the young woman appeared charming and genuine, Margarete's anxieties had come to the fore. Despite her desire to tell her story, despite all the years of frustration and silence that had passed, was it really safe to speak the truth, even now?

'Miss Bianchi?' Kristel gently prompted.

'It is true, I do have a notebook. But—'

The door opened and Lorenzo entered with the tea. Without a word, he laid it out on the table between them, poured two cups, then left the room silently again.

'You were saying?' Kristel asked. 'The notebook?'

'It does have information from that time,' Margarete began. 'But... but...'

Faced with the opportunity, Margarete was faltering. She wasn't sure she could trust Kristel with the notebook. Not yet... and, in any case, the notebook alone wasn't going to be enough. What she needed was Kristel's help to solve the mysteries it contained, but how could she tell her that? Kristel might think she'd been lured here under false pretences.

'Don't worry,' Kristel said finally. 'Let's not talk about the notebook yet. Why don't you start by telling me your story? Right from the very beginning. We can gradually work it out from there...'

Margarete stared back at her. Her own story? She thought back down the years, wondering where to start, where it had all begun.

'It all started when I was a nurse... I was very young and I didn't understand the terrible power the Nazis held...'

FIVE

MARGARETE

Charité Hospital, Berlin, 1933–38

Margarete was at home with her parents and her younger sister, Alicia, in their cramped tenement flat in a shabby quarter of central Berlin listening to the radio when the results of the election were announced – the Nazis had won a majority in the Reichstag.

Her father, Josef, was full of rage at the way the Nazis had intimidated the electorate into voting for them. 'They've been spreading malicious, alarmist rumours everywhere. They've been saying that the Social Democrats and Communists are out to destroy the fabric of German society. It's all plain lies.'

'And people have fallen for it...' Margarete's mother, Hilde, interjected shaking her head in dismay.

'They arrested anyone who dared to oppose them,' Josef went on, clenching his fists. 'Anyone who's left, that is, or hasn't fled abroad or gone into hiding. They've shut down every newspaper apart from their own, arrested so many people that they've had to build new prison camps just to house them. Is this what we fought for in the Great War?' By the time he finished, he was practically shouting, his face was flushed and he was breathing heavily.

'Hush, Josef,' Hilde said, glancing nervously at the flimsy front door of their apartment. 'You must stop talking like this. Walls have ears, you know.'

'I can say what I want in my own home,' Josef retorted, still in a loud voice, and Hilde looked at Margarete with despairing eyes.

'Mutti is right, Papa,' Margarete chimed in, worried that her father's strong views would get him into trouble. 'We agree with everything you say but you don't want to get yourself arrested too, do you?'

'Well, I agree with Papa,' Alicia piped up. 'It's obvious what is happening. The Nazis were determined to win the election by brute force and they've got what they wanted.'

'But don't say that to anyone at school,' Hilde told her in hushed tones. 'Promise me that much, Alicia.'

Margarete turned to her sister. 'From now on, you must be careful what you say. Otherwise we could all be arrested.' She'd seen so many arrests on the street; she knew this was a real concern.

'Be careful what you say, yes,' Josef said. 'But we all must remember one thing. Whatever happens, be true to yourself and to your own principles.'

His words struck a chord with Margarete and in the coming months and years when she'd be tested to the limit, she would repeat them to herself time and time again.

Margarete's life changed very little at first after the Nazi Party won the general election. She'd been working as a nursery nurse in the women's Charité Hospital in Berlin for several years by that time and she had recently gained her nursing qual-ification, the culmination of years of hard work, long hours, endless studying and ceaseless dedication. She adored caring for the newborns in the nursery. She had a real affinity with the babies, and she truly loved the work. It was her life.

It was tempting to forget that beyond the hospital gates there was unrest on the streets of Berlin, frequent and terrifying Nazi Party rallies, violence against Jews and anyone who opposed the Nazis and their henchmen – the brown-shirted Stormtroopers – but she came face to face with it herself each time she left the confines of the hospital to cross the city to visit her family. Her tram often rattled past groups of Brownshirts, kicking and punching people who lay motionless on the ground, throwing bricks at windows, or running mob-handed after unarmed civilians. It was terrifying, often she had to look away.

Life at the hospital went on as normal for a while, but a few months after the election, a new nursing sister was appointed by the Ministry of Public Health and Nursing to run the maternity ward at the Charité Hospital. The day she arrived was the day that everything changed. It was indelibly etched on Margarete's memory.

Margarete was in the nursery, busy feeding one of the newborn babies with a bottle. His mother had been unwell and was not producing any milk. She looked down at his tiny face, his soft skin with its covering of downy hair and his beady eyes and her heart melted. She stroked his cheek and cooed at him gently. Cradling a newborn in her arms, soothing their cries, she was at her happiest and most content. She knew she had a unique talent and affinity for caring for newborn babies. It was one good thing to have emerged from the years of poverty and hardship of her upbringing.

Margarete was the eldest in her family, and she'd helped her mother to care for her four siblings, only one of whom, her sister Alicia, had survived beyond infancy Looking down at the tiny baby boy in her arms that day reminded her of the baby brothers and sister who hadn't survived that she'd learned to care for. She would change nappies, fill and warm bottles, administer cod-liver oil, deal with colic and treat fevers by sponging down a hot baby with a wet cloth. All those skills were second nature to her when she'd started at the hospital, where the other nurses had to learn them from scratch.

Her childhood had taught her how to comfort babies and how to entertain them, to make them gurgle and smile and squeeze her finger in their tiny hands. She'd grown very attached to her baby brothers and sister, and each time a baby had been taken from them, Margarete had been grief-stricken. She would silently mourn each loss, crying herself to sleep at night in her tiny bedroom.

Caring for babies in the hospital, ensuring they were clean, well-fed and comfortable, was somehow a way of assuaging that grief, making up for the fact that she hadn't been able to save her baby brothers and sister. And she'd made a life here amongst the other nurses, many of whom were her friends. Her room-mate, Magdalena, a lovely, caring girl, was Polish and she'd picked up the rudiments of the language from her.

Margarete was deep in thought, thinking about those difficult days, cradling the baby in her arms, but when she looked up, she saw that the whole ward was stirring at the sight of a newcomer. It was the new nursing sister. She was walking through the ward with Professor Wagner, the newly appointed medical chief of the Women's Hospital. The two of them strutted between the beds to Matron's office and there was a ripple of excitement amongst the nurses.

The woman was a striking figure, tall and statuesque, with hair scraped back from her head, and she was wearing a uniform that no one had ever seen before. It reminded Margarete chillingly of the Stormtrooper uniform because it was the same mucky brown colour, with swastikas prominent on her breast pocket and emblazoned on her kerchief. But it was her eyes that were the most chilling of all. Eyes completely devoid of compassion or pity. She had the hard, slate-like gaze of a fanatic.

She spent a few minutes speaking to Matron in the office, then Matron emerged, looking flustered, and called all the staff to join them for a meeting – Margarete and three other nurses, together with the three auxiliary workers. Everyone looked at each other nervously before going in and taking seats.

The newcomer was standing in front of Matron's desk.

'Good morning, Fräuleins,' the woman said, without a hint of a smile. 'I am Jutta Koch, your new ward sister. I will be working alongside Professor Wagner from now on. I have been appointed by the Ministry and the Nazi Party to supervise healthcare on this ward.'

Margarete stole a glance at Matron. Matron's cheeks were flaming and her lips were pursed, but it was impossible to see her eyes. She was staring down at her stout shoes, but her fists were clenched.

'I understand from Matron that staff here are all members of der Caritasverband – the Catholic Nursing Association,' Fräulein Koch said and the girls nodded. With a sour smile, she went on, 'Well, I'm afraid I have to tell you that that organisa-tion is not acceptable to the Führer and the National Socialists. We want our nurses to be the guardians of a new era in medi-cine, to be pioneers in this new world, not hidebound by the stifling doctrines of the Catholic Church. To that end, a new organisation has been formed: the National Socialist Nursing Association. Some call us the Brown Sisters,' she said, still without even a hint of a smile. 'And everyone here must become a member of that organisation. You will be issued with new uniforms forthwith. I hope everyone has understood. I think the message is clear, but are there any questions?'

One of the nurses shot her hand up.

Margarete sighed. This girl, Lottie, had been one of the young nurses she'd overheard praising the Nazis over the past few months. One day, over lunch in the canteen, Margarete had overheard her saying: 'After all this poverty and turmoil, we need a strong leader and party to make us a proud nation again.'

Others sitting around the table had murmured their agreement, but Margarete had stared down at her plate, trying to keep her expression neutral. She was determined not to be drawn into a discussion about the Nazis because she couldn't trust what she might say. She vehemently disagreed with the girl, aligning with the views of the rest of her family; the Nazis seemed like dangerous, violent thugs to her. She'd witnessed as much when she'd crossed the city by tram and seen mobs of Brownshirts beating up innocent civilians, but she wasn't going to mention that. She felt that speaking her mind might have adverse consequences.

She tried to keep her expression neutral while Fräulein Koch nodded in Lottie's direction.

'I'd like to say welcome from all of us, Fräulein Koch,' Lottie simpered, 'and how pleased and honoured we are that you have come to guide us.'

Fräulein Koch's mouth twitched. 'Thank you. Now, I have the Association forms here for you all to sign, so if you can come forward, one by one...'

Margarete was appalled that she was being pressured into joining the Brown Sisters. It would be going against everything she stood for. She recalled once again the conversation in her own home on the day of the election. Now, with the eyes of every member of staff in the room upon her, Margarete put her own hand up. It was shaking as she held it there and, for a second, before all eyes swivelled towards her, she thought about putting it down, but again and again she recalled her father's words, *Be true to yourself*. This was her first test of that maxim.

Now Fräulein Koch's cold eyes were on her. 'Yes, Nurse?'

There was a pause, where Margarete considered asking a completely different question to the one she'd intended, but before she knew it, the words were already coming out of her mouth, surprising even her. 'Is membership of the Brown Sisters compulsory, Fräulein Koch?' Her voice was loud and clear.

There was a stunned silence, during which Margarete noticed Matron's head lift slightly. Their eyes locked together and Matron shook her head very slightly and frowned. It looked like a warning.

'Membership is not compulsory, Nurse... I didn't catch your name?' Fräulein Koch began.

'Nurse Weiss...'

'Ah, yes. Nurse *Weiss*, but I'm afraid that those who don't agree to join the Brown Sisters will no longer be able to continue nursing in this establishment. The choice is yours.'

Margarete was silenced. She felt her cheeks heating up in shame and panic and she stared down at her lap while the others got up from their seats with a scraping of chair legs on the wooden floor. One by one, they approached the desk. Starting with Lottie, they signed all the papers renouncing their membership of the Catholic Nursing Association and replacing it with membership of the Brown Sisters.

Margarete was keenly aware that Fräulein Koch and Professor Wagner were staring at her, waiting for her to make her decision. She felt the pressure of the moment and panic gripped her chest. What if, as a result of the question she'd asked Fräulein Koch, the SS or the Gestapo started to look into her background? She'd heard that they would stop at nothing to root out people who opposed them. What if they discovered that Mutti and Papa were less than enthusiastic about the new order, that Papa had even helped the Communists by distributing leaflets over the past few months, and that Alicia shared those views too? Her parents' age and frailty and Alicia's youth wouldn't protect them.

As if to echo Margarete's own thoughts, Fräulein Koch suddenly said, 'Fräulein Weiss! I understand that your *family* has fallen on hard times in recent years, that your father suffers from ill health and finds it difficult to provide for your sister and mother. It might be very hard indeed for them to manage without your nursing salary... have you thought about that?'

She stared into the woman's hard eyes and thought about her words. How did she know so much about her family? What was doubly shocking was that what Fräulein Koch had said was true. Her father had been injured in Northern France during the Great War, his lungs damaged by mustard gas, but although he was an invalid, he had tried his best to provide for his family. During the economic turmoil of the 1920s, he had often been without a steady income for months at a time. He would take any work he could get, though – in factories, in garages, on construction sites, on the railway, on the docks. If he wasn't in work, he would spend his days queuing for handouts of food or fuel from charitable institutions. It used to tear Margarete's heart to see him struggle up the stairs at the end of a long day, hauling a bag of potatoes or firewood, pausing at the top to lean on the banister, wheezing and gasping for breath. Margarete's income was a lifeline for the family, she didn't want to make their life any harder.

Looking into Fräulein Koch's eyes, it was plain to Margarete that there were suspicions about her family. She had often wondered how long they could continue as they were without attracting the attention of the authorities.

'Nurse Weiss! Did you hear what I said? What would your family do if you lost your job?'

So that was it. Margarete didn't need any more convincing that her family's safety and well-being hung by a thread and depended on her complete discretion. She got up and even though nausea rose in her throat and every nerve in her body screamed out in protest at what she had to do, she approached the desk on shaking legs. Her hands shook too as she signed the forms pledging her allegiance to the Brown Sisters.

When she looked up, Fräulein Koch was smiling smugly at her.

'Well done, Nurse Weiss. I knew you would see sense in the end. I'm hoping that from now on, our work together will be fruitful and positive.'

The next morning, when Margarete began her shift, there was no sign of Matron. Her belongings had been removed from the ward, and through the office window, Margarete noticed with a shudder that Fräulein Koch was sitting at Matron's desk.

Margarete asked Katherina, one of the nurses who'd been on duty overnight, if she knew what had happened to Matron.

Katherina shrugged. 'She must have decided she didn't fit in here anymore. Probably for the best. She was getting old and rather stuck in her ways, wasn't she?'

Margarete thought about Matron, about her professionalism and her strong work ethic, about how her rather severe manner had hidden a big, generous heart. She recalled how Matron had been the one who had first spotted Margarete's talents and her natural ability to care for babies. It was Matron who had interviewed Margarete for an auxiliary's job when she had turned up at the hospital – a naive teenager who'd had to leave school because her parents could no longer pay for her education. Matron had seen her commitment and enthusiasm and had appointed her straight away. Matron had lived for her work. How would she cope in her advancing years cut off from the hospital she'd devoted her life to?

During her break that morning, Margarete hurried back to the nurses' residence and climbed the stairs up to the top floor where Matron's flat was. She knocked on the door, but there was no reply so she knocked again, and when she tried the handle, she found that the door was locked.

Over the next few weeks, she returned many times to knock on Matron's door but to no avail.

One day, Fräulein Koch called her into her office and shut the door behind her.

'I understand that you've been trying to find Matron, Nurse Weiss. Please don't go up to her apartment again. Matron has left Berlin. She has retired from her post and moved out of the nurses' residence.'

Margarete was stunned.

'Where has she gone?' the question was on her lips before she could think properly.

'I have no idea. And I would advise you to forget all about her and others like her. She wasn't ready to move with the times, or to embrace all the exciting ideas about modern medicine that the Party has been pioneering. Anyone not ready to do that cannot expect to be part of our future.'

Margarete fell silent. She had heard about the 'exciting ideas about modern medicine' that Fräulein Koch was referring to. Since the Nazis had come to power and the senior hospital staff were replaced with appointees acceptable to the regime, Professor Wagner had given several lectures, which all the nurses had been required to attend. They were all about eugenics – the ideals of racial purity and the Nazis' desire to fill Germany with a master race of Aryans. Margarete had listened with horror but with scepticism too. She'd been unable to believe they were anything other than the ideological dreams of a fanatical regime. Surely no one could be seriously suggesting that those theories had any practical application? Perhaps Matron had felt the same way and had expressed as much to the wrong people. She was known for her plain speaking.

Margarete vowed that she wouldn't give up on Matron, that she would keep making enquiries about her until she had tracked her down. But try as she might, Margarete could find no trace of her. She asked for Matron's new address in the records office, but the clerks had no record of it. It was almost as if she had never existed and Margarete was left with a sick feeling in the pit of her stomach. How could a venerated elderly woman who had given valuable public service to the community for her entire life simply disappear?

As the months went by and those months became years, the mystery surrounding Matron didn't go away. Margarete remembered all the people who had disappeared during the election campaign and realised that there was nothing the regime would stop at to cleanse the country of opponents or undesirable elements and to indoctrinate the minds of its subjects. Perhaps poor Matron had ended up in one of those camps for simply expressing her views.

On the terrible day that several esteemed Jewish doctors who had worked at the hospital for many years were dismissed summarily, Margarete watched from the front window of the ward with tears in her eyes as they were escorted out through the front gates, carrying a few meagre belongings in boxes, stripped of their dignity as well as their livelihoods. She was horrified at the increasing marginalisation of the Jews generally, of how their businesses were being confiscated, how they were banned from education, from shops, from mixing in society and from practising their professions.

The work of the ward itself went on unchanged through all this. Margarete was grateful that at least the process of childbirth itself couldn't be tampered with. However, gradually and subtly, even the status of the women who were cared for on the ward began to change. In time, most of those who were being admitted were themselves either Nazi Party members, the wives of government officials or of SS Officers. Professor Wagner would pay a visit himself to the wives of the highest-ranking officers, his face wreathed in supercilious smiles.

'There is nothing more important than the birth of new members of the Aryan race,' Margarete overheard him telling the wife of an SS officer once in a simpering voice. 'The ovaries of fertile Aryan women are so precious, they should be the property of the state.'

Margarete felt so uncomfortable with these changes that she told her family she was thinking of looking for another job. By now, Alicia had left school and was working in a café a few blocks away from the apartment, but her wages were dismal despite the long hours. She had confided in Margarete that she had joined a group of other young people in secret who were opposed to the Nazis. Margarete was proud of Alicia for that, but terrified for her all the same.

Her mother looked alarmed at Margarete's news. 'I can see how it might be difficult for you to work in those conditions, daughter, but the money is good and regular.'

'Nonsense, Hilde!' said Josef, whose lung condition had become progressively worse and was now confined to the apartment. 'You should leave that appalling place, my girl. Don't worry about us, find another job. Somewhere you don't have to work for that shower, where you can be yourself... if such a place even exists anymore...' he trailed off. Then he began coughing and reached for a stained handkerchief. His words were soon drowned out in a coughing fit.

Feeling torn, Margarete began to look around as discreetly as she could for another post. Ideally, she wanted to find something that would still enable her to work with babies or children. But the more she looked, the more dismayed she was at what she discovered. All the hospitals in Berlin were now dominated by the Brown Sisters, apart from the Jewish Hospital, and it would be impossible for her to work there. She then looked for a job in a nursery or kindergarten, but found that with the Nazi drive for women to work in the home and nurture their family, more and more women were looking after their own babies. There were virtually no nurseries in existence. The kindergartens were run by the Nazi Party too. They were places where tiny children's heads were filled with Nazi propaganda from the moment they started. Margarete wondered, with mounting fear, if there was any aspect of life that the Nazis hadn't infiltrated.

After a few weeks of searching, she was forced to concede that she would have to find a job outside the nursing profession. If Alicia could work in a café, why shouldn't she do that, or something similar? It would mean returning to live at home and giving up the profession she'd worked so hard to become part of, but she was prepared for that. She eventually found a job in a department store near home and made her decision with a heavy heart.

On the day Margarete went to hand in her notice to Fräulein Koch, the other girls on the ward were buzzing with excitement and full of the news that there was a surprise visitor – a VIP, in fact – who was being shown around the hospital. Fräulein Koch was not in her office.

Margarete got on with her work, her resignation letter tucked in the pocket of her apron. Halfway through the morning, Fräulein Koch and Professor Wagner appeared on the ward, the important visitor walking between them. All the nurses lined up near the door to greet him and as he walked through the door, Margarete saw with a shock who he was.

She knew his rounded, moustachioed face from propaganda posters and newsreels. It was none other than Heinrich Himmler, the head of the SS. He had come to the hospital in full SS regalia: a grey uniform complete with insignia, a cap and polished black boots. A hush fell over the ward as he approached. He nodded and smiled at the line of nurses, before moving on to the patients. He stopped at the beds of some of the new mothers. Margarete could hear him congratulating the women on the important work they were doing producing Aryan babies for the good of the Fatherland. When that was over, Professor Wagner ushered him towards the nursery.

The nurses drifted back to work, and after a few minutes, Fräulein Koch, Professor Wagner and their important visitor went into the office and shut the door. Later that morning, as Margarete was feeding one of the babies, Fräulein Koch came to speak to her.

'Come to the office with me please, Nurse Weiss,' she said. 'Katherina can take care of that baby.'

Margarete looked up in alarm. 'Isn't Herr Himmler in the office?' she asked.

'He is. And he wants to speak to you.'

Shock washed through Margarete. 'To me?' she asked weakly.

'Yes, you, girl,' Fräulein Koch said impatiently. 'Come with me.'

Margarete quickly handed the wailing baby and the half-drunk bottle of milk to Katherina, and followed Fräulein Koch to the office. Her heart was pounding. Had they found something out about her parents, about Alicia's secret opposition group? Had they discovered that Margarete had been looking for another job? Was she actually going to be disciplined for that?

Fräulein Koch shut the door behind her. Himmler was seated behind the desk, Professor Wagner sat tensely in another chair.

'Take a seat, Nurse Weiss,' Himmler said, and Margarete obeyed, her mouth dry. She glanced at the Reichsführer. He leaned back in his chair, looking relaxed – as if he owned the place, in fact.

'Professor Wagner and Fräulein Koch tell me that you are the best maternity nurse there is in this hospital,' he began and Margarete tried to suppress a frown of confusion. 'I have been looking for somebody just like you to carry out some very important work for the good of the Fatherland.'

Margarete had no idea what to say in response, so she simply stared at him in silence.

'This work is just the beginning of a whole new programme that I am setting up in my ministry. The work is confidential, the German people aren't quite ready for it yet, but I am convinced that it is the right way forward.'

Margarete noticed that there was no warmth in his voice.

'It is a fascinating programme, my dear,' Professor Wagner put in. 'It is very much in line with some of the work I have been doing here in the hospital.'

Chills went through Margarete as she recalled his lectures on eugenics and the master race.

Himmler nodded towards Professor Wagner and went on, 'You will be running a maternity facility in Bavaria for women who have unfortunately become pregnant out of wedlock. We want to encourage them to keep their babies, not to give in to conventional pressure and terminate their pregnancies. To that end, we want to ensure they are offered excellent care in the most discreet of places, well away from the disapproving gaze of their neighbours and society at large.'

Margarete blinked at him. What he said didn't sound too bad, but...

'You, Nurse Weiss, have been chosen because we are confident of your ability to ensure the care of newborn babies. You seem to have a unique talent in that direction. There will, of course, be other nurses there under your leadership, as well as midwives.'

'Where is this... this facility?' Margarete muttered finally.

'In Bavaria. In a schloss, high up in the mountains. A beautiful building that has been equipped to the highest standards. It's in a very discreet location.'

Margarete swallowed, trying to process the information, to understand what was being asked of her. She knew she couldn't trust this man. How could she possibly avoid what they were suggesting?

'You have also been chosen, Nurse Weiss, because we know how important it is to *your family*, that you are able to provide for them,' Fräulein Koch said, with one of her knowing smiles.

Shock waves coursed through Margarete again. They knew something about her family, she was quite sure of that now. Margarete lifted her head and looked up at Fräulein Koch. She understood the message in those cold grey eyes.

SIX

KRISTEL

Trento, 2005

Kristel stepped out of the fuggy warmth of the care home into the ice-cold evening air. It was past eight o'clock and the inky sky was leaden with snow, not a star in sight. A chill breeze was blowing down from the mountains. It had snowed heavily as Kristel had driven down through Austria and up to the border town of Brenner earlier. The snowploughs and gritting lorries had been out in force, keeping the autobahn open. But once she'd cleared the border and headed on down the pass on the Italian side towards Trento, the snow had gradually eased off. But now it looked set to return.

She got into her car, started the engine and turned the heater and fan up high, pulling her coat and scarf around her tightly and rubbing her hands together for warmth. She would be late checking into the hotel that Nicole had booked for her, and she'd probably already missed dinner, but it didn't matter. She wasn't hungry. She'd not thought of food once during all those hours she'd sat in that upstairs room, listening to Margarete Weiss' story, spellbound by what she'd heard. She'd been transported back seventy years to 1930s Germany and the rise of the Nazis as Margarete had started to tell her about how she'd been coerced into working for them. Kristel's own needs and desires had seemed to fade away as she'd tried to imagine what it might have been like to have lived through those years and to have been forced to face the agonising choices Margarete and all her contemporaries had.

Margarete's German had sounded rusty and a little archaic to Kristel's modern ears, her accent chillingly like those heard on crackly wartime broadcasts. As the day had faded, Margarete had grown tired telling her story. Her voice had become hoarse and she had closed her eyes periodically, making Kristel think she'd gone to sleep. At around seven thirty, Margarete's supper had arrived and one of the carers had put it in front of her on a cloche-covered plate, but Margarete had left it untouched while she finished telling Kristel about Himmler's visit to the maternity ward at the hospital.

The heater had cleared the windscreen now, so Kristel pulled out of the care home car park onto the main road. She drove through the quiet, narrow streets to her hotel, which was near the medieval centre of the town.

She checked in at the desk, then went up to her room. When her luggage arrived, she, ordered a club sandwich and a coffee from room service. Once they'd arrived, she called Nicole, who was still at work in the studio.

'Kristel! Good to hear from you,' Nicole said. 'We've had such a response to your report. Calls have been coming in all day, on and off. So many people have come forward to tell their stories, most of them Lebensborn children. I'm about to email you with a summary. Some of them are extraordinary, many really heartbreaking. Your report obviously struck a chord with many, many people.'

'Thanks so much, Nicole. It's really heartening that so many people have responded,' Kristel said, scrolling through her emails, looking for Nicole's. 'I can't wait to read about them. I've only just got back from interviewing Margarete Weiss, otherwise I'd have called sooner.'

'Gosh. You must have been at the care home for four or five hours. Was it useful?'

'Incredible. Her memory of the 1930s is crystal clear, but she got tired quite quickly. I'm going back to speak to her again tomorrow. I have a feeling that it might take a few days.'

'I'll let Michel know. He's just left the office for the evening.'

'Thanks. I'll call him tomorrow morning before I go back to the care home.'

Kristel said goodbye to Nicole, took a bite of her sandwich and turned her attention to Nicole's email. Nicole had sent her the details of about ten people, some accompanied by photographs. All were in their sixties and looked at first glance like ordinary Germans, but peering closer, Kristel noticed that they all had that same look – a sadness in their eyes, a look of detachment, disappointment even.

She scrolled down to the summaries of their stories. The first told of a man who had spent years tracking down his father. He'd eventually discovered, to his dismay, from papers concealed by his adopted parents, that his father had been a high-ranking SS officer. Then there was the woman who discovered that her mother had lied to her for her entire life – telling her that her father was simply a common solider in the Wehrmacht who'd died in battle. He was in fact commandant of a concentration camp and had been sentenced to death for war crimes at the end of the war.

All the stories had a common thread, a child brought up in ignorance of the truth, searching desperately for some understanding of the past by uncovering their own personal history. But the real sadness here, Kristel realised, was that the truth was often as uncomfortable as not knowing.

With a sigh, she got out her tape recorder and sat down with her laptop at the desk under the window to type up her notes from Margarete's interview. She was tired, but she knew that if she didn't complete the task that evening, some of the nuance of what she'd heard might be lost. She sipped her coffee gratefully and was soon making progress with the transcript.

She'd been typing for about half an hour, and was so absorbed in Margarete's description of her early years at the Charité Hospital that when her mobile phone rang, she jumped. It was Joachim.

'How's Trento?' he asked. Hearing his voice, Kristel immediately felt guilty for not having been in touch with him. Her mind had been so full of her work that she hadn't even thought to call him.

'Well, it's dark now and freezing cold. It's threatening snow,' she replied. 'I haven't seen much of the town so far, but from what I have seen, it looks really beautiful. Surrounded by mountains. How's everything with you? How did the board meeting go?'

'Great, thanks. All good. The presentation seemed to go down well with the board. I just need to wait and see... There was some talk after the meeting though, something I need to speak to you about when you're back.'

'Really?' she asked, wondering why he might need to ask her advice about anything to do with his work. He never normally did. 'Can't we talk about it on the phone?'

There was a short silence. 'It would be better in person, Kris. When are you coming back?'

'I'm not sure,' she said, hoping he wasn't going to get annoyed again about her being away for work. 'It depends how long the interviews take. We didn't get too far today. Whatever it is, can't we talk about it now?'

Joachim cleared his throat. 'I suppose so... OK, here goes. The board were talking about a posting. To the Singapore office.

They think they need someone who's got a handle on the strategic aims of the business to shake things up out there... The Chairman took me aside after the meeting and asked if I'd be interested in the role myself. It would mean a pay rise, of course.'

'Singapore?' Kristel managed to say, swallowing hard, trying to process what this meant and to work out her own feelings at the same time. 'That's a very long way from Munich...'

'It is. I know it would be difficult for you to get a job out there. At least one as good as the one you've got now.'

'So, what are you saying?' She moved away from the desk to lie down on the bed. The conversation had suddenly become serious and she wanted to give it her full attention. The line was crackly and poor, but even so, she could sense Joachim's discomfort.

'I've been thinking about us, Kristel... You must have been too. We haven't really been getting on so well lately, have we? You know, we've been on a high since we met, we rushed into things headlong. I've been wondering lately if perhaps we decided about stuff a bit too soon.'

'Stuff?'

'Well, maybe neither of us is quite ready for such a big commitment. I know your career is important to you. Mine is to me. I realised this morning, when you went off, that I shouldn't try to tie you down or give you a hard time if you need to work long hours or go away for a while. I know that now. Perhaps... if I *were* to take this transfer, we might feel less pressured. We might be able to give each other a bit of space?'

Kristel opened her mouth to speak, but her throat was constricted with emotion and she had tears in her eyes. She was surprised; after all, only the day before they'd been discussing their wedding reception, but she realised gradually that the overwhelming emotion at hearing his words was one of sadness mixed with relief. Joachim was so right. And how characteristically brave of him to be able to broach the subject with her as he had.

'I think you might be right,' she said after a long pause. 'Look, why don't we talk about it when I get back in a couple of days? Can the board wait for an answer until then?'

'Of course. Let's do that, Kristel. Thanks for understanding.'

They carried on talking for fifteen minutes or so, exchanging news about their days, then said their goodbyes. Afterwards, Kristel lay on the bed staring up at the ceiling, going over and over the conversation in her mind. It was strange, now that everything was out in the open, she felt more tender towards Joachim than she had for weeks.

She went back to the laptop and finished typing up her notes from Margarete's interview, then wrote herself a memo. *Margarete Weiss has so much to tell me. She is desperate to tell her story, but she is so used to keeping it a secret that it must be hard for her. I can tell there's a lot she is instinctively holding back until she feels she can trust me completely. I'm looking forward to hearing the next instalment of her life tomorrow.*

Kristel took a long shower and lay down on the bed. Her mind was buzzing and she knew it would be pointless trying to go to sleep. Strangely, it was not Joachim but her mother, Greta, to whom she kept returning. If Kristel looked deep into her own heart and was honest with herself, she knew that Greta was the real reason she was here. If it hadn't been for certain unanswered questions about Greta's life, she probably wouldn't have started asking about the Lebensborn story or got interested in it at all.

There were so many unanswered questions about Greta and now that Kristel's father, Frank, had passed away, it would be even more difficult to get answers. Not that he would ever have discussed her mother in any depth. Anything Kristel had ever asked him about Greta would be met with a blank stare and a wave of the hand. 'It's a long time ago, Kristel darling. You could always ask your mother about it herself next time you speak to her.'

Kristel had never asked her mother those awkward questions about the past. Except that one disastrous time, after her father's funeral, which had ended in tears and recriminations. They very rarely met, and when they did, their exchanges were quite formal. Greta clearly wanted to keep Kristel at a distance and return to her solitary, ordered life in America as soon as she could.

All Kristel knew was that one day, shortly after the death of Greta's mother, Greta had upped and left Kristel and her father and taken a job in New York. Kristel had little memory of that time, perhaps she had blotted it out. After all, she had only been three years old. She had a vague memory of the terror and the pain of her mother leaving, screaming at the top of her voice, clinging to her mother's legs, tearing her tights as she tried to leave the apartment carrying two suitcases. But even now, if she closed her eyes and thought back to that day, the pain was still there, buried deep inside. It still shocked and bewildered her to think that a mother could do that to her own child.

Her poor father must have been devastated too. He'd had to pick himself up and get on with life. He'd brought Kristel up single-handed, juggling a demanding business career and caring for her at the same time. It can't have been easy for him. But he had hidden things from her too. She knew that now. Things she had only discovered after his sudden death a few months ago.

She'd been sorting through his apartment, going through the drawers of his desk, looking for any bills that might need settling or outstanding paperwork. In a locked drawer that she'd prised open with a kitchen knife, she'd found a stash of letters inside a shoebox. She'd sat back on her father's leather chair and opened them one by one.

As she had read them, the hairs on the back of her neck had stood up. The letters began a few months after Greta left and had arrived every six months or so thereafter. They were clearly in response to letters Kristel's father had sent. They were written in very friendly terms and chronicled every detail of Kristel's life.

Thank you for the photographs of Kristel at Kindergarten. Isn't she growing up!

It's good to know that Kristel did well in her end-of-year exams. She obviously has your brains, Frank!

How incredible that she's about to graduate from the Gymnasium. It doesn't seem possible. How the years have flown by. I'm so pleased that she's going to study journalism. She's always had an enquiring mind...

Kristel had read them through with her mouth open, shock washing through her. She'd been led to believe that her father and mother weren't in contact, and she'd assumed that Greta had no interest in her; she'd certainly done everything she could to distance herself from Kristel. So why had her father been writing to Greta on a regular basis with information about Kristel's life?

The very next day, stunned and hurt that her father could have hidden this from her, that he must have lied to her, or at least hidden the truth from her throughout her entire life, Kristel had begun to look for answers. She had started digging into her mother's early life for an explanation. And it was the clues she'd gleaned on that quest that were the primary reason she was now here in Trento interviewing a former member of the Brown Sisters, who, in some shape or form, was connected to the Lebensborn programme. Without that hunger for answers, Kristel might never have made the journey over the snow-covered Brenner Pass to interview Margarete Weiss. Now she felt as if she was standing on the edge of a precipice. She wasn't sure whether the truth would push her over the edge or set her free.

SEVEN

HEDDA

Munich, 2005

Hedda sat in the comfy chair in her apartment, in front of the electric fire, stroking the tiny lock of pale gold hair in its disintegrating ribbon. She was thinking back to those dark days in September 1942, that terrible moment when she'd seen her family home reduced to rubble by the Allied bombing raid on Munich. If she closed her eyes now, blotted out the sounds of the neighbours, she could still feel Sebastian's strong arms around her, holding her tight, while she screamed and sobbed and thumped his chest in pain and grief and frustration.

'I'll take you home to my place,' he said when she'd calmed down a little. 'My mother will be there. We can look after you.'

But Hedda resisted. 'No, I can't leave here. I need to go back to the house. What if... what if...?' Her mind was frantically running through the possibilities, trying to grasp onto hope by whatever means possible. What if, by some miracle, one of her family had survived the destruction of the house? It was just possible that her father had been out on an errand when the bombs fell, or that he'd been late getting home from work that day. What if her mother had taken her younger sister Clara and popped to her friend Dagmar's house round the corner to borrow some flour or potatoes for the evening meal? She might be just across the road, watching in horror as the remains of her house burned. Hedda needed to be there in case they came back. Or what if one of them was pulled alive from the rubble? She'd heard miracles like that could happen, from news reports of previous bombing raids in other parts of the city.

'I understand,' Sebastian said. 'I'll come back with you.'

So, with his arm around her shoulders, she huddled against him and allowed him to support her as they walked slowly in the direction of her home. She felt him stiffen and take a sharp breath as the devastated street came into view, the houses reduced to burning rubble, the searchlights, the fire engines, the frantic people running to and fro. They stopped a little distance away from the burning buildings, joining a small crowd of bewildered onlookers who were standing there in the chill of the evening, staring in disbelief at the piles of brick and dust that had been family homes less than half an hour beforehand.

With the aid of searchlights, rescue workers were digging in the rubble, sifting through the debris for survivors, and the firemen were still dousing the flames with long hoses that ran from their fire engine.

'I need to go to them,' Hedda said desperately, breaking free from Sebastian's arms and running towards the remains of her home.

A couple of firemen stood on the piles of rubble, bending down, throwing bricks aside, searching. Hedda reached the edge of the pile and began to climb onto it. She'd only gone a couple of steps before she stumbled and fell onto her knees, grazing them, twisting her ankle. Then she felt Sebastian's arms around her once more, pulling her back.

'I need to look for them myself,' she implored, struggling in his arms. 'I can't not try!'

One of the men working nearby looked up and, seeing her, held up a hand and motioned for her to go back. 'Get down. It's dangerous here. You could get injured, Fräulein.'

Reluctantly, she sank back into Sebastian's arms and allowed him to walk her away from the bombed-out buildings, limping and bruised, to where the crowd stood behind a newly erected rope barrier. They stood there, eyes smarting in the smoke, watching the rescuers' every move, until the men finally gave up their search. Hedda's feet and hands were numb with cold, but she hardly noticed.

One of the rescuers approached. 'We'll come back tomorrow at first light with better equipment. But we are quite sure there are no survivors in there. I'm very sorry, Fräulein.'

Hedda stared at the man, stunned, trying to take in his words. It was too much to process. Again, she felt Sebastian's arms around her and allowed him to guide her away from the scene. She moved beside him dumbly, like a sleepwalker. She didn't care where she went or what happened to her; at that moment, it felt as if her life was over.

'This is what the Führer has been warning against,' Sebastian muttered as they walked. 'The cynical targeting of civilian areas in our cities. The British will stop at nothing. They are an evil enemy.'

Hedda had no answer for him, reeling from the shock and pain of her loss as she was. Everything about the war seemed evil to her. Why had the bombers targeted the area? There were no arms factories or military installations for miles around. It was a cruel, pointless act. It had robbed Hedda of her entire family and, even worse, it had robbed her family and many others of their lives. What a senseless waste.

Sebastian's house was a large villa a few blocks away in one of the more expensive parts of the suburb. He showed her inside, through the tiled hallway and into a kitchen, where a maid in a black dress and white pinafore, a little white cap perched on her grey hair, stood at the sink. Hearing them enter, she turned round in surprise.

'This is Hedda, Gertrude,' Sebastian said. 'Her house has been destroyed in the raid and her family are missing. Can you get her something to eat and drink, please? We've been standing in the cold for hours.'

'Of course. How truly terrible, Fräulein! I heard the bombers. I have only just come back from the shelter myself. It was very close.'

Sebastian pulled out a chair and Hedda sat down at the table, still numb with shock and grief, her whole body trembling. The maid put a cup of hot milk in front of her, quickly followed by a bowl of soup and a hunk of bread. She sipped the milk gratefully.

'Eat the soup, Hedda. You've had a terrible shock. You must keep your strength up,' Sebastian said, draping a blanket around her shoulders.

She managed a couple of spoons of soup and gradually she began to thaw out. All the time, her mind was going over the pain and horror of her loss. How could she carry on without Mutti and Papa? Clara too? If only she'd come home earlier, perhaps she could have saved them...

'Gertrude, where's Mutti?' Sebastian asked, interrupting Hedda's thoughts.

'Oh, your mother's gone off to a reception with your father, I'm not sure where exactly. She said they would be late back. They left in the motor car well before the raid.'

Relieved that she wouldn't have to face another stranger that evening, Hedda forced the soup down.

'Why don't you stay here tonight?' Sebastian said. 'We have plenty of spare rooms.'

Hedda shook her head. 'I need to go to my aunt's place. She's my mother's sister. I need to tell her what's happened. I can stay there.'

'If you're sure. You'd be welcome to stay. But I understand if you need to go, I will come with you.'

When she'd finished eating, they crossed the city to where her aunt, Ursula, lived in an apartment with her husband and three young children near the main railway station. The trams weren't running because of the air raid damage to the electrical supplies, so they walked all the way, passing many bombed-out buildings, their façades crumbling onto the streets, exposing the insides of rooms, floors hanging precariously. In some places, firemen were still dousing flames by searchlight, searching through wrecked buildings for survivors.

The walk seemed to take forever; they made slow progress and it was after eleven o'clock when Hedda knocked on the door of her aunt's apartment. She had to knock several times before her aunt came to the door. She was wrapped in a dressing gown, her auburn hair tucked up in a hairnet.

'Hedda?' She peered out in the gloom. 'I was just going to bed. Whatever's the matter?'

'Oh, Auntie...' Hedda dissolved into tears.

Ursula stepped forward and put her arms around her, but Hedda found herself unable to say the words she needed to say. It was left to Sebastian to break the news that it was virtually certain that Hedda's entire family had perished in the bombing raid.

'Oh... my God!' Ursula wrapped her arms around Hedda and drew her inside, both of them sobbing.

Sebastian left her then and it was only afterwards when she looked back over that terrible evening that she realised he would have had to cross the city alone on foot all the way back to his house.

There was no choice but for Hedda to stay in the cramped flat with her aunt and her family, sharing a tiny bedroom with her eldest cousin, Gisela, who was six years old. The other two, boys, were four and five. Being with Gisela made Hedda think of Clara, who'd been only a couple of years older, and she pined for her loss.

At first, Aunt Ursula was kind and welcoming towards Hedda. Although Ursula and Hedda's mother hadn't been very close, Ursula was deeply saddened by the death of her sister and Hedda was grateful to at least have someone to share her grief with.

Ursula's husband, Edward, had always been brooding and gruff. Even before she'd had to move in, Hedda had the sense that he disapproved of her. Despite the tragic circumstances, he seemed to resent Hedda's presence in the apartment from the outset. He would make disparaging comments about the cost of food and fuel and the overcrowding in the apartment, which were clearly aimed at her. Luckily for Hedda, he wasn't at home much. Each day, he was up early and out to take a tram to his job as a foreman in a factory on the edge of the city that made parts for aircraft. Hedda was shocked when, on that first terrible morning after the bombing, as they were walking home from taking the children to school, Ursula told her that Edward was a member of the Nazi Party.

'He had to sign up,' she said defensively. 'All workers at the factory are party members, so it made sense to for him to join too. It's helped him get his promotion, actually.'

Hedda felt too weak and grief-stricken to express her disapproval at this news, and in any case, she wasn't sure that Aunt Ursula didn't have Nazi leanings too. She decided that she would keep her opinions to herself.

The service for the victims of the September bombings was held the following week in the Catholic church nearest to Hedda's old home. Hedda and Aunt Ursula went alone; Edward grudgingly stayed at home to look after the children. As they arrived at the church, Hedda's heart lifted to see Sebastian waiting there for her beside the door, looking smart in a dark suit and tie. He fell into step beside her as she walked into the church and found a pew.

'Thank you for coming,' she whispered. It was a comfort to feel him there beside her when the coffins of her family were carried down the aisle, along with those of the ten other victims of the bombings in that district, and the shock of her loss hit her afresh. He held her hand as she sobbed her way through the service.

After they had witnessed the coffins being lowered into their graves out in the windswept graveyard, Hedda walked between Aunt Ursula and Sebastian in a crowd of other mourners towards the cemetery gates. It was hard for Hedda to walk away from those three freshly dug graves. She felt as though she was leaving her whole life behind her there in that muddy corner.

'I know it's early days, but are you going back to college?' Sebastian asked gently.

'I'm not sure.' Hedda glanced at her aunt, aware that Ursula was keen on Hedda helping out with the children and earning her keep by doing other household chores in the daytime. During the miserable, grief-torn fortnight that she'd stayed at the apartment, there had been no mention of her resuming her studies. Now, Ursula shot her a warning look.

'Well, I hope you do,' Sebastian said. 'Whatever difficulties we face in our own lives, all young Germans have a responsibility to the Fatherland to keep up with their studies.'

When they reached Hedda and Ursula's tram stop, they said their goodbyes and Sebastian headed off in the direction of his own tram stop. Hedda stared after him, wondering what he meant, and why he'd said it in those terms. Despite the grief and sorrow of the day, she couldn't help but feel a glow of warmth that he'd been there with her.

On the way home, Aunt Ursula was silent for a while as the tram rattled towards the centre of the city but eventually she said, 'Your friend was right, you know. You should go back to college. I can manage at home, as long as you're prepared to help out during the evenings.'

Hedda smiled inwardly. Now she understood why Sebastian had said what he'd said. How clever he was. He must have picked up on Ursula's pro-Nazi stance and said those words in order to gain her approval for Hedda's return to college. Thinking about Sebastian was the one bright spot in her otherwise miserable existence and she clung to it like a port in a storm.

EIGHT

HEDDA

Munich, 1942

The following week, Hedda went back to class. She was glad to finally be getting out of the apartment and heading off across the city to college with her satchel over her shoulder. Aunt Ursula had lent her some of her cast-off clothes – all her own had been lost along with her family in the rubble of their home. She felt a little awkward and self-conscious dressed in a tight black skirt and knitted sweater that were at least ten years out of date, but she still had her red winter coat, the one Mutti and Papa had given her last Christmas.

The other girls glanced at her awkwardly when she approached the building, and she gradually realised that they had no idea what to say to her in the face of the tragedy she'd suffered. Many others in her class had lost family members since the war began; brothers and fathers had been killed in action, younger siblings, grandparents, even mothers had been cut down in previous bombing raids. But it was very rare for someone to have suffered the loss of an entire family in one evening as she had done. As she entered the building and went along the corridor towards the classroom, a few of her fellow pupils ignored her, others looked embarrassed when they saw her. Some even turned and walked in the opposite direction. She sensed that her presence was discomforting to them.

Only Beate and Elsa welcomed her that first morning. They put their arms around her and both said earnestly how sorry they were for her loss.

A couple of days later, though, Hedda even began to sense some sort of hostility radiating from her two best friends as well. She wondered at first if she was imagining it, and tried to put it down to being oversensitive. It was only when Sebastian came to speak to her one morning as they all arrived at college at the same time that she understood the source of this hostility. When she turned back to Beate and Elsa after speaking to him, the naked envy on both their faces was plain to see.

'He's been kind to me,' she explained when Sebastian had gone inside the building to his class. Even as she spoke, she wondered why she felt the need to explain, but she carried on. 'We're just friends. Sebastian helped me that evening... when... when...' Her eyes welled up and she felt hot tears on her cheeks.

Immediately, Beate's face softened and she came and put her arms around Hedda, hugging her tight. 'I'm so sorry, Hedda. There's no need to explain. Please don't cry. Come on... let's go into class.'

So, Hedda resumed her studies, and life slotted back into some sort of normality on the surface – although inside, her heart ached with sorrow. It was especially hard at the end of each day when classes were over and she had to set off towards Aunt Ursula's apartment. It was in the opposite direction to her old home. She missed those tram rides with Sebastian, she missed her mother's baking, the evenings by the fire with her father smoking his pipe and listening to the radio, she missed playing with her little sister. In fact, she missed everything about her old life.

On the second week back, when she was on her way home one evening, Hedda rounded a bend in the street after having said goodbye to Elsa and Beate and someone stepped out of the shadows in front of her. She recognised him immediately.

'Sebastian?'

He came close, rubbing his hands together in the freezing November air. 'I waited until you'd said goodbye to your friends. Can I walk you home?'

Her spirits rose, just seeing him there. 'Of course. That would be nice. Thank you.'

They began to walk side by side through the dark, narrow streets of the old town.

'How have you been?' he asked.

'All right. Fine,' Hedda replied, her voice neutral.

'It must be so hard for you,' Sebastian said. 'Apart from the terrible loss that you've suffered, your aunt's apartment looked pretty small to me.'

'It's not easy living there,' she admitted.

'I've got an idea. Why don't we go for a drink on the way there?' he asked.

'What, now?' Her heart sped up. What would Aunt Ursula say if she was late home?

'Yes, now,' he laughed. 'Unless... unless you don't want to?'

'No. No, I'd really like that... it's just...'

She didn't want to tell him how claustrophobic she found life in the apartment with Aunt Ursula and Uncle Edward, how she was treated as an unpaid servant-cum-nanny, how, once they'd eaten supper, her aunt and uncle would often go out to their rallies or clubs or bierkellers in the evenings, leaving her to wash the dishes and put the unruly children to bed.

'Don't worry about your aunt and uncle, Hedda,' he said. It was uncanny how he seemed to know what was on her mind.

'All right,' she said tentatively, 'but I mustn't be too late.'

He took her arm and turned off the main thoroughfare,

guiding her to a discreet little cellar bar tucked away deep in the ancient, cobbled streets of the old town. It was only a short walk away from her normal route to her aunt's place, but Hedda had never been that way before.

She hesitated in the doorway; she had never been in a bar before. Standing there looking down the steps into the alcoves of the vaulted bar itself, she noticed a group of SS officers seated at a table in the corner. For a second she froze in panic.

Following her eyes, Sebastian smiled reassuringly and said, 'Don't worry about them. Their HQ is nearby, they are off duty.'

He led her to a table on the opposite side of the cellar to the officers and ordered them each a large schnapps. Hedda had rarely drunk alcohol before, only sipped her father's beer or after dinner liqueur on the odd occasion, but she wasn't about to tell Sebastian that. She sipped the fiery drink tentatively, noticing how it burned in her gullet and within seconds made everything feel a little blurry around the edges. She quickly began to relax.

'How is everything *really* going at home?' Sebastian asked, leaning forward across the table and looking deep into her eyes. The sincerity of his look melted her reserve. What harm was there in telling him?

Hesitantly, she began to confide in him about life at the apartment. Once she began speaking, she realised what a relief it was to be able to talk to someone frankly about it. She told him how claustrophobic and cramped it was in the flat, how much work her aunt expected of her and how Uncle Edward did everything he could to make her life difficult and unpleasant.

'I know I'm not really welcome there,' she said. 'They'd probably prefer it if I'd been lost along with the rest of my family. Especially my uncle. But they can't really ask me to leave. I don't have anywhere else to go.'

'I'm so sorry, Hedda,' Sebastian said, taking her hand across the table. 'I would ask you to come and stay with us. The house is easily big enough, but I don't think you would agree.'

She tore her eyes away from his and looked down at the table, where a candle flickered, their hands entwined beside it. 'It's very kind of you but I couldn't possibly accept,' she replied. 'In any case, wouldn't your parents have something to say about it?'

He smiled. 'They wouldn't mind at all. They are very generous. Besides, they are often away. Father has to go back and forth to Berlin regularly and Mutti often travels with him.'

'Didn't you say your father runs a factory?' Hedda asked.

'Yes. He's an engineer by trade, an industrialist. He's a very good businessman, actually.'

Hedda thought about the sumptuous house, the uniformed maid, the chauffeur-driven car. The family were clearly very rich, and even Hedda knew that people didn't get to be rich or to stay rich under the Nazis without some sort of collaboration or compromise.

She eyed Sebastian in the candlelight. He looked so wholesome and innocent – with his perfect skin and clean features, his deep blue eyes and thick blond hair with its natural wave. Could he really be the son of Nazis? There were so many questions she wanted to ask him, but for some reason she couldn't bring herself to. Perhaps she didn't actually want to know the truth, perhaps she was just glad to have found a friend, someone who genuinely seemed to care about her. Why risk alienating him by probing into his background? What did his parents' views and lifestyle matter anyway? *They* weren't him, were they?

'Are you still going to the Hitler Youth meetings?' she asked him, skirting around the issue. Despite all the conversations they'd had on the tram on the way home and at her house when he used to come to tea, she'd never been sure about his stance on the Nazi regime. She didn't dare ask him his views directly, but perhaps if she approached it in this roundabout way, they would naturally emerge. And if he turned out to be a Nazi sympathiser, she knew she would have to distance herself from him. If he actually was, it would surely be easy for her to do.

'Yes. Of course,' he replied, still looking deeply into her eyes. 'Every Tuesday. I am an instructor now. Last weekend, we took a group of the younger boys out of town to the forest to practise shooting.'

Hedda swallowed, still unclear whether he was playing a role or if his enthusiasm was genuine. 'Oh, that must have been... interesting.' She chose her words carefully. 'Cold though, in this weather.'

He laughed and sat back in his chair, sliding his hand away from hers. 'It wasn't that bad, actually. It's good practice, a bit of hardship like that.'

He took a swig of his drink, tipping the glass upside-down.

'Practice? For what?'

He put the glass down on the table and beckoned to the waiter for another one.

'For the army, of course. The Wehrmacht. I will be signing up as soon as I've passed out of the Gymnasium. The end of the year. It's not long now.'

'Oh!' It was impossible for Hedda to hide her surprise and disappointment.

'I know. It's bad timing. Just as we were getting to know each other,' he said, leaning forward and smiling into her eyes again. 'But if I don't volunteer, I will be called up. At least this way it will be under my control. We will have a few weeks together before I go. And you don't have to worry, I'll make sure I don't get killed. I'll definitely be back.'

His words sent a little thrill through her. He was acknowledging that there was something special between them – that it wasn't just her – he felt it too. But she still wanted answers.

'Are you sure you actually want to fight?' she asked, probing again.

He glanced around quickly, but the SS officers were getting rowdy now; there was no chance of anyone hearing their conversation.

'We all have to fight, Hedda. Look what is happening to our cities, to our people. Your own family have been taken from you. Like thousands of others, innocent civilians killed in their own homes by the British bombings. The Allies have been determined to crush us since the Great War and the Treaty of Versailles. It is only through fighting back that we will be able to assert ourselves again. It's my responsibility as a young German to fight for my country. All my friends think that way.'

She stared at him, trying to read between the lines of what he said.

'I'm sure you would do the same if you had a choice,' he added.

'I suppose so,' she replied, torn once again. Because of the anger and grief and confusion she felt at the loss of her family, she realised that he was right. She *would* consider joining up to the Wehrmacht if she wasn't a girl. Not because she agreed with Hitler and the Nazi Party and what they were doing to Germany, but because she was German and would be prepared to stand up for her country against the bombing and killing of innocent civilians.

Two more drinks arrived and when she'd taken a couple more sips, Hedda realised that she was feeling dizzy now and when she spoke, her words came out slurred.

'I think I'd better go home now,' she said, putting the glass down. 'I can't actually finish this. I'm sorry, Sebastian.'

'Of course.' He drained his glass quickly.

The waiter came bustling over and Sebastian paid the bill.

Sebastian smiled at her as he opened the door onto the street and a blast of cold air enveloped them.

'You look so beautiful,' he said softly, touching her cheek.

The schnapps had made Hedda warm inside and his words intensified that feeling. She could feel her face glowing in the cold air. She looked up at him and smiled. Nobody had told her she was beautiful before, apart from her mother and father, of course. Hearing it from Sebastian's lips reminded her sharply of them and brought a lump to her throat.

They stepped out into the cold street and the door closed behind them, shutting out the light. There were no street lamps in the blackout. Sebastian put his arm around her shoulders and she leaned against him, happy to let him guide her through the dark alleyways to the familiar streets. Soon they were passing the Hauptbahnhof. Even in the gloom, she could hear the swastika banners fluttering from the portico. They hurried past the station entrance and turned into the street where her aunt and uncle's apartment was located. They walked along in silence and stopped outside the front door.

'Do you want me to come up to the apartment with you?' he asked.

Hedda shook her head. 'I'll be fine from here,' she said. The cold air seemed to have banished the effects of the alcohol.

'Goodbye, then, Hedda.' He drew her towards him and kissed her full on the lips. The initial surprise of feeling his lips on hers was quickly replaced with tingling pleasure and although she'd never kissed anyone like that before, she responded instinctively, slipping her arms around the back of his head and pulling him towards her, forgetting everything else in the pleasure of that moment.

When they parted, he stood and watched her go up the staircase and she waved before she turned the bend in the stairs. She carried on up to the apartment feeling euphoric and a little heady.

'Where have you been?' Ursula shouted as soon as she got through the front door of the apartment.

'I went for a quick drink with a friend.'

'Quick drink?' Ursula appeared in the hallway, she was getting dressed to go out. She was wearing a skimpy black dress and had a lipstick in her hand, curlers in her hair. She sniffed the air and frowned. 'You've been drinking alcohol!'

'I only had one.'

'Well, never mind. I don't have time to talk about that now. At least you're back. I've had to put the boys to bed myself, but I left the dishes for you. I've got to finish dressing – I'm late already.'

Hedda didn't mind doing the dishes and reading Gisela a story before tucking her up in bed. It gave her a chance to be alone and to think about what had happened that evening, to dream about Sebastian – the way he'd looked at her, called her beautiful, and the memory of his lips on hers.

When Gisela was safely asleep, Hedda went into the bathroom and took a long, hard look at herself in the mirror. Her skin was still glowing from the mixture of alcohol, cold air and excitement and her ice-blue eyes were sparkling and bright for the first time in months. She unplaited her thick blonde hair and let it tumble loose over her shoulders. She narrowed her eyes and tried to see herself as Sebastian might see her. Was she beautiful? She'd never really thought about it before, but she could still feel that glow of pleasure from his words. She drew herself up and smiled at herself in the mirror. If he thought she was beautiful, she must be.

NINE

HEDDA

Munich, 1942

From that day on, Hedda and Sebastian met in the same spot almost every evening after college and went for a couple of drinks before he walked her home. They sometimes went to the bar they'd been to on that first evening, sometimes others. All of them were tucked away discreetly in the little streets behind Marienplatz. There were often Nazi officers drinking and relaxing in a corner, and although the sight of them made her nervous initially, Hedda learned to ignore their presence. Sebastian always paid for the drinks; Hedda had almost no money of her own, but if she ever offered to contribute, he would wave her offer away – generosity seemed central to his nature.

During those evenings, they would talk about almost everything. Sebastian told her all about his life in Berlin, about his travels with his parents – before the war, they had visited many countries with his father's business. Hedda listened awestruck to his tales of New York, of London, of Paris and even India and Japan. His stories would transport her to another time and place, away from the horrors of the war and the bombings, her

grief, and her life of drudgery with Aunt Ursula. As long as she
didn't stay out late and was available to help with supper and
with putting the children to bed in the evening, her aunt didn't
seem to care about her outings.

They skirted around the subject of politics and the Nazi
regime. Even though Hedda was falling in love with Sebastian,
she still didn't feel confident enough to tell him what she
thought about what had been happening around her for most of
her life – the persecution of the Jews, the Nuremberg Laws
banning them from professions, the open hostility and persecution of them on the streets of her home city, the incarceration of
them and opponents of the regime in Dachau and other concentration camps. How could she tell him that on Kristallnacht,
when she'd been only thirteen, she had been shocked to the core
coming home from a shopping trip with her mother to see mobs
of ordinary Germans throwing stones at Jewish shops and
beating up Jews, and she'd gone home to cry. Her mother and
father had sat tight-lipped in the sitting room that evening,
shaking their heads and saying how they were ashamed to be
German.

She felt a little cowardly, ducking these issues, but she was
half afraid of finding out something about Sebastian that she
didn't want to know. He was as circumspect as she was, skirting
round difficult issues, never confronting them head-on. Besides,
she didn't want to spoil the world he had created for her on
those evening outings, the world he painted for her with his
stories. It lifted her heart and her spirits.

It was a couple of weeks before Christmas when he invited
her to his house.

'It would be nice to spend a whole evening together for
once,' he said. 'Come for supper and I will take you home on the
tram afterwards.'

'I'm not sure what my aunt might say,' Hedda replied, hesitating. She knew that Ursula didn't really care about her

welfare or about who she spent her time with, but she was keen on making sure Hedda was available to put the children to bed and to help out in the apartment.

'Just say you are going to study with a friend and that you might be late home. We *could* study together for a while so it wouldn't actually be a lie.'

When the appointed evening arrived, they met in their usual place, then walked together arm in arm to the tram stop. This was how it used to be, before her life had been ripped apart, Hedda reflected as they boarded the tram and found two empty seats side by side. It was the same familiar route and they sat together and chatted easily, just as they used to. When the tram rattled towards Hedda's old neighbourhood, she closed her eyes. She just couldn't look. Even though it was dark, she didn't want to risk even a glimpse of her old street. As she sat there with her eyes shut, she felt Sebastian's hand taking hers and she grasped onto it and held it until they reached the next stop.

Hedda was tingling with nerves and anticipation as they walked together along Sebastian's road towards his house. When he opened the front door with his key and they stepped into the dark hall, she realised that they were alone. He had told her that his parents were away in Berlin, but she had assumed that the maid would be there.

'Is Gertrude not here?' she asked.

'It's her night off. She's gone to see her sister in Augsburg. She'll be back in the morning.'

Hedda was a little surprised that Sebastian hadn't told her that they would be completely alone. But still, she supposed, she hadn't actually asked.

He switched on the light and took her through to the kitchen. 'I asked Gertrude to leave some food.'

He put down his bags and took some dishes out of the refrigerator: cold bratwurst, ham, potato salad and a loaf of bread. He also took out a large, covered tankard of cold beer.

'Let's eat in the drawing room. It's nicer in there. I'll light a fire.'

He stacked the food on a tray, along with plates, glasses and cutlery.

'Come on through,' he said, picking up the tray, and she followed him through the panelled hallway and into a high-ceilinged drawing room, luxuriously furnished with heavy oak chests and tables and classical art on the walls.

Sebastian put the tray on the coffee table, knelt down before the marble fireplace and lit the fire with the kindling and news-paper that had already been laid in the grate.

'Let me take your coat,' he said when he stood up.

Hedda shivered when he took it from her shoulders, not just from the cold, but from the touch of his fingers on her bare neck.

They sat down opposite each other on stuffed blue velvet sofas and ate the food and sipped their beers. Gradually, the warmth from the fire crept through the room and started to thaw Hedda out, but the conversation didn't flow between them as easily as it usually did. The large, empty house was intimidat-ing. To Hedda, it felt impersonal and she couldn't help comparing it to the house she'd grown up in, a little down at heel and shabby, and a bit cramped too, but always full of laughter and the sounds of family life.

But once she'd had a few sips of beer, she began to relax.

Sebastian cleared his throat. 'It's only a few weeks before I leave,' he said. 'I'm off in early January.'

'Oh!' They hadn't spoken about him leaving since that first evening. Hedda hadn't wanted to contemplate it. Just the thought of it sent panic waves through her. 'Where are you going?' she asked, trying not to sound as devastated as she felt.

'I don't know yet. Not to the Front straight away. I'll be going to training camp first, somewhere in Bavaria. Not too far away.' He put his knife and fork down and looked at her. 'I will miss you, Hedda.'

'I'll miss you too,' she said, swallowing hard. It came home to her how much his company meant to her now. Beate and Elsa seemed to have distanced themselves from her since she'd been meeting Sebastian. She'd kept it a secret from them, but perhaps they knew anyway. Certainly, neither of them had invited her to their homes after college or BDM meetings as they used to do.

Sebastian moved across to sit next to her and put his arms around her. She turned her face towards his and he kissed her hard on the lips. It felt more urgent, more passionate than his previous kisses. It ignited a flame deep inside Hedda and she found herself responding with equal passion.

'I love you, Hedda,' he kept murmuring as he unbuttoned her cardigan and slipped his hand inside her clothes.

She shivered as his cold fingers explored her breasts, but although this felt strange and new and she hadn't been prepared for what the evening might bring, now it was happening, she didn't want him to stop. Sebastian had become her world in recent weeks. Despite the fact that he was an enigma in so many ways, she knew she loved him, and she wanted to show him how much, especially as he would be gone in a few short weeks.

'Is this all right?' he asked, looking deep into her eyes and pushing her clothes aside.

'Yes,' she breathed. 'I love you, Sebastian.'

She closed her eyes as he moved on top of her and even though what followed made her gasp with pain, she was so filled with love and gratitude towards him that it seemed nothing beside the overwhelming feeling of joy and love that flooded through her, displacing the emptiness and despair she'd felt for so long.

. . .

Hedda held the lock of blonde hair between her arthritic fingers and smiled fondly. She was jolted out of her reverie by the sound of the downstairs neighbour's baby crying again. She fingered the lock of hair and tears came to her eyes at the injustice of it all. That poor little mite was yelling the place down and its parents didn't seem to care. Like so many people, they had no idea how lucky they were to be blessed with a child. They were so profligate with their good fortune. If it were *her* baby, she wouldn't let it cry for hours on end like that.

Her tears ran over recalling that evening in Sebastian's house. As she'd lain next to him, so utterly in love, she'd had no idea what was about to happen. That a baby was already growing inside her. That she would have no one to turn to. That very soon she would be on a train bound for a castle in southern Bavaria in the snow-capped mountains, hoping that it would be a safe place for her to have her child.

TEN

MARGARETE

Trento, 2005

In the morning, after the snowstorm of the previous evening, the sky was clear and bright, the snow on the far-off hills glistening in the morning sunlight. Even before breakfast, Margarete was out of bed and sitting beside the window, her eyes glued to the driveway. She was filled with a sense of anticipation tinged with apprehension, watching for a glimpse of that little red car turning into the entrance of the care home.

She heard the sound of the trolley in the corridor and one of the younger carers came in with her food. It was Sophia. Today was the first day she'd been on duty since Margarete's revelation. As she laid the bread rolls and slices of cheese and hard-boiled egg out on the table in front of Margarete, she said, 'I didn't know you were German, Margharita. You speak Italian so well. It was a big surprise to all of us.'

Margarete shrugged and muttered something indistinct. It pained her to know that they must have all been gossiping about her in the staffroom. Only Lorenzo seemed to understand that she needed time and space. She wasn't about to

reveal anything about her former life to the staff here, even
though she cared for them deeply and they had been good to
her, her cover was so ingrained in her behaviour. Hadn't she
spent the last sixty years perfecting her Italian identity?
These nurses would never understand. No one would, except
perhaps for Lorenzo, and that promising young woman,
Kristel Meyer. Kristel had intelligence and integrity.
Margarete, with her laser-sharp understanding of human
nature, had spotted that instantly. Although she'd been reluctant at first to trust Kristel, on reflection, she was sure she
could.

While she was eating her breakfast, the red car appeared on
the drive. And there was Kristel getting out of the driver's seat.
This time, she looked up at the front window and waved.
Margarete smiled and waved back with her napkin. It was good
to see her. In the few minutes it took for Kristel to sign in at the
front desk and make her way upstairs, Margarete had finished
her breakfast and dusted the crumbs off her clothes.

Sophia bustled in ahead of Kristel. 'Miss Meyer is here to
see you,' she said with a knowing smile, then whisked the breakfast tray away.

'How are you today, Miss Bianchi?' Kristel said, sitting
down in the chair beside Margarete's.

'Miss Weiss. Or better still, Margarete. Please call me
Margarete.'

Kristel beamed. She looked so much more relaxed this
morning, Margarete noted as she took out her notebook and
mini tape recorder and put it on the table between them.

'Are you OK to start?'

Margarete nodded.

'All right. Now, yesterday you were telling me how
Himmler recruited you to run a Lebensborn home in Bavaria.
Could you tell me more about that today?'

Margarete was a little disturbed that Kristel had dived

straight in with a mention of Himmler, but she answered as honestly as she could.

'Of course. Well, I had no choice but to agree to it. I was terrified that they knew about my family's anti-Nazi views. I left for Bavaria by train the following week. I was sad to say goodbye to my family, but I was going partly for their sakes, to protect them, but I didn't tell them that, of course. I told them that I'd been posted to a maternity home in Bavaria and that I would write as soon as I could.

'When I arrived at the castle, naive and inexperienced as I was, I quickly realised that behind the saccharine exterior of helping women and caring for babies, it was part of the most heinous experiment the world has ever known. I was briefed on arrival by the doctor in charge – Doctor Finkel. He was quite frank with me about the aims of the place.'

It was early afternoon on a beautiful, sunny day in June 1938 when the black Mercedes, the staff car that had collected Margarete from the station at Füssen, skirted a lake, rounded a bend in the road and the castle first came into view. Margarete gasped when she caught sight of it there on the mountainside above the road. It was a breathtaking spectacle – like something out of a fairy tale. Pale stone walls with red roofs, it soared through the pine forest towards the sky, with its many round towers and spires and crenelated bowers. It seemed to perch precariously on the side of the mountain, standing out against the backdrop of craggy rocks and peaks behind it and the bright blue cloudless sky. The sun glittered and twinkled on its many windows.

'It's beautiful,' Margarete said to the driver, who seemed friendly enough.

'It is quite a sight, miss,' he replied. 'Of course, it wasn't always so grand. It had been shut up for years. The owner,

Count Von Essenberg, couldn't afford to keep all the rooms open. The old place has had a revamp since the Ministry took it over.'

He turned the car off the road, and in through some elaborate wrought-iron gates. Then, engine roaring, they began to climb the steep driveway that twisted and turned its way up the mountainside, until finally they arrived in a large square courtyard in front of the castle. It was even more impressive close up, a little intimidating even.

The driver came round to let Margarete out of the back seat, then took her suitcases out of the boot. She looked towards the building and noticed a tall figure dressed in a white coat, holding a clipboard, standing in the arched doorway.

'Nurse Weiss? I am Doctor Finkel,' the man said, striding forward to greet her.

She held out her hand to shake his, but instead of taking it, he raised his right hand in the rigid Nazi salute.

'Heil Hitler,' he barked.

Self-consciously, Margarete lifted her own hand and returned the gesture as perfunctorily as she could.

'Heil,' she muttered.

'I have been waiting for your arrival,' Doctor Finkel said, frowning and peering at her through wire-rimmed, pebble glasses. 'Your train was a little late. Come inside, please.'

He took her by the arm, guided her up the front steps and through the great oak doorway.

The driver carried Margarete's bags inside the cavernous entrance hall and left them there, clicking his heels together and saluting in the same way before leaving the building and shutting the door.

Margarete looked around the vaulted entrance hall in awe. Giant wrought-iron candelabra hung from the ceiling. Huge, gilt-framed oil paintings of landscapes adorned the stone walls, alongside stuffed deer heads and antlers, hunting spears and guns. It was impressive but a little unsettling too.

'Please follow me, Nurse Weiss. Somebody will take your bags to your room,' Doctor Finkel said, setting off down a high-ceilinged corridor at a brisk pace.

Margarete followed him along the long stone passage, itself decorated with hunting memorabilia, and into a large office, filled with bookshelves, neatly labelled filing cabinets, an imposing desk and leather button chairs.

'Would you like some refreshment, Nurse Weiss? It is a little late for coffee. I'm afraid you've missed lunch too, but afternoon tea will be served in the staff dining room in about an hour. But if you'd like a cold drink now?'

'Just some water, please,' Margarete said.

The doctor rang a bell on the wall and a maid appeared almost instantly and took his order.

'Do take a seat, Nurse Weiss.' The doctor gestured to a chair opposite the desk. 'I will brief you on the programme we are running here at Schloss Schwanburg and what will be expected of you.'

Margarete sat down feeling a little nervous, and the doctor leaned back in his chair and put his fingertips together.

'You have come highly recommended by Reichsführer Himmler, Nurse Weiss,' he said.

Margarete hid the shudder that passed through her at the notion that she should be associated in any way with that man, the leader of the brutal SS. He was known to have personally established the Dachau concentration camp and was also doubt-less responsible for countless barbarous policies and acts of cruelty.

The maid came into the room bringing a jug of water and glasses on a tray and there was a pause while she poured and handed Margarete a glass.

'The Reichsführer himself set up the Lebensborn

programme in 1935,' Doctor Finkel continued when they were alone again. 'This establishment here in the castle falls within that programme. Initially, its purpose was to ensure that SS officers married women of impeccable Aryan descent and produced as many children as they could, but in the years since its inception, it has developed well beyond those initial aims.'

He smiled, but the smile didn't reach his eyes, and another shudder went through Margarete, despite the heat of the day.

'The Reichsführer is concerned that many racially valuable babies are being lost through needless terminations, simply because their mothers are unmarried. It is his wish to encourage those women to keep their babies to increase the stock of Aryan children in the Fatherland.'

'I see.' Margarete nodded and tried to keep her face neutral. The way Doctor Finkel described the programme made it sound quite different and far more sinister than the way it had been introduced to her in Fräulein Koch's office the previous week.

'Our role here is to offer single women of Aryan blood a place to give birth in comfort and privacy. That is, of course, provided their ancestry and that of the father of their child has been checked, is racially pure and free from the stain of Judaism, Slavic blood or other undesirable elements,' he virtually spat these last words, betraying his own views about people he deemed racially impure.

'Oh...' Margarete muttered, trying to hide her disgust at his words.

'We test the young women as soon as they arrive and if either they or their partner don't meet our strict criteria, we are unable to help them, and they are asked to leave immediately.'

'What sort of tests are those, Doctor Finkel?' she asked. Prickles of discomfort were running through her at each sentence the doctor uttered. This was very different from what she had been led to expect.

'Oh – the tests are very rigorous, you'll be glad to hear, Nurse. We carefully measure their skull and the distance between their eyes and ensure that they conform to various other physical criteria. We also investigate their ancestry in great depth – in fact, when they arrive, they must bring with them a certificate of racial purity. But we check carefully the veracity of that document. We also seek to ensure that there is no disability, mental illness or congenital defects running in their families. Of course, all that is my job, Nurse Weiss,' he smiled. 'Your predecessor, Sister Bach, was never involved in the initial testing.'

'Sister Bach? Is she no longer working here?'

The doctor cleared his throat and his eyes flickered away from Margarete and down to the papers on his polished desk for a second. 'No, I'm afraid Sister Bach had to leave the castle rather suddenly.'

'Oh?' Margarete had asked before she could stop herself.

'You don't need to know the details, Nurse Weiss,' he said, peering at her sharply. 'Now, your job will be to supervise the nursery and the maternity ward. I know you are a nursery nurse by training. We have a trained midwife here for the births, but you will oversee her work and that of the nursery nurses... All of it is under my overall direction, of course.'

Margarete frowned but said nothing. She was finding it increasingly hard to take all this in, and her mind was very distracted now. The set-up at the castle was not what she'd expected at all and alarm bells were ringing in her head. The racial purity tests sounded very strange, and she was also wondering about Sister Bach and why she'd had to leave so suddenly.

Doctor Finkel stood up briskly. 'Now I've outlined what our purpose is here, I will show you round the building. I'm very proud of the important work we do here, our contribution to the Fatherland, Nurse Weiss. We are a dedicated, serious team and

I think you will fit in very nicely indeed. Now, come along.
Please follow me.'

Her nerves taut, Margarete obediently followed the doctor
out of the office, back along the passage to the entrance hall, and
up the wide, sweeping central staircase. At the front of the
castle, in a large, square bedroom with an elaborate plasterwork
ceiling, four young women rested in hospital beds.

Doctor Finkel strode into the room in front of Margarete
and clapped his hands. The girls stiffened visibly and sat up
straight.

'Heil Hitler, ladies,' he boomed, saluting again. 'I have
brought someone to meet you. This is Nurse Weiss, who has
come all the way from the Charité Hospital in Berlin to take
charge of your care here at Schloss Schwanburg.'

'Welcome, Nurse Weiss,' the girls chorused in unison, but
none of them smiled.

'Thank you. Now, Nurse Weiss, these young ladies are
resting in this small ward up here because they are either very
close to their delivery date, or they have been encountering difficulties with their pregnancies. I won't introduce you personally
to each of them because... Oh, I should have reiterated, but I
assumed that the Reichsführer or Fräulein Koch would have
told you in advance... we operate on a no-names basis here.
Apart from the staff, of course. That is in order to give these
girls the confidentiality and privacy they deserve.'

'I see...' Margarete replied, once again rendered speechless
at yet another bizarre regulation.

She looked around the beds at the faces of the girls lying
there, propped up on pristine white pillows. All of them
looked a few years younger than Margarete herself. They were
probably aged between eighteen and twenty-one. Younger
than most of the mothers she'd worked with at Charité. These
girls all looked similar to each other – with blonde hair and
blue eyes – but she noticed too that they looked tired and a

little nervous, pale with blue smudges under their eyes. That was natural during the later stages of pregnancy, but she noticed with concern that none of them looked happy or contented.

'Most of our young ladies are taking the air out in the garden. The mountain air here at Schwanburg is as healthy as anywhere in the Reich. Come and have a look...'

Doctor Finkel beckoned her to the window and, pushing aside the elaborate lacy floral curtains, he pointed down to a huge lawn. It was surrounded by colourful flower beds and mown in neat strips. Several young women – about ten, Margarete guessed – in various stages of pregnancy sat in deckchairs, reading magazines or chatting in groups, or wandered together on the neat gravel paths around the edge of the lawn.

'I will introduce you to them later. In the meantime, I will show you the delivery room and nursery.'

Margarete smiled goodbye to the four nameless young women who barely looked at her, and followed Doctor Finkel along another corridor to a room with swing glass doors at the far end. Inside, Margarete was again stunned by what she saw: a state-of-the-art delivery room – a high bed with stirrups, spotlights, monitors and every conceivable type of equipment that might be needed during a delivery. All of it polished and pristine, scrupulously clean.

'As you'll see, Nurse Weiss, no expense has been spared in equipping the building for the very important and delicate job we do here,' Doctor Finkel said.

'It's incredible,' she replied, thinking of the worn-out, outdated equipment in the busy delivery room at Charité, that, due to lack of funding, hadn't been replaced for a long time.

As she was wondering at it, a stout, middle-aged woman appeared from a doorway at the far end of the room. She was dressed in a nurse's uniform, starched white apron and tall cap.

'Ah, Nurse Ekert,' Doctor Finkel said and introduced Margarete.

The woman gave the Heil Hitler salute unsmilingly.

'Welcome, Nurse Weiss,' she said. 'I am a qualified midwife and have been present at all the births that have taken place at the castle so far.'

'And how many is that?' Margarete asked.

'Forty-five,' Nurse Ekert replied. 'Since we were set up at the beginning of last year. Regular, but not overwhelming. Quite manageable with our small staff numbers. Of course, with the latest changes to the programme, we are expecting to increase our production considerably.'

'Changes?' Margarete asked, turning towards the doctor, at the same time wondering at the use of the word 'production'. She caught Doctor Finkel exchanging a warning look with Nurse Ekert.

'I haven't explained the latest brainchild of our esteemed Reichsführer to Nurse Weiss yet,' Doctor Finkel said hastily. 'I was going to wait until I showed her the entertainment suites on the second floor. But since you have raised the subject, Nurse Ekert, I will explain as I take Nurse Weiss along to the nursery wing. Come this way, Nurse Weiss, and I will talk as we go.'

He ushered Margarete swiftly out of the delivery room and back along the corridor.

'Now, let me explain,' he said as they walked slowly along a panelled corridor hung with works of art of the classical kind favoured by the Nazis, 'The Reichsführer has found that the numbers of babies born into our new programme haven't been quite what he'd hoped. He is concerned about the dwindling numbers of the master race. So, he is pioneering a new initiative. At the moment, it is not yet in operation here at Schloss Schwanburg, but we are expecting it to begin in the next couple of months. That's why it is so important for us to have a reliable and presentable head of nursing at the helm.'

Margarete watched his face, wondering what fantastical Nazi policy he was about to reveal to her. She wasn't sure she really wanted to know, but of course, she had no choice but to listen to him.

'The idea is for the castle here to become a meeting place for suitable young people of both sexes – the young men will be drawn from the ranks of the SS and the young women mainly recruited through the BDM movement. They can come and stay here, meet in congenial surroundings and... well... nature will take its course. The young women will, of course, be offered a home here until they give birth or alternatively will be able to stay at home for a few months and return here to the castle for the birth. It is up to them. We do find, though, that we are ahead of our time, and that German society isn't yet prepared to accept unmarried mothers into its heart, so they are often better off spending the whole nine months under our care.'

'And what about the babies?' Margarete asked, the hairs on the back of her neck rising in horror at what she was now hearing. 'What will happen to them?'

'Oh, the normal rules of the programme will apply. When they arrive, once they have proved their racial purity, the young women will sign a form relinquishing rights to their babies on their birth. Their babies will become the property of the Führer.'

'Property of the Führer?' she repeated, trying to keep the horror from her voice. 'What happens to them?'

'They are placed with deserving party members who are childless or wish to adopt. Their suitability is vetted rigorously beforehand, of course. We have so far placed all the babies born at Schloss Schwanburg. Now, here is the nursery, Nurse Weiss.'

He pushed open some double doors and they entered a sun-filled room with five white cots lined up on either side. Only three of them were occupied and the tiny babies inside were sleeping peacefully, snuggled under snow-white blankets. A young woman with blonde plaits wound tightly round her head came to greet them with the usual Heil Hitler salute. Doctor Finkel introduced her as Nurse Helena Jung. Margarete was disturbed to see that Helena, although a lot younger than Nurse Ekert, was equally severe-looking. Again, Margarete noticed that the nursery was a lot better equipped than the one she had just left, even though it catered for far fewer babies.

'I will show you to your quarters now,' Doctor Finkel said as they left the nursery.

Margarete followed him through the corridors and up a winding staircase to an upper floor, her mind going over and over the disturbing information he'd shared with her. At the top of the staircase, they were met by a middle-aged man in brown overalls, his oiled grey hair plastered to his head.

'Good afternoon, Holge. Nurse Weiss, meet Holge Schwartz. He is the caretaker of the castle. If you have any problems with your accommodation, you should ask him.'

'Good afternoon, Fräulein.' The man did the usual salute and rested his cold eyes on her face. 'As the doctor said, I am here to ensure the place runs like clockwork. Your room is ready for you – at the end of the corridor,' he said, pointing. 'Everything should be shipshape in there.'

Doctor Finkel took her to the room and opened the door. As they stepped inside, Margarete caught sight of the caretaker still standing at the top of the stone staircase, watching her.

The doctor closed the door. 'Yes, Holge keeps us on our toes. He actually works for the owner of the castle, Count Von Essenburg. The Count is now an officer in the SS, fighting for the Fatherland in France, and he has kindly given over the castle to the Ministry for the use of the Lebensborn programme in his absence. If you ever need Holge, his rooms are in the tower at the end of the corridor here.

'Now, I see your cases are already here. If you'd like to freshen up and then make your way down to the front hall in ten minutes, I will meet you there and show you to the dining room for afternoon tea. I will show you the second floor later. The refurbishment of that floor has just been completed. That is where the officers and young women will be staying when we move into the next phase of the programme. I will leave you alone to get settled in.'

When the door had closed behind the doctor, Margarete looked round at her room. Large and functional, with a wooden bed and heavy, walnut furniture, the walls were painted white. Above the bed was a framed propaganda poster that she had seen displayed on public buildings in Berlin. It was of a voluptuous mother holding a baby. Both were lustrous and healthy-looking, the woman dressed like a milkmaid in a periwinkle-blue dress that matched her eyes. Behind them was a cornfield, farm horses silhouetted on the horizon. The slogan on the poster was '*Mutter und Kind*'. Mother and child.

Margarete turned away from it and went to the window and threw it open. The view was stunning, over the tops of the fir trees and down layers of hills to a shimmering lake; it lifted her heart for just a moment. But when she looked directly beneath her, she could see the lawn and the heads of the girls there, killing time while they waited to give birth.

She drew in gulps of the fresh air, unbuttoned her blouse, went to the sink and splashed herself with cold water. Then she sat down on the bed, put her head in her hands, and breathed deeply, trying to calm herself.

After a couple of minutes, there was a knock at the door. Margarete quickly buttoned her blouse and answered it. To her surprise, the caretaker stood there.

He looked her up and down. 'Nurse Weiss, I heard the doctor say that he would meet you downstairs for afternoon tea. Could I remind you that tea is served at four o'clock and it is already two minutes past. The doctor doesn't like lateness. I could show you the way down, if you like?'

'No... no...' she stammered, realising she must have lost track of time. 'It's quite all right, I will go now.'

She went out into the passage and pulled the door shut, wondering where the key was, but not wanting to ask. Then she nodded to the caretaker and walked towards the stairs. As she put her foot on the top step, she glanced back along the corridor. With a shock, she saw that the caretaker was still standing there in front of the door to her room, watching her go.

Margarete hurried down the stairs towards the front hall, her mind in turmoil. Whatever had she let herself in for? Everything the sinister doctor had said had gone against all her instincts, both as a nurse and as a human being. How could she ever be part of this abhorrent experiment? How could she work in this place and face her conscience and her family? How could she retain her humanity? In her desperation, she started to think about possible escape routes, but she kept returning to the same point in her mind. It was all very well for her to consider risking everything by refusing to co-operate, or even by running away, but she couldn't risk the lives of her family back in Berlin. They were relying on her. Not only for money, but for her discretion, too. She was only too aware that the Party knew where to find them.

Margarete reached the vaulted castle hall and there was Doctor Finkel waiting for her at the bottom of the stairs, tapping his hand impatiently on the newel post.

'Ah, Nurse Weiss. There you are,' he said, making a show of glancing at his watch. 'Come, let us go along to tea.'

'Yes, Doctor,' she said, her eyes downcast, and she followed him towards the dining room, her shoulders drooping and her spirits lower than she'd ever felt in her life before.

ELEVEN

KRISTEL

Trento, 2005

Kristel left Margarete's room in the Our Lady of Mercy care home and wandered along the passage towards the stairs. It was late, she'd lost track of time, and it was already dark outside; she'd been listening to Margarete's story on and off since the morning. She was reflecting on what she'd heard, on what Margarete had told her about her time at the Charité Hospital in Berlin and her early days at the Lebensborn castle in the summer of 1938. It was incredible to think that the old lady with the kind eyes had once actually worked as a nurse for the Nazis. Until that point, that period in her country's history had just existed for Kristel as a terrible, shameful era, but listening to Margarete, who was a real, living, breathing woman, made it come alive for her in a way that it never had before.

When she'd started telling Kristel about her arrival at the castle, she'd said, 'So that was it, the Lebensborn programme. I was at the centre of it, Kristel.' Her eyes had been misty as she had looked down and taken a blue-covered notebook from the table into her hands. Was this the notebook she had mentioned?

Had she managed to write down the names of all the babies and their birth mothers in the hope that one day she would be able to reunite them?

Kristel was so deep in thought, heading for the stairs, that she didn't see the young care worker, Lorenzo, approaching with a tray of evening drinks for the residents. She walked straight into him, and the tray clattered to the floor, tea and coffee flying everywhere.

'Oh! I'm so sorry,' Lorenzo said. 'Just look at your coat! I'm so clumsy.'

'Not at all. It was completely my fault,' Kristel said, glancing at the broken cups on the floor, the coffee stains on the front of Lorenzo's starched white overall, feeling foolish and clumsy herself. 'Let me help you clear this up.'

She knelt down and began picking up pieces of broken china, while Lorenzo went to the kitchen and reappeared a minute later with cloths, a mop and bucket and a bin bag for the debris. He knelt down too and together they put the broken china into the bin bag, then he handed her a damp cloth and she sponged down her coat and got to her feet.

'If you give me your coat, I'll take it to the dry-cleaner's tomorrow morning,' he said. 'It's my day off and I'll have plenty of time.'

'No, really. There's no need,' Kristel replied. 'It was my fault. And the coat doesn't need cleaning at all. Look, I've sponged the worst of it off. I'll give it another go back at the hotel. Are you sure *you* are all right though?'

He shrugged and pulled a face, looking down at the brown stains on his pristine white coat. Her eyes met his and they both laughed. 'This can be washed, it's no problem. I have a spare one in the staffroom.'

'I'd best be getting back to my hotel,' she said. 'I'll see you tomorrow.'

'Not tomorrow, it's my day off.'

'Of course. You said! How silly of me. I'm not thinking straight.'

'Let me show you out,' he offered, and she noticed how kind his gentle brown eyes were. Like all the staff here, he was clearly a generous, caring person.

They walked downstairs together.

'How are your interviews going with Margarete?' he asked.

'Very well, thank you. She has an incredible memory for detail, and she really wants to tell her story.'

'She is a wonderful lady,' Lorenzo said, 'but she gets very fed up and frustrated sometimes. Since you've been coming here, her spirits have really picked up. She has no one to visit her normally. No family at all.'

'How very sad,' Kristel replied, reflecting on his words and feeling Margarete's loneliness and pain. If she'd had no visitors, it must have meant that Margarete had never married, or had any children. On the other hand, perhaps it meant that she'd had to leave any family she had behind in Germany. There was still so much that Margarete hadn't told her, so much of the story yet to come. Kristel was desperate to hear it, but she was determined not to rush Margarete.

Lorenzo opened the front door. A blast of snow blew in from outside, showering them both in icy white crystals. They looked at each other and laughed again.

'I guess we're both jinxed this evening,' Lorenzo said, dusting snow off his overall. 'I hope you'll still be here the day after tomorrow when I'm working again?'

'I hope so too,' Kristel said. 'I think I will. I'll probably be coming back to talk to Margarete for at least another couple of days.'

'Are you all right getting to the car? It looks slippery out there.'

'I'll be fine. Thanks.'

Kristel made her way to the car, got inside and switched on

the engine, turning the fan up high to clear the windscreen. As the snow cleared, she could see that Lorenzo was still standing in the doorway, watching solicitously, making sure she got away all right. She smiled and waved. How refreshing he was, she thought, with his ready smile and easy, uncomplicated manner. Despite her conversations and growing closeness with Margarete, Kristel realised that she'd been feeling a little alone here in Trento and the light-hearted conversation with Lorenzo had made her feel less lonely. She had the surprising thought that she'd like to get to know him better.

Back at the hotel, Kristel ordered a burger and a glass of red wine from room service, and after she'd eaten, she got down to writing up her interview notes. As she listened to Margarete's reedy voice on the tape, she realised that she was really making progress with Margarete, that Margarete was now comfortable in her presence and didn't seem to be holding back. Perhaps, in due course, she would reveal the precious notebook.

Kristel's mind went back again to her own reasons for wanting to do the research. She recalled the shock and hurt of finding her mother's letters to her father after his death. She'd been even more desperate then to know why her mother had run away when she was a tiny child. After all, if her parents had been on good terms and able to exchange friendly letters about their daughter, why had Greta walked out like that and been at pains to distance herself from her daughter ever since?

Now, Kristel laid her pen down and put her head in her hands. The memory of the time she'd plucked up courage and confronted her mother about those letters was both painful and humiliating.

Greta had come over to Munich from America for Frank's funeral, although she'd declined the offer to stay at Kristel's flat.

'I'm much better off at the Sofitel,' Greta had said on the phone. 'You wouldn't want me around. I'm very demanding, and I don't sleep at all well. I'd be sure to disturb you.'

'Well, if you don't want to stay at my place, you could always stay at Dad's,' Kristel had suggested. 'There'd be no one to disturb you there.'

'Oh, Kristel! I couldn't possibly stay there,' Greta had exclaimed, and Kristel had heard the shudder in her voice at the very thought. She'd wondered then why her mother would find the suggestion of staying in her father's apartment so abhorrent if they'd truly been good friends. But she'd accepted Greta's wishes.

It was after the funeral was over, when they were at the wake at the hotel that Kristel had organised in memory of her father, and all the guests had drifted away that, at last, she was alone with her mother.

'One more drink?' Kristel had said, taking a bottle of wine and moving to a quiet corner of the room. 'There's something I want to ask you.'

'Nothing too difficult, I hope,' Greta had replied, looking nervous.

As she'd followed her mother across the room, Kristel had reflected on how young and elegant Greta always managed to look. Her silvery blonde hair was always perfectly coiffed, and she was as effortlessly stylish as ever in a black jacket and calf-length skirt over high-heeled boots. She looked more like a fashion model for mature women's clothes than a university lecturer.

They had sat in the corner, under a window looking out over a windswept square, where autumn leaves swirled around and the sky was growing dark.

Kristel had taken a gulp of wine and looked into her mother's eyes. It had been a difficult, draining day already, but since Greta was actually there in front of her, she knew she had to confront her about what had been puzzling her for weeks.

Greta had sipped her wine too and glanced at her watch.

'This won't take too long, I hope. I need to go and pack for my flight.'

Kristel had put her glass down. 'No, not too long. It's just that... when I was going through Papa's paperwork, I found some letters. Some letters from *you* actually... to Papa. I wanted to ask you about them.'

Greta's face had blanched and when she had put her glass down, Kristel saw that her hands were shaking. 'Letters?' she'd asked.

'Yes, Mutti. You must know about them. You wrote them... to Papa. They were all about me. He must have been writing to you regularly, sending you pictures and news. Don't tell me you don't know about them.'

'You shouldn't ever read other people's letters, Kristel,' Greta had said, frowning.

'I needed to look through his things to sort them out, and once I'd started reading, I couldn't stop. And you know that's not the point...' she finished, irritated by her mother's reaction.

'Frank promised he wouldn't keep them,' Greta had muttered.

'Why? Why would he promise that? And why, if you two were in touch about me, did you make it seem as though you had nothing to do with each other?'

Greta had blinked several times but remained silent, the fingers of her left hand at her throat, fiddling with a brooch on her collar, as if it was too tight and she needed some air.

'And why did you distance yourself from me, Mutti? Why did you run away when I was a little girl and refuse to be there for me when I was growing up? I need to know these things now that he's gone.'

Kristel had never dared bring this up directly with her mother before and she couldn't believe that she was doing so now, but the words were spilling from her mouth like water from a burst dam. They were unstoppable, despite the expression on her mother's face, appalled and horrified. She had flinched at each word as if she was being physically struck.

'I... I can't talk about it now, Kristel,' Greta had said, taking a large gulp of wine and setting the glass down shakily.

'Well, when *can* you talk about it? We've just buried Papa. When would be a better time to talk about these things, Mutti?' Kristel felt on edge after all the emotional upheaval of the day She was determined not to back down.

'Well, certainly not now. There isn't time and I'm not prepared to discuss it. You've blindsided me, Kristel. I need to go and get ready for my flight.'

'What does your flight matter?' Kristel asked, exasperated. 'This is about my life, your life. It's more important than missing a flight.'

Greta had burst into tears then, sobbing into a handker-chief. 'I can't talk about it to you, Kristel. I won't. Don't ever ask me again,' she implored, and with that, she'd gathered her things and rushed out of the room without a backward glance. Kristel had watched her go, tears in her own eyes.

She had thought long and hard about her mother's behaviour; her lack of empathy and the coldness towards her, realising that it could well have its roots deep in Greta's own past. She could barely remember her maternal grandmother, Greta's mother, who had died a couple of months before Greta walked out. All Kristel knew was that Greta had grown up in a small town in Bavaria. She'd left home to go to university and had never returned, but her parents had remained in the town until their deaths. Greta's father had died before Kristel was even born, so she'd never met him, but she'd seen photographs of a severe-looking man, evidently once handsome, who had run to seed in his old age. She'd searched through her father's flat, but apart from their marriage certificate, there was no informa-tion about Greta there at all.

Kristel's reporter's instincts had come to the fore and two

days after her father's funeral, she had travelled by train to the small Bavarian town of Mittenwald to see if she could find any clues about her mother's childhood. She had a small map of the local area and the address of Greta's birth as given on her marriage certificate.

The house was easy to find. It wasn't too far from the station, in a leafy, affluent-looking part of town, where the large houses, built like Alpine hunting lodges, were set well apart in huge gardens. It was a big, sprawling residence, probably a hundred years old at least. It had the appearance of having been the house of someone with wealth and influence.

Gathering her courage, Kristel had knocked on the door, which was eventually opened by an elderly lady wearing an apron over a black dress.

'Good afternoon?' The woman had looked at Kristel enquiringly. 'The owners, Herr and Frau Trudinger, live in Munich and only come here at weekends. So, if you are looking for them, you will need to come back on Saturday.'

'No... no, I wasn't looking for them. I'm actually researching some family history. My mother once lived in this house.'

The woman had drawn herself up and frowned. 'How long ago would that be, please? Herr and Frau Trudinger have owned this house for thirty years. I am their housekeeper.'

'Oh, it would have been before that. My mother was born in 1943 and lived here until she was about eighteen, I believe. Her own mother, Bettina Oberman, lived here, or at least in this town, I think, until she died about thirty-two years ago.'

The old lady's face had dropped. 'Frau Oberman... really? Would you like to come in? My memory isn't perfect, but I've lived in this town all my life. I could tell you a little bit about the Obermans if that would help?'

'Oh yes, please. If you have time. That would help a lot.'

Intrigued, Kristel had followed the old lady inside, through a panelled hallway and into a traditional Bavarian kitchen, with a red tiled floor, carved wooden cupboards, a cuckoo clock and gingham curtains and tablecloths. The windows looked out over the windswept garden, along the bottom of which flowed the fast-running river Isar and beyond the snow-capped mountains. The old lady seemed only too glad to have a visitor. She made Kristel coffee and offered her cookies before sitting down opposite her at the table.

'Herr and Frau Oberman came to live in the town in the mid-1930s, if I remember correctly, a few years before the war,' she began. 'You might not know this, and it might be hard for you to hear, but Herr Oberman was sent here by the Nazi Party. He was in fact appointed by them as an important town official. Everyone was afraid of him. He ruled with a rod of iron. His first act, with the help of the local Gestapo, was to track down everyone who had ever been part of another political party and to send them to "protective custody". That meant to Dachau,' she said bitterly.

'No!' Kristel had said, her hand flying to her mouth. She had stared at the old lady in disbelief, shock washing through her in waves. How could this be? For her own flesh and blood to have been Nazis was unthinkable. She'd been prepared to admit the shame of being German, but to think that her own family had actually been part of that evil regime made her recoil in horror and shame.

'Many evil things happened in this town, overseen by Herr Max Oberman,' the housekeeper had continued. 'He granted many of the top Nazis citizenship, just to show his loyalty to them. And photographs of the town were used in propaganda posters, promoting country life. They even shot one of their propaganda films here.'

Kristel had been speechless. Was this what lay at the root of Greta's strange behaviour? Had she discovered this when her mother had died and been so ashamed that she'd been unable to continue living as a wife and mother to Frank and Kristel?

'My mother must have been born here,' she eventually remarked. 'But she would have been too young to know what was going on.'

'Indeed. I was only a child at the time, but I remember they had a little daughter during the war years,' the old lady had replied. 'It was all very strange and there was a lot of gossip about it. There was no sign that Frau Oberman was expecting. In fact, she looked too old to bear children. Then one day there she was, pushing a pram around the village as proud as punch.'

Kristel had frowned, shocked once again, and the old lady went on.

'There were a lot of rumours about it, but no one dared to ask her. People said that the baby was adopted. And when the little girl grew older, everyone could see that she didn't look a bit like her parents. They were stocky and dark-haired, but the little girl was tall for her age and very fair. Like you, my dear.'

'Adopted?' Kristel had muttered, her mind racing. Had Greta known this? Was it the discovery of this fact that had sent her away? 'Do you know what happened to them, after the war?'

'After the war, everyone was re-educated by the Americans. Somehow, Herr Oberman managed to convince the American authorities that he'd not been part of the Nazi movement, that he'd been forced to work for them, that he was just a passive follower. That meant he wasn't sent for trial or detained in prison, he was simply ordered to undertake re-education. People in the town who knew what he'd stood for were very angry and shunned him. He tried to get elected onto the town council after the war, but nobody voted for him. The pair of them lived in this house until the end of their days, outcasts from the town.' Her tone was critical, judgemental even.

'And what about my mother?' Kristel had managed to ask, and the old lady had looked at her with curiosity.

'Is your mother still alive, my dear? She must only be in her early sixties surely?'

'She is... but she has never told me any of this. She lives in America now and I hardly ever see her. It's hard to explain, but... well, my father died recently, and I want to find out more about my family history.'

'It's a shame that you're not close,' the woman said, looking at Kristel with sympathy. 'I can't remember her ever coming back to visit once she left school. She must have been about eighteen then. In the early 1960s, I suppose. No, as far as I'm aware, she didn't come back.'

'Apart from when my grandmother died,' Kristel had said. 'I believe that she came back then. At least, she did, according to my father.'

'Perhaps she did. All I know is that no one cared for Frau Oberman. Memories are long in places like this. So, I don't know anyone who went to her funeral.'

Kristel had left the house in a state of shock. She'd wandered around the pretty little town, with its backdrop of mountains and Alpine-style buildings, trying to imagine Greta growing up there under the dark shadow of the Nazis. Since she'd left Germany, Greta had made a name for herself in academic circles, lecturing on and promoting human rights worldwide. Kristel had read some of her articles; they were impressive, but in none of them had she ever alluded to her upbringing. Even so, it must have been that knowledge that had inspired her in that direction.

Kristel had gone back to Munich on the train and reflected deeply about what she'd heard. Back at home, she'd started to look into adoptions under the Nazis and how a Nazi official in small-town Bavaria might have come to adopt a baby girl. She had stumbled across the Lebensborn programme. It was something she'd never heard about before that day and reading about it had sent chills right through her. And from that moment on, she'd wanted to find out as much about it as she could. Not just because she realised that through her efforts and her ability to bring things to light through the medium of television, she might be able to help people find out more about their past, perhaps even track down lost relatives, but also because along the way, she hoped she would be able to get to the root of her own mother's past.

She had wondered if her father had known about Greta's upbringing and the question marks surrounding her family and her antecedents. If he had, why hadn't he told her about it? Perhaps, like Joachim, he didn't want to delve into the past too much, for fear of the horrors he might uncover. Or perhaps he hadn't known at all. Perhaps Greta had never even spoken of it to her own husband.

Now, sitting in her hotel room in Trento, thinking back over the past ten months or so since her father died, Kristel recalled that it was the day after her trip to Mittenwald that she had first met Joachim. It seemed unbelievable that it was so recent.

He had been introduced to her at a party by a mutual friend and they had hit it off instantly. She was attracted by his smouldering good looks and his easy charm. He'd asked her out the following evening for a meal and within a week they were an item. Within six weeks, she had moved into his apartment and shortly after that he'd asked her to marry him.

Joachim had been right to observe that they'd flung themselves headlong into the relationship without looking back. Now that she was away from him, thinking back over those months, she could see that after her father's death and the traumatic scene with her mother, she'd felt very alone. She'd been desperate for someone to love her and take care of her and Joachim had stepped into the breach. She also realised now that she was attracted by his calm, orderly lifestyle. There was something soothing about it. It contrasted deeply with the chaos in her own life that she was trying to get away from.

His career was on an upward trajectory; his apartment, his life and everything about him seemed under control. Except that now she could see that there was something missing between them, that she'd projected onto him qualities that she wanted to see rather than ones he actually possessed. They rarely laughed together now and over recent weeks they had often argued. Little resentments had become big ones.

Kristel sighed. It was good that he would be going to Singapore. It would give them both a chance to think clearly about the future, and now that she was grieving less, she felt more confident about being able to make good decisions for herself.

TWELVE

MARGARETE

Schloss Schwanburg, Bavaria, 1938

During those first few months in the early summer of 1938, all Margarete's initial fears about the programme she'd been co-opted to work on were confirmed. How naive she'd been when she'd listened to Professor Wagner's lectures on eugenics at the hospital in the early days of the regime and had thought they were flights of fancy, that they would never have any practical application. She could see now that what was happening at the castle *was* the practical application of his theories. That the Lebensborn programme was eugenics in operation and now she was part of it.

Margarete found herself trying to gauge whether any of the other nurses had similar qualms to herself. There were four nurses in the home, including Nurse Ekert, and they all lived in the local area. They struck her as humourless but efficient and none of them gave an inkling that they were anything other than completely invested in the programme.

On her second working day, a new expectant mother

arrived at the castle. Margarete's job was to greet the young woman and help her to settle in.

Margarete met the girl in the entrance hall, where she stood beside her suitcases looking exhausted and a little nervous. She was sweetly pretty with perfect skin, big blue eyes and an innocent smile and, of course, the trademark blonde plaits. Margarete showed her up to her quarters: a light, airy room on the first floor, a few doors along from the ward that Margarete had visited with Doctor Finkel on the first day. The girl let slip her real name – Heidi – during the first few minutes of conversation.

'It's lovely here,' Heidi said, sitting down on the bed and arching her back. 'So different from home. Gosh, this baby is really heavy! My back is killing me and my poor legs are so swollen, just from the train journey.'

'When is your due date?' Margarete asked her, eyeing the girl's swollen belly hidden by the voluminous smock dress.

'A week from now,' Heidi replied. 'And the sooner it is over, the better. I'm dreading the birth!' Then her face took on an anguished look. 'Will it hurt very much, Nurse Weiss?'

Margarete sat down on the bed beside her. 'It is a natural process, Heidi. There will be some discomfort of course, but please don't worry. The doctor and midwife will be with you every step of the way.'

What she didn't tell her, and what she'd discovered to her dismay during her first proper discussion with the midwife, Nurse Ekert, was that both Nurse Ekert and Doctor Finkel strongly discouraged the use of pain relief during the births under their supervision.

'Good German women don't need such decadent aids!' the midwife had told her sternly. 'Pain relief is for weaklings and for the inferior races. No, we keep the gas and air in reserve for emergencies. All our girls are strong and healthy. They come from the best stock. They are happy to go through with it without using unnecessary drugs.'

Heidi looked back at Margarete and smiled. 'I'm so glad you're here, Nurse Weiss,' she said. 'It's comforting to see a friendly face. But the lady who was here when I came a few months back was lovely too. Sister Bach, her name was. Where is she?'

'I'm afraid Sister Bach doesn't work here anymore. I'm her replacement,' Margarete replied, still wondering herself what had happened to Sister Bach. All her subtle questions about her predecessor's whereabouts had met with blank looks and evasive answers.

'Oh, that's a shame. She was so nice. Some of the others are a bit frightening.'

Margarete smiled and patted her hand. 'I'm here to look after you and your baby, Heidi. Now, Doctor Finkel has asked me to take you along to his office for some tests. Are you ready to go?'

'Yes. Oh, I've just remembered. I've brought my certificates.' Straining to bend down, Heidi picked up her handbag which was on the floor and took out three large brown envelopes. 'This one has some general papers inside. This one is for me and this one for Heinz. Our family doctor certified my certificate. It's not quite as good as Heinz's though,' she smiled apologetically. 'His goes back at least two hundred years. His ancestry is perfect.'

'I'm sure,' Margarete murmured, taking the envelopes and looking into Heidi's eyes. Did she really believe in all this talk of racial purity? Margarete supposed she must, or she wouldn't be here. All the young women she'd spoken to here had been of the same mind. They'd been brainwashed, she knew, by everything they had seen and read since childhood, by the relentless Nazi message pumped daily through the news media, and by their local BDM officials. All the same, Margarete felt compelled to ask more questions.

'Have you thought about what will happen when your baby is born?' she asked tentatively.

Heidi nodded. 'Of course. They told me when I was here before. I will be able to look after the baby and nurse it for the first ten days, then it will be placed with a new family. A good Nazi family who are able to give it a good home and raise it properly.'

'And how do you feel about that?' Margarete asked and Heidi returned her look with a vacant stare.

'I'm pleased to be able to do my duty for the Führer and the Fatherland,' she parroted. 'I thought it was unfortunate at first that I became pregnant, but since my family doctor told us about Lebensborn, it has all turned out very well. Heinz and I will be contributing to the stock of Aryan babies in the Reich.'

'Right,' said Margarete, realising she was getting nowhere and standing up from the bed. 'Now, if you feel any qualms about it, or you just want to talk about it, at any point, either now or after the birth, I'm the person to speak to.'

Heidi frowned at her as she heaved herself up and off the bed. 'I don't think I will, but thank you anyway,' she said, and, not for the first time in the two days she'd been at the castle, Margarete made a mental note to be very careful of what she said. These girls were all loyal to the Nazi Party, some of them were probably even party members themselves, and if she stepped out of line, or even hinted to anyone that she wasn't fully invested in what was happening here at Schloss Schwan-burg, they would inform on her as easily as breathing.

Margarete walked with Heidi along the corridor and down the stairs. A group of girls in varying stages of pregnancy was coming up in the opposite direction.

'Good afternoon, Nurse Weiss,' the girls chorused, and Margarete nodded back to them.

The day before, she'd been taken by Nurse Ekert to a large, comfortable lounge, referred to by the staff as the common room, on the first floor, and had met the pregnant girls in residence aside from the four she had already met in the ward. They had been sitting round playing card games and reading magazines. They had all greeted her with Heil Hitler salutes, although had remained seated. But what had disturbed Margarete most about meeting them was that none of them had expressed any regret about what was planned for their babies. At least not in that setting. She wondered how they would feel after the birth though, when they held their babies in their arms for the first time.

The three young mothers who had already given birth, and had a separate, smaller sitting room adjoining the nursery, had seemed less sure of themselves. Freda, Gunhild and Sophia were sitting nursing their babies when Margarete had been shown into the nursery for the second time that morning. She knew their names from the record book in the office, although she'd been told not to use names when addressing the girls. All three looked pale and exhausted, but were giving a good impression of putting a brave face on their situation.

Margarete had sat down between Freda and Sophia and had waited until Nurse Ekert had left the room before asking them how they were feeling.

'A little tired,' the first one, Gunhild, had ventured with a nervous smile. Her baby had dropped off the breast and began to wail. She had turned her attention back to it.

'I was in labour for three days,' Sophia had said. 'My baby was born yesterday morning. I'm very tired, but Doctor Finkel says I will feel better soon. He has prescribed cod-liver oil and vitamins.'

'My baby is a week old now,' Freda had said. 'They have already found him a new home. He will go in two days' time.'

'Oh, Freda,' Margarete couldn't help herself saying. 'How do you feel about that?'

Freda had glanced at her, and Margarete had seen a flash of panic in her eyes, but the girl had quickly composed herself.

'I'm happy that my baby will be going to a good family who will care for him and give him a good life.'

Margarete had smiled at the girl, who was holding her tiny baby to her breast, and tried to keep the pity and concern from her eyes. Did Freda really think this? Margarete didn't want to risk exposing herself by saying any more, so she had simply patted Freda's arm and said, 'Well, I'm here if you would like to talk about it. I'm sure it will take some... some adjusting for you.'

Now, she reached Doctor Finkel's office with Heidi.

'Come in, Nurse Weiss, come in, Fräulein,' he said. 'Nurse Weiss, perhaps you would like to sit in on the tests I need to perform on the Fräulein? I think you will find it most interesting.'

'Yes, Doctor,' she said, sitting down beside Heidi, keen to learn about his unorthodox methods.

'Now, Fräulein, do you have the paperwork we need? That is, your own and the father's family tree, the affidavit you have sworn attesting that he is the father of your child, and the health certificates signed by your family doctors?'

Heidi nodded and handed the envelopes over the desk.

There was a strained silence in the room as Doctor Finkel tore open the envelopes and perused the contents, frowning and sniffing slightly as he read. Heidi sat rigidly watching him. The clock on the wall ticked loudly and the sound of laughter floated up from the gardens, where the other girls were sitting out on the lawn.

The doctor cleared his throat and pushed his glasses up his nose. 'Good. This all seems to be in order,' he said. 'Now, Fräulein, if you would kindly sign the consent form that we discussed last time.' He pushed a form towards Heidi over the desk. From where she sat, Margarete was just able to scan the words.

I, Heidi Schmidt, hereby consent to transferring the guardianship and all rights that go with that status in relation to my unborn child, due on 4 July 1938, to the Lebensborn programme.

Heidi took the pen the doctor held out and scribbled her signature on the dotted line. Margarete couldn't help noticing how she put her tongue between her lips to concentrate and how round the letters of her signature were. It struck her then that Heidi was little more than a child herself.

'Thank you,' Doctor Finkel said, taking back the form and glancing at it. 'The Reich is indebted to you and girls like you. Now, you know what our esteemed Reichsführer says about Lebensborn mothers, don't you?'

Heidi nodded. 'Oh yes. I read it on the leaflet you gave me. *Every mother of good blood shall be holy to us.*'

A smile stretched across the doctor's thin lips. 'Correct! Now let us get on with the final tests I need to carry out. Just a formality, of course, but I do need to perform them once more for the record.'

Margarete watched in horrified silence as the doctor pulled out a fat record book and began a series of physical tests on Heidi.

First, he looked into her mouth with a torch and a metal implement to hold down her tongue, paying particular attention to her teeth and gums. He then made notes scrupulously in his book of what he saw.

Then he moved onto Heidi's face, measuring the length of her nose, the width and height of her forehead, her chin, the length of her neck. He paid particular attention to her ears, measuring their size, the size of the earlobe and the distance of the ear from her skull. He examined her hands and nails and once again made meticulous notes.

Lastly, he asked Heidi to remove her shoes, and he looked at her feet. Then he asked her to walk across the room and back and made more notes in his book while she was doing so. Heidi accepted all this patiently and with good grace.

After more scribbling in his book, Doctor Finkel looked up and beamed at Heidi. 'I'm very pleased to say, Fräulein, that you have passed all the final tests for Aryan racial purity with flying colours. Now, please go and join the other young women in the common room and make sure you eat well and take plenty of rest over the next few days. The midwife will come and talk to you later on today to help you prepare for the birth of your child.'

Margarete escorted Heidi from the doctor's office. She glanced sideways at Heidi to try to gauge her reaction, and was dismayed to see that Heidi looked relaxed and happy, without a care in the world. How accepting she was of everything that was happening to her and around her!

'I'm so pleased that I passed those tests,' she said to Margarete as they went up the stairs to the common room. 'What a relief. And I'm so happy to be here.'

Margarete couldn't help wondering if she would still be happy when the harsh reality of having to part with her newborn baby finally kicked in.

Two days later, Doctor Finkel asked Margarete to be present at the first adoption to take place since she'd arrived at the castle.

'It will be good for you to see the process in practice,' he said with one of his thin-lipped smiles. 'It is a wonderful experience, handing over a newborn to its new family. It makes everything we do here worthwhile. I would like you to ensure, of course, that the baby is dressed and ready to go, and that the mother has said her goodbyes and has already left for the station when the parents arrive. We've had a couple of incidents where things haven't run totally smoothly,' he remarked, frowning. 'Most upsetting for all concerned. I'm determined that that shouldn't happen again.'

Margarete looked at him enquiringly. This was the first instance of anyone mentioning anything running less than perfectly here at Schloss Schwanburg, or of any of the girls being unhappy at parting with their babies. Perhaps it had had something to do with Sister Bach? Was that the reason she had left?

But the doctor didn't elaborate further, and simply said dismissively, 'Very well then, Nurse. I will see you back here in my office at midday,' and Margarete left to go up to the nursery.

Freda's baby boy had been bathed and changed and wrapped in a white shawl. The young nursery nurse, Helena, sat cradling him, feeding him milk from a bottle.

'Where is Freda?' Margarete asked.

'She is in her room,' the young woman replied.

Margarete went along the corridor to Freda's room. When she knocked, Freda said 'Hello' in a weak voice and Margarete went inside. Freda was sitting on the bed. It was the first time Margarete had seen her fully dressed. There were two suitcases beside her on the floor and a light summer coat laid on top of them.

'Are you all right, Freda?' Margarete asked, her own heart swelling with emotion at the very idea of a mother parting with her newborn.

Freda's face was white, the skin under her eyes still bruised with exhaustion. When Freda looked back at her, Margarete saw that her eyes were bloodshot, as if she'd been crying.

'I'm all right, thank you, Nurse,' Freda replied, looking away and down in her lap.

Margarete sat down beside her on the bed and slipped her arm around Freda's shoulders. She felt Freda stiffen. 'It must be tough for you, saying goodbye to your little boy,' Margarete ventured, and she felt Freda shudder and let out a stifled sob.

'I can't do it,' she said. 'I'm not going back into the nursery. I can't bear to see him again. If only I'd have known how much I would fall in love with him...'

'Oh, Freda.' Margarete held her tight, fighting back her own tears. 'Would you like me to have a word with Doctor Finkel? Perhaps something can be done.'

She felt Freda go rigid. '*Could* something be done, do you think? I've been wondering...'

'Wait here,' Margarete said without reflecting too much on what she was about to do. She was acting from pure instinct. Not as head of healthcare here at Schloss Schwanburg, but as a woman, as a human being. She rushed out of Freda's room, ran along the corridors, pounded down the staircase and along the flagstone passage to Doctor Finkel's room, where she knocked firmly on the door and went straight inside without waiting for a reply.

'Nurse Weiss?' Doctor Finkel was straightening his tie in a mirror at the far end of the room. She was surprised to see him without his white coat. He was wearing a dark suit, and his grey hair was freshly oiled, plastered to his head to cover his bald patch.

'I've just been speaking to Freda,' Margarete said breathlessly. 'She is extremely upset at leaving her baby. I was just wondering if there's anything that can be done... to enable her to... to perhaps keep her baby, instead of sending him to strangers?'

Doctor Finkel's face clouded over. 'Nurse Weiss! I am surprised that you have seen fit to pose that question. The girl has signed away her rights to the child. She did that well before the birth, and there is no going back now. I repeat: no going back.'

'But, Doctor—'

He came towards her, his face reddening with anger. 'I would advise you not to persist with this. I have explained what we are here for, and you need to follow orders, Nurse, or there will be consequences. The baby's new parents are on their way here right now. They will arrive in the next half-hour.'

'But—'

'I have already ordered a car to take Freda to the station. It will be here any minute. I advise you to ensure she gets into that car and the driver will do the rest.'

'Do the rest?' Margarete asked weakly.

'He will make quite sure that she departs on the train. And that will be an end to it.'

'But, Doctor—'

'Nurse Weiss, I have already warned you. I am prepared to accept that this is the first time you've encountered the reality of an adoption process, so I'm going to be lenient on this occasion. You will soon get used to the drill. Now, go straight back to the young lady's room and bring her down to the front hall to wait for the car. The sooner she is gone, the better.'

'It seems so... so inhumane,' she burst out before she could stop herself.

'Nurse Weiss! What is happening here is government policy. Do I take it that you are against government policy? That is a very serious offence. Treason, in fact. One that could have serious consequences for you and your family. Now, if this continues, I will be forced to make a report to the Ministry and Reichsführer Himmler about you. Once again, I advise you to think carefully about the consequences that might have for your family.'

Margarete hung her head. Those words had finally hit home with her. She knew what he meant, and she knew that he and whoever his superiors were in the Party and the Ministry wouldn't hesitate to carry out their threats. Without saying another word, she turned on her heel and left the room.

Guilt weighed her down as she went slowly up the stairs to Freda's room. She'd given the girl hope and now she was going to dash it. How could she live with herself?

Freda looked up as she entered, a spark of hope in her eyes.

Margarete shook her head slowly. 'I'm so sorry, Freda.'

'It's all right,' Freda said, biting back tears. 'I knew he wouldn't help.'

'Look,' Margarete said on an impulse, 'why don't you give me your address and I will see if there's anything at all I can do? If there is, I will let you know.'

Freda shook her head, bitterness written all over her face. 'There is nothing you *can* do. I'm going to go home and put this behind me. I need to forget all about this place and that I ever had a baby. It's the only way I'll be able to make it through.'

She got up from the bed and picked up one of the suitcases.

'Don't do that, Freda, I'll send one of the porters. Please, let me help you.' Margarete put her arm on Freda's to give her support, but Freda shook it off and drew herself up.

'I can manage. I don't need your help.'

She left the room, holding her head high, and walked unsteadily along the corridor towards the top of the stairs. Margarete trailed behind her, feeling wretched, berating herself, knowing that her actions had only made matters worse.

Freda went downstairs slowly, leaning on the banisters, and sat on one of the wooden benches in the great hallway. Margarete went off to the servants' quarters to find someone to collect the cases. When she returned, the black Mercedes was parked at the bottom of the front steps. Freda was already outside and being helped into the back seat by the driver. Margarete went outside.

'Goodbye, Freda,' she said. 'And I'm so, so sorry.'

'Goodbye, Nurse Weiss,' Freda said, not meeting her eye.

The cases were loaded in the boot, the doors slammed and the car pulled away. Margarete stood on the bottom step, watching the back window of the car as it drew away, Freda's white face staring back at the castle where she was leaving so much behind.

THIRTEEN

MARGARETE

Schloss Schwanburg, 1938

Within seconds of Freda's car disappearing through the castle gates, the bonnet of another black limousine was nosing through the front entrance. Chills coursed through Margarete when she noticed the antenna on the bonnet, from which fluttered a swastika flag. This must be the good Nazi family that Doctor Finkel had told her about, coming to take Freda's baby away. Clearly the husband was either an SS officer or some high-ranking official in the Nazi Party itself. A wave of terror passed through her just thinking about it and nausea rose in her throat. She needed to get inside quickly; she didn't want to be the one to greet the couple when the car drew up at the front door.

As she hurried up the steps, she was shocked to see the care-taker, Holge Schwartz, standing at the top. His arms were folded and he was standing there motionless, watching her, his eyes narrowed, just as he'd watched her the first day she'd arrived at the castle.

'Feeling all right, Nurse?' he asked, his tone as cold as his expression.

'Quite all right,' she said briskly and rushed past him. Then she ran across the hallway and down the corridor to the office which had been allotted to her, a few doors along from Doctor Finkel's. She went inside, slammed the door shut and locked it, breathing heavily, then went over and sat down behind her desk. She could hold back no longer; she took a great, shuddering sob and let the tears fall.

Margarete knew she had only minutes to compose herself before Doctor Finkel called her through to witness the adoption, but in those few minutes, she made a decision. Despite what Freda had said about needing to forget her baby and put all this behind her, Margarete wanted to make sure she had made a note of Freda's details and those of the baby, in case the records somehow disappeared at some point in the future.

She quickly found the ledger in her desk that contained the personal details of all the girls at the home, together with their assumed names. She hurried out to the stationery cupboard on the corridor and found a fresh, government-issue, blue notebook. Back in the office, she closed and locked the door and into the notebook, on the first page, she copied Freda's name and address, the date she had given birth to her baby, the fact that it was a boy, and the date of the adoption. The opposite page she left blank. She would find out the name and address of the adopting family from Doctor Finkel's records somehow, then complete it. She bit her nail, wondering how she would manage that. She would have to get into Doctor Finkel's office when he was not around. He kept the ledger of the adopting families under lock and key in his desk.

It was the only thing Margarete could think of to do that might be of use to Freda and her baby in the future, whatever that future might hold.

A sudden loud knock on the door made her start. That must be Doctor Finkel summoning her to his room.

'One moment!' She hastily shoved the notebook to the back

of the bottom drawer of the desk, locked it and put the key in her purse. Then she wiped her eyes, blew her nose, took a deep breath and went to open the door.

Over the next half-hour, Margarete witnessed the middle-aged couple who had come for Freda's baby complete the forms Doctor Finkel put in front of them while being plied with drinks and snacks. Margarete watched the doctor with concealed contempt. She'd already known he was fully invested in the Nazi cause, but what she hadn't been prepared for was how obsequious and grovelling he would be towards the couple because of their rank.

The man was dressed in SS uniform and although their names were not spoken out loud, Margarete recognised him from the local newspaper she'd read over breakfast and the propaganda posters which were pasted around the station at Füssen as a high-ranking SS official – the local leader, in fact. The wife was over-dressed, in heavy make-up and a tight-fitting royal blue suit, high heels and a hat with an elaborate feather display perched on her blonde curls. She was tall and well-built, the perfect embodiment of Aryan blood, just like all the wives of SS officers Margarete had ever seen.

'There is no need for you to produce your certificates of racial purity,' Doctor Finkel said. 'That is already established, given your membership of the SS.'

'And, of course, my wife had to prove hers before we were married,' the officer said and his wife looked at him with a proud smile on her ruby-red lips.

'Of course, of course. Now, may I offer you some alcoholic refreshment, now we have the formalities over and done with? Champagne perhaps?'

The man nodded, and soon one of the kitchen maids had brought a bottle of champagne complete with ice bucket and white cloth and the doctor was uncorking the bottle.

'Nurse Weiss,' Doctor Finkel turned his gaze towards her

for the first time since she'd entered the room, 'while our esteemed guests are toasting their new family member, would you go and collect the baby from the nursery, please?'

Margarete was only too glad to be able to leave the over-heated room, walk away from it and up to the nursery. There, she looked down at Freda's baby in his cot, innocent and unknowing. If only his future could be different. With a lump in her throat, she picked him up from the cot, wrapped him in warm blankets and carried him downstairs, together with the bag that had been packed by the nursery nurse with his nappies, clothes and other essentials. Looking down into his little face snuggled beneath the snow-white blanket, with his little fuzz of blond hair, she felt like a traitor.

Crossing the hall downstairs, she paused for a second and glanced towards the front door. She had a fleeting impulse to take the baby, run out of the door, down the drive and away from the castle. Perhaps she'd be able to find Freda and return him to her. She could remember the address by heart. But, sigh-ing, she put those thoughts aside. She knew that wasn't possible if she and Freda were to remain alive. There was no escaping the iron grip of the Lebensborn programme and the Nazi Party. She would have to find other ways of doing what she could to alleviate the suffering that she knew was being caused by what was happening here. It was the only way she could survive.

When she got back to Doctor Finkel's office, Margarete sat down with the baby on her lap, dreading what was coming next, hoping against hope for a change of plan.

'Well, Nurse Weiss, what are you waiting for? Give the baby to its new mother,' Doctor Finkel barked impatiently.

It broke Margarete's heart to hand Freda's baby over to the woman, who clearly didn't know how to hold him. As he left Margarete's arms, he began to cry and the woman looked alarmed.

'You just need to support his head and rock him gently,'

Margarete explained, and the woman began to rock the baby with jerky movements, which made the baby cry even louder.

'Now, now, not to worry. He will settle down very soon,' Doctor Finkel reassured. 'You can leave us now, Nurse Weiss. I think your presence is unsettling the baby.'

Margarete got up and walked to the door, once again feeling a traitor for leaving the baby, who was still wailing at the top of his voice.

That evening, when she had finished her work and was sitting alone in her room, Margarete felt drained by everything that had happened that day. She had watched from an upstairs window as the SS couple got into the back of their big, black car holding Freda's baby and she'd had her last glimpse of the little bundle of white blankets before the door was slammed shut by the driver and the car pulled away. After the high emotion of the day, she didn't feel like going down to supper in the staff dining room. She could hardly keep the tears from her eyes, but she knew that she had to maintain appearances. If she didn't go to the dining room, questions would be asked, assumptions made.

Gathering all her courage, Margarete headed downstairs and took her place at the long table as she had done each meal-time at the castle so far, between Nurse Ekert and the young nursery nurse. Mechanically, and with a forced smile, she joined in their conversation while they were served their food – schnitzel and salad – by the kitchen staff. Doctor Finkel sat at the head of the table, presiding over proceedings as he always did.

'It was a very good day's work today,' he said, addressing the whole table. 'Another of our Lebensborn babies has been dispatched to a family of good blood. That is what we are here for, what we work towards tirelessly every day. So, may I congratulate you all. Very well done to everyone involved.'

A little round of applause burst forth. Margarete stared

down at her plate, not wanting to indulge in the congratulatory talk, but what Doctor Finkel said next made her scalp prickle with horror and her stomach churn.

'And next week we are expecting our first honoured guests to arrive. Our SS officers and our young women of Aryan stock, hand-picked for the honour of giving a baby to the Führer by local BDM leaders. The second floor of the castle is ready to receive them, their rooms are prepared, and the kitchen staff are busy cooking up a feast for the first evening. The young people will all stay here together for a week. After that, the officers will depart, but the young ladies will remain at the castle, so that we can monitor the results. I hope everyone is prepared for this,' he said, beaming from ear to ear and looking round at the assembled company. 'It is the next step in the Reichsführer's brilliant vision for this programme.'

As soon as the meal was over and Doctor Finkel had departed to his home in one of the gatehouses on the perimeter of the estate, Margarete said goodnight to the other staff. She crossed the shadowy entrance hall and tiptoed along the downstairs corridor towards the doctor's office. The corridor was dark, and she didn't want to put the lights on for fear of alerting the caretaker. Instead, she had brought a tiny torch which she used to use at the Charité Hospital for walking between the hospital and the nurses' quarters.

The doctor's office was locked, as she'd suspected it would be. It was a simple matter for Margarete to walk over to the key safe on the wall at the end of the corridor and open it with the key that had been issued to her for her own use. With trembling hands, she took the key to Doctor Finkel's office off its hook, closed the safe up again and walked back to the doctor's door, her heart pounding.

The key turned easily in the lock, but it seemed to make a loud metallic scraping sound, which echoed in the stone corridor. Margarete froze and waited, holding her breath, listening with dread for the sound of footsteps coming towards her. But no one came, and after a few moments, she pushed the door open and went inside, locking it behind her again as a precaution.

She knew exactly where Doctor Finkel kept the ledger containing the names and addresses of the adopting families: in the middle drawer of his desk. She went straight to it, but when she tried to open the drawer, as she'd half feared, it too was locked shut. She racked her brains, wondering where he might keep the key. Perhaps he took it home with him at night? She rummaged through the other desk drawers, which were unlocked, shining her torch into each one in turn, but could find nothing. Then she turned to the filing cabinets, pulling each drawer open methodically, but they were all crammed full of files of medical records. It took her a good fifteen minutes to get through all the drawers, but when she'd finished, she was still no nearer finding the key.

Margarete looked around wildly, wondering where to search next. In desperation, she went over to the sink in the corner and opened the cabinet underneath it. That was where Doctor Finkel kept his instruments – the measuring devices, the thermometers, the magnifying glasses, the monitors – some of which she'd seen him use on Heidi. She shuddered, seeing them there, glinting in the light of her torch. One by one, she took out all the trays and containers under the sink and went through them, but there was nothing resembling a key.

She glanced around desperately, running out of ideas as to where he might have hidden it. On the opposite wall was a high bookcase, filled with medical tomes and encyclopaedias. Margarete quickly went over to it and ran her hand along the tops of all the books. On the second shelf her hand paused on a volume of Hitler's *Mein Kampf*, sitting in pride of place in the middle of the bookcase. She felt a tiny key. Her heart leapt and her hand closed around it. She hurried back to the desk. Her hands were shaking so much that she almost dropped the key, but to her relief, it fitted in the lock and the drawer slid open.

She pulled out the large black book that lay in the drawer and opened it out on the desk. There were the lists of names and addresses of the adopting families. She scanned them quickly. There were around forty altogether at a quick guess. This corresponded to what Nurse Ekert had told her on her first day. Forty-five Lebensborn babies had been born at the castle since the programme began two years previously.

Margarete ran her finger down the columns to the entry made that day. As she'd thought, the entry listed the name of an SS officer, Herr Dieter Frank, and his wife, Johanna. Their address was given in Schwangau – a village not far from the castle. Margarete scribbled it down on a piece of paper and slid it into her pocket.

She was about to close the black book when she noticed a couple of strange entries. These weren't the addresses of SS officers, but instead, in the address column beside the entries for certain babies, was written the address of a children's hospital in Munich. Running her eyes back through the columns, she saw that there were at least five babies with a similar entry. Perhaps she could ask Nurse Ekert about that, although the nurse was as tight-lipped and unforthcoming as the doctor.

Still puzzled, Margarete slid the book back in the drawer, locked it up and returned the key to the bookcase. Then she crept over to the door and put her ear to it, her heart still thumping. The door was very thick, and she knew that she wouldn't be able to hear whether someone was outside in the corridor. Suppose the caretaker had followed her from the dining room, had heard the sound of the key in the lock and come to investigate? She had no way of knowing. She drew herself up, her mouth dry. This was the risk she had taken in entering the doctor's office. If she was going to do what her conscience told her she must do, there would be many times like this ahead.

Taking a deep breath, Margarete turned the handle and eased the door open. Putting her head through, she looked up and down the corridor. To her intense relief, the corridor was empty. She locked the door, tiptoed back to the key safe and returned the doctor's key to its hook. On an impulse, she took out the key to her own office and went to the door, unlocked it and put the light on. It would be a useful pretext if anyone apprehended her. There was her cardigan hanging on the back of her chair. She grabbed it, and, turning the light back off, she left the room, locked it up and returned the key to the key safe then made her way back towards the main hall.

As she reached the end of the corridor, her heart missed a beat. The caretaker stepped out of the shadows.

'Nurse Weiss! I was just doing my evening rounds. What are you doing down here at this time? Office hours were over a long time ago.'

'I was just fetching my cardigan from my office. I left it there earlier,' she replied, thanking her own foresight.

'Yes, the evenings can be quite chilly at this time of year.' He peered closer. 'You are shivering, Nurse Weiss,' he said, and he was right. There were goosebumps on her arms.

She swallowed and looked him in the eye, determined not to let him see how afraid she was of him.

'Could I ask, though, why did you not switch the corridor light on?' he said.

'I didn't think I needed to... I know the way...' she replied.

'But still... I think I will just go down to Doctor Finkel's office myself and check that everything is in order in there,' he said, not taking his eyes off her face.

It was an effort not to react when, all the time, she was wondering whether she'd left any trace that she'd been inside the office. Had she locked the drawers up properly? Had she put everything back in the cupboard in the exact order she'd taken them out?

'Goodnight then, Nurse Weiss,' the caretaker said, still looking at her through narrowed eyes. 'And do take care as you go up the stairs. Remember to switch the light on to the third-floor staircase, won't you? Those stairs can be treacherous in the dark.'

Margarete hurried away from him, shivering even more now, her heart pounding. She went straight up to her room, where she took the paper with the SS officer's address on out of her pocket and hid it under her mattress. In the morning, she would copy the couple's details into her notebook, but if it was found in the meantime, she knew it would be the end. Not just for her, but for her family too.

She lay down on the bed and closed her eyes, letting out a shuddering sob, partly of relief and partly through fear of what the future might hold.

FOURTEEN

MARGARETE

The following week, Heidi's baby was born. Heidi had asked for Margarete to be present at the birth. 'You make me feel safe, Nurse Weiss. I don't think I could manage it without you,' she'd said, looking at Margarete with her big, blue eyes.

'Nonsense, Heidi! As I said, it's a natural process but I'd be delighted to be with you during the birth if that's what you want.'

Doctor Finkel was less than enthusiastic about Margarete's attendance.

'It's against protocol to have an extra person present. Lebensborn rules are strict about it. Only one midwife and one doctor should be in attendance.'

'Perhaps I could attend a birth just this once, Doctor, just as I attended the adoption recently. Perhaps it could be part of my training?' she'd suggested.

He'd thought for a while.

'I suppose I could permit that,' he relented.

As things turned out, Margarete was very glad that she had

offered to be there. Heidi was completely unprepared for the pain of childbirth and from the very first contraction was grasping Margarete's hand with an iron-like grip and yelling out in pain. She fought against what was happening to her body every inch of the way, for the full twenty-four hours it took for her baby girl to be born. All her squirming and resistance seemed to serve to slow the process down. As time wore on, when it got too much for her to bear, she asked repeatedly for something to help with the pain, but each time, the doctor shook his head.

'This is all quite normal, my dear. You are doing very well as you are. There is absolutely no need for artificial pain relief, take it from me.'

Heidi's progress wasn't helped by the fact that Doctor Finkel and Nurse Ekert insisted on her lying down on her back with her legs up in stirrups. From the births Margarete had witnessed at Charité, she knew that mothers who were able to move about and stay upright during labour had easier, quicker births. Doctor Finkel and Nurse Ekert stuck rigidly to their old-fashioned beliefs and when Margarete tentatively suggested that Heidi should be encouraged to get up and move around, Doctor Finkel said, 'Nurse Weiss, you are here simply to observe, not to participate or offer suggestions. You are a nursery nurse, not a midwife. I can assure you, Nurse Ekert and I know what we are doing. If you persist in criticising, I will have to ask you to leave.'

After that, Margarete restrained herself. She knew Heidi needed her there so she didn't want to be asked to leave, but all the while, she was having to bite back the words.

By the time the baby was finally born at midnight on the second day, Heidi was limp and exhausted, a shivering wreck, her hair and nightgown sodden with sweat. The baby girl did not emerge yelling. She looked limp too and an unhealthy colour. She was very slow to take her first breath. Margarete watched anxiously as Nurse Ekert patted the baby repeatedly on the back. All the time, the midwife was shaking her head, her forehead drawn up in a frown. She and the doctor exchanged worried looks, then the nurse hurried the baby through to the adjoining room, where, through a window in the door, Margarete could see her working furiously on the newborn.

'What's happening? Can I see my baby?' Heidi asked, barely able to lift her head from the sodden pillow.

'Not right now. Nurse Ekert is tending to her,' Doctor Finkel said. 'You can hold her as soon as the nurse has finished. I will just go and check on her progress.'

'Let me clean you up,' Margarete offered, holding a glass of water out to the girl. Heidi sipped gratefully, then sank back on the pillows. Margarete filled a bowl of water and brought flannels and towels. She took Heidi's sodden nightdress off and sponged her down before slipping a fresh gown over her head.

The door opened and Nurse Ekert came back holding the baby, who was wrapped in towels. She handed her to Heidi. 'Put her to the breast straight away,' she ordered.

Margarete helped Heidi ease the baby onto her breast, but the baby didn't suckle. Her face had a pallid blue colour and her eyes were closed.

'Is she all right?' Heidi asked anxiously.

'She will be fine. She is recovering from the birth, just as you are,' Doctor Finkel said. 'Now, I need to go and write up my notes.'

He left the room and Nurse Ekert busied herself clearing up. Margarete watched the baby, trying to keep the anxiety from her eyes. She'd seen babies like this in the Charité Hospital. It was clear to Margarete that she'd not had enough oxygen during the birth. Such babies often had lasting effects, were slow to learn or suffered from other physical ailments.

'I will call her Hannah, after my mother,' Heidi said as the baby took her first tentative sucks from the nipple.

'You have no need to name the baby. Her new family will do that,' Nurse Ekert said from across the room.

Heidi opened her mouth to protest, but Margarete put her fingers to her lips and shook her head. She had already told the other new mothers that they could name their babies, and that they could cuddle them and show them love, but only when they were alone.

Later, Margarete helped Heidi settle Hannah in a freshly made cot in the nursery and supported her as she walked back to her own room. Heidi collapsed, exhausted, onto her bed.

'You did very well, Heidi,' Margarete said, giving the girl a hug. 'And your baby is beautiful.'

'Thank you, Nurse Weiss. I couldn't have done it without you there.'

Closing the door, Margarete didn't have the heart to tell Heidi how worried she was for her baby. She decided to keep it to herself for now and let the new mother relax and recover from the birth.

A few days later, the young SS officers and new Lebensborn recruits descended on the castle. Margarete watched them arrive from the window above the front entrance. Car after car drew up in the courtyard and disgorged young, athletic-looking officers. Tall and blond-haired, they bounded energetically up the front steps. They were all decked out in grey SS uniforms, complete with leather boots and full regalia. Even from where she stood, Margarete could hear Doctor Finkel's fawning voice greeting them in the entrance hall with his usual oily compliments. The castle stewards were waiting to show them up to the second floor and to their rooms, which were all situated along one wing. As the door to that wing closed, the first car arrived from the station carrying a group of BDM girls. Reluctantly, Margarete made her way down to the front hall to greet them as she'd been ordered by Doctor Finkel.

The first four girls were coming through the front door carrying their bags as she reached the bottom of the stairs. She couldn't help a sharp intake of breath at the sight of them there. They were all bright-eyed and a little nervous. Like the officers, they were in uniform – all wearing their BDM uniforms, plain brown skirts, white blouses with a Nazi emblem on the sleeve, a brown kerchief round their necks. With white ankle socks and sandals to complete the picture, they looked impossibly young and innocent. Were these girls even younger than the pregnant girls and young mothers who were already in residence? she wondered, dreading what she would have to do.

Doctor Finkel was so enthused by this new development that he had insisted on greeting the young women himself, but he had asked Margarete to help show them to their rooms. She went to collect the first group of four girls.

She greeted them and explained who she was, then showed them upstairs and along the wing on the second floor that had been allotted for their accommodation. The girls were all excited and exuberant, exclaiming at the beauty of the castle and how fortunate they were to be there. Margarete wondered how much they had been told about what they were actually here for. If they knew everything, why were they so ebulliently happy, with shining eyes and flushed cheeks?

As she opened the door to each room, a collective gasp went up from the group and whichever girl the room was allotted to burst inside and rushed to sit on the bed, testing the mattress.

When Margarete was alone with the last one in the group, a fragile-looking girl with fine features, she decided to ask some questions.

'How do you feel about what is planned for your trip to the castle?'

The girl looked at her steadily with her cool blue eyes and

gave a mechanical reply. 'I'm happy to be able to do something for the Führer and the Fatherland. I'm very much looking forward to having a child for the Führer.'

They had reached the girl's room now. Margarete opened the door and the girl went inside and put her bags on the floor. Margarete followed her inside and shut the door.

'Has anyone actually explained to you what that will involve?' Margarete asked.

'Of course,' the girl said, sitting down on the bed. 'Our BDM leader told all of us. We know what to expect. Tonight, we will choose our mates and when we are on the tenth day after our period, we will sleep with them for three nights. If we become pregnant, we can either stay at the castle, or go home for a time until our babies are due.'

As she spoke she didn't give an inkling that she had any qualms about what would occur over the next couple of weeks. Margarete was aghast that this slip of a girl was taking all this in her stride. It was one thing getting pregnant by mistake, like the other girls here so far, quite another to offer one's body voluntarily for the purpose of bearing a child for the state. Outraged as Margarete was, she hesitated, ever aware that she needed to be very careful what she said, especially to these girls who had clearly been hand-picked by the BDM for their loyalty to the Nazi cause.

'What do your parents think about this?' she asked.

The girl's smile vanished, and she frowned. 'They tried to stop me coming. My father said I was too young, my mother said I should wait until I'm married. They don't understand the new ideas, they are stuck in the past. I took no notice of them and came anyway.'

Margarete sighed. She wanted to ask the girl how old she was, but stopped short of that. She would be able to look through the details later when Doctor Finkel showed her the records. This story was all too common – the control and influ-

ence parents used to have over their offspring had been systematically and ruthlessly replaced via propaganda, school, the
Hitler Youth and the BDM, by loyalty to the Reich.

'Look,' Margarete said, 'if you have any hesitation or worries
about this yourself, come and speak to me. I'll be around the
whole time you are here. Motherhood is a big step, and you
might have some questions. I will say the same to all the girls
who arrive here today.'

The girl shrugged and gave her a suspicious look, which told
Margarete she had gone far enough. She left the room and went
to the next door along, where she knocked and went inside.

Taking a calculated risk, Margarete took the girls aside and
said the same thing to every one of them. Each of them gave her
the same quizzical look. That look said they had no idea why
she might be concerned about them, that they had made their
decision and were fully aware of what they were doing. They
made her feel as though her questions were unwelcome. Ten
girls arrived at the castle that afternoon and ten SS officers,
although Margarete didn't meet any of the young men until the
evening reception.

That evening, Doctor Finkel had asked Margarete to be
present at the feast when the new visitors would meet each
other for the first time. Getting ready in her room, she looked at
herself in the mirror, feeling sick to her stomach at the thought
of what the evening would bring. She contemplated making an
excuse not to go, and saying she felt ill, but she knew that would
arouse the doctor's suspicions.

With a heavy heart, she went down to the first floor again
and along to the vast reception room, which Doctor Finkel had
proudly told her had once been the Count's ballroom. It had
recently been refurbished at considerable expense by the
Lebensborn programme. The vast room was resplendent, with a
domed ceiling painted navy blue with a huge, golden sun in the
middle from which hung an elaborate brass chandelier lit with

dozens of flickering candles. On the walls were colourful murals, medieval hunting scenes and tableaux depicting Bavarian mythology, all of which were lit by spotlights to display their colours. At one end of the room, a long table was laden with food and several of the castle's maids and stewards stood there in uniform ready to serve the young people.

The youngsters were already milling about, holding glasses of sparkling wine or tankards of beer. The officers were still dressed in full uniform, but the girls had been transformed since they arrived. They had all changed out of their BDM uniforms and into pretty summer dresses in pastel colours. Many of them had applied a touch of make-up to their faces and they looked a lot older than they had when they'd first arrived. Margarete was surprised that Doctor Finkel had allowed it though; make-up was scorned as decadent by Nazi ideology. But either the doctor hadn't noticed or had decided to overlook this transgression in the interests of increasing the attractiveness of the girls in the eyes of the officers.

Stewards were circulating, handing out drinks and already some of the girls were looking flushed and bright-eyed.

After a few minutes, Doctor Finkel silenced the room by tapping a spoon on a glass. He then addressed the assembled company.

'Welcome, everyone, to our beautiful castle. I'd like to thank you all for coming and for putting your faith in the Lebensborn programme. We are all here by virtue of the generosity and brilliant vision of the Reichsführer himself. This is a brave vision, one that will advance the cause of the master race. You are all generous and selfless to have volunteered to further this pioneering cause in the way that you have.'

Margarete shuddered inwardly as she looked round at the shining faces of the young people applauding Doctor Finkel's words. They were clearly all completely committed to the cause. Margarete put her glass down and sidled out of the room, unable to stomach staying there a moment longer. Instead, she went along to the nursery to take a look at Heidi's baby girl. She was surprised to see Heidi sitting in the room beside the nursery, nursing the baby herself, an anxious look on her face.

'Hello, Nurse Weiss.' She looked up as Margarete entered. 'I'm so pleased you've come. I'm worried about Hannah. She isn't feeding properly, and she doesn't seem quite right.'

Margarete took the baby in her arms and, cradling her, examined her face. Her skin was pallid, and her eyes closed. Her breathing was irregular and her body felt floppy and unresponsive. There was clearly something wrong, but Margarete didn't want to alarm Heidi.

'Perhaps she isn't hungry at the moment. Why don't you put her back in the nursery to sleep and get some rest yourself? You look very tired.'

'Are you sure nothing is wrong?' Heidi was looking at her anxiously.

'I think she needs to sleep. Go back to bed, Heidi. I will ask Doctor Finkel to come and examine her, but please don't worry.'

Margarete helped Heidi take Hannah back to the nursery and settle her in her cot. Heidi bent down and kissed the baby, then Margarete led Heidi back to her room.

'Get some sleep yourself, Heidi,' she said.

With a heavy heart, Margarete made her way back to the ballroom, where everyone was now eating, seated at the tables that were set out round the perimeter of the room. Doctor Finkel was speaking to the kitchen staff at the buffet table. Margarete approached him.

'Doctor Finkel, I'm very worried about the baby that was born two days ago. She is unresponsive and not feeding properly.'

Doctor Finkel turned to face her with a look of exasperation. 'Not now, Nurse. Can't you see I'm busy?'

'I wouldn't ask unless I was sure it was important, but the

baby's breathing is irregular and she isn't responding to normal stimuli. I think you should come and take a look at her.'

'All right,' the doctor said irritably.

They hurried along to the nursery together and Doctor Finkel picked Hannah up. He took her into the side room, laid her on a table there and performed some tests on her – her heartbeat, her breathing, her reactions. Margarete watched him anxiously.

After a few minutes, he looked up. 'It's as I thought. The baby must have suffered brain damage at birth. She won't be fit for adoption. I will decide what is to be done with her tomorrow. Now, I really must get back to the reception and so must you, Nurse Weiss.'

'I will make sure she's settled first,' Margarete said, taking the baby from the doctor and cradling her in her arms, a niggling worry in the back of her mind. What did the doctor mean, that he would decide what was to be done with the baby?

Carefully, she laid Hannah down to sleep again, stroking her cold brow, tucking the blankets around her. Then she tiptoed out of the nursery and, instead of going back to the reception, in a small act of rebellion, went upstairs to her room.

In the morning, as soon as she was dressed, Margarete headed straight down to the nursery before she'd even taken breakfast. The nursery nurse who had been on duty overnight was just packing her things, ready to leave. Margarete went over to Hannah's cot and peered inside: the cot was empty.

'Where's the baby girl who was in this cot?' she asked the nursery nurse.

'Oh, Doctor Finkel came and collected her before dawn. An ambulance came from Munich to take her away.'

Shock washed through Margarete, and she rushed out of the nursery, down the stairs and ran along to the doctor's office, where she raced in without knocking. 'What's happened to the baby girl?' she asked.

Doctor Finkel looked up from his desk, exasperated. 'Sit down, Nurse Weiss,' he said. 'I do wish you would stop bursting into my office. I decided to send her to the facility in Munich where I've sent other babies who weren't going to make the grade.'

'Facility?'

'Yes. That is where she will be cared for appropriately. Now, please don't ask any more questions about it. That is my decision, and I would be grateful if you would inform the mother that the baby has been sent to its new home. She can be discharged straight away. There is no need for her to stay any longer here at government expense. We need to turn our attention to the next two adoptions which are booked in for this week and, of course, to our young guests, who must take priority now.'

There were so many questions Margarete wanted to ask, so many things about baby Hannah being sent off like that that made her feel deeply uncomfortable, but she knew it was no use persisting with Doctor Finkel at that moment.

She left the room, feeling wretched and powerless, and went up the stairs with dread in her heart. How could she tell Heidi that she would never see her baby again, that her baby hadn't 'made the grade' and had been sent to a special facility in Munich? None of it felt right, and Margarete hated the fact that she had to be part of all this; that there was no escape.

FIFTEEN

MARGARETE

Schloss Schwanburg, Bavaria, 1938

When Margarete sat down on Heidi's bed and told her that her precious baby had been sent to a medical facility in Munich, Heidi's face crumbled, and she burst into tears.

'What will happen to her?' she kept asking, tears streaming down her cheeks.

'I'm sure she will get the best care available,' Margarete replied, trying to convince herself of that fact as much as Heidi. But there was so much she didn't understand and didn't trust about what was going on here at Schloss Schwanburg.

After her early morning visit to the nursery, she'd managed to slip into Doctor Finkel's room while he was at breakfast. She had looked again at the entry he'd made beside the entry for Heidi's baby: *Born weak and feeble. Usual responses absent or slow. Clearly brain damaged. Discharged to the aa medical facility in Munich for further assessment.*

She'd stared at those words in horror. They filled her with anxiety and fear in equal measure. Why had the doctor seen fit to send the baby away covertly before dawn without informing either Heidi or herself about it? It must be because he'd known she would object and that what he was doing was somehow wrong and not in the best interests of the child.

While she was in his room, knowing Doctor Finkel was elsewhere, and that Holge Schwartz was doing his morning rounds of the castle grounds, she'd taken the opportunity to slip the ledger of adoptive parents out of the desk drawer and had copied down the remaining details of all the babies that had been born since the programme had started at Schloss Schwanburg. She wrote out the names and addresses of all the adopting families and the babies they had taken, identified by the mothers' names in the ledger. Afterwards, she'd rushed through to her own office, slipped the page into her notebook and concealed it in its usual place in her bedroom.

Margarete thought about the words she'd seen in the ledger about Hannah as Heidi sobbed in her arms that morning. But, gradually, with soothing words, she finally managed to calm Heidi down.

'You're not to worry. Your baby is going to a hospital where she will get the special care she needs,' she repeated.

Eventually, Heidi sank back on her bed. The fight had gone out of her and it looked as though she'd reluctantly accepted the situation.

Leaving her to rest, Margarete returned to the nursery to feed and change the remaining babies. It was a busy morning, and she got caught up helping a mother breastfeeding in the side room. Before she knew it, it was past twelve o'clock and already lunchtime. She decided to look in on Heidi on her way to the dining room.

When Margarete entered her room, Heidi was lying unconscious on the bed, fully clothed. Her suitcase was packed and waiting beside her. Margarete tried to shake her awake, but she was in a deep sleep. She rushed straight back to the nursery.

'Nurse Ekert,' she asked sharply, 'whatever's wrong with

Heidi? She's out cold. And her bag is packed. What on earth has happened?'

The woman lifted her head, her mouth drawn up in a defensive line. 'May I remind you, Nurse Weiss, that we don't use the girls' real names? But actually, Doctor Finkel had to give her a shot of sedative. She started to make a fuss. She has taken her baby's departure very badly. We can't have that going on with all the young people we have staying here, it will sap morale.'

'Well, I'm not surprised she was upset!' Margarete snapped. 'The baby was taken before dawn without her having a chance to say goodbye. And, by the way, what *is* this facility that babies are sent to in Munich, Nurse Ekert? I've never heard of it before.'

The midwife pursed her lips and Margarete was surprised to see colour creeping into her chubby cheeks. 'It is where weaker babies are sent to be dealt with appropriately by suitably qualified doctors, that's all I know,' she said.

'And do they come back here when they're better? Do they still go for adoption?'

The midwife shook her head and drew herself up. 'I know nothing about it, and I don't ask. It is better that you don't ask either, Nurse Weiss. It is Nazi policy that babies with health problems should go there, and who are we to question that?'

Infuriated and deeply troubled, Margarete left the nursery and went straight back to Heidi's room. To her astonishment, Heidi was no longer lying on the bed, but her suitcase was still on the floor. Margarete rushed to the top of the stairs and stopped dead, staring downstairs, stunned by what she saw. Holge Schwartz, the caretaker, was halfway down the stairs, carrying Heidi in his arms, her legs and arms flopping freely.

'Whatever are you doing, Herr Schwartz?' Margarete yelled.

Holge didn't stop walking down the stairs and he didn't turn

round. 'The car has come to take this patient home and Doctor
Finkel asked me to take her out to it,' he said.

Margarete began to run down the stairs after him. 'You can't
just send her off like that. She's unconscious, anything could
happen.'

Holge got to the bottom of the stairs. He turned and looked
up at Margarete scornfully. 'The doctor has asked me to accompany her to make sure she gets home safely. So, when she wakes
up on the journey, I will be there to take care of her.'

'You?' Margarete asked, appalled, thinking of how terrified
Heidi would be when she awoke and saw that she was in a car
with a strange man. 'I will go with her.'

Doctor Finkel suddenly emerged from the corridor into the
hall. 'There is no need for that, Nurse Weiss. The young
woman will be perfectly safe with Holge. It is high time she left
the premises, she's caused quite enough trouble as it is. Now,
could I please ask you to return to your duties in the nursery.
You have no need to concern yourself any further with that
young woman.'

Margarete went back to her work, but she would never
forget the sight of Heidi being carried out to the car by Holge
Schwartz, or Heidi's expression of love when she'd looked down
at her baby girl. What had happened to baby Hannah? Where
was she now? The poor little thing, deprived of a mother's love
she so needed and deserved.

Over the next few months, babies were born at regular intervals
at Schloss Schwanburg. The births took place, just as Heidi's
baby had, under the strict medical supervision of Doctor Finkel
and Nurse Ekert and Margarete was excluded. It troubled
Margarete deeply that after the birth the babies were put
through rigorous physical testing to ensure they met the criteria
for racial purity. If any were born with physical or congenital

ailments, they were removed quickly and taken away by ambulance to the 'facility' in Munich that baby Hannah had been sent to. If they passed the tests, on the other hand, Nazi Party members, families of SS officers or other Nazi high officials were found to adopt them.

Margarete hated being part of this. Her heart broke every time she stood at an upstairs window and watched a smug Nazi couple getting into one of those sinister black limousines, holding a tiny bundle she'd cared for since birth. But she had to carry on, she had no choice.

In the ninth month after the first batch of officers and BDM members had stayed at the castle, nine healthy babies were born. One of the BDM girls had failed to conceive and had been sent home under a cloud, but the others had all become pregnant during that week. Some of the girls had gone home for a few months, but others had stayed the entire nine months at the castle, relaxing in the gardens and the common rooms, being cared for by the multitude of castle staff and eating plentifully despite the hardships at home.

It was a busy time for Doctor Finkel and Nurse Ekert, who sometimes had to deal with two deliveries a day. Margarete was rushed off her feet too, caring for the newborn babies in the nursery, yet she was grateful for the distraction of being busy. If she thought too much about what she was doing, she felt she would go mad.

By then, the country was at war with Britain and food was becoming scarcer for civilians. But the war, the reality of the outside world, hardly impinged upon life at the castle. For the officers who came to stay there, it was a welcome respite to life at the Front, and for the girls who joined them, a change from the privations of civilian life in wartime Germany.

Although it was difficult to get news at the castle, the only newspapers being those controlled by the Party, Margarete did her best to read between the lines of the propaganda. She followed the progress of current events with growing horror, appalled when Hitler invaded Czechoslovakia in direct breach of his promises to other world leaders, and afterwards had overrun Poland, tipping the country into full-scale war.

As the days and months slid by, and those months turned into years, there were regular repeats of the first experiment with SS officers and girls recruited by the BDM. There was also the usual procession of unmarried Aryan mothers coming to the castle to give birth.

Margarete felt very alone and very afraid as she carried out her duties, caring for the newborn babies in the nursery. She did her best for them, despite detesting the fact that she was there under duress, working for the Nazis, whom she feared and despised. Despite her love of the babies and delight in the work, every hour of every day was tinged with dread. She was acutely aware that all those beautiful babies were going to be taken from their mothers and brought up by fervent Nazis. She couldn't escape that thought as she cared for them. It weighed heavily on her heart and on her conscience too. But she was afraid of Doctor Finkel, afraid of Nurse Ekert and all the other staff and especially afraid of Holge Schwartz, the sinister caretaker who appeared to watch her every movement with suspicious eyes.

To add to the fear, time and time again, Margarete bore witness to distressing scenes when the young mothers realised the full implications of being parted from their babies. Although they had come to the castle knowing what would happen after they gave birth, and were fully invested in the Nazi cause, having been indoctrinated with propaganda from an early age, when they faced the harsh reality of parting with their babies, most, like Freda and Heidi, found the wrench very hard to bear.

Margarete carried on doing the only thing she could for the mothers and their babies: making a note of the mothers' details and addresses, the date of birth and sex of their babies, and the details and addresses of their adoptive parents. The deeper she got into creating those records, the more afraid she became of discovery, especially as Holge seemed to constantly have her in his sights, frequently appearing in the corridor when she had slipped out of Doctor Finkel's office. The caretaker often asked pointed questions about what she was doing. More than once, he referred to her family in a threatening way. Once, he came up close to her, looming over her and said with a sly smile, 'I hope your family are grateful for your sacrifices for them and for all the valuable work you are doing here for the Lebensborn programme.'

He left no doubt in her mind that this was a thinly veiled threat. As he'd slunk away, down the stone passage, she had felt sick with fear.

Shortly after that, he almost discovered her notebook. She was in her office, busy copying out babies' details from the ledger, when there was a brief knock at the door.

'Wait a moment,' she said, but a bolt of shock coursed through her when she realised that she had forgotten to turn the key in the lock. The next second, Holge had entered her office. She looked up from her notebook, trying to keep the guilt from her face, hoping desperately that he wouldn't come close enough to see what she was doing.

'Sorry to disturb your important work, Nurse Weiss,' he said facetiously, his eyes on her desk. 'But I need to order stationery. Do you require anything?'

'No... no... it's quite all right,' she replied, willing him to leave.

'Those blue notebooks, they are extremely useful. Do you need any more of them? I noticed one had been taken from the stationery cupboard.'

'No... no, it's fine,' she said, colour creeping into her cheeks. She had taken the second notebook from the cupboard without filling in a slip to say she'd done it, hardly imagining that it would matter or even come to light.

'All right then...' Holge said, backing out of the room slowly, his eyes still on her desk. 'I will leave you to it.'

He closed the door and Margarete ran over to it and turned the key quietly in the lock, then stood with her back to the door, her heart pounding. She determined that she must be more careful; she needed to work out a code for the notebook in case it was ever discovered.

That evening, Margarete took two novels out of the lining of her suitcase that was stored under her bed. She had brought them from Berlin. They were both banned by the Nazis, and she had read them so many times, she virtually knew them by heart. *The Great Gatsby* and *Death in Venice*, two books that Frau Lessing, the wife of the family doctor, had given her before books were destroyed in book-burning ceremonies across the country, ordered by the Nazis.

With the help of the two novels, Margarete began developing a code to use in her notebooks for every letter of the alphabet, based on the page and line of the book in which each letter appeared. Then, she painstakingly rewrote every word of the lists she had compiled so far, taking the further precautionary step of splitting them up into two notebooks – one for the mother's details and one for the details of the adoptive parents. This time, she didn't make the mistake of taking one from the stationery cupboard, she found an old one buried in a bottom drawer of her desk. Instead of keeping them in the locked drawer in her desk, she kept them in the void underneath the drawer for added safety – although she knew that nothing would prevent their discovery if anyone suspected her actions and was determined to find them.

Twice a year, when she was permitted to take her annual leave, Margarete made the long train journey home to Berlin. She was always grateful for the chance to leave the castle behind her, even if it was only temporary and she would have to return. Her father's health was deteriorating fast – he was virtually bedridden by 1939 – but his hatred of the Nazi regime and everything that was happening in Germany, including the waging of total war, was undimmed.

'Not only have those bullyboys whipped up racial hatred and driven thousands of Jews to leave the country, but now they've confiscated their businesses and their property and they are shipping those who are left off to work in camps in appalling conditions.'

Alicia shared her father's rabid hatred of the Nazis and she quietly confided in Margarete that she was now working actively for the German resistance in Berlin, taking many risks to spread the word of peace by distributing leaflets. She was also helping Jews to escape the country or the camps, helping communists, gypsies, homosexuals to hide or to flee to safety. Margarete was full of admiration for Alicia's bravery, but full of fear too.

In turn, she told her sister a little about what went on at the castle. Alicia was appalled at what she heard.

'How can you work there, for them? Doing that?' Alicia asked. 'It's abhorrent.'

'I have no choice,' Margarete said. 'Every time I step out of line, they mention my family. You are on their radar, you know, Alicia. They know about what you do.'

Alicia scoffed. 'They might think they know, but they have no proof. Until they catch us red-handed, they only have their suspicions.'

Margarete couldn't get Alicia to understand that she hated what she was doing at Schloss Schwanburg, but she was trapped in her work at the castle precisely because of what Alicia and her father stood for. On the train back to Füssen, she reflected on how ironic it was that her sister disapproved of what she was doing when it was Alicia and her parents she was trying to protect all the time by staying there.

As the war dragged on, Doctor Finkel's duties took him

away from the castle for long periods at a time. He was often summoned to the Ministry for meetings and conferences to work on new strategies for Lebensborn. Margarete was aware that Lebensborn homes were opening up all over Germany and also in territories occupied by the Germans, such as Norway and France. There were other plans afoot too for the programme, which were shrouded in mystery. Margarete knew that the Nazis would stop at nothing to expand the population of the so-called master race, but she couldn't guess the full extent of their ruthless pursuit of this aim.

One day, towards the end of 1942, Doctor Finkel summoned Margarete into his office. She was surprised to see that he was not alone. Another man was sitting opposite him with his back to the door. Her scalp prickled. Was this Reichsführer Himmler? Doctor Finkel was always talking about him in favourable terms and saying how much the Reichsführer approved of the work of Schloss Schwanburg, but Margarete lived in fear of him visiting the castle. As she moved into the room on unsteady legs and the man turned round, she put her fears aside. There was something fresh about the look in his eyes that struck her, something different.

'Nurse Weiss, this is Doctor Tomas Müller,' Doctor Finkel said.

The man got up from his chair and held out his hand for Margarete to shake. He was tall and slim, with dark blond hair and blue eyes.

'Doctor Müller has come from the children's hospital in Munich to cover for me while I am in Berlin for the next couple of weeks and he will then stay on to assist He is a highly regarded obstetrician.'

Margarete looked nervously up into the newcomer's gaze and her breath caught in her throat. He was actually smiling at her – a genuine smile that reached right to his eyes.

'Good afternoon, Nurse Weiss. Doctor Finkel has been singing your praises.'

'Really?' she asked, surprised.

'Of course,' Doctor Finkel said, giving her a loaded look. 'We are a tight team here at Schloss Schwanburg and Nurse Weiss runs the nursery like clockwork.'

Margarete realised that Doctor Finkel was determined to present a united front to the newcomer, despite whatever differences they may have had.

'Well, I look forward to working with you, Nurse Weiss,' Doctor Müller said.

'Do sit down, Nurse Weiss,' Doctor Finkel instructed. 'I thought it would be useful for you to be here while I explain our work to Doctor Müller.'

Margarete sat down and listened while Doctor Finkel described what Müller's duties would entail. Doctor Müller listened patiently, his intelligent dark eyes taking it all in, but occasionally he interrupted Doctor Finkel, asking him to explain more precisely what he meant. Margarete was heartened to hear him querying some of the practices which she herself had great difficulty coming to terms with.

'We don't administer pain relief during the births,' Doctor Finkel said at one point and Doctor Müller visibly stiffened and frowned.

'Really, Herr Doctor? What purpose does that serve?'

Doctor Finkel looked surprised to be challenged by someone he clearly regarded as his inferior. He took a pained breath. 'Well, these girls are at the pinnacle of health, Doctor Müller. They are all prime specimens of Aryan womanhood. They are young, fit and healthy. The Führer encourages a natural approach to womanhood and all it entails, so we have taken the decision that giving birth naturally without pain relief is the best interpretation of the Nazi ideal.'

Doctor Müller leaned back in his chair, rubbing his chin,

and he shook his head thoughtfully. 'With respect, Doctor Finkel, I would have thought that if you are a young woman, barely out of your teens, becoming pregnant and giving birth for the Fatherland, when you know that you will be parting with your baby very shortly after its birth is already a traumatic experience. The kindest thing to do would be to make that experience as pain-free and stress-free as possible.'

Doctor Finkel pursed his lips. 'Of course, when you are in charge, you must do as you see fit, Doctor Müller. But I fear you may encounter some resistance from our senior midwife, Nurse Ekert, in the matter.'

Doctor Müller raised his eyebrows and the discussion moved on. Doctor Finkel spoke about the routines of the nursery, how although the young mothers were allowed to breast-feed their babies, they were not encouraged to cuddle them, to pick them up when they cried, or to show them any emotion. Once more, Doctor Müller stopped him.

'But what is the purpose of that rule, Doctor Finkel? It seems very harsh.'

Doctor Finkel frowned and looked at Doctor Müller as if he were an imbecile. 'Doctor Müller, I'm surprised you are asking questions like this. I understood you to have been recommended by the Ministry. Surely you are aware of the rudiments of Nazi ideology on such matters, and the teachings of Doctor Johanna Haarer? Cuddling and pandering to babies softens and spoils them. They should be isolated for long periods at the earliest opportunity and left to cry alone at night. We want our children to grow up tough, to be hardy, to be good soldiers for the Fatherland.'

Margarete was staring down at her lap while Doctor Finkel was speaking, pursing her lips. This was something she felt very strongly about herself. When she was on duty in the nursery, she always encouraged the young mothers to cuddle their babies and to pick them up if they cried. She was convinced that the

Nazi teachings were wrong and deeply damaging to babies. She'd had several disagreements with Nurse Ekert about it, and she had no intention of bowing down to such harsh ideology. However, she couldn't challenge Doctor Finkel about it directly.

'Well, let us move on... I have to explain about the testing of babies at birth and our policy regarding those who do not pass our post-birth testing... Nurse Weiss, would you leave us now, please? From here on in, our discussion will touch on purely medical matters.'

Margarete left the meeting heartened by Doctor Müller's questioning attitude, but troubled about what they were currently discussing. As she walked away, she comforted herself with the thought that at least this man seemed sympathetic. She was grateful that at last there was someone who seemed to share her concerns. She returned to the nursery feeling a little more optimistic, looking forward to Doctor Finkel's absence and the prospect of working with Doctor Müller.

In the morning, her heart lifted as she stood at her bedroom window watching Doctor Finkel's black car with its Nazi insignia draw away from the castle in the billowing morning mist. Seeing him depart was as if a cloud had lifted, and she went to get ready for the day, wondering what it would bring.

When she arrived in the nursery, Nurse Ekert was banging around, steaming with anger. 'That man!' she stormed. 'He had the nerve to come in here and tell Jutta, the ward sister, that she mustn't let the babies cry. He's breaching protocol on his very first day.'

'Let's give him a chance, shall we?' Margarete replied. She was pleased that Doctor Müller was following through with his ideas rather than just espousing them.

'I knew you'd say that. You're just the same yourself.'

'Everything all right, ladies?' Doctor Müller put his head round the door and grinned at Margarete. As her eyes met his, she felt a connection with him that she'd not felt with anyone since she'd started work at the castle.

Just then, a bell in one of the expectant mothers' rooms shrilled.

'That must be Ingrid,' Nurse Ekert said. 'Her baby is due in three days' time. Perhaps she's started early.'

'Excellent!' Doctor Müller said, rubbing his hands together. 'A great way to get started. Please bring her along to the delivery room, if that's the case, Nurse.'

Soon, the midwife reappeared, helping a pale-looking Ingrid along. The girl, who was only eighteen, was clutching her belly, pain and fear etched on her face.

In the delivery room, Margarete watched on as Doctor Müller spoke gently to the girl. He sat her down and explained what was happening to her body.

'You're not to worry, Ingrid. This is all quite natural, and when things get difficult, we will give you something to help with the pain.' He looked up and nodded towards Nurse Ekert. 'Get the gas and air ready please, Nurse. Pethidine too. We want Ingrid to be as comfortable as possible.'

'Doctor Finkel doesn't give pain relief during labour, Doctor,' Nurse Ekert replied, folding her arms.

'I'm aware of that but I'm in charge here now, Nurse, and I have a different approach. Now could you please fetch them and get the gas and air ready for Ingrid while we get her up onto the bed. Nurse Weiss, could you help, please?'

Nurse Ekert bustled away, huffing.

Margarete took one of Ingrid's arms and they both lifted her up onto the bed.

'Now, Ingrid, I'm going to examine you quickly, but after that, if it feels more comfortable, you are free to get down from the bed, to stand up, lie down, move about. Do whatever feels best for you. If you are upright, the baby will come more quickly.'

Margarete couldn't help smiling at Doctor Müller's words, and although Nurse Ekert was bristling with disapproval, Margarete stayed throughout Ingrid's labour, pleased to be able to comfort the girl, to rub her back when she asked, to help her take the gas and air and to support her when she needed to lean against someone. The labour was shorter than any other Margarete had witnessed at the castle and, afterwards, Ingrid burst into tears when she saw her baby boy and held him in her arms.

'Thank you, Doctor,' she said, smiling up at Doctor Müller. 'For helping me. I couldn't have done it without you.'

Margarete was pleasantly surprised that Doctor Müller was still on the ward with mother and baby rather than hurrying away as soon as the birth was over as Doctor Finkel always did.

At the end of the long day, after Nurse Ekert had finally left the castle, setting off for her home in Füssen on her old-fashioned bicycle, Doctor Müller asked Margarete into his office.

When she entered, she was surprised that he strode over and locked the door.

'I wanted to speak to you, Nurse Weiss,' he said, 'because I sensed as soon as I arrived that you share some of my concerns about what is happening here.'

He spoke in hushed tones, gesturing to Margarete to sit down. From the look on his face, she knew that she finally had an ally but part of her hesitated, she was so programmed to be cautious that she wondered if this was some kind of trick. She sat down and waited for him to go on before she committed herself.

'But you need to be a bit careful,' he said, leaning forward. 'We both do. Do you know what happened to your predecessor? Sister Bach?'

Margarete shook her head, her heart in her mouth.

'She was removed from her post by the Gestapo,' he said.

'Sent off to Dachau. Pronounced an enemy of the state. I don't know if she's still alive or not.'

'How do you know this?' Margarete faltered, shock making it hard to speak.

'Finkel told me when I arrived yesterday. He told me a lot that made my blood run cold, to be honest. He was speaking quite freely, worried about deserters from the programme. He clearly thought that he had an ally in me.'

Margarete's heart was pounding now, the news about Sister Bach had sent her nerves into overdrive. Was that what had happened to Matron at the Charité Hospital too?

'What did she do?' Margarete asked finally. 'Sister Bach. What did she do?'

'She was constantly critical of the programme apparently. Then she helped a young mother to run away with her baby. That's when Finkel called in the Gestapo. They took Sister Bach away in the dead of night.'

Margarete's hand flew to her mouth but she was filled with admiration for Sister Bach. She must have been very brave to have put herself at risk like that.

'What happened to the mother and baby?' she asked.

'They got away apparently. The Gestapo haven't been able to track them down, but they won't stop looking, you can be sure of that.'

Margarete swallowed, her eyes fixed on Tomas Müller's, aware that this was a turning point for her. Hadn't she vowed to be brave? Be true to herself, just as her father had said? *Sometimes you have to take risks*, she told herself.

Doctor Müller leaned back in his chair, still looking at her intently. 'When Finkel sent you out of the room yesterday, he told me what happens to those babies who are born with physical or developmental problems,' he said, still watching the impact of his words. 'He sends them off to a special hospital run by Aktion T4.'

'Aktion T4?' Margarete repeated. 'What is that?'

He leaned forward and as he spoke, she could see the horror in his eyes. 'Aktion T4 is a Nazi programme of enforced euthanasia. Babies and children who those monsters deem unworthy of life are sent there. They might have some physical or mental problem, sometimes quite minor. There, they are systematically eradicated. They might be starved to death or helped on their way by lethal injection. Afterwards, their family is told that they died of natural causes.'

'No!' Margarete let out an involuntary sob and broke down, doubling up on the chair, bile flooding into her mouth. This was unthinkable. How could anyone even consider harming an innocent baby? This must have been the fate of Heidi's beautiful baby, Hannah, and all those other babies born into the programme who were deemed less than perfect. In her gut, she had suspected something like this, but her heart had refused to accept it. How stupid she'd been. How naive!

'Nurse Weiss... Margarete... if you don't mind me calling you by your first name. We need to be strong,' Doctor Müller said. 'Over the years working for the Nazis, it has been very difficult to hold true to my principles and to my oath. I've done my utmost to do what I became a doctor for. While I'm in charge here, even if for a short time, I intend to continue to do that. No babies will be signed off by me to Aktion 4, mothers won't be forced to sign away their rights if they don't want to, and we won't be holding any soirées for SS officers and BDM girls. I suspect that you've already been doing what you can to alleviate suffering here. Is that right, Margarete?'

Margarete hesitated again, but just for a second this time. Slowly, she nodded.

'I've done what I can. I've been encouraging the girls to cuddle and comfort their babies, to pick them up when they cry. I tell them that they can use their first names, and... and... I've noted down details of all the adoptions in my notebooks.'

She watched his face warily. He smiled. 'I thought so. Well done. You're very brave. Now, with two of us, it will be a little easier. You will carry on and help me with this, won't you? It's not going to be plain sailing.'

Margarete looked at him through a blur of tears. 'Of course,' she said. 'Of course I'll help you, Doctor Müller. I'm so glad you're here.'

SIXTEEN

HEDDA

Bavaria, 1943

The train was making its way south from Munich, rattling through dense evergreen forests, past picture-book Bavarian villages, through rolling, fertile farmland. Up ahead, in the distance, Hedda could just about make out the shape of some jagged mountains on the horizon. They must be nearly there.

Nervously, she fingered Sebastian's letter in her lap. How many times had she read it now? It didn't matter, it gave her comfort.

She hadn't wanted to write to him at first, but Aunt Ursula had insisted. Having no one else to turn to, she'd been forced to tell her aunt of her predicament, once she was quite sure that she was expecting. It would have been impossible to speak to Beate or Elsa. They were so jealous of her relationship with Sebastian, she just couldn't imagine how they might react. But when she did pluck up the courage to broach the subject with Ursula, her aunt was less than sympathetic.

'I know a woman...' Ursula had said once she'd got over her initial shock at the news. 'She lives not too far away from here.

We can go to her,and she will sort you out. She doesn't come cheap though so you must go to lover boy and ask him for the money.'

'He doesn't even know about it,' Hedda had said miserably. 'He's away now, in the Wehrmacht. Fighting in Russia.'

'Well, I'm sure you can write to him there. I've seen those letters arrive that you whisk away to your bedroom. They're from him, aren't they?'

'Yes,' Hedda had whispered, thinking about the stash of letters from Sebastian hidden in her underwear drawer. She'd been quite disconcerted by the letters though. They were full of tales of bravado on the Eastern Front and Sebastian seemed to revel in the triumphal acts of violence and warfare he was engaged in. She was surprised at their tone, but she was so in love, she was prepared to forgive him anything. It must be the shock of being in combat that had caused him to react like that.

She'd dreaded telling Sebastian about her condition and she'd dreaded even more asking him for money to get rid of their baby. How could she even think about getting rid of that tiny, innocent being growing inside her, the living embodiment of their love?

'Well, if he won't pay, we can go to his parents and ask *them* for the money,' Aunt Ursula had said, interrupting her thoughts.

Hedda had looked up sharply. 'No! I would never do that. And I'm not even sure if I want to... to go to your woman.'

'As I see it, you haven't much choice,' Ursula had replied. 'Babies born out of wedlock are shunned in the Third Reich. I don't know if you've noticed, but the Führer is very keen on the idea of children being brought into the world and nurtured in a caring, traditional family. You won't get very far without a husband nowadays, Hedda Jenner. Now, write to your fancy man this evening and let's have done with it.'

At that point, a pan on the stove had begun to smoke.

Ursula had sworn and dived across the kitchen to take it off the heat.

'Now look what you've made me do! And, by the way, don't you *dare* breathe a word of any of this to your uncle, or you'll be straight out on your ear.'

Hedda had written to Sebastian that very evening with a heavy heart, telling him about the baby growing inside her. He had written back to her within a few days. It was that letter she now clasped in her hands as she made her journey south.

'There is a place you can go, where you will be safe,' he'd written. 'A castle in Bavaria. My officer told me about it. I am due some leave from the Front in March, so I will be able to meet you there for a couple of days. It's part of a special initiative where girls of good blood can give birth in safety. You and the baby will be taken care of.'

He'd followed that up with another letter giving her the address of the castle near Füssen and the date and time of the train she should take there from Munich.

'There will be a car to meet you at the station. It will take you straight up to the castle so you're not to worry.'

The other girls on the train had quietened down now and Hedda guessed that like her, they were growing more nervous the closer they got to their destination. The train ran through the foothills of the Alps, with their rugged, rocky peaks and past still mountain lakes surrounded by fir trees. The further south they went, the more dramatic the landscape became. She could see snow on the tops of the hills now, contrasting starkly with the bright blue sky.

It was snowing when the train finally steamed into Füssen station and Hedda pulled her coat tightly around her as she got down from the carriage, crossed the platform and looked about her for the car Sebastian had promised. To her relief, there were actually two big black cars waiting, parked in front of the station steps, and her heart leapt to see Sebastian standing beside one of them.

He was dressed in a grey greatcoat and military cap and his face lit up when he saw her. But running forward into his arms, seeing the silver skull badge on his cap and the insignia on his epaulettes, she realised with shock that the uniform he was wearing was that of an officer of the SS. She knew the SS to be uniquely brutal, responsible for extermination and torture on a grand scale. So different from the Wehrmacht, the regular army.

He hugged her tight, then released her, held her at arm's length and looked into her eyes. 'I'm so glad you've come, Hedda. I've been very worried about you,' he said. Then he picked up her suitcase and opened the car door. 'Come on, get in. The driver will take us up to the castle.'

He went to stow her case in the boot and, watching him through the back window, she noticed the three girls from the train getting into the car behind theirs.

On their way up to the castle, through the small town of Füssen, along the shores of a mountain lake, then up a winding road through thick forest, Sebastian talked excitedly. 'I'm so pleased that you agreed to come here, Hedda. As I said in my letter, my senior officer told me all about this initiative. It's called the Lebensborn programme.'

'Lebensborn?'

It meant 'spring of life'; it had been spoken about at the BDM meetings. One evening at the beginning of the war, a fierce-looking woman had come to recruit girls of Aryan blood to volunteer to have a baby for the Fatherland. The woman had had no takers from Hedda's group; they had all been outraged and bewildered at such a notion, that seemed contrary to everything they'd learned in their Nazi philosophy lessons about the importance of the nuclear family. The woman had gone away disgruntled and empty-handed. Now, Hedda wondered what the Lebensborn programme had to do with her baby.

Sebastian turned to her smiling, his blue eyes looking brighter than ever in the winter sunshine. His SS cap was on his lap and her eyes kept straying to the insignia, to that chilling skull badge on the front. 'Yes, Lebensborn. Isn't it an inspiring name? It's a programme to encourage Aryan women to give birth to their babies whatever their circumstances. Women just like you.'

Things suddenly became clear to Hedda as the car crawled up the icy road towards a white fairy-tale castle set high on rocks amongst the trees, its steep roofs covered in snow. She fell silent, suddenly filled with dread. This wasn't what she was expecting at all. How hadn't she realised that this was where he was taking her? Even on the train, she'd guessed where the group of girls were bound for, but she hadn't connected it to herself. How could she have been so naive? But she suppressed her worries. She knew better than to overreact. Despite that, there was one question she couldn't resist asking him.

'That uniform you're wearing,' she said. 'I didn't know you were signing up for the SS. You said you were in the Wehrmacht.'

'Ah... I had the chance to transfer when I arrived at the recruitment centre. Some of us were fortunate enough to be selected for the Waffen-SS training camp. My father put in a word for me.'

'Your father?'

'Yes... he has a lot of influence in party circles. Of course, they owe him a favour... with the family factories producing as much as they do for the war effort.'

The car was pulling between giant wooden gates, driving under a gatehouse and into a huge square courtyard. Hedda swallowed hard.

'You never actually told me what your father's factories produce,' she said weakly.

'Oh, weapons of course. Weapons and tanks... they used to

make tractors and industrial machinery before the war, but all that has changed in the past couple of years. The firm has been expanding, working round the clock. New premises have been opened in Munich. That's what my father was posted there to oversee.' There was a note of pride in his voice.

She stared at him wordlessly, as the car drew up in front of the castle entrance. What a fool she'd been. This was what she had avoided confronting all along. She had deliberately ducked the truth. Why hadn't she actually asked him at the time? But in her heart, she knew the answer to that question. She'd been so alone, so bereft, and Sebastian had shown her kindness and love. He'd been everything to her. She'd pinned all her hopes and dreams onto him. She'd seen in him everything she'd wanted to see and been blind to the truth.

But there was no time for regrets. The car had stopped, and the driver was getting out to open the door for her. Hedda got out of the back seat, gasping as the icy mountain air wrapped itself around her. A freezing wind whipped round her legs. She looked at the great building looming up in front of her, full of apprehension and regret. Sebastian took her arm and guided her up the front steps and into a cavernous hall. At least there was a roaring fire in a huge open grate at one end, but its heat hardly seemed to have an impact on the temperature of the room. She looked around her at the intimidating surroundings, overawed and frightened. She felt trapped. This place was miles from anywhere, completely secluded. It must be why it had been chosen.

A man approached, his footsteps echoing in the passageway. He wore a white coat and carried a clipboard. At first, Hedda couldn't see his eyes, the light from the fire reflected in his pebble glasses. But when she could, they were as cold as the icy wind in the courtyard.

'Good afternoon, Miss Jenner. I am Doctor Finkel,' he said. 'Medical Director of the Lebensborn programme here.

Welcome to Schloss Schwanburg. If you'd like to follow me, I will show you to your room and tomorrow, I will carry out your preliminary tests.'

'I will see you soon, Hedda,' Sebastian said. 'There's a drinks reception at six o'clock, I'll see you there.' She stared after him, confused. What was he thinking, bringing her here?

She followed the doctor reluctantly up the long flight of stairs and along a carpeted corridor lined with doors. He opened one near the end. 'This is where you will stay,' he said. 'My head of nursing, Nurse Weiss, is away for a couple of days, that's why I'm showing you to your room.'

Hedda peeped inside. The room was large and square and sumptuously furnished. There was a washbasin in one corner, a large double bed on one side with an elaborate walnut head-board, a dressing table on the other and a sofa in the window in red velvet to match the curtains. 'It's beautiful,' she couldn't help saying, despite how uncomfortable she was feeling, but she was amazed at the luxury. It was such a contrast to the difficulties and privations she'd suffered in recent years.

'It is indeed. We've had all the rooms on this wing refurbished for the young ladies on the programme,' the doctor commented. 'Your luggage will be up shortly. Now, at six o'clock, do come along to the ballroom. It's where all the other young people will be gathering. Three of the young ladies came on your train, I believe,' he added.

Hedda felt trapped. She shouldn't be here, she didn't want to be part of this, she wasn't like those girls on the train. She needed to tell him straight away before there was any more misunderstanding. She took a deep breath.

'Herr doctor,' she began, 'there must be some mistake. I didn't agree to be part of this programme, I should really leave.'

The doctor frowned. 'Please don't worry, Miss Jenner. Lots of our young mothers feel a little apprehensive at first. There is really no need. As I said, I will explain everything tomorrow morning. We can talk about it properly then.'

Before she could protest, the doctor had left the room.

Hedda sank down on the bed and put her head in her hands. A sob rose in her chest. How could this have happened to her? How could she have become part of this Nazi-promoted programme? She crossed the room and splashed water on her face in an attempt to calm down.

A steward brought her suitcases and miserably, she changed into one of her winter dresses, a red one which she knew suited her complexion. She hoped it would cheer her up. Looking in the long mirror, she was surprised at how good she looked, the red fabric contrasting with her blonde hair. Her cheeks were full of colour.

At six o'clock, out of curiosity and, despite everything, still wanting to be with Sebastian, she wanted to talk to him, to persuade him, to talk him round. She wandered along to the ballroom where young men and girls of about her age were standing around, chatting in groups.

Sebastian detached himself from one group and came over to her, kissing her on both cheeks. 'You look beautiful,' he said, whisking a glass of champagne from a passing steward and hanging it to her. 'Relax, Hedda, everything will be all right. You'll see.'

Hedda sipped the champagne uncertainly. Would it harm her baby? She wasn't sure and she told herself she would only have one glass.

'Shall we go and eat?' Sebastian asked. 'There's a buffet over there. Why don't you go and sit down at that table in the window and I will get you a plate of your favourite foods?'

'All right.' She let him guide her to a table set for two in one of the bay windows. Despite everything, it felt good to feel his hand on the small of her back, to know he was looking after her, for this evening at least.

Hedda sat down and watched the others laughing and chatting in groups a little stiffly. How strange, she thought, meeting someone like that, just for the purpose of getting pregnant, sleeping together, then going your separate ways. The conversations looked forced, the girls' faces were flushed, the young officers, all in full uniform, were drinking beer at an alarming rate. They were probably finding the whole occasion as awkward as it looked.

Sebastian returned with the food. Hedda stared at the plate. She hadn't eaten so well for months. There was poached salmon, coddled eggs, many types of vegetables, roast potatoes and a creamy sauce. Her mouth watered.

As they ate, Sebastian talked about his training camp, about how well he was doing in weapons training and about the action he'd already seen on the Eastern Front.

'We took a village,' he said proudly. 'The Red Army had been staying there, but we drove them out. We burned the buildings to the ground, took all the animals to feed our men.'

Hedda stopped eating. 'What happened to the villagers?'

'Oh, we let them escape into the forest,' he replied, but she could see in his eyes he wasn't telling her everything.

He carried on talking, of the triumphs of the training camp, of the exploits on the Front. He was full of Nazi propaganda about the glories of war, the supremacy of the Reich. He sounded so different from the Sebastian she remembered. Had he changed, or was she viewing him differently now? Was he just displaying his true colours?

As he talked and as the evening wore on, she was dimly aware of some of the couples peeling off and leaving the room. Just the sight of them going off together made her flesh crawl.

'You know, now I'm an SS officer, Hedda,' Sebastian went on, 'I've realised that this is my true calling. I want to focus on my career, make a success of it.' He took her hand on the table and looked into her eyes. 'You know, what has happened to us is providence,' he said. 'It's an ideal opportunity for us to provide a baby for the Reich. It will stand me in very good stead in the eyes of my superiors.'

'What?' Hedda asked, appalled at what she was hearing. 'Is that what matters to you? Really? You didn't tell me what was really happening at this place when you asked me to come here.'

'But I knew you would come round. Think about it, Hedda. It is the ideal solution to a sticky problem.'

'I thought... I thought...' She wanted to tell him that she'd thought he would look after her, help her to keep the baby, that he would ask her to marry him. But those hopes seemed so hollow now. Now it came to it, she saw how gullible she had been and she couldn't tell him those things. Not this Sebastian with his SS uniform, wearing his Nazi credentials on his sleeve. She fell silent, deeply troubled.

'We can talk it all through with the doctor in the morning,' Sebastian said, tucking into his food again, indicating that was an end to the matter as far as he was concerned.

After the meal, a string quartet arrived and played some slow waltzes. Some of the couples danced together, twirling round in the middle of the room.

Sebastian held out his hand. 'Come on. We've never actually danced together, Hedda.'

Reluctantly, she stood up and allowed him to gather her in his arms, to hold her tight as they moved together round the dance floor. Tears were stinging her eyes. She felt so alone. She mourned for that old feeling she'd once had when he'd held her to him and had made her feel safe, but that feeling had gone. It was replaced with revulsion and mistrust. She recoiled from his touch now, knowing what he really was.

They danced until it grew late and the ballroom was virtually empty.

'Let me take you to your room,' he said, and she allowed him to take her arm and guide her along the corridor to her door. He put his hand on the handle, 'I can't wait to hold you in my arms again, Hedda.'

She put her hand on his. 'No!' she said. 'I don't want you to come in.'

Shock registered on his face, which then gradually turned to annoyance. 'I've travelled hundreds of miles especially to be with you,' he said. 'Especially for this.'

'You didn't tell me what this place was,' said Hedda, her voice shaking. 'You said you'd look after me, but you want to give our baby away. I don't trust you anymore.'

'What choice is there? You can't look after a baby alone where you live.'

'I thought... I thought...' Still she couldn't tell him. What was the point anyway?

'You thought I would marry you and we would live happily ever after? Do you think my family would allow that? A girl from a tenement block with no prospects?' he scoffed.

She stared at his face blankly, too humiliated, too shamed to retaliate.

'Go away,' she muttered. 'I never want to see you again.'

'Have it your own way then, Hedda,' he said angrily, his face growing red. 'Be alone and see what happens to you. You will never cope. Your grasping aunt and uncle won't help you, you'll be an outcast. Just another pathetic, poverty-stricken pauper living on the streets.'

With that, he left her standing there and strode away along the passage, the click of the heels of his high leather boots sounding on the boards until they faded away.

Shaking with anger and shame, Hedda rushed inside the room, locked it and threw herself on the bed, sobbing inconsolably. The tears kept on coming until finally she cried herself to sleep.

When she awoke in the morning, she was lying on top of

the bed shivering, still wearing the red dress she'd been so proud of the evening before.

Feeling wretched and blurry with exhaustion, Hedda washed and dressed. She was confused and reeling with the exchange with Sebastian. She had no clear plan. There was a knock on the door and a maid appeared with a breakfast tray.

'Doctor Finkel sent this for you. He said once you've finished, to go straight down to his office. It's on the ground floor. I can show you the way if you ring the bell.'

Hedda had no appetite, but she forced down a buttered roll and drank some coffee. Then she rang for the maid. She followed the girl downstairs, along a long, echoing corridor and into a large office lined with bookshelves. She would have to leave, to go back to Munich and appeal to Aunt Ursula for her help.

Doctor Finkel looked up when she entered and motioned to Hedda to sit down opposite his desk. Out of the huge window behind the desk, she could see the evergreen forest on the mountain opposite, its trees heavy with snow. It would have been beautiful if she hadn't been so afraid, so convinced that she'd made a terrible mistake coming here.

'Now, SS-Untersturmführer Sebastian Dietrich, the father of your child, has produced his bloodline and medical details for me,' the doctor began, looking sternly at Hedda. 'And I have to say it is impeccable. Do you have yours to hand, Miss Jenner?'

Hedda shook her head. 'No... I didn't know...'

'Well, no matter. We were very strict about it in the early days of the programme. Very strict indeed. But it is wartime now, and we have had to relax our standards a little. What you can do for me though,' he went on, shoving a piece of paper under her nose, 'is complete this blank family tree with details of your immediate antecedents. Please note down for me if there are any known cases of hereditary disease in your family, or any blood that is Jewish, Slavic or non-Aryan. If not, we will then be able to accept you onto the programme, and you can supply me with your doctor's certificates at a later date.'

'But...?' She swallowed. She felt such a fool. A weak, powerless fool.

'Now, I need to check that you pass the Aryan tests,' said the doctor, ignoring her. He produced some odd-looking instruments, came round from behind his desk and began to measure her head, her face, examine her legs, her toes, her ears and teeth.

She wished the floor would open up and swallow her, she felt so wretched and humiliated, and so furious with herself for getting into this situation, but within minutes, she was even more humiliated when Doctor Finkel asked her to remove her underwear and get onto the trolley in the corner of the room. She lay back and stared up at the ceiling, her face burning with embarrassment while the doctor prodded and poked between her legs, felt her abdomen and even her breasts.

'All seems to be in order,' he said, going over to the sink to wash his hands. 'You can get dressed now.'

Hedda pulled on her underwear and went back to sit on the chair. She was near to tears now. She couldn't look at the doctor, she just wanted to get out of there.

'Your baby is progressing nicely. You are approximately three months pregnant. So, it will be born in September this year. That is a very good time for our programme. Now, I need you to sign this form so that your baby may be cared for after its birth,' he said, pushing another piece of paper across the table.

'What's this?' she asked, in her panic the words were blurring beneath her eyes.

'As I said,' the doctor replied with a touch of impatience, 'it is so that the programme will be able to take care of your baby after it is born.'

'But... but I want to keep my baby,' Hedda said. There, the words were out.

'That's not what Untersturmführer Dietrich has told us,'

Doctor Finkel said, peering at her and frowning deeply. 'He said that you were coming into the programme in order to provide a baby for the Fatherland. Is that not the case, Miss Jenner? You *are* a good Nazi, aren't you?'

Hedda froze. The room around her seemed to revolve, she felt as though she couldn't breathe and dark spots were appearing before her eyes, growing bigger and bigger and blotting out the light.

When she came to, she was lying on the trolley in the corner of the room again. She felt sick and desperately weak. As she sat up, the room revolved again, then, slowly, Doctor Finkel came into focus.

'Ah, Miss Jenner. You had a dizzy spell. Now, we were discussing your care during the birth of your child and that of your baby. You need to sign this form please so that we will be able to provide that care.'

Doctor Finkel put the form in front of her and handed her a pen. Her thoughts blurry, she scribbled her signature on the dotted line. She just wanted to get out of there and go and lie down on the bed upstairs and the sooner she complied with the doctor's wishes, the sooner that would be.

'Thank you! Now, one of the nurses is coming to take you upstairs, so you can rest. You can either stay here for the duration of your pregnancy or you can go home and return for the birth. It is up to you. We can discuss it later.'

The door opened and a nurse entered. She was large and flabby, her jaw was set, her mouth turned down at the corners and her grey eyes unsmiling.

'Ah, Nurse Ekert. Miss Jenner has been feeling unwell. Could you take her up to her room, please?'

'Of course, Doctor.' The nurse came over to the trolley and helped Hedda down, then she put a strong arm around Hedda's shoulders and propelled her towards the door. Out in the corridor, she said, 'I expect you had too much to drink at the party last night. It's not advisable, you know. It's not good for your baby.'

'I'm sorry,' Hedda muttered, feeling guilt-stricken. 'I only had one small glass.'

They walked slowly and in silence along the corridor towards the great hall and as they reached the end, Hedda stopped dead.

'Whatever's the matter?' the nurse asked.

There was Sebastian crossing the hall in his grey greatcoat and jackboots, his SS cap under his arm. A steward scurried behind him with his luggage.

'Hurry up, man,' he was saying to the steward, 'I don't want to miss the train.'

Then he strode out of the open doorway and ran down the steps towards a waiting limousine, the winter sunlight catching on his blond hair.

Stunned, Hedda watched him go, struggling with overwhelming feelings of being betrayed. She was glad in a way that he was leaving, after what she now knew about him, but things could have developed so differently.

Hedda allowed the nurse to guide her with her iron grip across the hallway and up the stairs, along the carpeted passages to her room.

'The doctor said to get some rest,' the nurse said.

Hedda went over and sank onto the bed, grateful for the softness of the counterpane and pillows. Her whole body was overcome with exhaustion.

'I will ask Nurse Weiss to come and talk to you. She is our head of nursing here. She has been away for a few days, but she is back this morning. She will help you decide about whether to go home or not.'

'I don't want to see anyone,' Hedda said wearily, and she meant it. What was the point of talking to anyone else? She couldn't trust any of them, she felt so alone.

'Well, you'll need to make your decision soon so arrangements can be made. If you're going to stay at the castle, you won't be able to keep this room. This is for the visiting BDM girls. You were lucky to get it, since you don't strictly qualify as one of them.'

Hedda didn't reply. She didn't care about the room, she just wanted the woman to go and leave her in peace. She buried her head in the soft pillows. Finally, she heard the nurse leave the room and shut the door. She closed her eyes and drifted off, the image of Sebastian striding across the hall to his waiting car going round and round in her mind.

When Hedda awoke an hour or so later, someone was knocking gently at the door. She turned over, pulled the pillow over her head and ignored it. If she didn't answer, perhaps they would go away. But the knocking continued. Finally, Hedda hauled herself out of bed and crossed the room to open the door.

A young woman, a few years older than Hedda herself, in nurse's uniform, striped dress, white pinafore and starched white cap, stood there on the step, but she didn't look like any of the other nurses Hedda had encountered so far. She had a sweet face, with kind, blue eyes. Her straw-blonde hair, the same colour as Hedda's own, was tucked up into her cap. She was smiling.

'I'm so sorry to disturb you, Hedda,' she said, 'but I understand you've been feeling a little concerned. I thought it would be good to have a chat. I'm Nurse Weiss, by the way. Margarete Weiss.'

Hedda was about to say she didn't want to talk and close the door in Margarete's face, but something in the nurse's eyes made her hesitate. Perhaps it would be good to talk after all. She pulled the door open wide and Margarete came inside. They sat on the sofa in the window overlooking a square garden, where snow covered the lawn and the bushes. Beyond the garden, the craggy outcrops of the hills behind the castle rose up dramatically.

'You know about Lebensborn, don't you, Hedda?' Margarete asked gently. 'What it's all about?'

Hedda nodded. 'We were told all about it at our BDM meetings but I didn't know that I was coming to a Lebensborn home,' she confessed. 'My boyfriend... Sebastian. He didn't tell me the truth. He told me he'd found somewhere safe where I could have my baby. I thought... I thought...' Her voice trailed off and she fought back tears. She felt Margarete's hand on her arm.

'Don't worry, Hedda. Take a deep breath. Take your time.' There was something warm and encouraging in Margarete's tone. Something she hadn't heard since she'd lost her parents.

'I thought we would be together...' Then she lowered her voice. 'I didn't even know he was in the SS until he met me at the station yesterday.'

Margarete was looking at her with concern in her eyes. 'There's obviously been some misunderstanding. I'll try my best to help you, Hedda. What did Doctor Finkel say?'

'He told me that I can't change my mind.'

'Did you actually sign any papers?'

Slowly, Hedda nodded and turned to look at Margarete, and when she saw the expression on Margarete's face, she realised that she'd made a terrible mistake.

SEVENTEEN

MARGARETE

Schloss Schwanburg, 1943

From the first day that Doctor Tomas Müller arrived at Schloss Schwanburg, Margarete was relieved to know that she had an ally. Although she was acutely aware that what she was doing was risky, it somehow felt less daunting and dangerous now that she was no longer acting alone.

As she had already been doing for several years, she carried on copying the names and details of babies, mothers and adoptive parents in code into her two secret notebooks. There were so many entries by that time that the notebooks were over three-quarters full.

For those two weeks while Doctor Finkel was away at his conference in Berlin, things at the castle ran smoothly with Tomas Müller at the helm. Margarete even began to take pleasure in her work for the first time since she'd arrived at Schloss Schwanburg. It reminded her of how much she used to enjoy caring for the babies at Charité, when the horrors of eugenics and the Lebensborn programme hadn't been there to overshadow everything.

There was only one adoption during that fortnight and Margarete was present when Doctor Müller spoke to the young mother about it beforehand. He called her into Doctor Finkel's office where he was working.

'Anneliese,' he began, 'I'm aware that you've signed papers to agree to your baby being transferred to the guardianship of the Reich. I just wanted to find out if you were still happy with that decision?'

Anneliese looked at him with startled blue eyes. 'Of course, Doctor. I agreed to have a child for the Führer. That's why I signed that form.'

'Yes, I know that,' Tomas's gaze flicked over towards Margarete and she returned his look and gave him a reassuring smile. 'I just wanted to check that you stand by that decision now that the baby has been born. I want to be sure that you haven't changed your mind.'

The girl stared at him. Suspicion narrowed her eyes now and she was frowning. 'I don't understand, Herr Doctor,' she said. 'When I signed the form, Doctor Finkel told me that I couldn't change my decision.'

'In principle that is correct,' Tomas replied. 'But in reality, if you were really unhappy, I'm sure that something could be done.'

'No, Herr Doctor,' she said instantly, eyes snapping. 'I am happy with my decision. I don't want to keep my baby. And I don't understand why you are asking me these questions. The baby is the property of the Reich, isn't he? Surely that is a sacred bond that cannot be broken?'

Margarete shot Tomas a warning look. This girl was clearly indoctrinated by Nazi ideology and fully committed to giving her baby away to the Fatherland. There was nothing anyone could say to shake her from that position.

'We understand, Anneliese,' Margarete said smoothly. 'The

adoption will go ahead. You don't need to worry, the doctor was just checking with you.'

Annaliese's face cleared and she smiled conspiratorially. 'Oh, I see, Herr Doctor. You were testing my resolve! Well, I'm happy to say that my resolve is solid. My love for the Führer couldn't be greater. I have made the biggest sacrifice a woman can make for him and for the Fatherland.' She stood up and thrust her right arm forward in a rigid salute. 'Heil Hitler,' she said and while Margarete was wondering quite how to respond, the girl promptly left the room.

'You need to be careful,' Margarete whispered to Tomas once the girl's footsteps had echoed away down the corridor. 'Almost all these girls are like this. Don't forget, they've been peddled this propaganda from childhood. They know nothing else. If you go too far, one of them might even inform on you.'

'I know it is risky but I have to ask the question, Margarete,' he said. 'I couldn't live with myself if I didn't give them a chance.'

After Ingrid's baby was born, there were no further births at the castle during that fortnight, but Margarete and Tomas made a pledge.

'I'm determined to stop babies being sent to T4,' Tomas said. 'And I know what I need to do. If in the future, a baby is born with any physical problems, I will falsify the test results and sign a certificate saying that the baby is healthy.'

'Are you sure you'll be able to do that?' Margarete asked, feeling nervous for him at the very thought of the risks he would be taking.

'Of course. It has to be done. I will be as careful as I can, but I can't let any more babies go to their deaths that way.'

Margarete looked at him full of admiration for his bravery. The idea that those beautiful babies who had problems at birth were sent to their certain deaths, that trained medical staff who had taken an oath to protect life were instrumental in the deaths of innocent children, often kept her awake at night. That she was part of the same programme that carried out these 'mercy killings' made her feel ashamed. She couldn't reconcile any of it with her training and with everything else she'd learned about the duties of her profession. Nor did she want to. But, until now, the only thing she'd been able to do was to make entries in her notebooks.

'I will help you in any way that I can,' she said.

'Thank you. I know I can count on you, Margarete.'

She and Tomas agreed that they were both ready to step up their efforts to assist any of the mothers who might ask for their help.

Margarete subtly approached all the young mothers, as she had been doing since the very start, checking they knew what they were doing. Like Anneliese, most of the girls were so brainwashed that they were more than happy to go along with the programme, delivering up their babies for adoption by Nazi families then going back to their lives. On occasion though, Margarete would see a flicker of hurt and confusion in a girl's eyes at what they'd let themselves in for once they'd experienced the pull of affection their newborns exerted on them. She knew that one day they would look back on this and regret what they'd done. That's why she needed to compile her notebooks.

She continued trying to help in small ways, to make the girls' lives and those of their babies as comfortable as possible. She didn't enforce the strict routines and rules she was meant to follow in the nursery, which discouraged the showing of love and emotion, and she allowed the girls to call each other by their own names, something else that was strictly forbidden.

She and Tomas took care to hide their new-found alliance from the other staff. They were discreet, often conferring in secret at the end of the day in Tomas's office, comparing notes and ensuring they had both done whatever they possibly could to alleviate the suffering of mothers and babies. After each of their meetings, Margarete left with a warm glow, a feeling that at last she had someone to share this with and that she was doing something positive to counteract all the harm that was being done at Schloss Schwanburg.

It was at the end of the first week that she realised with shock that she was developing feelings for Tomas Müller. Her heart would lift whenever he came into the room. She would often find herself resting her eyes adoringly on his face and if he happened to catch her doing it, colour would flood her cheeks and she would look away in confusion.

It was the first time anything like this had happened to Margarete. She'd been very young when she'd entered the cloistered world of the nurses' residence at the Charité Hospital and since then her life had been devoted to her work, given over completely to the care of babies. She'd had no need for friends outside the hospital and although she'd caught one or two of the doctors appraising her with admiring eyes, she'd never felt that way about anyone before this.

Now, when she went to bed at night, she would lie awake thinking about Tomas, going over their conversations, reliving every smile they'd exchanged, every look of encouragement he'd given her. She didn't even know if he was married or single, he'd never mentioned his family. With his striking good looks and his caring temperament, she would be surprised if he was alone. She berated herself for falling for him, but it didn't seem to be a choice she'd had. Some external force seemed to have taken over her emotions and her senses and she felt powerless to stop it.

The day before Doctor Finkel was due back, Tomas was in Margarete's office at the end of the day. She was showing him her notebooks.

'These are valuable documents,' he said, poring over the coded words in her lists. 'You are so brave to be doing this,

Margarete. It's refreshing to find someone who is prepared to stand up for justice amongst all this horror. The way ordinary people just go along with the cruelty and unfairness of the Nazi regime is astonishing.'

She looked up at him and smiled into his eyes. 'I couldn't have lived with myself if I hadn't at least tried to do something. It doesn't seem very much though,' she reflected, 'in the great scheme of things.'

'You wait and see. Your bravery will be rewarded. One day, these lists will be used to reunite mothers with their children. This madness can't last for ever.'

'I hope you're right,' she said. 'I sincerely hope you're right.'

'Once Finkel is back, we can carry on what we've started during this fortnight,' he said, 'Only more discreetly. It will be difficult to pull the wool over Finkel's eyes, but I will volunteer to be present at more of the births, to free him up for his other duties. It will then be me who writes up the certificates. That should make things a little easier.'

'Just let me know what I can do to help. I'm right behind you, all the way,' Margarete replied. She caught him looking at her then and her heart leapt when she saw that the expression in his eyes looked soft, misty even, full of longing. Was it possible that he was feeling about her the way she'd only just acknowledged she was feeling about him?

She looked away instantly, her cheeks aflame, but then he took her chin in his hands and kissed her on the lips. She was completely unprepared for this, for the rush of pleasure it gave her. Her whole body felt as though it was on fire and she responded to his kiss. Time seemed to stand still.

When he finally pulled away, Tomas said, 'I've been wanting to do that ever since the first day here, when I realised you were good and kind and brave. Not to mention beautiful.'

Margarete had no words. No one had ever said she was beautiful before, except her father and mother of course.

'You do feel the same way about me, don't you?' Tomas asked, a note of anxiety in his voice.

'Yes... yes. Of course I do. I think about you all the time,' she stumbled, and they kissed again, for even longer this time.

'I was worried that you might be... be married,' she said when their lips parted.

He shook his head. 'I was married once,' he said. 'For two years. But my wife was killed during an air raid three years ago...'

'I'm so, so sorry,' Margarete said, seeing how grief shadowed his eyes as he spoke those words.

'It was a terrible blow,' he confessed quietly. 'It's taken me a long time to come to any sort of peace with it. You are the only person I've felt anything for since then.'

There was a sudden knock on the door and they sprang apart.

'Come in?' Margarete managed to say, smoothing her hair down quickly.

The door opened and Holge Schwartz stood there, his expression as inscrutable as ever.

'Dinner is served in the dining room. It is past seven o'clock. The staff won't start eating without you there at the head of the table, Doctor Müller. The food is getting cold. I said I would come and find you.'

'Of course,' Tomas said, his voice calm and authoritative. 'We were just going over some notes in advance of Doctor Finkel returning. We must have lost track of time.'

They left the office and followed Holge through the castle to the dining room. Feeling Tomas's arm brushing against her own as she walked beside him filled Margarete with an overwhelming sense of well-being. There was something else she was feeling too, which she realised quickly was love.

. . .

After Doctor Finkel returned, Margarete and Tomas carried on helping the girls and babies as best they could. Tomas took great risks to ensure all the babies passed the Aryan tests, falsifying the results right under Doctor Finkel's nose, although he was still concerned about them being adopted by SS families. Tomas had little influence over who the babies were placed with – Doctor Finkel took this duty back on his return, revelling in placing babies with the highest-ranking members of the SS.

Most evenings, after dinner, when the day staff, including Doctor Finkel, had gone home, Holge had retired to his room and the night nurse was overseeing the nursery, Margarete would hurry through the darkened corridors to visit Tomas in his rooms. They weren't on the third floor where Margarete, Holge and members of the castle staff were lodged, but in one of the round towers of the castle, overlooking a waterfall that thundered through the ravine below.

In front of a roaring fire, and over a glass of wine or schnapps, they would talk about what had happened that day, and exchange information about what they had each been able to do to sabotage the programme. They also spoke about their lives. Margarete confided the truth about her lowly childhood and the anti-Nazi views of her family, and how afraid she was for their safety. Tomas told her how he'd grown up on a farm in Bavaria, how from an early age he'd wanted to care for the sick animals. He had a talent for it, and when he was older, he realised he had a calling to tend to sick people too.

'And I've never forgotten that that was the reason I went to medical school and became a doctor. So many of my profession have become tainted with Nazi doctrine, with eugenics and with the idea of the master race. They think that is justification for departing from their oaths. They have lost their perspective. I think it's important to remind myself each and every day of why I'm doing this job.'

When they said goodnight, they would kiss, and as time

went on, their kisses became more passionate, until one day, Tomas murmured as she was leaving, 'I hate saying goodnight to you, Margarete. I always long to hold you when you've gone. Why don't you stay here with me? Stay the night?'

Margarete hesitated. Staying with him was a big step, but she wanted Tomas with every nerve and every sinew of her body. She'd had to force herself to leave every evening and she longed for his touch each time she'd lain in her bed alone.

'I want to, Tomas, but I can't help being afraid,' she admitted. 'What if Holge finds out I'm not in my room? He's always snooping around.'

They both knew that if Holge discovered their liaison he wouldn't hesitate to report them to Doctor Finkel. What they were doing was strictly forbidden and discovery would have severe consequences for them both.

Tomas thought for a moment.

'I could come to your room. He will never find out that I'm in there, but if he knocks on the door, you would be there to answer it.'

So that is what they did. Margarete left Tomas's room alone and made her way back through the dark corridors to her own room, and Tomas followed a few minutes later. She opened the door the instant he knocked and locked it behind him. He took her in his arms and kissed her again and they fell on the narrow bed together. Then they made love for the first time, gently and tenderly.

In the morning, when Margarete awoke entwined in Tomas's arms, her heart soared to see him there beside her, blinking awake in the grey light of dawn. After they'd kissed, Tomas got out of bed, dressed quickly and, checking there was no one in the corridor, slipped away as discreetly as he'd arrived.

That morning, Doctor Finkel called Margarete and Tomas into his office.

'I've got something important to say to you both,' he began.

Margarete and Tomas exchanged a furtive look. Had they been discovered?

'We are very fortunate. Reichsführer Himmler is going to pay us a visit here tomorrow. And while he is here, he is going to perform a naming ceremony for the new babies currently in our care. It will be a great privilege. I have asked Holge to ensure the ballroom is made ready and I expect both of you to attend and ensure the rest of the staff are there too.'

Margarete glanced at Tomas. His expression was calm and serious, but she could tell that the news had perturbed him.

Later, he told her why. 'I've only been at one of these cere-monies before, but they are the most bizarre, disturbing occa-sions imaginable, and I'd hoped never to have attend one again. Have there not been any at the castle before?'

'There have been a few since I've been here, but I've either been at home on leave or on duty in the nursery. I've never attended one.'

'Then prepare yourself for something very unsettling,' he said.

The next morning, Margarete watched from the nursery window as a black limousine drew up in the courtyard, bearing the swastika standard on the bonnet. The tall, erect figure of Heinrich Himmler got out of the back seat when the driver opened the door. Just the sight of the top of his head sent chills through Margarete.

She left the window and went to check on the babies, speaking to the nursery nurses and the young mothers to check they were ready. They were all dressed in their best clothes, ready to go along with their babies to the ballroom.

Margarete waited a few minutes, allowing time for Doctor Finkel to greet Himmler and bring him upstairs, then she led the group of mothers, babies and nurses to the ballroom. When she entered, she took a sharp intake of breath. Huge swastika flags were draped from poles in each corner of the vast room.

Rows of chairs were set out for the staff and for Himmler's driver and aides, and at one end of the room what looked like an altar had been set up, draped in yet another swastika. Tall vases of flowers stood on either side and a large portrait of Adolf Hitler was displayed on the altar itself.

Everyone took their seats, the four mothers and newborns in the front row. Margarete sat beside Tomas on the second row. Doctor Finkel joined Himmler at the altar. He cleared his throat.

'Good morning, everyone, and a very warm welcome to our esteemed special guest, Reichsführer Himmler, whom we are deeply honoured to have here to name our new babies today. This ceremony is a sacred occasion, in which our newborn babies are welcomed into the society of the SS and given their names. In the Third Reich, as we all know, this replaces and transcends any previous such ceremonies held by the Church... Now, before we proceed, I believe the Reichsführer would like to say a few words.'

Doctor Finkel bowed to Himmler, who stepped forward and said, 'Good morning. I am honoured to be here today to welcome these young lives into the world of the Third Reich. But, firstly, I would like to thank these brave young mothers, fine examples of Aryan womanhood, for their sacrifice for the greater good of the master race. We are humbled by your example... Now, if you would like to bring your babies up in turn, I will perform the ceremony...'

Margarete watched in deep discomfort as one by one, the young mothers carried their babies to the front and held them out to the Reichsführer. Himmler dipped his fingers in a bowl of water on the altar and made a sign on the babies' foreheads. She could barely believe she was watching this bizarre, twisted ritual, much less that she was a part of it.

She dropped her gaze, unable to watch anymore, feeling wretched and helpless as she often did when she realised how caught up in this great, inescapable machine she was. But then she felt Tomas's hand on the chair beside her, their fingertips touched and she felt reassured by the feel of him.

'Don't despair, Margarete,' he whispered. 'We have each other now.'

EIGHTEEN

KRISTEL

Trento, 2005

On her third day in Trento, when Kristel was eating breakfast in the dining room of her hotel, her mobile phone rang. It was Ginetta from Our Lady of Mercy.

'I'm afraid Miss Bianchi... or should I say Miss Weiss... isn't feeling up to much this morning,' the nurse said. 'It might be better if perhaps you could come along this afternoon instead?'

'Oh dear,' Kristel said, feeling a little guilty that her interviews might have been tiring Margarete. 'Nothing serious, I hope?'

'Not really. She often has these nervous turns. It is nothing physical. I'm hoping that if she rests this morning, she will be able to see you this afternoon.'

'There's no hurry. I can wait until tomorrow.'

'We know that you are here in Trento especially to see her. We don't want to waste your time. I will call you around lunchtime and let you know how she is then.'

Kristel thanked her, sent her best wishes to Margarete and ended the call. She hoped the old lady was going to feel better soon. Perhaps all the talk about the past and the never-ending stress she'd been under for all those years at Schloss Schwanburg had brought this on. There was so much for Margarete to process and talking about it must have been so difficult.

Kristel could have spent the morning in her room finalising her notes, but instead, she decided to take the morning off and to have a walk around Trento. She'd had no time to see the town since she'd arrived and she knew it was a fascinating place. She'd read there was a medieval town centre, a fabulous cathedral, a castle and even underground Roman ruins. At the hotel reception, she asked for a map of the town. She went back up to her room and wrapped up warm, then set off to explore.

Behind the hotel, Kristel found an alley that led up to the cobbled streets of the medieval town centre. As she headed up it, she took a deep breath of the fresh mountain air. How good it felt to be getting away from her work for a while. She realised as she turned right at the top of the alleyway and wandered through the cobbled streets of the town centre towards the duomo that she'd become slightly obsessed with Margarete's story since she'd arrived here. It was so inextricably linked with her own quest for the truth about her mother that she'd lost her usual perspective and hadn't been able to think about much else. Other than about Joachim, of course.

They hadn't spoken since the conversation about Singapore. She hadn't wanted to speak to him, she'd needed some space to think about the future. Now, pausing to look in a shop window full of bottles of liqueur and Italian delicacies, decked out with red ribbons and holly, she wondered when he would actually be leaving. Would it be before Christmas, which was only a few weeks away? She felt a little empty thinking about it, but she knew that some time apart would be for the best. Thank goodness they hadn't actually sent out their wedding invitations or booked the venue.

The cobbled streets soon opened out into a huge square,

with an elaborate fountain in the middle. The vista before her took her breath away. On the opposite side stood a beautiful white stone church with a detailed façade, complete with two round towers, one either end. The taller one had an onion-shaped dome. Kristel crossed the square and joined a long queue of sightseers which snaked out of the main door. She shuffled slowly forward with them into the church.

Inside, she wandered around, admiring the symmetry of the building, the soaring vaulted ceilings and the intricate frescos. It felt strange sightseeing alone; she couldn't help thinking back to the holiday she and Joachim had taken in Rome in the summer. They'd explored the streets arm in arm, marvelling at the incredible Coliseum, eating at intimate cafés in back streets. But she drew herself up and put those thoughts aside. There was no point hankering after those heady days of their early romance. Things had changed dramatically between them since then. Now she needed to be positive and strong.

When she'd finished looking round and went outside, it was snowing again. She hurried across the square to the shelter of a cloistered walkway which ran in front of a row of shops. There was a café inside that looked warm and inviting. Kristel hovered at the steamed-up window. It was full of locals, mostly young people, drinking coffee and eating pastries.

She pushed the door aside and went in, the steamy atmosphere enveloping her and warming her instantly. Approaching the counter, she paused, surprised. She knew the face of the young man serving. It was Lorenzo.

He smiled broadly when he saw her, showing a line of perfect white teeth. 'Hello, Kristel! Not at Our Lady of Mercy this morning?'

She explained that Margarete was feeling low and he instantly looked concerned.

'Oh no! Poor Margarete. She sometimes has these episodes, poor lady. Her nerves are a bit fragile.'

'Yes, I'm hoping she'll be better this afternoon so I can go then.'

'I hope so too. What can I get you to drink?'

Kristel asked for a cappuccino. 'I didn't know you had another job,' she remarked.

'I don't really. My father owns this place, and they are short-staffed today. I sometimes help out on my days off from the care home. I enjoy it, to be honest.'

'It's a great café,' she said, looking round admiringly at the low-ceilinged room. Every table was full and the place was buzzing with conversation, jazz music playing on the sound system.

'It attracts students from the university on their breaks between lectures,' Lorenzo explained. 'It's a good location. And Papa prides himself on his cakes. Would you like a slice of torta di grano saraceno? It's a local speciality.'

'What's that?' she asked, smiling.

'Buckwheat and nut sponge, filled with blueberry jam,' he replied, reaching inside the counter display and taking out a moist-looking cake. 'In fact, it's probably actually Austro-German in origin. You know that Trento was once part of the Austrian empire before the First World War?'

'I had a vague idea,' she said. 'But you're obviously the expert!'

'So, you will have a slice? On the house, of course,' he said, cutting a generous portion.

'That's very kind of you. It looks delicious. How could I refuse?'

'I will bring it to the table. Look, there's a group just leaving now, over by the window.'

Kristel went across and sat down at the table beside the window with a view across the square towards the duomo. Lorenzo followed her and put her steaming cappuccino and plate of cake down in front of her before clearing away the empty cups.

'I'll try not to spill anything this time,' he said, with a gleam of amusement in his eyes. 'Has the coat recovered by the way? It looks OK.'

'It's fine, thank you,' she replied. 'And it was my fault entirely.'

'Not at all. Enjoy your coffee and cake,' he said, returning to the counter to serve a couple who had just arrived.

Kristel sank her teeth into the light, moist sponge that tasted slightly nutty and was melt-in-the-mouth delicious. Her gloomy thoughts in the church had completely dissipated. Seeing a familiar, friendly face and the light-hearted exchange with Lorenzo had lifted her spirits.

When he'd finished serving, Lorenzo came over to her table again.

'Do you mind if I sit down with you for a moment? I've been thinking about Margarete.'

'Not at all,' Kristel said, and he sat down opposite her.

'It's just that I know having to admit to everyone that she's German has had a big impact on her. I could see it in her eyes when she first spoke to me about it. I think she might feel a bit ashamed – that she's let people down. She's worried that we are all talking about her behind her back.'

Kristel sipped her cappuccino and reflected on his words. She'd been so focused on what Margarete had to tell her about the war that she hadn't thought about this angle before. But she could see now that it was probably true.

'It must have been a huge thing for her to admit,' Kristel acknowledged. 'That she's basically been living a lie for the past sixty years.'

'Of course. And the strain of it has probably got to her. She is ninety, you know, and not in the best of health.'

'Hmm, perhaps I should give her a break. I could go back to Munich and return in a few days. I can see that she wants to talk, but it does seem too big strain on her. And there's something else. She seems to be reluctant to show me her notebook for some reason. I know she has some important information in it – that's partly why I came down to Trento to interview her. But each time I ask her about it, she seems to sidestep the issue.'

'That's strange,' remarked Lorenzo, 'Although, as you say, she does want to talk. Would you like me to have a word with her about the notebook? She sometimes confides in me.'

'If you think it would help and wouldn't upset her and make things worse,' Kristel said, frowning in thought. 'It's a fine balance between giving her the chance to tell her story and the whole thing upsetting her. I can see why the past is distressing for her. What she went through as a young woman must be hard for her to talk about. She has to relive it all again when she tells her story.'

'I could come along with you this afternoon. I'll be finished here by about one thirty. I could see if she's OK and have a word with her about the notebook if that would help?'

'Are you sure? It is your afternoon off, Lorenzo.' She was sincerely grateful to him for the offer, but she didn't want to put him out.

He shrugged. 'I don't have anything else to do.' He leaned forward. 'And I think what you're doing is amazing, to be honest. Giving Margarete the chance to tell her story. Some people might automatically assume that she was part of it all. They don't understand that there were a lot of Germans who hated the Nazis and were forced to co-operate.'

'You're right. It's a lot more complicated than people think,' Kristel said with a shudder, thinking about her own mother growing up the daughter of a Nazi official in small-town Bavaria. Greta seemed to have spent the rest of her life trying to make amends for something that was beyond her control.

'Margarete was very brave coming forward like she did. She could have hidden for the rest of her life,' Lorenzo said.

'I get the feeling that she's been wanting to do something for a very long time, but that she hasn't had the opportunity before,' Kristel replied.

When Kristel had finished her coffee and cake, she got up to leave. They agreed that she would text Lorenzo when she'd heard from Ginetta. He said he would pick her up in his car.

'There's no point going up there separately,' he noted. 'And I think you will like my car!'

It was still snowing when Kristel went out into the cold air, but the coffee and the atmosphere of the café had warmed her through and she could feel her cheeks glowing. On Lorenzo's recommendation, she headed up to the castle. It was perched on a hill overlooking the town. She spent the next couple of hours wandering through its palatial rooms, admiring the fabulous painted ceilings and frescos. She walked through the cloistered courtyard and gazed at the views of the town and surrounding mountains from the castle balconies. She breathed in the clean mountain air and gazed at the beauty all around her. How different this was from the urban hustle and bustle of Munich.

She was heading back to her hotel when Ginetta called.

'Margarete feels a little better now. She would be happy to see you this afternoon.'

'That's great news,' Kristel said, relieved. 'Oh, by the way, I bumped into Lorenzo this morning. He offered to come along with me. He thinks it might help Margarete to talk.'

'That's wonderful,' Ginetta said. 'Margarete likes and trusts Lorenzo. Of all the staff in the home, he is definitely her favourite. He is so wonderful with the residents. I'm glad he's coming with you, it should help Margarete to feel more relaxed.'

Kristel walked back to the hotel, texted Lorenzo and bought a panini in the bar. When she was eating, her mobile rang. To her surprise, it was Joachim.

'Sorry to call at lunchtime, but there's something I wanted to let you know,' he said, sounding a long way away.

'It's OK. What is it?'

'They want me to go out to Singapore before Christmas, apparently. There's some sort of crisis brewing out there. They need me to go as soon as possible. When are you coming back from Trento?'

She paused, letting the news sink in, surprised that it didn't affect her as she thought it might have done.

'I'm not sure yet. I think the old lady still has a fair amount to talk about.'

'Don't the studio want you back in Munich?'

'They're being very patient. Michel said I should spend as long as it takes to get this story. But if you're going to leave in the next few days, I will definitely come back to say goodbye.'

'I don't know the exact date yet,' he said. 'I'll let you know.'

'I've been thinking, Joachim. If you are going to be away for a while, I need to move out of your apartment. I can go back to Dad's place. You will probably want to let it out.'

There was a short silence at the other end of the line, then he said, 'You don't have to, you know... It makes it all sound so final.'

'Does it?' she asked. 'It's not really final, is it though? I just thought we were giving each other some space. Me staying in your apartment wouldn't be giving either of us space.'

'All right. Whatever is best for you. We'll be able to talk it through when you come back to Munich.'

'I *would* come back today, but this assignment is really important to me, Joachim. And to a lot of other people.'

'Who exactly is this old woman you're talking to?' he asked.

'She was a nursery nurse who worked for the Nazis in the Lebensborn programme. She's got some information in a note-book, but she wants to tell me her story first. I get the impression that she needs to feel she can trust me.'

Joachim was silent at the other end of the line, then he said, 'She could be a war criminal, you know. Thousands of them flocked through Austria and into Italy through the Brenner Pass in 1945. I read about it once...'

'I thought you weren't interested in the war,' Kristel probed gently, half teasing.

'It's more complicated than that. You know that,' he replied. 'But why else would your old German lady who knows about the Lebensborn programme be living in Italy, posing as an Italian?'

Kristel thought about it for a moment. 'I'm sure she's not a war criminal, Joachim. She tried to work against the regime, but the very fact that she was part of the Lebensborn programme probably put her in danger from the Allies at the end of the war. That must be why she kept it secret for so long. And why she's finding it so difficult to dredge up the past now.'

After they'd said goodbye, Kristel thought about Joachim's words. How typical of him to think that Margarete might be a war criminal, assuming blindly that as she'd worked for the Nazis, she would automatically be one of them. That black-and-white attitude was what she and Lorenzo had been discussing in the café earlier.

With a sigh, she finished her panini. Then, glancing at her watch, she noticed that it was just after two o'clock. Lorenzo would be along very soon.

She went to the reception and looked out of the glass doors into the hotel car park. A tiny black car, a vintage Fiat 500, was parked outside the front door. Kristel's heart lifted when she saw that Lorenzo was leaning against the driver's door, smoking a cigarette. He was wearing jeans and a padded ski jacket, a woolly hat pulled down over his dark curls. She watched him for a moment, thinking how attractive he looked, then she pushed the door open and walked out to meet him.

When he lifted his head and saw her coming towards him, a broad smile spread across his face.

NINETEEN

When Margarete left Hedda's room on the first floor of Schloss Schwanburg that morning after their talk, Hedda felt her spirits lift, just a little. Knowing that there was someone prepared to help her stopped her feeling quite so desperate. Margarete had reassured her that the forms she had signed would already be locked away in Doctor Finkel's cabinet, but when the time came, she would help Hedda as best she could if Hedda wanted to keep her baby.

Hedda could tell that Margarete was genuine from the look in her eyes. She'd known that from the start. There had been an instant connection between them, as if they were kindred spirits. On that basis, she decided to go home to Munich for a few months. There was nothing for her to do at Schloss Schwanburg. It was in the middle of nowhere, and she found the whole place and what it stood for very distasteful. So, she packed her suitcase and called for one of the castle staff to arrange her trip. She would go back to her aunt and uncle's and plead with them to let her stay.

Before she left, Doctor Finkel came to see her.

'I need your address in Munich please, Fräulein Jenner,' he said. 'Someone from the Lebensborn programme will come to see you to check you over and make sure you are all right.'

As she scribbled down her address, Hedda sensed the noose of the Lebensborn programme tightening around her neck. Despite that, when she left the castle, later that day, she felt reassured that when she returned, Margarete would help her. When Hedda's car drew out through the gatehouse, Margarete was standing in the door of the castle waving. Behind her stood another doctor, a younger man, who looked altogether kinder and more human than Doctor Finkel. Perhaps he would help her too and everything would be all right after all?

When she arrived back at the apartment in Munich, her aunt wasn't at all pleased to see her.

'I didn't think you were coming back,' Ursula said, looking frazzled. She was in the middle of preparing tea for the children. 'I don't know what we're going to say to Edward when your baby starts to show. I can't believe you're actually going ahead and having it.'

Hedda said, 'I'm sure Uncle Edward will be fine about it. I'm part of the Lebensborn programme now. And that is official Nazi policy.'

Ursula narrowed her eyes in suspicion. 'Lebensborn? What's that?'

'There's a big movement to encourage young Aryan women not to terminate their pregnancies. It's Heinrich Himmler's brainchild apparently. They offer you care in homes all over the country.'

'I've never heard of it. You must be making it up. It is completely contrary to Nazi policy on the family.'

'I'm surprised you don't know about it, with all your links to the Party,' was all Hedda could think of to say in response.

Ursula shrugged. 'As long as you're not going to bring

another mouth into this home, I don't care where you go when the time comes,' she said.

Hedda looked at her aunt. She felt very alone.

The next morning, Hedda trudged the streets of the city centre looking for work. She'd decided not to go back to college. She wouldn't be able to cope with the taunting of the others when she could no longer hide her growing belly. But she couldn't stay in the apartment either, no matter how much Ursula angled to get her to help out again. She needed to work. She didn't want to be reliant on Ursula and Edward, especially once the baby was born. She wanted to be able to support herself and her child. If she saved enough money, perhaps she would even be able to rent a room of her own.

She eventually found a job selling newspapers from a kiosk next to the tram stop in Marienplatz. The scruffy old man who ran it looked her up and down and said frankly, 'The woman who helped out here before was a Jew. None of us knew until she was taken away by the Gestapo last month. She'd managed to hide it from everyone. She was sneaky, that one. You're not Jewish, are you?' he asked, peering at her. 'No... no. I can see that you couldn't possibly be.'

Even though it was almost April by then and the weather was improving by the day, it was still chilly standing there in the newspaper kiosk for hours on end. Hedda didn't mind the job. She enjoyed passing the time of day with customers, even getting to know some of the regulars. From there, she had a bird's eye view of the city centre. She would see people hurrying to work and about their business, the Gestapo and SS officers parading up and down the square at regular intervals, Alsatians straining at the leash. There was rarely anyone who came here to stroll around for pleasure. She could see how subdued and frightened people were. But it had always been like this, for as long as Hedda could remember. It was only the fact that she'd been brought up by enlightened and free-thinking parents that made her see things

differently from most of her generation, she realised. She thanked
her lucky stars for her parents and wondered how her mother and
Aunt Ursula could have turned out so differently.

Glancing at the headlines of every paper she sold, she was
not surprised that people were cowed. They only had one
source of information – the Nazi-run newspapers, *Volkischer
Beobachter* and *Der Sturmer*. Both were full of bile and hatred,
antisemitic articles and trumpeting of Germany's achievements
in the war. Apparently, the Wehrmacht was pushing back the
Russians on the Southeastern Front, making huge gains daily. It
was impossible to know whether any of it was true, but it was
unsettling all the same.

The old man who ran the newsstand, Herr Hertzog, was a
grumpy old antisemite himself. She learned to ignore his hate-
filled outbursts. But as well as that, he was lazy and careless and
often left Hedda alone for long periods at a time. She was
grateful for the solitude, it allowed her to think – about her
family, about Sebastian and about the baby growing inside her.

Over the weeks of the spring and summer of 1943, Hedda
gradually began to accumulate some savings and by the time her
belly was so large she couldn't hide it any longer, she'd saved up
quite a sum.

One day, Herr Hertzog greeted her as she arrived at work, a
thunderous expression on his unshaven face. 'I've been
watching you walking across the square, Fräulein Jenner. You're
expecting a baby, aren't you?'

Before she'd had time to say anything, he said, 'You're fired.
Don't come to work here anymore, casting shame on my business. I trusted you, but you've let me down. You're as bad as the
one before you. Don't let me see you here again,' he virtually
spat at her. Hedda was shocked at his vitriol.

She wandered back to the apartment. Ursula was still in
bed. She'd been feeling unwell for the past few days. The

doctor had told her it was anaemia and that she should eat plenty of meat and greens and take it easy. Ursula was doing her best to comply with his instructions, but it wasn't easy with the all deprivations of war. Hedda was reluctant to tell her she'd lost her job, but as soon as Ursula saw her, without even asking why she'd come home, she propped herself up on her elbows and said, 'The kitchen floor needs cleaning, and after that you can go down to the market and find some potatoes for this evening.'

Hedda complied without protest, but she was groaning inwardly. She was back where she didn't want to be, her aunt's dogsbody again. She had been contributing some of her wages to the household budget, so Ursula had stopped making so many demands of her. But perhaps it was fair, she reflected, if she could no longer do so, that she should take on more of a share of the housework.

With a sigh, she got the mop and bucket out of the cupboard, filled the bucket with water and began to mop the floor. As she worked, she dreamed of escaping all this and finding a home of her own. In her mind's eye, it was in a little village somewhere, away from the city. Like one of the picturesque ones, full of painted wooden cottages surrounded by meadows that she had passed on the train from the castle. But she knew in her heart that it was a pipe dream. It was never going to be possible. She would just have to grit her teeth and put up with living with her aunt and uncle until she could figure something else out.

Two days later, there was a knock at the door. When Hedda opened it, a grim-faced woman stood out on the landing. She wore some sort of uniform, with swastikas on her lapels, and she carried a black doctor's bag.

'Hedda Jenner?' the woman asked.

Hedda nodded.

'I'm from the Lebensborn programme. I've come to check you over. Is there somewhere private we can go?'

Reluctantly, Hedda took her through to the tiny bedroom she shared with her young cousin.

'Hedda? Who's that?' Ursula called from her bed.

'Someone for me, Aunty,' she said and closed the bedroom door behind them.

'Lie down on the bed. I need to examine you,' the woman said, and proceeded to prod Hedda with cold hands. Then she listened to her heart through a stethoscope and took her blood pressure. 'All is proceeding normally,' she advised. 'What date are you going back to Schloss Schwanburg?'

'Sometime in late August, I suppose,' Hedda replied. She dreaded returning to the castle but there seemed to be no alternative. It would be impossible to stay here and the visit from this woman demonstrated to her again that the Lebensborn noose was tightening around her neck.

'You'll need to be more precise. Doctor Finkel wants to know when you're coming back. Shall I put down the twentieth?' the woman scowled.

'All right...' she said, feeling even more trapped.

The woman scribbled in a notebook. Then she looked at Hedda and said, 'I take it you will stay here until then?'

Hedda nodded.

'Now, if you want to go anywhere else, or leave the city, even for a few days, you must get permission in advance from the Ministry. Here's my telephone number.' She thrust a card into Hedda's hand. Then she picked up her bag and went to the door.

Hedda pulled her clothes on hastily and showed the woman out of the apartment. Then she stood behind the door and let her heartbeat slow down.

Ursula took full advantage of Hedda now that she was no longer going out to work. Once more, Hedda found herself taking the children to school, fetching food from the market, doing the housework and preparing the evening meal and clearing up after it. She found the physical demands on her particularly hard now her baby was growing. It made her slower than before, and Ursula would often shout at her from her bedroom.

'What are you doing? Haven't you even finished cleaning the stove yet?'

'You need to get down to the shops and queue. Potatoes are short at the moment. You might need to make cauliflower soup tonight.'

Hedda put up with her aunt's demands because she really had no choice, but all the time, she worried about what would happen once her baby was born. But things were difficult for everyone. Rationing and wartime shortages made life a struggle, and they lived under the constant threat of bombing raids. Many evenings, the local Nazi block warden would knock at the door and tell the family that they must go down to the communal air-raid shelter. They would all troop downstairs to the sound of sirens, together with the neighbours, to a smelly underground shelter near the Hauptbahnhof, where everyone would cram in together for several hours until the raid was over. For Hedda, each raid would bring back the memory of that terrible evening her home had been hit. The sound of planes overhead and the crash of bombs would make her sweat and tremble and cover her ears. It was a miracle, Uncle Edward remarked each time, that their apartment block had never been hit, though many buildings around it were reduced to piles of smoking rubble.

But there was another problem, closer to home, that made Hedda's stomach churn with anxiety. One day when she was struggling back from the vegetable market with a heavy bag, a neighbour from along the corridor stood at the top of the stairs watching her come up, her hands on her hips. The woman was known to be a troublemaker and had been at the forefront of ensuring the few Jewish residents were flushed from the apartment block.

'I don't know how you've got the nerve to show your face,' she said when Hedda reached the landing and paused for breath. 'Everyone in the block is talking about you, you know. Hey... I'm talking to you!' She stood in front of Hedda, blocking her way.

Hedda met her eye. 'Let me past, please,' she said.

'I don't know what your aunt and uncle think they are doing, harbouring a whore like you. There's no place for the likes of you in the new Reich.'

'You don't know what you're talking about,' Hedda couldn't resist saying, but she wasn't about to explain Lebensborn to this woman. She didn't want to be identified with that either.

'Oh, don't I? I know all about Nazi policy, the importance of the family. A woman's place... you are a disgrace. You should be taken away to Dachau like others who don't fall into line.'

Hedda pushed past the woman and carried on to the flat, but when she got inside and dropped her bags, she was shaking all over. How long would it be before her uncle discovered her condition?

That woman was the first, but she had clearly been spreading her malice amongst the neighbours, because the same thing happened most times Hedda left the apartment, even when she was bringing her cousins home from school. It was mostly women, sometimes children, who would push into her and call her a whore. The children would run away laughing, but the women would usually deliver a lecture about morality.

One day, she arrived back from fetching her aunt's medicines from the chemist's and her uncle was home early from the factory. He called Hedda into the kitchen, white-lipped with rage.

'A neighbour shouted at me on the stairs just now. Told me I was a traitor for harbouring a hussy like you. I didn't know what she meant, so I asked her. I have never been so humiliated in all my life. To trick us like that... I can see it now that I'm looking at you properly. There's no hiding it. I must be a fool. A trusting fool.'

'I didn't lie,' she said. 'I didn't have anywhere to go.'

'Your aunt is mortified,' Edward said, nodding in the direction of the bedroom.

'She knew about it all along,' Hedda retorted. 'Right from the start.'

'Don't peddle your foul lies with me,' he shouted. 'You're a disgrace and I won't have you looking after my children, filling their heads with your immoral ideas. I've packed your bag for you. It's in the hallway. I don't want to see you again, or your bastard brat.'

Hedda surprised herself. She didn't feel like crying at all. She was angry and indignant and wanted to get out of there as much as they wanted her out. 'You'll have to do your own cooking and cleaning now,' she said, throwing the medicines down on the table, walking with as much dignity as she could muster out into the hall, picking up her suitcase. She couldn't leave without saying goodbye to the children. When Gisela heard she was leaving, she burst into tears and the boys looked crestfallen too.

'You'll come back though, won't you?' Gisela asked, sobbing.

'We'll miss you,' Jonas, the older boy, said and Timm, the youngest, clung to her legs, trying to stop her from leaving.

'One day, perhaps,' Hedda replied.

All three followed her into the hall, where she ruffled their hair and said goodbye to them, picked up her suitcase and left the apartment, without saying a word to her aunt.

. . .

The baby was crying in the downstairs flat again as Hedda resurfaced from her reverie into the past. It was a past that she'd never been able to share with Hari. She'd felt too ashamed of everything after the war: of being involved with an SS officer, of being part of the Lebensborn programme. And it felt better to keep the pain deep inside. She just couldn't bring herself to tell him about it. Perhaps, she reflected, things might have been different between them if she'd ever been able to share those dark times with him. Now, listening to that poor baby screaming his head off downstairs, Hedda wondered how different their lives might have been if she and Hari had been able to have a child. She would have lavished care and love on it and it would have stopped her descent into depression.

Hedda thought about pouring herself another glass of schnapps, but resisted the urge. On an impulse, she got up, switched the electric fire off, pulled on her coat and boots and left the flat. It was cold outside on the open walkway. She pulled her coat around her and made her way along to the staircase at the end, then down the stairs and back along to the front door of the downstairs neighbours. There, the sound of the baby crying was even louder. She had to knock three times to make herself heard.

The door opened a crack and the young woman peeped through. Hedda had never seen her up close before and she was shocked at the dark rings round her eyes, her gaunt, exhausted face.

'Is everything all right?' Hedda asked.

The woman glared at her. 'Who are you? Social services?'

'No. I'm your upstairs neighbour. I... just wanted to know if... well, if you'd like any help.' The words sounded insulting now they were actually coming out of her mouth. She hadn't known what she was going to say when she was coming down the steps.

'Who's that, Inge?' a male voice shouted from inside the flat and the woman flinched visibly.

'Just a nosy old bag from upstairs.'

'Tell her to get lost.'

'We're all right,' the woman said. 'We don't need your help.' Then she closed the door in Hedda's face.

Hedda pushed the letterbox open and said, 'Well, you know where I am if you need me,' then straightened up and walked away. She wasn't surprised. What had she been thinking of, interfering like that?

She let herself back into the flat, gave Max his evening meal and milk, had another quick shot of Schnapps, then went through to the bathroom and got ready for bed. Before she got into bed though, she went through to the living room and fetched the tiny scrap of baby hair with its fading ribbon and put it on her bedstand. She wanted to remember now, not to bury the past. Kristel Meyer's report on the TV had brought it all alive for her once more. So vividly it was as if she was back there again in the 1940s. For years, she'd wanted to bury it deep inside, but she no longer felt that way. Tomorrow, perhaps, she would have the courage to pick up the phone and call the TV station.

TWENTY

MARGARETE

Trento, 2005

Margarete didn't know what had come over her that morning. She had no appetite and didn't want to eat breakfast. She pushed it away when Sophia put it in front of her. A little later, Ginetta came to see her, bending down and peering into Margarete's face, her kind, dark eyes full of concern.

'You are shaking all over, Margarete,' she said, squeezing her hand, which was icy cold. 'What's the matter? You can tell me.'

Margarete shook her head and muttered something she knew to be incoherent. She'd been speaking so much German over the past few days, delving so deep into the past which always replayed in her mind in German, that her Italian brain seemed to have switched itself off. But Ginetta was right, she was shaking. The radiator in her room was belting out heat, but she just couldn't get warm.

She'd had a terrible night and had hardly slept a wink. She'd been unable to calm her mind. All the memories had kept on resurfacing, like a film on a never-ending loop, as did the terrible guilt she felt at not having done more, and the pain that she always experienced too when she thought back to those days.

It wasn't surprising that she felt dizzy and disoriented. Going back to those years was a physical as well as a mental and emotional effort. It was taking every ounce of her energy to speak to Kristel. And it didn't help that she didn't know the girl very well. Kristel was clearly an intelligent, sensitive person, but despite Margarete's long-held desire to tell her story, it still felt as though she was speaking to a stranger. Something deep inside that she didn't fully understand was preventing her from handing over the notebook too. The notebook she'd harboured all these years and what she'd used to entice Kristel to come to Trento to see her. But now her confidence in the notebook had deserted her. She kept wondering how useful it would actually be when it came down to it.

She took the sedative that Ginetta offered her. As Ginetta pulled the curtains across the window and left the room, closing the door gently, Margarete lay back in her recliner. Gradually, her mind settled down, her thoughts became blurry and she drifted off to sleep.

She awoke a couple of hours later feeling a lot better. The anxieties that had been consuming her had all but disappeared. She rang the bell on the wall beside her and Ginetta appeared almost instantly. She told Margarete that Kristel was coming after lunch if she felt up to seeing her.

'Yes, I'm much better now,' Margarete said.

'Oh, and by the way,' Ginetta added, 'Lorenzo is coming along with her to sit in on the interview. So, you'll have a friendly face by your side when you tell your story.'

Margarete relaxed. 'That's good,' she said simply, smiling at the thought of Lorenzo. It would be good to have him there. She always found his presence very reassuring.

She ate the soup that Ginetta brought for her. She was ravenous now, having missed breakfast, and she ate quickly.

Ginetta took away her dishes, and Margarete turned her attention to watching the front drive from her vantage point in the window. Soon, she spotted Lorenzo's black Fiat 500 pull into the drive. Lorenzo got out of the driver's side and Kristel emerged from the passenger's side. They were both laughing. Margarete's heart lifted just to see them. It was so good to see young people enjoying themselves.

Within a few minutes, there was a tap on the door and Lorenzo put his head around.

'Can I have a quick word, Margarete?'

'Of course.'

He came and sat down beside Margarete and looked into her eyes.

'Kristel and I thought it might help you to tell your story if I sat in on your interviews with her,' he said.

'Yes... Ginetta told me. It is a difficult story to tell, and it might help if you were there. You always understand me so well, Lorenzo... Oh, but I am speaking to Kristel in German. Do you speak German?'

'I worked in Germany for a while during my travels,' he said. 'I can't say I'm fluent, but I can understand more than I can speak.'

Margarete beamed. 'Well, that's fine then.'

She sensed that Lorenzo was hesitating.

'There is something else, though, Margarete.'

'Oh? What's that?'

'Well, Kristel mentioned that you have a notebook but that you haven't shown it to her yet. She thinks it could be very useful for her research. Do you think you could show it to her at some point soon, or is there a reason you want to keep it to yourself?'

'Oh,' Margarete said, looking away from him and twisting her hands in her lap. The notebook was right there, by her side. She'd kept it close all those years in the hope that someday it would be needed. Just looking at it took her straight back to Schloss Schwanburg and her office, the way her hands would sweat whenever she wrote anything in its pages, knowing the consequences of it being found. 'I *will* give it to Kristel in due course, of course I will. But there's a lot I need to explain to her first, otherwise she won't understand about it. When I've explained everything, I will give it to her.'

'Well, that's good to know,' Lorenzo said. 'So, are you ready to see her? Shall I go and get her now?'

'Of course,' Margarete replied.

Lorenzo fetched Kristel and they sat down next to each other opposite Margarete. Kristel took her tape recorder out of her bag, put it on the coffee table between them and switched it on. Margarete couldn't help noticing how much better Kristel looked today. There was colour in her cheeks and her eyes were dancing with life. On her previous visits to the care home, she'd always looked a little forlorn.

'You were telling me about Tomas, Margarete,' Kristel began.

Margarete closed her eyes. Even now, if she wanted to, she could still feel the warmth of his arms around her, holding her tight, and hear his voice. She'd never forgotten the sound of it, or the way just hearing it would make her feel.

'Tomas and I did everything we could to sabotage what was happening at Schloss Schwanburg,' Margarete began. 'Tomas took terrible risks. Whenever he could, he tried to make sure that when babies were adopted, they went to people who were just party members, rather than SS officials.

'But the big risk he took was signing those certificates to prevent babies with health problems from being sent to the T4 programme in Munich. He saved the lives of many babies like that. We just had to hope and pray that Doctor Finkel wouldn't look too closely at the certificates or take it upon himself to examine those babies. But for the time being, Finkel trusted

Tomas. He knew Tomas from when they'd worked together before and he had no reason not to trust him.'

'Were you afraid you would get caught?' Kristel asked.

'Of course. All the time. We were living on a knife edge. We watched Finkel like hawks for any change of mood or sign of suspicion on his part. Because he probably wouldn't have said anything to us. He would have just called in the Gestapo or the SS if he had any suspicions. So, it could have happened at any time, out of the blue.'

'And what about your relationship with Tomas? How did that develop?'

'We fell deeply in love,' Margarete said. She felt no awkwardness saying this. She was not ashamed of her relationship with Tomas, it was the purest, most loving, most honest thing she'd ever done in her life. Nothing else had come close to it. 'We saw each other whenever we could. He would stay with me in my room most nights. We had to creep around to avoid discovery. Of course, we knew we were taking risks, but it was worth it. We needed each other. We were partners in our quest to help the mothers and babies, as well as lovers. Our lives were inextricably entwined from the day he arrived at the castle. I suppose the claustrophobic environment and the risks we were taking in defying the programme intensified our love. We felt we were each other's port in a storm.'

'Do you think Finkel ever suspected what you were doing?'

'We had many tense moments. He would often call Tomas into his office abruptly without giving a reason. We would instantly panic and think we had been discovered, but usually it was just Finkel's manner. He was very imperious. But one day Doctor Finkel called Tomas in and told him that Himmler was going to pay another visit. Finkel said that he'd been looking at the paperwork in preparation for the visit and it didn't add up.

'When Tomas came out of his office, he was as white as a sheet. That night, after Finkel had gone home, we both went in there and checked through all the recent records to make sure they were coherent. We concluded that there was nothing wrong or out of place and that Finkel had just said what he'd said to test Tomas. But it made us very wary. From that moment on, we knew he was suspicious.

'When Himmler came the following day, Finkel took him into his office and they were closeted in there together for a couple of hours. Tomas couldn't sit still during that whole time. He was like a cat on hot bricks, convinced Finkel would have spotted something that we'd missed and be informing on us to Himmler. But when the office door opened, and they finally came out, they were all smiles.

'After that, Finkel paraded Himmler around the castle proudly again, introducing him to staff and the young mothers, and Himmler presided over another chilling naming ceremony. It was hard to watch, knowing this ritual was to admit these poor innocent babies into the church of the SS.'

'What date was that, roughly?' Kristel asked.

Margarete thought for a moment. 'That was probably the early spring of 1943. After that, Tomas and I managed to get away for a weekend together. Our leave coincided, so I told Doctor Finkel I was going to Berlin to see my family and Tomas said he was off to see his parents on the farm. In fact, we met in a little town on Lake Constance and spent a glorious few days... I still treasure those precious moments we had together.'

Margarete paused, remembering. She was back there in her mind, reliving their walks around the lake, their arms entwined, those long afternoons making love in their hotel room, eating in the hotel restaurant, pretending they were a respectable married couple.

'When I got back on the Monday, a young girl called Hedda Jenner had arrived. That was the first time she came to Schloss Schwanburg, in the early days of her pregnancy. As soon as I saw her, I liked her instantly. She looked a little vulnerable, because she'd just been let down by the SS officer who was the father of her child, but she had a refreshing honesty about her. She'd had a hard time, that was clear, but she was prepared to stand up for what was right. That was very rare in those days.

'Hedda was unusual amongst those girls, in that she hadn't really known what she was letting herself in for. Many of the others had volunteered to give the Führer a child and were fully signed up to the Nazi agenda. But Hedda wasn't like that at all. She was an innocent.'

TWENTY-ONE

HEDDA

Schloss Schwanburg, 1943

Hedda arrived back at Schloss Schwanburg in the middle of August 1943. She'd walked straight to Munich Hauptbahnhof from her aunt's apartment, still shaking from the argument with her uncle. She'd used some of her precious savings to buy a ticket and had got on a train at Munich to Füssen. When the train steamed into Füssen station that time, there was no black car waiting to greet her, but the stationmaster took pity on her and said he would find her a taxi to the castle.

To Hedda's surprise, it wasn't a car but a pony and cart, but the weather was beautiful. Riding past the glittering lake and up the winding drive to the castle through the scented pine woods was a magical experience. The carter was a gruff old man and didn't speak once during the hour-long journey. Perhaps he felt it best not to ask questions about the schloss and what went on there. But his silence suited Hedda. She sat back on the wooden seat, closed her eyes, enjoying the swaying of the cart and the sounds of birdsong and the clop-clop of the horse's hooves.

When she opened her eyes again, they were moving through a grassy oasis in the middle of the forest, full of wild flowers, with caramel-coloured cattle grazing the long grass. Despite her trepidation at returning to the castle, Hedda's spirits lifted at the beauty of her surroundings. This was a far cry from Munich, with its bombed-out buildings, its empty shops and frightened people.

When the cart clip-clopped into the castle courtyard, Hedda paid the carter and stood in front of the door, taking in the beauty all around her. The ornate façade of the white castle rose up before her. Everything was silent apart from the roaring of the waterfall in the valley beside the castle and as she listened, she could hear the faint sound of female voices laughing. Perhaps the other expectant mothers were out in the gardens somewhere. She had one last moment of doubt as she stood there. Was this the right thing to be doing?

Taking a deep breath, Hedda pulled on a huge, rope bell-pull beside the door. A bell echoed somewhere deep inside the castle corridors. After a pause, she heard footsteps. A man opened the door and looked her up and down. She didn't remember him from her first visit.

'I'm Holge Schwartz, the caretaker here,' he said in a gruff tone. 'Are they expecting you?'

'Not quite yet. I came a bit early,' Hedda admitted.

'I'll tell Doctor Finkel,' the caretaker replied and took her suitcase. 'Sit down over there. Oh... what's your name?'

Hedda told him and went to sit down on the wooden bench. She waited, her nerves jumpy, intimidated now by the palatial surroundings. Had she done the right thing coming back? Where was Margarete Weiss? There was no sign of her yet, but Hedda hoped fervently that she was still working at the castle. Margarete's promise to help her was what had given her the confidence to return.

Soon, Hedda heard footsteps approaching down a passage behind her and Doctor Finkel appeared in his white coat.

'Ah, Miss Jenner. So, you did come back,' he said with a smug smile. He consulted his clipboard. 'I'm afraid you are a few weeks early and we are almost full to capacity at the moment. I hope you don't mind sharing a room with another young lady?'

'Of course not,' Hedda said. She was used to cramped conditions. At least she wouldn't be sharing with her cousin Gisela any longer, who tended to wake her up by jumping on her bed in the mornings, which lately had made Hedda anxious for the safety of her baby.

'Well, come along then. I'll show you to your room, and tomorrow morning, I will examine you, see how your pregnancy is progressing. I had a favourable report from the Lebensborn officer in Munich.'

She followed him up two flights of stairs, realising that the plush rooms on the second floor were reserved for visiting BDM girls and SS officers. The decor and the rooms higher up looked shabbier and altogether less impressive.

Doctor Finkel knocked on a door halfway along a corridor. A sullen, female voice said, 'Come in,' and Doctor Finkel pushed the door open.

'I'm afraid you're going to have to share your room from now on, Caro,' he said. 'We've had an unexpected arrival.' He beckoned Hedda inside the room. 'There – you can sleep in that bed,' he instructed, waving to a single bed on one side of the room. 'Right, I will leave you to it. Dinner is at seven o'clock in the dining room on the ground floor. The caretaker will bring your luggage up.'

Hedda sat on the bed and, once Doctor Finkel had gone, turned her attention to her new roommate. Like Hedda, she had blonde hair and pale skin. She was reclining on her bed, flicking through a fashion magazine. She was clearly in the last stages of pregnancy.

'I'm Charlotte,' she announced, barely looking up from her magazine. 'We're not supposed to know each other's real names, but I don't care about that. What's your name?'

'Hedda,' she replied, taking off her sandals that were chafing in the heat. 'I don't mind about that either.'

'But don't let on to Finkel that you know my name. When's your baby due?' Charlotte asked.

'Oh, not until next month. I had nowhere to go, so I had to come here.'

'Thrown out of home?' Charlotte asked, appraising her with cool blue eyes.

'Yes,' admitted Hedda.

'It's not uncommon. My parents were understanding, but I know that many aren't.'

Hedda didn't answer. She didn't want to think about the distressing scene with her uncle or the ugly, threatening taunts from the neighbours.

'How did it happen for you?' Charlotte asked. 'Was it here in the castle?'

'What?' Hedda asked.

'How did you get pregnant?'

'Oh. Oh no, it wasn't here. I was already expecting when I first came here. I was... I was with someone. He's now in the SS and arranged for me to come here once he found out about the pregnancy. But we're not together any longer,' she said bitterly. She thought about Sebastian. She hadn't heard from him since she'd left the castle the first time, and she'd tried to put him out of her mind.

'At least it wasn't like what happened to me,' Charlotte said, putting her magazine down and looking at Hedda properly for the first time. 'I didn't really understand what I was letting myself in for when I agreed to come. The woman who came to the BDM to recruit us made it all sound so glamorous and heroic to have a baby for the Führer. I agreed because a couple of the other girls from my group wanted to come, and I didn't want to miss out. But once we got here...' She trailed off.

'You don't have to tell me if you don't want to,' said Hedda.

'No! I want to talk about it. I need... I need to get it out.'

'All right. I'm listening.' Hedda swung her legs onto the bed and leaned back on the pillows.

'We were all quite excited about coming. Apart from BDM camping trips, none of us had been away from home for more than a weekend before, and it seemed like an adventure. But when we got here, everything changed. We were told to get into our best dresses and go to the ballroom and to choose a partner from the SS officers there.

'When we were actually there in the ballroom with them, it all started to seem a bit frightening. As I looked around the room, all the men looked much older than us and very intimidating. Not a bit like the boys we knew at home. We didn't really have any choice though. I chose one man who looked a bit less serious than some of them there and after we'd eaten and had a couple of glasses of champagne, we went to my room.

'I wasn't at all prepared for what happened. No one had explained anything about it to us, although we had a vague idea that it would be romantic and lovely. When we got into the room, I didn't really want to go through with it, but I felt I had no choice. He pushed me down on the bed and went at me like a wild animal. I had no idea it would hurt like it did. As soon as he'd started, I asked him to stop, but he seemed possessed. He wasn't listening to me. Nothing in the world would have stopped him. I had no choice but to put up with it. When he'd finished though, he looked a bit embarrassed. He hardly said anything to me. He just left me lying there and went off to his room.' She trailed off and Hedda sensed her sadness at what had happened.

'Oh, how terrible for you,' Hedda said, remembering the visible awkwardness between the BDM girls and the SS officers she'd witnessed the first time she'd come to the castle.

'It happened again the next night and several times after that too. I'm not sure he even wanted to do it. It didn't look as though he enjoyed it. It was probably as much a chore for him as it was for me.'

'Oh, Charlotte. It must feel terrible.'

'It does. Terrible. But the worst thing was, we girls had to sign something saying we agreed that our babies would be under the guardianship of the Fatherland when they were born. I just signed it, not thinking much about it, but now I've changed my mind,' she said, determination in her tone.

'Really?'

Charlotte nodded. 'Yes, despite everything that happened, it is still my baby. My flesh and blood. I don't want it to be sent to some SS family and never to see it again.'

'Me too,' Hedda said with feeling. It was a shock to her to find that Charlotte felt exactly as she did. Apart from Margarete, Charlotte was the first person she felt she would be happy to confide in. 'I want to keep my baby as well,' Hedda admitted, 'but I signed something too. I didn't really realise what I was signing. I was at a very low ebb and Doctor Finkel sort of tricked me.'

'There is one nurse who has said she will try to help me though,' Charlotte confessed. 'Nurse Weiss. She is very kind and I really think she hates what is going on here and wants to help girls who want to be helped. But most of them don't.'

There was a knock at the door and Charlotte stopped talking immediately.

Hedda went to answer it. It was Holge Schwartz with her suitcase. She took it from him and closed the door again.

'*He's* someone you definitely can't trust,' Charlotte said.

'I'm sure he's a spy for Doctor Finkel. I've seen him watching people, listening to conversations so he can report back.'

'He does look untrustworthy,' Hedda agreed. 'Just one look at his eyes...'

Charlotte pulled a face, imitating Holge's narrow-eyed, shifty look, and both girls laughed, dissolving any remaining tension left between them. For the first time, Hedda felt a ray of hope. Perhaps her stay here wasn't going to be so bad after all.

Later, they went downstairs to eat in the dining room and Charlotte introduced Hedda to the other girls on the table. Hedda knew, though, that the girls weren't using their proper names. None of them looked any less than fanatical about what they were doing and their commitment to provide a baby for the Führer. By the end of the meal, Hedda was thanking her lucky stars that Charlotte was her roommate and not one of the others.

After supper, Hedda and Charlotte took a stroll round the garden. It was wonderful to breathe in the fresh, mountain air, the evening scents from the roses in the garden, and to hear the sound of the waterfall in the ravine and the birdsong at dusk. But Charlotte was soon tired, so they went back to the room and lay on their beds and talked some more. Charlotte told her that she came from Augsburg and that her father was away fighting in the Wehrmacht.

'He's in Russia at the moment. We haven't heard from him for weeks, but I pray every day that he is keeping safe.'

In turn, Hedda told her about the loss of her entire family that one terrible evening in September 1942.

'That's why I turned to Sebastian, I suppose,' she said. 'He seemed so kind. But later I realised I was blind to the other side to him. I saw it when we came to this castle, though. By then he'd joined the SS.'

Suddenly, Charlotte drew in a sharp breath and put her hand on her back.

'Are you all right?' Hedda asked. Charlotte's face was pale, her eyes terrified.

'I don't know. I think it might have started.'

'The baby?'

Charlotte nodded.

'I'll go and fetch someone.'

Hedda hurried down to the nursery, hoping that Margarete would be there. But there was only the grim-faced nurse Hedda remembered as Nurse Ekert.

'I think Charlotte has gone into labour...' she said breathlessly.

'Charlotte? Charlotte? We don't use real names here. I shouldn't have to remind you of that. We call her Caro. And you are Helga. Remember?'

'Of course. But she is in labour. She wanted Nurse Weiss.'

'Nurse Weiss is off duty this evening. She will have to make do with me and Doctor Finkel.'

'What about the other doctor? Charlotte... I mean Caro ... mentioned a Doctor Müller to me.'

'What is wrong with you, girl? He is off duty, too. Now, let's go and see how Caro is...'

The nurse set off ahead of Hedda back to the room and when Hedda caught up with her there, she was already bringing Charlotte out. Charlotte was sweating profusely. Her hands were clutching her belly and she kept crying out in pain.

'No need to make a fuss,' Nurse Ekert said impatiently. 'And Helga, you can stay in your room. You're not needed.'

Hedda followed them a short distance and watched them make their slow progress down the stairs. She leaned on the banister, watching them walk along the landing below towards the maternity suite next to the nursery. As she watched, someone came hurrying along the lower landing. Hedda realised it was Nurse Weiss.

'Let me see to this girl, Nurse Ekert,' Hedda heard her say. 'We agreed that I would look after her.'

'We agreed no such thing. You are off duty, Nurse. You have been working round the clock and need a rest. Doctor Finkel and I will look after her.'

Instinctively, Hedda began to walk down the stairs. Then Doctor Finkel appeared on the scene, rushing up the stairs from the ground floor.

'You can go back up to your room immediately,' he said, glaring up at Hedda. 'And, Nurse Weiss, we have no need of your help. I instruct you to return to your room until your morning shift.'

'But, Doctor...' Nurse Weiss protested.

'Your room. Immediately, Nurse Weiss. Please don't disobey my orders or I may have to inform Herr Himmler that you have been less than co-operative lately and you know what that would mean.'

By now, Charlotte had been ushered into the delivery room and Doctor Finkel disappeared in that direction too. Nurse Weiss was still there on the landing. She stood biting her nail, then she turned to walk upstairs and saw Hedda standing half-way up.

'Hedda! How wonderful to see you back. Are you all right?'

'Yes,' said Hedda, lowering her voice, 'but I'm worried about Charlotte. She told me she wants to keep her baby.'

'I know. I wanted to be there during the birth, but you saw what happened. It's proved impossible. But I will be there for her in the morning.'

'Will you help me too?' Hedda asked. She was even more worried now, seeing Charlotte's pain and the way Doctor Finkel and Nurse Ekert had taken over.

'Of course,' Margarete said, smiling and laying a hand on Hedda's arm. 'I told you I would, didn't I? When your time comes. Now, go and get some rest and I will see you in the morning.'

Reluctantly, Hedda heaved herself back upstairs and lay on the bed and closed her eyes. It had been a long day and she fell asleep almost immediately.

In the morning, she awoke to the sound of shouting and crying. There was a commotion in the corridor. She couldn't hear what was being said, but it was a girl's voice she could hear, wailing and protesting. Hedda crept out of bed and listened at the door, but the screaming and crying were incoherent. She realised that the echoes were coming from the front hall by that time, then the voices moved outside. Hedda rushed to the front window that looked over the courtyard and pushed it open.

With a bolt of shock, she saw that it was Charlotte howling and screaming. She was dressed in a hospital gown and was being bundled into a black SS vehicle by two guards, struggling and crying out all the time.

Hedda hurried downstairs herself, although it was difficult in her condition. She crossed the hall as quickly as she could and made for the front door. She wanted to see Charlotte, give her some words of comfort. But before she could reach the door, Doctor Finkel appeared from nowhere and stood in front of her, barring her way.

'You are not going anywhere,' he said. 'Let her go. She has been making a dreadful fuss and she needs to go home.'

'Why?' Hedda asked.

'Go back to your room. You will find out in due course,' he said coldly, then strode over and slammed the front door shut.

Hedda stood there, shock coursing through her, tears in her eyes. Through the thick door, she could hear the sound of the car door slam, the engine starting up and rumbling away through the gatehouse.

Defeated, she walked wearily back across the hallway, up the stairs to her room and lay down on the bed. She noticed that

Charlotte's things had been removed and her suitcase had gone. Someone must have come in while Hedda had been asleep and taken them away. Chills went through her at the thought of that dreadful, sly caretaker coming in secretly and watching her sleeping.

There was a knock on the door. She looked up, startled, but the visitor was Margarete.

'Are you all right, Hedda?' she asked, coming in and sitting down on the bed.

'What happened to Charlotte?' Hedda asked through her tears. She noticed that Margarete's eyes were red. She must have been crying too. 'Why did they send her away like that?'

'Doctor Finkel doesn't like a fuss and Charlotte was hysterical.'

'But why?'

Margarete hesitated. Hedda watched her face and it was clear that Margarete was trying to decide how much to tell her. In the end, she said, 'Charlotte's baby boy was born with some physical problems and he was sent to hospital immediately. Charlotte didn't want him to go. She was worried she might not see him again.'

'And will she?' Hedda asked.

Margarete looked down at her lap. 'I can't say,' but Hedda knew she was hiding something. 'I wish I could have been there,' Margarete went on, almost to herself. 'I told her I would help her, but I failed her. They wouldn't let me go to her.'

'You will help *me* though, won't you, Nurse Weiss?' Hedda asked, alarmed.

It was slowly dawning on her that it could be difficult if not impossible for Margarete to help her. What if the same thing happened to her baby? What if she could never hold the baby, if it was whisked away just as Charlotte's baby had been and she was sent away, hysterical and distraught?

'I will do whatever I can, Hedda. I need to make sure I'm on duty when your baby comes. Now, I'm really sorry, but I must go down to the nursery and check on the babies. I'm late for my shift.'

She squeezed Hedda's arm tenderly and stood up to go.

Hedda watched her walk to the door and turn to say good-bye, but when she did, Hedda noticed with a bolt of shock that Margarete's own stomach was visibly swelling underneath her neat uniform.

TWENTY-TWO

MARGARETE

Trento, 2005

'I still feel guilty about what happened to Charlotte all these years later,' Margarete told Kristel, her eyes shadowed with decades-old grief. 'And all the others I wanted to help but couldn't... Tomas and I protested to Doctor Finkel about what had happened. We wanted to be there for Charlotte when she gave birth, but he must have known it was imminent and had changed our shifts at short notice. He was definitely suspicious of us, but he had no proof that we were doing anything against the rules. After the birth, though, he must have suspected somehow that we were going to help Charlotte leave with her baby, because he went into the nursery in the middle of the night and insisted on removing the baby to Munich.

'When we complained to him about the way Charlotte and her baby had been treated, he told us that he was acting within the rules of the programme, and if we didn't like it, we could take our complaint to Herr Himmler himself, but he didn't think we would get very far with that.'

Kristel and Lorenzo had been listening, gripped by

Margarete's story, but now she had to stop talking. What was to follow would take all her strength to tell and she wasn't sure she was strong enough to talk about it that day.

'What was wrong with Charlotte's baby?' Kristel asked, horror and incredulity etched on her face.

Margarete shook her head. 'I'm not sure precisely and Doctor Finkel put down on his notes that he had weak lungs. Finkel was quite capable of trumping up false stories when it suited him. So that poor little mite was sent off to Aktion T4, when there was likely nothing much wrong with him.'

Margarete fell silent, thinking about that tiny, innocent baby, sent for 'mercy euthanasia', and all the others who had gone that way too. Then her thoughts turned to Hedda.

A few weeks after Charlotte had left the castle, Hedda finally went into labour. She was out in the garden when it happened, reclining in a basket chair with a book, basking in the late afternoon sunshine. Margarete and Tomas had ensured they were both on duty that day. One of the other girls came to the nursery to tell Margarete that Hedda's baby was coming. Margarete rushed out to the garden, calling into Tomas's office to collect him on the way, but Doctor Finkel was already there, taking charge in his imperious way.

'Doctor Müller, there is no need for you to attend this birth,' Doctor Finkel said coldly, seeing Tomas arrive in the garden. 'I will allow Nurse Weiss to be present for this birth, alongside Nurse Ekert, but you need to be on call for the other patients, Doctor Müller.'

'But, Doctor Finkel, I thought we agreed that I would be present at this birth.'

'Did we? Well, if we did, I'm afraid I've changed my mind. Please resume your duties in the castle straight away, Doctor Müller.'

Margarete exchanged exasperated glances with Tomas, but this wasn't totally unexpected. They'd hoped that at least one of them would be there for Hedda during the birth and they'd achieved that. With an exasperated sigh, Tomas turned and walked back to the castle.

Margarete was all too aware of her own condition. She would be giving birth too in the next few months. It had become really important to her to ensure the girls suffered as little as possible during the births. She thought fondly of how she'd told Tomas about her pregnancy. His initial surprise had quickly turned to delight and he'd taken her in his arms and held her tight for a long time.

'We can't tell a soul,' he'd said when he'd let her go. 'We'd surely both be punished severely, and they would try to take our baby.'

Doctor Finkel had disappeared into the building so Margarete helped Hedda walk through the gardens, into the castle, across the great hallway and up the stairs to the delivery room. It took a long time because every few minutes they had to stop for a contraction to pass. Hedda would grasp onto Margarete's hands fiercely, puffing and panting until it was over.

'Try to keep your breathing steady,' Margarete urged. 'That will help with the pain,' but Hedda was already panicking, clearly not remotely prepared for the strength and severity of the pain of labour.

Once they got into the delivery room, Nurse Ekert took charge. She insisted on Hedda lying down on the bed and putting her feet up in the stirrups. It reminded Margarete of the birth of Heidi's baby.

'Is that strictly necessary?' she asked. Nurse Ekert ignored her and she bit her tongue to stop herself intervening again. She knew from experience that her protests would be futile.

Hedda lay back on the pillows, her face bathed in sweat, her hair sticking to her forehead. She already looked exhausted, and she'd only been in labour for half an hour or so.

Margarete watched her anxiously, worried that she wouldn't have the strength to see it through, but she hid her fears and smiled at Hedda. She held Hedda's hand and tried to encourage her with positive words, but Hedda seemed to have gone into a fearful reverie; she was no longer listening or taking notice of anything around her.

The labour went on for a long time, well into the small hours. Like Heidi, Hedda seemed to give up, to be trying to fight against what was happening to her body. Margarete knew this was because she was lying on her back and that gravity was against her. She tried to keep Hedda's spirits up, and got her to sit up and sip water at regular intervals to keep her hydrated. It was a warm evening and the air was stifling in the delivery room. Margarete felt hot and sticky, suddenly able to feel the weight of her own baby. Her legs ached and she longed for a rest, but she knew she had to be there for Hedda.

When the baby's head finally appeared, in the middle of the night, Hedda was too exhausted to push. She just lay back, whimpering with the pain of the heaviest contractions.

Doctor Finkel and Nurse Ekert exchanged worried glances.

Doctor Finkel said, 'I'll have to use forceps. We need to get that baby out now.'

He produced an outsized pair of silver forceps from the cabinet. Margarete blanched when she saw them. They looked far too big and cumbersome for the job, but Doctor Finkel proceeded to insert them inside Hedda around the baby's head. Hedda yelled out in pain and gripped Margarete's hand with extraordinary force.

'Stop that fuss,' Nurse Ekert admonished. 'The doctor needs to do this because you're not pushing properly.'

Doctor Finkel continued to manipulate the forceps and Hedda writhed around on the bed in agony until he finally dragged the baby out. It started yelling instantly and Margarete smiled into Hedda's eyes, relieved.

'It's a girl,' he said. Nurse Ekert whisked the baby away to clean her and Hedda lay back, sobbing and panting. 'It's over now. Clean her up, Nurse Weiss.'

Gently, Margarete sponged Hedda's sweating body and changed her robe. When Nurse Ekert came back and handed Hedda the baby, Hedda looked down at the little face with its beady blue eyes and smiled for the first time in hours.

'She's beautiful,' she said. 'I will call her Evelina after my mother.'

'No names,' Doctor Finkel chided. 'Her name will be chosen by the family who takes her.'

Margarete watched Hedda, worried that she might have an outburst about keeping her baby, but she didn't. She must have known better than to give the game away. She was looking down at her baby, smiling, her eyes full of love, totally absorbed with the tiny new life in her arms.

Once Margarete was sure that Hedda was able to feed the baby, she left, exhausted with the stress and strain of the past few hours, and went upstairs to her room.

Soon, Tomas joined her. He took her in his arms and kissed her.

'You look very tired, my darling. Are you all right?' he asked, his face full of concern. 'Perhaps you should take things a bit easier, in your condition.' He smiled proudly, caressing her swelling belly.

'I'm all right, Tomas. But it was terrible for Hedda. They made her lie down as usual and she couldn't push. Finkel ended up using forceps.' She shivered, recalling the doctor's barbarity.

Tomas's face fell. 'I bet he was brutal with them,' he said. 'Poor Hedda.'

'It was excruciatingly painful for her,' Margarete replied, thinking about Hedda's animal howls during the delivery.

'We will need to act quickly,' he said. 'If Finkel suspects anything, he will take the baby away without warning.'

They had already discussed their plan with Hedda. It had been Tomas's idea. He was due some leave in the next few days, and was planning to drive to see his parents on their farm near the Austrian border. Hedda and her baby would leave the castle in the evening, when most of the staff had gone home and when Holge was on his rounds of the estate. Margarete would create some distraction for the night nurse. They would be hidden in the boot of Tomas's car until they were well clear of the castle. He would drive them to the family farm and find them somewhere to stay nearby.

'There are farm workers' cottages on our farm. She might be able to have one of those,' he suggested. 'I'm sure my parents will be happy to help when I tell them what is happening here.'

'It's a big risk,' Margarete said. 'What if you're caught? I couldn't bear for that to happen, Tomas.'

He kissed her on the lips then and stroked her hair, looking into her eyes. 'Have faith in me, Margarete. We all need to be prepared to take risks.'

The next day, Hedda was encouraged to take her baby outside to the garden for some air. Tomas had been walking round the grounds with his camera, photographing the castle and gardens. 'I want to show the castle to my family when I go home on leave,' he explained. 'My father's very interested in history. But let's have a picture of you and your baby, Hedda,' he said on an impulse, looking around to make sure Doctor Finkel or anyone else in authority wasn't nearby. It would have been strictly forbidden to photograph any of the babies at Schloss Schwanburg. 'Why don't I take one of you and Hedda, Margarete?'

Margarete smiled a little reluctantly, but wasn't about to deny Tomas that pleasure. She stood beside Hedda in front of the flowering roses. Glancing across at Hedda, she realised how alike she and Hedda looked. They were about the same height, both were slight with blonde hair, and uniform features, but Hedda was about ten years younger than Margarete and her face still had the round innocence of a teenager, whereas Margarete's lines were more sculpted and mature.

Tomas snapped the photograph and stepped back. 'I'll go up to my room and develop it straight away,' he said, 'so you can take it with you when you leave.'

He said that deliberately so the other girls in the garden would hear, Margarete thought. He was sowing the seeds for Hedda's escape plan.

The next day, in the evening, Tomas and Margarete went to Hedda's room and presented her with the photograph. Hedda was delighted when she saw it. Her eyes lit up.

'I will always remember you, Margarete. You've been so kind to me,' Hedda said. 'Thank you for everything.'

Margarete smiled nervously. Their plan hadn't been executed yet and who knew what could happen between now and Tuesday, in two days' time, when Tomas's leave was due? Those forty-eight hours stretched before her and seemed endless. How would her nerves stand the wait? She didn't want to think about the repercussions for herself and for Tomas if it all went wrong. She didn't mind so much for herself, but her worst fear was not seeing him again. How could she bear that, especially now that she was carrying his child?

On Monday morning, Doctor Finkel called Tomas and Margarete into his office.

'An opportunity has come up for two places on a symposium on racial theory in Munich. I would like you both to attend. Here at Schloss Schwanburg, we risk being a little detached from the centre. We don't want you to become cut off from Nazi politics altogether, now do we?'

They stared at him.

'When is the symposium?' Margarete ventured, trying not to sound thrown by this latest blow.

'It starts tomorrow morning, but you will need to leave today and stay in Munich overnight. It begins quite early, so there will be no time to travel up there in the morning.'

'But, Doctor Finkel,' Tomas protested without looking at Margarete, 'you know that I am due to go on leave on tomorrow. My parents are expecting me. It's been a very long time since I've seen them.'

'Yes, I'm well aware of that, Doctor Müller,' he said, staring at Tomas coldly, 'but this is a unique opportunity that I wouldn't want you to miss out on. In fact, the Reichsführer, Herr Himmler himself, particularly requested your and Nurse Weiss's presence at the symposium. He will be delivering the keynote speech and is looking forward to you being there. You can take your leave on your return.'

'How many days is it?' Tomas asked.

'It will last two days, but I'd also like you to attend some meetings at the Ministry on my behalf. You can come back on Friday and then you can take your leave with your family,' he said with an air of finality. 'So, please go to your rooms and pack now,' he went on when neither of them replied. 'The car is already waiting to take you both to Munich. You will stay at the Hotel Vier Jahreszeiten. I think you both will be very comfortable there.'

Was there something pointed in his voice when he said that? Did he know about their relationship? All Margarete could think of was that this turn of events put their plan to help Hedda escape with her baby in serious jeopardy.

They left the office together but were unable to say a word to each other as Holge was waiting outside the room and followed them down the corridor a couple of steps behind. Margarete's mind was racing, and she realised that she was shaking all over. How could this be happening, after all their careful planning?

She was desperate to visit Hedda and tell her what was going on. There might be some way of Hedda holding off her baby's adoption and her own departure from the castle. If only it could be delayed until the weekend.

But Holge followed Margarete up to her room and waited outside the door. She threw some random clothes into her suitcase, hardly noticing what she packed. She hoped and prayed that Tomas would have a chance to go and see Hedda, to let her know that their plan would have to be postponed. Holge couldn't be in two places at once.

When she'd finished packing, Margarete emerged from the room with her suitcase and Holge escorted her downstairs and across the hall to the open door. A big black car was waiting in the courtyard, its engine already running, and Margarete's heart lurched when she saw the two Gestapo officers stood beside the car and a Gestapo driver installed in the driving seat. Was this it? Were they were being taken to a concentration camp without even being told? If they were, what would that mean for the innocent life growing inside her?

'Get in, please, Nurse Weiss,' one of the officers said, holding the back door open and taking her case. She had no choice but to slide into the back seat.

In a few minutes, Tomas came out of the front door and got in beside her. Glancing at him, she saw that he looked nervous. Then they were speeding under the gatehouse and out of the courtyard.

'He knows, doesn't he?' she whispered to Tomas.

'I don't know. Perhaps this is just a precaution.' There was a wariness in his voice that belied his words.

'Did you speak to Hedda?'

He nodded. 'I told her we will be back at on Friday, but she was distraught. And she is right to be. This is Finkel's way of thwarting our plans.'

'We've let her down,' Margarete said, biting her nail. 'Just like Charlotte.'

'Don't give up on her, Margarete, not yet.'

She stared bitterly out at the calm waters of the mountain lake they were skirting now, hardly noticing the beauty of the landscape. She suddenly worried about her notebooks. They were under lock and key in her wardrobe, but did Holge have another key? She went hot and cold thinking about it. She was wondering too what the next days would bring for Hedda, and for them. Why were they being taken by the Gestapo? Would the car be heading straight past Munich and on to the concentration camp at Dachau? She wouldn't be surprised. If Finkel was suspicious, why didn't he just have them put away? Perhaps he was playing the long game though, toying with them for some bizarre reason of his own.

But the car didn't head to Dachau, it went straight through the city centre of Munich to Maximilianstrasse and the Hotel Vier Jahreszeiten.

Driving through the city, Margarete stared in horror at the bombsites they passed, the once proud buildings that had been reduced to rubble, the children in rags picking through rubbish heaps. She was stunned. Although she'd seen some evidence of bombing from the train last time she'd been home to Berlin, this was on an altogether different scale. Could the Nazis really say they were winning the war?

The hotel, however, was sumptuous and elegant, a favourite with the Nazi elite, and Margarete and Tomas discovered that their rooms were on the same corridor. How wonderful it would have been if they could have stayed the night together, revelled in that chance to be together, just as they had on their trip to Lake Constance. But they were both wary. They knew that it was highly possible that they were being watched, that their rooms could well be bugged. Although it was tempting, they didn't want to leave anything to chance.

So, while they were in the city, they treated each other like colleagues and only spoke freely when they were completely sure they were alone. And even then, they were careful what they said and spoke in whispers.

The symposium, held at the Bavarian Ministry of Health, was a series of lectures introduced by Reichsführer Himmler, each given by a different senior Nazi doctor. As when she'd listened to Professor Wagner's lectures at the Charité Hospital, Margarete recoiled at what she was hearing about the superiority of the Aryan race, about eugenics and the mercy killing of those with disabilities.

But unlike back then, this time she knew it wasn't just theory. She knew that these inhuman practices were being carried out all over the country by medical professionals, so keen to gain favour with the Nazis, or simply to save their own skins, that they would break their oaths and participate in the killing of innocent patients. She could hardly bear to listen to these complacent men, preaching this hate-filled propaganda as if it were science. She knew that Tomas felt the same, by the way he buried his face in his hands at regular intervals, clenched his fists, or shook his head in denial.

Margarete was not expected to attend the meetings that Tomas went to on Doctor Finkel's behalf at the Ministry on the Thursday. Instead, she decided to take a walk around the city. Once again, she was appalled at the poverty visible on every street, the children in rags playing on bombsites, the women queuing for food beside empty shops, the piles of rubble on the roads and pavements and the ruins of the collapsed buildings.

She didn't know Munich well, so she headed for somewhere she had heard of; Marienplatz and the town hall. When she arrived, she was dismayed but not surprised to see swastika flags festooned from every façade. It depressed her to be there. But when she turned round to go back to the hotel, she could have sworn that a man in a raincoat smoking a cigarette a few paces from her turned away from her. Each time she turned round as she hurried back through the streets, he was there, a few paces behind her. There was no doubt in her mind now: they were on to her and Tomas.

That evening, when they met in the corridor before going down to dinner, Tomas looked around to check they were alone and bent to peck her cheek.

'Be careful,' she hissed, drawing away from him. 'We're being watched. I'm sure I was followed when I went out earlier.'

Tomas's eyes widened in shock. 'My God! Will they stop at nothing? I'm sorry, Margarete, I'll be more careful. I had no idea.'

The next morning, the same car came to the hotel to take them back to the castle. Margarete was glad to get into the back seat and be heading south out of the city towards the mountains once again. She couldn't wait to get back and find out how Hedda was. It was all she thought about throughout the four-hour journey. She and Tomas hardly spoke, although having him there by her side was reassuring. She ached to lay her head on his shoulder or take his hand in hers, but she knew it wasn't worth the risk.

When the car finally ground its way up the steep castle drive and drew up at the gatehouse, Margarete got straight out and, without waiting for her luggage, rushed inside and up the stairs two at a time. She went directly to Hedda's room and burst inside without knocking.

Margarete let out a cry. The beds were made up neatly and there were no clothes or books scattered about the room anymore. She'd known this would happen, even though she'd tried to convince herself that everything would work out. She collapsed down on the bed sobbing, guilt rushing through her at the thought that yet again she'd failed to help a vulnerable young mother. Worse than that, she'd given Hedda hope.

Margarete looked up, hearing the door open behind her, and there was Tomas. He locked the door shut behind him, came to her and picked her up from the bed and held her in his arms, stroking her hair.

'Don't take it so hard, Margarete. We failed this time, but we must carry on with what we're doing, or at least I must continue on my own until the birth of our child. Even if it's just small steps, we can't ever let them beat us.'

Margarete looked at him and tried to smile but in the back of her mind was the niggling worry that Finkel might have suspected they'd tried to help Hedda. And if he'd suspected that, what else did he know?

TWENTY-THREE

KRISTEL

Trento, 2005

Lorenzo drove Kristel back to her hotel at the end of the day, when Margarete had grown too tired to talk any more.

'How do you think the interview went today?' he asked after they'd set off from the care home.

'Good,' she replied. 'Better than before. It was good to have you there, Lorenzo. Margarete obviously likes and trusts you.'

'She is a lovely lady. It's sobering to hear what she went through,' he said. 'I had no idea, she hid it so well.'

He drove on round the ring road, then through the narrow streets of the town centre which were still slushy with snow, arriving at the hotel within minutes.

'Would you like to come in for a drink?' Kristel asked on an impulse, not wanting to say goodbye and not wanting to spend the entire evening alone yet again.

'That would be good,' he said, manoeuvring the car into a parking space. 'I've never been in this hotel before.'

They went inside, across the lobby and into the hotel bar. It was virtually empty. Just one couple sitting beside the window deep in conversation and a couple of businessmen talking loudly at the bar. Kristel ordered an Aperol and Lorenzo a beer. They chose a corner table.

It felt nice to have some company for once. Especially this company. Kristel sipped her drink and smiled at Lorenzo. His face was perfectly symmetrical with high cheekbones and smile lines around his enigmatic, intelligent eyes. He was constantly smiling.

'Amazing that you've not been in here before if you live in Trento,' Kristel said.

Lorenzo laughed. 'Well, residents don't normally spend a lot of time in tourist hotels, do they? I've spent quite a bit of time in other hotels though, in other places.'

'Really? Have you done a lot of travelling?'

'Yes. After my degree, I decided to see the world. South America, the States, India, South-East Asia, China, Australia, even Germany...' he said, with a teasing smile. 'I worked there for a while. In Munich actually, teaching Italian.'

'How interesting! Why did you come home?' Kristel asked.

'My mother's not well,' he said, suddenly serious. 'Cancer. It's being treated now, but when she was diagnosed it was a very scary time. I wanted to be here for her.'

'Oh, I'm so sorry,' Kristel said with feeling, remembering her father's sudden and swift illness. 'That must be terrible.'

For once, Lorenzo wasn't smiling. He toyed with his glass. 'She's over the worst, but the treatment took it out of her. She used to have so much energy. I'm hoping that will come back one day. Papa needed my support too. Mama's always been the strong one, he was close to crumbling at one point.'

'Do think you will stay here now?' Kristel asked.

He smiled and shrugged. 'I will always have itchy feet. I love seeing new places, meeting different people, but for the time being I'm happy to be here. I like working at the care home. It's very rewarding working with people like Margarete who have seen so much of life.'

'I admire that,' Kristel said, and she meant it. How different Lorenzo was from all the men she knew in Munich. Career-obsessed, ambitious, materialistic, and she included Joachim in that. It was refreshing to find someone who didn't seem to care about any of that. Lorenzo seemed happy to live a freewheeling, low-key life, to do a poorly paid but rewarding job, and to be there for his parents when they needed him.

'I'm not sure it's that admirable,' he replied. 'What *you're* doing is admirable. It's amazing. To bring the past alive like that, to help so many people.'

'We haven't helped that many people yet. A few maybe. We've certainly tried to shine a light on what happened back then.'

'Well, I'm certainly in awe of what you're doing,' Lorenzo said, raising his glass to hers.

At that moment, Kristel's phone rang and, glancing at the screen, her heart sank when she saw it was Joachim. She had no desire to talk to him. Especially not at that moment.

'Take it, if you need to,' Lorenzo said.

'It's fine, it can wait,' Kristel replied, switching the phone off and putting it into her bag. But seeing Joachim's name had interrupted the flow of conversation and soured the moment for her. Now, Kristel felt a little awkwardness had crept between her and Lorenzo. Perhaps he guessed that she had someone back in Munich. She was certainly wondering if he had someone here in Trento. Then she berated herself for the thought. She shouldn't be thinking like that. She and Joachim were still together, although every day that passed made her more and more convinced that things were over between them and that she had no wish to be with him when he returned from Singapore.

'Was that work?' Lorenzo asked.

She shook her head and didn't elaborate, but he must have taken her silence to mean that she didn't want to talk about it. He quickly moved the conversation on.

'How did you get interested in the Lebensborn programme?' he asked.

There was a look of genuine curiosity in his eyes. He wasn't just asking for the sake of making conversation. She suddenly had the urge to unburden herself to this man whom she hardly knew but whom she knew she could trust implicitly and who was a good listener. She picked up her glass to take another sip and realised that she'd almost finished her drink.

'It's a long story,' she said.

He took her glass from her hand and stood up.

'You look as if you'd like to talk about it. I'll get another round in.'

When he came back with fresh drinks, Kristel took a sip of her Aperol and then a deep breath.

'I strongly suspect that my mother is a Lebensborn child,' she said and went on to tell him about how Greta had walked out when Kristel was only three years old, about how she'd always distanced herself from her daughter, and about the letters she'd found after her father's death. Finally, she told him about her trip to Mittenwald and what she'd discovered there. All the time, he listened intently, not interrupting once, his gentle eyes on her face. 'It was that that convinced me,' she finished. 'Finding out that my mother had been brought up in an SS family and that the neighbours thought she had appeared from nowhere. I strongly believe that she found something out about it before she left and it was that which prompted her to go. It was only a couple of months after her mother – or adoptive mother, I should say – died.'

'Have you told her that you went to her home town?' Lorenzo asked.

Kristel shook her head. 'Not yet. I'm looking for something concrete to point to first. At the moment, it's just supposition.'

'I can see now why the Lebensborn story is so close to your heart. Why you pursue it with such fervour,' Lorenzo said. 'I really hope you find your answers and that it brings you closer to your mother.'

'Somehow I don't think we'll ever be close,' Kristel replied sadly. 'She's just not like that. I read somewhere once – and Margarete has also mentioned to me – that the Nazi thinking about childcare was never to show them any emotion. Never to pick them up or cuddle them and to leave them to cry in order to harden them up. If my mother was raised like that, it's probably impossible for her to show emotion or to be close to me.'

'How very sad,' Lorenzo remarked. 'The repercussions of that evil regime continue to be felt decades after it fell.'

Kristel asked him then about his own family, about what had happened to them during the war. He told her proudly that his grandfather had been in the Italian Resistance, had lived in caves in the hills behind Trento and sabotaged German operations from behind their lines.

'There's a plaque in his memory in the cathedral,' he said.

'You must be so proud,' Kristel reflected, swirling her glass. 'A bit different to a mother brought up by the SS.'

'We can't help where we come from, Kristel,' Lorenzo said. 'And it sounds, from what you've said, that your mother has gone out of her way to live a life that redresses the balance.'

'That's true,' Kristel said, finishing her drink. She felt a little light-headed now. 'I think I should order some food. I haven't eaten much today. What about you?'

'I'd love to, but I really need to be heading home. Mama will be making pasta for me. The evening meal is one of the things she loves to focus on and she doesn't like us to miss it.'

'Of course,' Kristel said, a little disappointed that he was about to head off.

'You should come along,' Lorenzo said. 'I've told my parents all about you and I'm sure they would love to meet you.'

'That's very kind,' she said, genuinely touched by the offer. 'Another time perhaps. But I really need to write up the notes of today's interview while they are fresh in my mind.'

'All right. Let's fix up another evening for you to come round.' He stood up. 'But I really must be going now. It's been a real pleasure talking to you, Kristel.'

She stood up too and walked him to the door. There, they stood awkwardly together for a moment, before he put his hands on her shoulders and kissed her on both cheeks. She watched him walk to his car, start the engine and reverse out of the parking space, waving him off and feeling flushed with pleasure.

TWENTY-FOUR

HEDDA

Munich, 2005

The morning after Kristel Meyer's broadcast, Hedda was tucking into her breakfast when there was a knock at her apartment door. She looked up, trying to see through the frosted glass who the caller was. This was unusual. She wasn't expecting any deliveries. Perhaps it was someone to read the gas meter or perhaps the postman? She pulled her dressing gown around her ample frame and went to open the door.

She blinked in surprise. It was the young woman from downstairs, her bleached hair looking even more artificial in the morning light and her exaggerated eyeliner making her sallow skin look even paler. She wore a leather jacket decorated with studs and chains over a grubby T-shirt. She was holding her baby in one arm and a canvas bag over the other shoulder.

'Inge?' Hedda said, using her name for the first time.

'If you really want to help,' the young woman said, 'you could look after him for me this morning. I've got a hospital appointment and last time I took him, he screamed the place down.'

Hedda was suddenly wide awake. 'Of course. I'd be happy to. I'm not going anywhere this morning... What time will you be back?'

Inge shrugged. 'Lunchtime-ish?'

'Well, don't hurry back on my account. Take your time. I'm sure I'll be perfectly fine with little...?'

'Leon. It's Leon.'

Inge handed her the bag. 'There are nappies in there, wipes and bottles. I'm sure you'll manage.' Then she paused. 'You've had your own children, haven't you?'

Hedda stared at her, shock at the directness of the question and its meaning rushing through her.

'Yes. Of course. Yes. I had a daughter.'

Inge nodded but didn't smile. She handed her the baby and Hedda took him carefully. She held him against her shoulder and watched Inge making her way along the corridor. Then she took the baby inside her apartment and sat down with him in the armchair, rocking him gently, cradling him in her lap. He seemed happy and contented this morning, just gurgling away. She held out her hand and he gripped her thumb in his tiny fist. Then he looked up at her and gave her a toothless smile. His eyes were so bright, like little buttons. Hedda was entranced. She held the baby close to her and buried her face in his fuzz of hair. That smell! That lovely, musky, baby smell. It brought all those memories flooding back...

It was September 1943 and Hedda was sitting on the train, watching the rolling green Bavarian countryside slide by through the window. There was no sign of the war here. Everything was the epitome of bucolic calm, but the beauty all around her meant nothing to her. She was distraught, broken, and she didn't think she would ever feel whole again.

She'd known something wasn't right when Doctor Müller

came to see her early one morning, three days after her baby was born. He looked anxious. He came into the room and spoke quietly to her.

'I'm so sorry, Hedda. Margarete and I have been ordered to go to Munich for a few days.'

Hedda stared at him. 'So? What does that mean? Won't you be able to help me?'

'I'm so sorry. Finkel has given us no choice. We will come back as soon as we can, though. If you can just sit tight...' He hovered by the door. 'I'm sorry, but I have to go. The car is waiting in the courtyard.'

Hedda had known then that the carefully laid plans they had made for him to take her to his family farm would never come to fruition.

When he'd gone, she paced around her room in a panic. Surely their plans had been discovered, or at the very least Doctor Finkel was suspicious. He knew that she and Margarete had become close, and from the looks he gave them and the odd comment he dropped, she was aware that he didn't approve.

It suddenly struck her that it was possible that Margarete and Doctor Müller had been taken away by the SS or the Gestapo and shock shot through her at that realisation. They could be on their way to an interrogation centre or a concentration camp that very moment. She clenched her fists and took a deep breath to calm herself down, praying that she was wrong.

Well, if the plan had been thwarted, she would have to think of something else. She was on her own now. She wasn't prepared to wait until Doctor Müller and Margarete returned. She needed to save Evelina. All that mattered to her was her beautiful daughter. These last few days spent with Evelina had been filled with love. She knew she couldn't give her up.

For the next couple of hours, she considered and rejected plan after plan. Ultimately, she decided, there was only one thing she could do and that would be to take her baby from the nursery and simply walk out of the castle. But where would she go? How would she get far enough away before they discovered her? And what would they do to her if they found her? Hedda went hot and cold just thinking about it. She knew, though, that there was no time to lose.

That evening, she stood at one of the front windows of the castle, watching for Doctor Finkel's car to leave, but she waited for half an hour and there was no sign of it. She wondered if she'd missed it and wandered downstairs to the hall to see if she could spot him. Her heart missed a beat as she heard footsteps in the corridor and Finkel emerged, carrying his briefcase. He stopped when he saw Hedda standing there.

'What are you doing down here, Helga?' he asked and she couldn't help the colour from rising to her cheeks.

'I just needed to stretch my legs,' she muttered.

'Well, you have the whole of the upstairs corridors and the nursery. There is no need for you to come down here,' he snapped. 'Now, go back upstairs, where you belong.'

She bowed her head and walked back to her room. Every exchange with him made her flesh creep, but at least she now knew that he was on his way home. This was her best chance. Even though there was a night nurse in the nursery and Holge Schwartz prowled around the castle, she would have to act when neither of them was looking.

She knew it wouldn't work if she simply walked out of the front door and down the drive, but she had seen a track behind the castle that led up to a bridge over the waterfall. There were some old outbuildings up there beside the bridge. They looked run-down and disused. She would stay there until it got light, and in the morning, she would find a way of walking into Füssen and catching a train. She couldn't go back to Munich, that would be the first place they would look for her, but she would get off the train somewhere else along the line and find a place to stay. She had her savings with her from the kiosk job. They would tide her over for a few weeks.

Hedda glanced at her belongings. There was no way she'd be able to carry a suitcase, but she would need to take a few things. She bundled some light clothes up in a scarf. It was lucky that the weather was still warm. She also slipped into her pocket the lock of Evelina's hair she'd snipped from her head the day after she was born. She'd taken it to her room so that she could remind herself of her baby even though she wasn't allowed to have her by her side.

Her stomach churning with nerves at the audacity of what she was about to do, she went over and over her plan. It wasn't perfect, she knew that, but it was the only thing she could think of. She had to do something. And she had to do it that very day. The longer she left it, the more likely it was that baby Evelina would be whisked away from her.

It was hard to act naturally at supper time. She had no appetite for food, but she did her best to force down some of the roasted pork and boiled potatoes, knowing that it could be a while before her next meal. The other young mothers at the table were chatting away about inconsequential things as they did every meal time. Hedda thought them silly and empty-headed at the best of times, but today, their chatter grated on her nerves even more than usual. She remained silent, focusing on her food.

After a while, one of them said, 'Are you all right today, Helga? You seem rather preoccupied.'

'I'm fine,' Hedda replied, forcing a smile, and did her best for the rest of the mealtime to feign interest in the conversation, even interjecting with some comments about hairstyles and autumn fashions.

After the meal, she went back to her room, picked up the small pack she'd tied in her scarf, and a water bottle with a stopper from the dressing table. Then, shutting the door firmly behind her, she made her way downstairs and along the corridor towards the nursery. She paused at one of the windows that looked over the courtyard. There was Nurse Ekert, pedalling off down the drive on her sturdy bicycle. Now was the time to act.

Her nerves jangling, Hedda went along to the nursery and sidled into the room. The night nurse, a very young woman from the nearby village, was bending over one of the cots, settling one of the babies. She was focused on her task, so Hedda went quickly through into the adjoining nursing room and put her pack there, hidden between two chairs, then she went back into the nursery and bent over Evelina's cot. The baby was sound asleep, her little mouth open. She was making tiny snoring sounds. Hedda's heart squeezed with love for her. Gently, she picked her up out of the cot and held her close.

'Is everything all right, Helga?' the nursery nurse said.

'Yes. Nurse Weiss told me to give her a feed last thing at night to help her sleep through,' Hedda replied.

The nurse frowned. 'Really? That's not usual practice... are you quite sure?'

'Oh yes. Nurse Weiss was quite firm about it.'

Evelina had woken now and had started to cry.

'I won't be long,' Hedda said, taking the baby through to the nursing room and sitting down in a chair next to the door.

She let the baby suckle for a while. She looked down at Evelina's contented face. She was so perfect, so precious. How could the other girls give up their babies so easily? She was about to get up and leave the room when the nursery nurse came and stood in the doorway.

'How are you getting on?' she asked.

'Fine, thank you.'

'I really am surprised that Nurse Weiss advised you to do this. It's not normal practice at all.'

Hedda didn't know what to say, so she remained silent. She wondered how long the girl was going to stand there watching her with that critical expression on her face. But, to her relief, after a few moments, one of the other babies began to cry, so the nurse left Hedda alone.

Hedda listened for any sign of her returning, but when she was sure that the nursery nurse was occupied, she picked up her pack and crept out of the door.

Out on the landing, she looked around to check she was alone. She knew there was a back staircase in the tower at the end of the corridor that led down to the kitchens, so, holding the baby tight, she ran as fast as she could to the end of the corridor. There were no lights on, but she found the door to the tower quite easily. It opened at once and she went through and shut it behind her.

There were only tiny slit-like windows in the tower, but there was a full moon that night, which cast a ghostly light on the stone steps. Hedda crept down the spiral staircase, feeling her way down by the walls. The steps were uneven and once or twice she almost slipped, her heart thumping even faster in her chest when she did.

At last, she reached the bottom of the staircase and let herself out into a passage that led through to the kitchen. She stood there for a second, trying to locate the door that led out to a rear yard. She could hear the kitchen staff washing up, laughing and chatting, banging saucepans and plates about. The outside door was closer to the kitchen than she'd hoped, but she had no choice. She tiptoed across to it. At that point, she was in full view of the open kitchen door and if any of the staff had chosen that moment to come out of the kitchen, they would have seen her, but, thankfully, nobody did.

Hedda pulled the bolts back slowly and eased the door open. Of course, it squeaked, but there was so much noise going on in the kitchen that nobody noticed.

She was outside then, in a service yard, full of wooden crates and bottles and piles of firewood. She knew from her walks around the grounds that the track that wound up behind the castle went past the entrance to the yard. She crossed the yard quickly and then she was on the track, guided by the light of the moon. All she could hear was the rushing of the river in the valley below and the roaring of the waterfall down the ravine. She walked quickly, holding Evelina tightly to her. Luckily, the baby was quiet. It was a mild evening, warm for September. Hedda was thankful it wasn't winter.

It didn't take her long to reach the bridge. She walked onto it, pausing to look back at the castle. Despite everything that had happened there, the sight of it was still impressive, its round towers and ramparts soaring up from the mountainside, its steep roofs shining white in the moonlight, pinpricks of light spilling from behind blackout curtains in its many windows. She was grateful to be getting away from there, from the horrors and injustices of the place.

Hedda looked down at the waterfall, thundering over a ravine directly beneath her, and shuddered at the sight of it. She held Evelina even tighter to her chest as she crossed to the other side of the bridge and went straight to the ramshackle outbuilding beside it. She found a rotting door and pushed it open. It smelled damp inside. She guessed it must once have been a hut for hunters or foresters. It was empty now, apart from some piles of wood in one corner. It didn't look very promising, but it would have to do. After all, it was only for a few hours.

Evelina was growing restless now, so Hedda spread out her scarf on the hard earth floor and sat down on it and nursed the baby. As soon as it was light, she would leave the hut and find a route through the forest down to Füssen, then she would walk to the station and find a train. It didn't matter if she didn't get any sleep at all, she told herself. All she needed to do was to sit here quietly until morning.

She must have drifted off to sleep at some point, because

when she awoke, Evelina was stirring, light was coming through the slats of the shack, and there were terrifying sounds coming from outside. The shouts of men and the baying of dogs. Shaking with panic, Hedda gathered up her things and huddled behind the pile of logs, clutching Evelina to her, her heart in her mouth. Perhaps they were hunters after a deer, although it was very early for that. But within seconds the door of the hut burst open and an Alsatian bounded towards her, growling, its teeth bared. Hedda let out a scream and the dog was pulled back by its handler.

'Here she is!'

It was Holge Schwartz and a group of other men in uniform. They looked like Gestapo, but Hedda only got a fleeting glimpse of them. Everything happened in a blur. She was bundled out of the hut, Evelina was yanked from her arms and all she could hear were her own screams, and the rushing of the waterfall beneath her. She was dragged back to the castle, fighting all the way. She could hear Evelina's yells and it tore her heart to hear her baby in distress. She had nothing to lose then, she knew her plan had failed and that Evelina would be taken from her. She was taken directly to Doctor Finkel's room.

Doctor Finkel was there behind his desk, immaculate as ever, his face like thunder. 'You have done it now, my girl,' he seethed, as the men dragging her pushed her roughly down in a chair. 'What made you think you could leave like that and take the baby with you?'

Hedda remained silent. All she could think of was Evelina. Where had they taken her?

'Let me remind you, she is not yours to take. You have signed away any rights you might have had to her. She is now the property of the state and trying to remove her from here without permission is a criminal act.'

Hedda bowed her head and stared down at her shaking

knees, doing her best to calm down. Hysteria wasn't going to work with Doctor Finkel.

'I'm afraid I'm going to have to take some drastic steps to prevent this from happening again.'

Doctor Finkel came out from behind his desk and moved towards her. It was only when he was right in front of her and lunged at her arm that she saw he had a needle in his hand. There was a sharp pain in her arm and within seconds the room was tipping sideways and everything was going black.

That was two days ago. Someone must have carried her up to her room and laid her on her bed. She was unconscious for hours. Every time she surfaced, someone gave her another shot and she sank back into oblivion again. When finally, she was allowed to wake, Doctor Finkel was by her side. He put his cold hand on her arm and gave her a supercilious smile, making her flesh crawl.

'We have packed your bags and when you are dressed, we will put you on the train back to Munich,' he said. 'Your baby will be sent to a family with excellent Nazi credentials. They are arriving in a few hours. You can forget any of this ever happened.'

She felt too weak, too confused to argue. She registered in the deepest part of her being that she would never see her baby again.

Hedda watched the countryside roll by the train window and couldn't stop the tears falling. The train would be arriving in Munich soon and she had no choice but to go back to Aunt Ursula's. Now she was no longer pregnant, they might take her in. And when she was stronger, she would be able to leave and find a place of her own. She wondered where her baby was at that moment. Was she being cared for? Was she missing her mother's touch? It was agony not knowing, but one day, she vowed, she would find out.

TWENTY-FIVE

MARGARETE

Schloss Schwanburg, 1943

It took Margarete a while to find the name and address of Evelina's adoptive parents. It was difficult to get inside Doctor Finkel's room even after he had gone home in the evenings. Holge would often be lurking around in the corridor, making it impossible for her. The first time she tried, she entered the corridor just after Doctor Finkel had left the building. There was no one around, but just as she opened the key cupboard to get the key to the room out, she heard footsteps behind her. Turning, she saw Holge approaching. She immediately replaced the key on the hook and closed the cupboard.

'Can I help you, Nurse Weiss?' he asked.

She felt the colour creep into her cheeks. He had caught her red-handed. Her mind raced, wondering what she could say.

'I need to go inside Doctor Finkel's room for a moment. I believe I may have left my stethoscope on his desk when I was in there earlier,' she said. 'I can't seem to find it anywhere.'

He stared at her, frowning. 'That is most irregular, Nurse Weiss. Can't it wait until the morning when the doctor is back?'

'No,' she said, boldly looking him in the eye. 'I need to check on one of the newborns who has a slight fever.'

With a sigh, Holge himself went to the key cupboard, took Doctor Finkel's key from the hook and opened the door to the office. He waved Margarete inside, but stood in the doorway watching her while she made a show of looking on the desk and shelves.

'I'm afraid it's not there,' she said. 'I'll check upstairs again. Perhaps I left it in my room.'

She left, thwarted, while he replaced the key in the cupboard.

But the following week, she managed to get inside the office while Holge was out in the grounds, chatting to one of the gardeners. She retrieved the key to Finkel's desk, took the ledger out and copied down the name and address, her heart thumping.

Then she went upstairs to Tomas's room and knocked gently on the door.

When he opened it and saw her there, he took her in his arms. 'We need to get you away from here,' he said, holding her close and kissing her hair. 'You won't be able to hide your condition for much longer.'

Margarete had been wearing looser and looser skirts, but she knew he was right. If Doctor Finkel found out about her pregnancy, there would be serious repercussions for both of them. 'I know. I won't be able to fool people much longer. I saw Nurse Ekert staring at me yesterday, I hope she hasn't guessed the truth.'

'I'm going to persuade Finkel that you are exhausted and should be given three months off on health grounds. It's going to be tricky and I know he will object. You've not had much leave since you arrived here, have you?'

She shook her head. 'Only the odd couple of days here and there. And my father is very ill now too. It would be good to spend some time with him.' It would be wonderful to see Alicia and Mutti too. How she'd missed them, these past few months.

'All right, I will speak to Finkel. I'll have to pitch it carefully though. We don't want him deciding to examine you himself!'

Margarete shuddered and her eyes widened at the thought. 'No. That would be truly terrible.'

That afternoon, while Tomas spoke to Doctor Finkel, Margarete waited anxiously in her office. It seemed to take a long time, but at last Tomas came into the room and sat down with a sigh opposite her.

'He's finally agreed, although it was an uphill struggle,' he said. 'I said that your father is very ill and that is taking its toll on you. I reminded him how hard you've been working lately and how you've had so little leave since you've been here. He agreed to you leaving at the end of this week.'

Later, as Margarete packed, she wrestled with her feelings. It would be good to get away from the scene of so much trauma and heartache and to have her baby well away from prying eyes at the castle. She had told her family her news on her last trip home, and they were all delighted for her.

'If you need to go back to work after the birth, Margarete, we can care for your baby here,' her mother had told her. 'It would be a pleasure to return the favour you did for me so many times in the past.' Margarete instantly knew that she was alluding to how Margarete had spent a large part of her childhood caring for her younger brothers and sisters. She had put her arms around her mother then and held her tight, tears in her eyes, thinking of the tragedy and sadness that surrounded her memories of those years.

Now she was looking forward to the birth of her child, but that feeling of anticipation was tinged with a sense of sadness that Tomas wouldn't be there with her.

'I'm sad too,' he said, looking into her eyes and stroking her cheek a couple of days before she was due to leave. 'But I will be with you in spirit every second of the day, and I will come and visit you as soon as I can after the birth. But it will take a lot for Finkel to let me go away while you're not here.'

'You're right,' she said. 'But we can write to each other. I will ask Mutti or Alicia to address the envelopes though, or Holge will recognise my writing.'

Tomas kissed her. 'You think of everything, Margarete,' he said. 'I'm not sure I can bear to part with you, but this seems to be the only way. And it won't be long before we're together again.'

'I wish we could have done more for the babies,' Margarete confessed.

'We have done a lot, Margarete. Please hold onto the thought that many babies would have been sent for euthanasia if we hadn't intervened. And your notebooks are so important. You've risked so much for them.'

She nodded. 'I just wish I could have done more.'

On the day she left in the black Ministry car, Tomas stood beside Doctor Finkel on the front steps alongside Nurse Ekert to say a formal goodbye. It felt awkward having to leave him with a Heil Hitler salute, as she did with the others, but as their eyes met, she saw the warmth of his love in his. The memory of his hot skin against hers the night before came back to her and she felt the blood rush to her cheeks. She looked back through the rear window of the car at them standing on the castle steps as the vehicle drew away. She wished it didn't have to be like this and that she and Tomas could have been together properly at this momentous time in their lives, but she was doing this for their baby; one day they would be together.

Alicia came to meet Margarete at the Anhalter Bahnhof station in Berlin, and Margarete's heart soared to see her sister's face in the crowd. They rushed to each other and embraced for a long time. Margarete couldn't help noticing that Alicia had grown thinner since she'd last seen her.

'How are you all?' Margarete asked as they walked towards the tram stop together, Alicia carrying her suitcase.

'Papa is in a bad way. He's going downhill all the time. And food is getting harder and harder to get every day, but we're struggling on. They are both looking forward to seeing you, Margarete. They've been talking of little else for days.'

The tram rattled towards their district just west of the centre and Margarete was shocked to see, just as she had in Munich, the evidence of Allied bombing raids: wrecked buildings lying in heaps of rubble, destroyed churches, shops and apartment blocks, often with their inside walls and upper floors exposed to the street.

'There have been a few bombing raids here,' Alicia explained. 'There were two last week, a couple of nights apart. Lots of areas have been destroyed. We could see the firestorms from the apartment. We were terrified one of them would hit us and it was really frightening. Did you read about it?'

'Of course not,' Margarete said, keeping her voice down. 'You know all we get in the papers is Nazi propaganda. They are never going to report anything like that. That's why it's all the more shocking to actually be here and to see it as it is.'

She felt a stab of guilt that her family had had to deal with all this. She'd had no sense of the scale of things before. Was this a safe place to be giving birth?

'I'm still doing what I can for the Resistance, distributing leaflets wherever possible, helping Jewish families in hiding. But I've also been helping out in the shelters, for the homeless,' Alicia said. 'So many people have lost their homes through the bombing raids. Children have been orphaned. They have nothing.'

'You're so brave,' Margarete said.

'I'm not brave, I'm just doing what needs to be done. I'm sure you're doing what you can too, aren't you?' Alicia asked with a sideways glance.

'Of course, but sometimes I think it's a losing battle.'

When they arrived at the tenement block and struggled up the stairs, Margarete was shocked at how thin both her parents looked and how much her father had deteriorated since her last visit, only a few months before. She embraced them both, crying tears of joy, glad to be home at last.

'You are definitely showing now, my darling,' her mother said, holding her tight. 'It's good that you came away when you did.'

Margarete quickly slipped back into the daily routine of the household, helping her mother to queue for food, clean the apartment, prepare the evening meal and care for her father. Sometimes it felt as though she'd never been away and that Schloss Schwanburg and everything that had happened there was just a mirage. But her growing girth was a constant reminder that it wasn't all a dream, and that within a few weeks, she would become a mother and her life would change for ever.

She prayed for a letter from Tomas, watching anxiously from the window as the postman approached the apartment block each day. After a few days, her prayers were answered, and thereafter she and Tomas wrote to each other almost every day. His letters were full of loving words and news of everyday events at the castle. More babies were born and adopted, and Tomas mentioned in thinly disguised terms that he'd had to forge at least two certificates recently to prevent babies with physical problems from being sent to Aktion T4. Margarete worried for him. She knew he had to do it, but each time he did, he was putting himself at risk, putting his own life on the line.

Margarete had been at home for almost two months when Tomas's letters stopped coming. She'd always waited for him to confirm he'd received one of hers and that he'd destroyed it before writing back, in case any of the letters went astray. But, suddenly, he stopped responding. She thought back over his past few letters. She thought about the forged certificates. Perhaps Finkel had discovered what he'd done? She felt sick at the thought. Or perhaps there was some other explanation for his silence? Perhaps he'd fallen out of love with her? No, how could that be possible? His last letter had been full of protestations of love.

She barely slept that night, thinking about it, and in the morning, when she awoke there was another, even more pressing matter on her mind. Intense pains were gripping her lower abdomen and radiating up through her torso. How could this be? Her baby was at least a month early. Perhaps the stress of the previous day had brought it on. But there was no doubt about it, she was in labour, and judging by the length of time between contractions, she was already quite well advanced.

Margarete staggered out into the hallway and knocked on her parents' bedroom door. 'Mutti, my baby is coming,' she said.

Her mother rushed out in her nightgown, pulling on a coat, her eyes bleary with sleep. 'I will go and get Doctor Lessing. Just sit yourself down in the living room and take it easy. I won't be long.'

The labour was short and swift. Margarete had watched so many babies being born that she knew all the stages intimately and she knew what would help her and what would slow things down. But, even so, she still hadn't anticipated the intensity of the pain her body would have to withstand, and its severity shocked and surprised her. Her mind strayed many times to Tomas between contractions. She yearned for him, and she feared for him too. If only he could have been here to witness the birth of their child, to hold her hand, to mop her brow. Where was he now? Was he in his room at Schloss Schwanburg thinking about her, perhaps even writing her a letter that very moment? Or was he in some Gestapo cell somewhere being beaten and tortured, or lying in a bunk in a concentration camp? If only she knew he was safe.

Clutching her mother's hand tightly, half delirious with pain, she called out Tomas's name again and again.

'It's all right, my darling,' her mother kept saying, while Alicia mopped her brow and massaged her shoulders.

The baby came in the middle of the afternoon and Doctor Lessing, who had delivered Margarete herself and all her siblings, handed the screaming bundle to her wrapped in a sheet.

'It's a girl, Margarete. A beautiful girl. Well done.'

Margarete looked down into her daughter's face and tiny beady eyes looked up at her. She felt an instant connection with the little soul in her arms. She could see Tomas in her face and in her colouring.

'I will call her Tomasina,' she said. 'After her father.'

TWENTY-SIX

HEDDA

Munich, 1943

When Hedda arrived back in Munich from Schloss Schwanburg, it took all her courage to return to her aunt and uncle's flat. But she had no choice. Still feeling weak from her ordeal at the hands of the Gestapo, she dragged her suitcase through the streets, noticing how even in the few months that she'd been at the castle there had been more bombing raids. More buildings had now been reduced to heaps of rubble, where stray dogs rooted for food scraps and children climbed on broken walls.

When she knocked on the apartment door, Ursula answered. She looked only mildly surprised to see Hedda, but pulled back the door and let her in.

'Where is your baby?' Ursula asked instantly.

Hedda's eyes welled with tears. 'They took her. For adoption,' she muttered.

Her aunt handed her a cup of hot soup and sat her down at the table. 'It's probably for the best,' she said. 'After all, you had no way of caring for her yourself.'

Hedda didn't reply. Her aunt wouldn't understand, she'd never had to give up a child, so Hedda decided there was no point in discussing it with her. The only way she could see to deal with her situation was to bottle up her grief and get on with life. She wasn't the only one. She only had to look around her to see so many people who were suffering; losing family members in bombing raids or in battle, being dragged off to concentration camps or work camps, freezing to death or being shot down on the Eastern Front in Russia. Her loss was a drop in the ocean in comparison with so much human suffering. But even so, she couldn't get the image of Evelina's face out of her mind: her soft skin, her silky, blonde hair. She would take out the little snip of hair she'd cut from Evelina's head and stroke it, conjuring up memories of the musky smell of her baby skin.

'Your uncle is working long shifts at the factory,' Aunt Ursula said. 'They are stepping up weapons production for the war effort. So, he's not here at the moment. In fact, on his evenings off, he is often at fundraising rallies for the Party. I will talk to him about you coming back. As long as you're willing to help out with the chores again?'

'Of course,' Hedda sighed. What else could she expect?

So, Hedda's life resumed much the same as it had been before she'd gone to Schloss Schwanburg. Each morning, she got her cousins' breakfast, took them to school, then returned and worked hard in the apartment. Her cousins had been delighted to see her back; the boys jumped on her with glee when they came home from school that day and Gisela put her arms around her and kissed her on the cheek. Even her uncle accepted her presence without comment. He seemed too preoc-cupied to concern himself with her.

Although Hedda busied herself about the apartment, trying to lose herself in day-to-day tasks, she was sinking deeper and deeper into depression. She could not get over how her baby had been taken from her, and the longing occupied her mind from morning until night. It obsessed her, but it also made her feel powerless and frustrated. She wondered too about Sebastian, despite the fact that the thought of him repulsed her now. He was still her baby's father. Was he back in Russia on the front line, brutalising civilians again?

And there was something else looming on the horizon. During the second week, Ursula asked Hedda if she would go along to a Nazi fundraising rally with her.

'What about the boys? Don't you want me to look after them?' Hedda asked, looking for an excuse not to go.

'They're coming too. They are both in the junior branch of the Hitler youth now and they love coming along to rallies.'

'I think I'll stay at home anyway,' Hedda replied. 'I don't feel up to company. I'm still feeling a little fragile after the birth, you know.'

Her aunt looked at her with raised eyebrows, hands on her hips. 'You need to do your bit for the Fatherland, Hedda. Your Führer needs your help more than ever now. Stay at home tonight, but I will expect you to come along next time.'

That was something Hedda simply could not do. After her treatment at Nazi hands, after they had taken her baby, and with everything she knew about them, how could she go along to rallies as if she was a believer in the cause? It would feel like a betrayal of everything she'd been through. But she knew that her aunt and uncle would make life very difficult for her if she didn't comply with their wishes.

Two days later, the subject arose again. This time, it was her uncle asking her to go to a Nazi meeting.

'I think I'll just stay at home,' she said.

'That isn't an option, I'm afraid,' her uncle replied. 'You've brought enough trouble on this family already and I'm not having people saying I'm harbouring an enemy of the regime in my home. Either you come this evening or I will be telling the block warden that you have anti-Nazi views and letting them deal with you.'

The block warden was a poisonous-looking woman whose job it was to ensure everyone in her allocated neighbourhood was complying with Nazi rules and ideology. Hedda had seen her going from door to door, checking up on people, writing notes on a clipboard. She'd also seen her accompany members of the Gestapo to knock on people's doors and drag them away, never to be seen again.

'I won't come this evening, Uncle, but you can say I'm unwell. Tomorrow I will leave, I don't want to put you at risk by being here.'

'As you wish,' he said coldly and left with the rest of the family for the meeting.

There was no choice for Hedda but to find a job and move out of the apartment. The next morning, she went out and started tramping the streets looking for a job. She had no luck in the shops and businesses around. The shortages of war and the destruction of the bombings meant that most were struggling just to stay open. No one had enough funds to employ a new member of staff. But there was a small labour exchange near the Hauptbahnhof and, without holding out much hope, Hedda went inside and completed a form.

'There are no jobs around here, I'm afraid,' the young woman behind the desk told her. 'But there are one or two openings in Berlin for someone who can type. Would you be prepared to travel?'

'Of course,' Hedda replied, nerves rushing through her at the thought of leaving the place where she'd grown up and everything she'd ever known, but at least she wouldn't be at the mercy of her aunt and uncle anymore.

The next morning, she was heading off on the train to Berlin with no regrets. She had packed her belongings yet again and heaved her suitcase out into the hallway.

'Good luck, Hedda,' her aunt had said grudgingly, but Hedda could see the relief in her eyes. Her uncle hadn't bothered to get up from his armchair. The children had clung to her, crying.

'Don't go, Hedda,' Gisela had kept saying.

'I must,' she'd replied. 'Now please let me go or I'll miss my train.'

In Berlin, Hedda found a women's hostel to lodge in where there were many single women like herself who had lost family to the war and were trying to make their way in the world. She went from there by tram daily to the headquarters of Schering Pharmaceuticals in Wedding and typed up letters and reports for the managers all day. Her life was boring and routine, but she welcomed the chance to lead a simple, ordinary existence. She just wanted to forget everything that had happened and move on, but there was always a part of her that wondered about little Evelina and where she was at any given moment.

She followed the events of the war with horrified fascination, constantly willing the Allies to win through. When, in April 1945, the Russians finally broke into Berlin and the city became a war zone, Hedda and the other girls from the hostel sheltered in the cellar for days listening to the shelling and fighting in the streets outside. From a ventilation slit, they watched in awe as Russian tanks rolled through the city. The next day, a Russian soldier pulled open the door to the cellar and told them it was safe to come out. They struggled out onto a street that was unrecognisable from when they'd gone down to hide. People staggered about in clouds of dust in the post-apocalyptic landscape. The buildings were razed to the ground, piles of rubble replacing them. Any walls that remained standing were riddled with bullet holes. Despite the devastation, Hedda was pleased. All this meant that at last, for the first time in her memory, Germany was free of the Nazis. But all the same, this pleasure was tainted by the loss of Evelina, which ate at her constantly.

It was at a charity event for returning German soldiers that she met Hari. She knew as soon as she saw him that there was something special about him, something that set him apart from all the other soldiers in the room. He was dressed in rags and emaciated from months of starvation on the Eastern Front. Hedda was in charge of a stall that was doling out new clothes. He approached the stall and started rummaging through the second-hand clothes.

'Can I help you with something?' Hedda asked and he looked up into her eyes. As soon as their eyes met, she knew that Hari was a kindred spirit.

'Anything would do,' he said. 'I've got literally nothing. While I was away, my home was bombed.'

'Oh no. That's terrible,' she said, and her heart went out to him as she recalled her own experience. 'How about these trousers? They look as though they might fit you.' She held up a pair of grey, plaid trousers that were at least clean and free from holes.

He spent a long time trying them on behind a curtain, together with a couple of cotton shirts, coming out each time to seek her opinion. She wondered, after a while, if he was prolonging his time there in order to speak to her. She didn't mind if he was, she was enjoying speaking to him.

At the end of the afternoon, he went off with a bundle of clothes under his arm, but he came back the following day. 'I forgot about shoes,' he said, smiling into her eyes.

While she dug out all the shoes that would fit him, they got talking and Hedda realised that Hari was an intelligent, thoughtful person who'd had no desire to fight.

'Honestly, it was totally alien to my nature. I'm just a simple scientist at heart. I was terrified of battle. It's a miracle I survived really. I never wanted to fire my gun at all.'

She smiled at him, thinking of Sebastian and the way he had revelled in the killing. It was Hari's pacifist streak that drew her to him powerfully. That and his beautiful, dark eyes that lit up whenever they rested on her face.

That second afternoon, he asked if he could see her again.

'We could go to the Botanical Gardens. A lot has been destroyed by the bombings, but they are rebuilding the museum already. It would be a nice place to spend an afternoon.' For the first time since she'd lost Evelina, she found herself having something to look forward to.

She met him outside the gates the following day at 2 p.m. and he guided her around the remains of the gardens, pointing out different plants and interesting facts about them. It was an unusual place to meet, but the choice was typical of Hari and his unique take on the world. As they walked around the flower beds arm in arm, to the sound of hammers and saws of builders working on the museum, she realised that she'd never met anyone who made her feel quite so safe before, anyone she trusted as much.

She wasn't ready for love, she wasn't ready to forgive herself, but Hari was kind and patient and he brought her out of her shell with humour and love. They married in a quiet ceremony in September 1945 with only a few friends and colleagues in attendance. Hedda didn't invite her aunt and uncle. They hadn't been in touch since she'd walked out of the apartment in 1944, so she didn't even tell them she was getting married.

When she and Hari emerged from the church together that day, Hedda felt happiness for the first time in a long while. She knew she was starting a new chapter in her life. All she wanted to do was to put the past behind her, and at that moment she decided that Hari didn't ever need to know about Lebensborn or what had happened to her at Schloss Schwanburg. She didn't want him to know that she'd slept with an SS Officer and borne his child. How could she ever explain that to Hari? He would never trust her again. She felt as though she'd been given a second chance at happiness and she didn't want to jeopardise that, although she would carry the memory of Evelina in her heart forever.

Now all these years later, Hedda sat cradling the neighbour's baby, Leon, to her, rocking him back and forth, reliving those memories. He had been good, he'd hardly cried at all. He'd taken a bottle, chuckled when she'd changed his nappy, and had lain happily on a towel in front of the fire while she dangled objects above him to amuse him. She loved the way he reached out and tried to bat the objects aside and how his little face broke into a delightful smile.

If only she and Hari had been able to have children. How different their lives would have been. He wouldn't have lived out his years alone, estranged from her because of the depth of her pain.

For years, they had tried to conceive, but she suffered many miscarriages. She could never carry a baby to term. That had intensified her grief about baby Evelina. She blamed herself for her inability to have a child, thinking she was being punished for what had happened during the war. She was sure that the bungled forceps delivery by Doctor Finkel had damaged her for life.

The years wore on. In 1960, Hedda became pregnant again. Hari was ecstatic when she told him, covering her face with kisses. 'At last, Hedda. Let's hope and pray that this time we will be lucky.'

He made her rest up from that day and waited on her hand and foot so she didn't have to exert herself. She could see how excited he was and how having a child would mean everything to him, but in the pit of her stomach was that old familiar dread that her body was damaged, that she'd never be able to have another child.

Sure enough, at six months, she awoke in the night to stomach cramps and when she got out of bed, she saw that the sheets were stained with blood. Hari rushed her to hospital, but it was too late – a stillborn baby girl was born in the middle of the night.

Two days later, they went back to the empty house. Hedda stood in the doorway of the nursery that Hari had lovingly decorated and felt numb with grief. She knew that was the end, and that she would never try for another child. Losing yet another baby had exerted such a physical and emotional strain on her.

She felt Hari's arms around her. 'Don't blame yourself, Hedda,' he said and she turned angrily towards him.

'Of course I do. It's all my fault,' she cried, running into her bedroom and throwing herself onto the bed.

He came and put his arms around her again, but she shrugged them off.

'I need to be alone,' she said and heard him leave the room quietly. Poor Hari, he would never understand, and she would never be able to tell him the truth.

That moment was the point at which Hedda began to withdraw from him. He was clearly mystified and hurt. He tried everything he could to get close to her again, but she rejected all his attempts. How could she let him into her heart when it was so broken? And she could never tell him why, it was too late and far too painful.

She began to long for Evelina. Where was she now? She must be a teenager. Was she in college? Where was she living? The pain of knowing that she was out there in the world oblivious to Hedda's existence was almost as bad as the grief of losing the baby.

Eventually, Hedda decided to try to find out what had happened to baby Evelina. Still wanting to hide the darkness of those years from him, she told Hari she was going to see a friend in Munich. Then she travelled back to Schloss Schwanburg alone. It was strange, all those years later, taking the train from Munich Hauptbahnhof to Füssen, looking out at the farms and villages which were unaltered since the war years. The closer she drew to Füssen, the more nervous she became. Was she doing the right thing? But something was compelling her to do this, whatever the consequences.

When she arrived at Füssen, she took a taxi up to the castle. She had no idea what to expect, but she hoped that there were some records remaining there that would enable her to finally track down her daughter.

The taxi dropped Hedda at the gatehouse. The place looked shabby and run-down, paint peeling from the window frames, ivy running wild over the walls. The once pristine garden was overgrown too, as if no one had tended it for years. It was a deep contrast to how the place had looked during the war years.

Nerves made her hands shake as she pulled hard on the bell-pull and listened to a distant bell echoing somewhere in the depths of the castle. No one came for what seemed like an age and Hedda was about to turn away and start her long walk back to the station when she heard footsteps shuffling and the sound of the bolts being drawn back.

The door creaked open and the wizened, grey face of a very old man peered out at her. Then he pulled the door back and straightened up. 'Yes? What can I do for you?'

With a start, she realised it was Holge Schwartz, the care-taker who had been the one who had tracked her down when she'd tried to escape with Evelina. Her blood ran cold in her veins at the sight of him. She'd thought he would have been arrested at the end of the war. He was the last person she had expected to see. But now she was here, and the door was open, she wasn't going to give up.

'I have come to see if you have any records from the war years,' she said.

'Who is asking?' His jaw jutted out, aggressively. She could see he was as belligerent as ever.

'My name is... was... Hedda Jenner. I had a baby girl here in September 1943. She was adopted and I was made to leave. I would like to find her now. So, if you have any records from back then...?'

Holge held out his hand as if stopping a train. 'You can stop there. There are no records from that time at all. They were all burned at the end of the war. You won't find anything to help you. I suggest you forget all about it.'

'Is there anyone else who might help me? Doctor Finkel? Nurse Ekert? Nurse Weiss? Doctor Müller?'

He shook his head and smiled an evil smile, displaying rotten teeth.

'None of them are here anymore. At the end of the war, they vanished into thin air. You are wasting your time, miss. I suggest you go home and forget any of it ever happened.'

He slammed the door in her face and she stood there, helpless, anger boiling inside her. She wanted to scream and shout, just as she'd done when they took Evelina from her.

TWENTY-SEVEN

MARGARETE

Schloss Schwanburg, 1944

Less than a month after the birth of her baby girl, Margarete found herself getting off a train at Füssen station after a long journey south from Berlin. Doctor Finkel had written to her at her parents' apartment to say that she must report back to work without delay, that three months' sabbatical was quite long enough, and that she was needed urgently at the castle.

She'd been devastated to leave Tomasina behind. Before she left, she'd held the tiny baby tight and had showered the plump little face with dozens of kisses. But Margarete knew her daughter would be in the best of hands with her mother and vowed to return to see her little girl as soon as she could.

As she walked out of the station at Füssen, her heart sank to see a black car waiting for her on the forecourt. Those sinister black vehicles represented the stifling grasp of the programme. Seeing it there reminded her that she was back within the control of Lebensborn again, and of everything she had been so glad to be away from for the past three months. Everything except Tomas.

She'd still had no word from him, and because he hadn't written to her after her last letter to him, she had been unable to take the risk of writing to tell him about the birth of their daughter. She worried constantly about what might have happened to him, waking up in cold sweats in the middle of the night, imagining him languishing in a cell, or being worked to death by the SS in a factory or a labour camp somewhere. Although she was living in dread at what she might find out, not knowing why Tomas hadn't responded to her letters was tearing her apart. At least going back to the castle she would have a chance of discovering what had happened to him. Perhaps knowing the truth would be better than living in that state of constant limbo.

The car roared up the final twists and turns of the castle drive, passed under the arch of the gatehouse and pulled up in the courtyard. Margarete's spirits sank yet again to see Doctor Finkel waiting for her on the front step with his clipboard. He was immaculately dressed as ever, his grey hair slicked back with oil. She had an incredible sense of déjà vu. It felt so much like the very first time she'd arrived at the castle back in 1938. How much more she knew about the place and what it stood for now, she reflected. She wondered if she'd known as much back then, she would ever have allowed herself to be persuaded to be part of it all. However, she hadn't had much choice about it at the time, she reminded herself, with Himmler's threats about her family fresh in her mind.

Doctor Finkel ushered her inside, took her straight to his office and sat her down opposite his desk.

'I asked you back to Schloss Schwanburg because I wanted to brief you about the next stages of the Lebensborn programme,' he said. 'I am pleased to say that the success of the programme has meant that it has proliferated and expanded way beyond the borders of our beloved Third Reich. Your skills and experience will prove vital in that expansion, Nurse Weiss. The fact is, you are to be posted abroad to another Lebensborn home in one of our occupied territories. You are being sent to Norway, to be precise.'

'Oh,' Margarete gasped in surprise, her mind going into overdrive, running over and over what that would mean for her and for Tomasina.

'We have recruited another senior nurse to fill your post here. She will be arriving later in the week. We also have a new doctor here too,' he said, glancing down at his papers.

'New doctor?' Her scalp prickled. So, her fears were confirmed. Tomas was no longer here. Where could he be? 'What about Doctor Müller?' she asked with trepidation.

Doctor Finkel cleared his throat. 'Ah... Doctor Müller proved unworthy of his role, I'm afraid,' he said coldly. 'I discovered a number of health certificates he'd signed off that bore no relation to the physical state of the children they described. That meant that babies who were less than physically perfect had been sent out for adoption, thus tainting the name of the programme in the eyes of the public and, more importantly, in the eyes of the SS. He has left a damaging legacy and one which I sought to distance myself from as soon as I possibly could.'

'So... where is Doctor Müller now?' Margarete asked.

Doctor Finkel eyed her with his sharp gaze. 'It is really no business of yours, Nurse Weiss, but since you and the doctor were colleagues, I understand that you might be concerned about him. So, I shall tell you the unvarnished truth. Doctor Müller was questioned here at the castle by the Gestapo and then taken into custody in Gestapo HQ in Munich. I believe he has since been transported to Dachau.'

An involuntary gasp flew from Margarete's mouth at the shock of his words. Everything around her seemed to go into a blur and for a moment she thought she might faint. How could she bear this? Her dear Tomas, the noblest, kindest, bravest man she'd ever known, being starved and beaten by the SS sadists who ran that camp. He would never get to see his beautiful baby girl now.

'You have gone quite pale, Nurse Weiss.' Doctor Finkel's voice broke into her thoughts and she was aware that his critical eyes were fixed on her face. 'I can only suppose that it is through your natural kindness and concern for a former colleague, and I'm prepared to overlook it on this occasion. Doctor Müller's behaviour and actions put the whole programme in jeopardy, so you should not waste your sympathy on him. Now, let us get on with the business of the day – I need to tell you all about the important developments of the programme and what your duties will consist of in Norway. You will stay here tonight, then start on your onward journey tomorrow morning.'

But Margarete was hardly listening to what Doctor Finkel went on to say. She was thinking of Tomas, the father of her child, the only man she'd ever loved, with his beautiful eyes and gentle touch. Her heart ached for him, her mind ran wild imagining what might be happening to him that very moment. How could she go on working for the programme, for the very beasts who had handed him over to those sadists?

But there was little time for grief. The next morning, she was off again, whisked away in that black car back to Füssen station. There, she got a train back to Munich, from where, the following day, she was transported by air to Oslo. She went through the motions, barely noticing the journey. She was an empty shell – a husk of her former self. She didn't know how to carry on, she had no idea how she would ever get over losing Tomas, but she didn't know how to escape from the programme either. If she tried anything, they would surely take her family, and that would be worse than ever now. Baby Tomasina would have nobody.

. . .

Margarete had been talking to Kristel and Lorenzo for what felt like hours. She tailed off, drained by reliving the most difficult part of her past.

'How long were you in Norway?' Kristel asked gently after a pause.

'I don't know. A few months. Perhaps a little more. Terrible things happened there too. I can't begin to describe them.'

'And your daughter, Tomasina? What happened to her?'

Margarete closed her eyes and waved the question away. 'I can't talk about her. Please forgive me. I cannot. It is just too painful.'

'I understand,' Kristel said. 'Perhaps another time, when you're feeling stronger maybe?'

Margarete didn't reply. Hadn't she told them enough?

'And what happened when you went back to Germany?' Kristel asked, once again after a lengthy pause. 'Were you still with the Lebensborn at that point?'

Margarete nodded, the shadows of memories passing her eyes. 'Dreadful things had happened while I was away...' she said, almost to herself. 'But when I came back from Norway, I was sent to manage another home. This one was very different from Schloss Schwanburg and the Lebensborn home I managed in Norway.'

'Different?'

'Well, it wasn't a maternity home. It was a testing and Germanisation centre.'

Kristel's eyes widened. 'A Germanisation centre?' she repeated, an involuntary shudder passing through her. 'I don't know what that is. Perhaps we can talk about that another time too?'

'It was an evil place. I'm not sure I want to.'

Kristel said, 'I understand... but what about your notebooks?'

Of course. Margarete had known she would have to return to them at some point.

'Before I tell you about them, I should mention that I tried to track Hedda Jenner down. When I returned to Germany from Norway, I passed through Munich again. I had her address with me of course, it was in my notebook.

'I went to the apartment where her aunt and uncle lived. It was a squalid place, in a terrible area, poorly kept and filthy. I was nervous about going into the block and when I neared the apartment, I could hear shouting coming from inside. A man and a woman were arguing hammer and tongs. I had to knock several times before anyone heard me. Eventually, the woman came to the door. She looked rather brash, with dyed red hair. I could tell from the way she looked at me that she was an aggressive woman. It was obviously the Aunt Ursula that Hedda had spoken to me about. I told her I was looking for Hedda, that I was with the Lebensborn programme.

'She started swearing at *me* then, hurling insult after insult at me. I was quite shocked and started to back away. "You ruined my niece, corrupted her, turned her against us. If it wasn't for you, she would still be alive," she said.

'I couldn't believe what I was hearing. I stood there, my mouth open. The woman lunged towards me and shouted at me: "Yes, she's dead. Took her own life. A few weeks after she came back from your rotten castle. Square that with your conscience, and your precious programme."

'I turned around and walked away, trembling with shock. At that point, I was at rock bottom. I had lost Tomas and I'd failed Hedda terribly. I knew that it was because of me that she died.'

'That's so sad, Margarete,' Kristel said, leaning forward and taking Margarete's hand. 'What a terrible thing to happen. But you shouldn't have blamed yourself. You did what you could.'

Margarete stared at her. 'Yes. But it wasn't enough, was it? And I've had to live with that for the rest of my life.'

'It wasn't your fault, Margarete,' Lorenzo said. 'You were incredibly brave... writing those notebooks.'

'Ah... the notebooks,' Margarete said. 'I suppose now I must tell you what happened to them, and the reason why I have never been able to use them to unite mothers and children as I'd intended.'

One day, in April 1945, Margarete was called away from the home she was managing near Berlin. The orders came right from the top – Heinrich Himmler had signed them personally. Margarete knew that the war was almost over. She understood, reading between the headlines of the news reports, that Hitler had retreated to his bunker under the Chancellery in Berlin and that the Allies had crossed the Rhine and were already overrunning western Germany and closing in on German cities. She felt relief at the news, but it was tempered by everything she'd seen and the thought of those she'd lost.

The orders told her to pack her bags and report back to Schloss Schwanburg without delay. There was an SS car waiting outside her building to take her there. She left the home she was managing with mixed feelings. She didn't want to give up on the children there, but she was leaving the place in the capable hands of her deputy, whom she trusted.

'If the Allies arrive, whatever you do, don't evacuate the home. The children will have a better chance of surviving and finding their families if they are left where they are,' she told her. She realised that leaving the home as it was would provide useful evidence for the Allies too. They would instantly see what Lebensborn was all about. Those in charge of that evil programme would surely be punished, although would anyone ever believe that she'd tried to work against it?

The driver rushed her straight to Bavaria, through a devastated landscape, towns and villages that had been blown apart, some of them just piles of bricks. They drove past columns of refugees travelling with all their worldly goods, including furniture piled on handcarts or old prams. They were fleeing the advance of the front line, she realised, but where they were going, she had no idea. Would this mean that Tomas had been released from Dachau and that they would be reunited one day?

It was chaos at Schloss Schwanburg when Margarete arrived. She carried her secret notebooks with her, as she always did. She'd taken kept them by her side wherever she'd been. Many black SS cars, just like the one she'd arrived in were drawn up in the courtyard. When she entered the great hall, it was thronging with restless people, sitting around on their luggage, waiting. She quickly realised that there were no mothers and babies here any longer, but she spotted some of the former staff, including Doctor Finkel and Nurse Ekert. Several middle-ranking SS officers and their families had also taken up residence and were frantically debating how to save their own skins. They were all terrified that the Allies were going to overrun the place and that they would be captured. It was no less than they deserved, Margarete thought.

As she passed through the hall, Margarete overheard some of their fevered discussions. They were all making plans for their escape down the Brenner Pass, through Austria and into Italy. Cars were setting off from the castle at regular intervals to take them and their families away.

Through the back windows, she saw that a huge bonfire was burning out on the lawn. Margarete was shocked to see Holge Schwartz. He kept emerging from the building with armfuls of files, throwing them on the blaze. Papers were going up in smoke. She knew that the castle records were being destroyed. Watching the fires, her heart sank. Would the world ever know what had happened here? She thought of her notebooks then and how much more important they had become.

An officer with a clipboard told Margarete to report to an SS administrative officer who had an office in the cellars of the castle. She went down the dungeon-like stone steps and made her way along the vaulted passages to where the man sat behind a desk in a cave-like office. When she entered, he looked her up and down, found her name on his list, then handed her some false identity papers. She looked down at the Italian passport. Margharita Bianca, the Italian version of herself, smiled back at her from the photograph.

'Wait upstairs in the hall with the others. A car will soon arrive to take you. You will be travelling with an SS officer and his family.'

Margarete wasn't sure that she wanted to share a car with a member of the SS. She didn't want to be associated with them in any way. She knew that running away with them would make it look as though she was working for them and aligned with their views. How could she avoid that happening?

Margarete picked up her bag, and as she turned to leave, the man must have seen something in her eyes that he found suspicious, because without warning he stood up.

'Halt!' he said, making her start. 'I need to search you before you leave.'

Her heart was pounding against her ribs when he came up to her, drawing a gun from the holster on his hip. He grabbed her bag and started to riffle through it. As she'd dreaded, he found one of the two notebooks straight away, lifting it out, flicking through the pages and holding it up to her face with a malicious smile.

'What is this? About to betray the Fatherland?' he asked, peering at her with narrowed eyes.

She shook her head quickly. 'No! No! It is only a few notes,' she said, 'It's just a game I play to amuse myself,' but she knew that guilt was written all over her face.

She had the other notebook tucked inside her underwear.

She'd done that in the last few minutes as a precaution, suddenly worried that she might be searched before she left. He started to frisk her, from the shoulders downwards. He was almost at her waist. Margarete knew she couldn't let that happen. She didn't know what came over her – the man had a gun – but she shoved him aside with a violent push. The gun dropped from his hand and she ran hell for leather out of the door and along the underground passage.

As her feet pounded on the flagstones, Margarete could hear the man running after her, yelling for her to stop. Her heart was in her mouth. Rounding a bend in the passage, she saw a ventilation shaft built into the wall. Without pausing for thought, she climbed up inside it and hid a little way up round a bend. She waited, listening. Then she heard the man's footsteps running past. She knew there was only one way to save herself from there. She turned and crawled up the shaft. It was steep, but only a few metres long. When she reached the top, she broke the flimsy mesh grille that covered it and clambered out into the castle grounds.

Straightening up and looking around her, she gauged instantly where she was. She was near the edge of the castle grounds, almost at the ravine. She could hear the waterfall thundering over it. Walking slowly, under the cover of the trees, Margarete managed to find her way through the trees and across the bridge to an old disused building beside the waterfall. There, she rested for a short time, recovering from the panic of the encounter with the SS officer, allowing her heartbeat to slow down.

When she was able, she pushed on, through the forest, down the hill and back to the main road. She knew she had to avoid the station at Füssen and the centre of the town. The SS and their dogs would be waiting for her.

As she walked, she decided that the safest thing to do would

be to make her own way down to Italy. One day she would
come back, she told herself, and look for Tomas. She wasn't sure
of the way, and she had very little money with her, but, using
the sun as a guide, she headed south. She figured that if she just
kept going south, she would get to Italy one day.

It took a couple of weeks. Sometimes, Margarete managed
to hitch lifts on lorries and with other assorted Germans who
were streaming out of Germany. Then, before she got to the
Italian border at Brenner, she left the roads behind and struck
out on foot through the mountains. She wanted to avoid the
border post at Brenner, not trusting her papers. There was a
well-trodden path through the hills. Along the route, Margarete
met many people leaving Germany that way.

Some nights, she slept out in the open, on others she stayed
in mountain refuges. Luckily, it was early spring and the
weather was fine. She kept the one notebook she'd managed to
save with her, but she was furious that the second one had been
taken from her by the SS – the one with the details of the adoptive parents. Without that, she knew that all her efforts would
be fruitless.

She walked for days, scavenging on scraps and bits of bread
that kind locals handed out. She had no Italian money and
could only say a few words of Italian. But she struggled on until
she found a little town on the Brenta river, just south of the
Dolomites – Bassano del Grappa. It was an attractive place in
the shadow of the mountains, and as soon as she entered the
main square, and a local café owner greeted her warmly and,
seeing her condition, offered her food, Margarete decided to
make it her home.

'After the war,' Margarete told Kristel and Lorenzo, 'I managed
to find a cleaning job in a small hospital in the town. I made a

huge effort to learn Italian. I needed to blend in. Secretly, alone
in my lodgings, I followed the Nuremberg Trials in the newspapers, and saw some of those responsible for the Lebensborn
programme sentenced: Doctor Finkel, Jutta Koch, Professor
Wagner. But their sentences seemed too lenient. I still planned
to go back to Germany one day, but was too afraid at that point.
But every day I pined for Tomas, for Tomasina, for my family.

'I was terrified of being discovered. I knew that no one
would believe I'd tried to do anything against the Lebensborn
programme and in their eyes, I would look as guilty as Doctor
Finkel and the others. I felt powerless to change that, just as I
had throughout the Nazi era. Most frustrating of all, I couldn't
remember any of the names and addresses of the adoptive
parents, no matter how hard I tried. Ever since that time, I've
been haunted by what happened during the war and by the fact
that all those babies were separated from their mothers at birth
– many, like Charlotte's and Hedda's, forcibly.

'I vowed to do everything I possibly could to make amends.
As soon as I could speak enough Italian, I managed to find a job
working in a Catholic orphanage high up in the Dolomites
behind Bassano. I threw myself into my work. I was glad to be
working alongside people who cared deeply about the babies
and children there. Even though I knew I was doing valuable
work, I still could not erase those terrible memories and my
regrets for what happened during the war. Caring for the babies
brought back bittersweet memories of my own daughter, of her
tiny eyes looking up at me, of her perfect skin, the smell of her.

'A few years after the war, when it felt safe to do so, I think
it was in the early 1950s, I took some leave and travelled back to
Bavaria, to Schloss Schwanburg. I wanted to see if, by some
miracle, any records had remained, from which I might have
been able to piece together the addresses of the adoptive
parents.

'I walked up the hill from Füssen to the castle, memories of my time there flooding back to me all the while. As I got closer to the castle, I saw that the place had gone to rack and ruin. The paintwork was shabby, the gardens overgrown, the once pristine walls covered in ivy and lichen. It felt very odd being back there. I stood in the courtyard, which was eerily silent. It took a lot of courage to ring the bell.

'I was astonished when Holge Schwartz, the old caretaker, opened the door. He recognised me instantly and glared at me. I remembered how he used to spy on me and Tomas, and how he'd worked against us.

'"You! What are you doing back here?" he said. "You worked with Müller, that worthless doctor, against the programme, didn't you? He was your lover, wasn't he? Well, I saw to it that he got his just deserts in Dachau. I know for a fact that he didn't survive that place. Your betrayal has not been forgotten or forgiven, Weiss. You should know that there are people who are still after you. The Third Reich lives on in some people's hearts, you know. There is a silent minority who are doing their best to keep the flame alight. So, why don't you just get lost now. There is nothing for you here. If you don't turn around and start walking back the way you came, I will make a few calls to my old associates. They will be very interested to talk to you."

'I didn't need to hear any more. I turned on my heel and walked quickly away, my dreams of finding any remaining records there thwarted. My head was reeling and my heart heavy for my darling Tomas. I would never hold him again, kiss his face, feel the touch of his hand on my hair. I couldn't bear to think of how he'd suffered, how he might have died in pain in that terrible place. My world was shattered now. I had lost everything I'd once held dear.

'I went straight back to Füssen and got on a train. I felt

angry and defeated. And ever since that day, no matter what I have done to make amends, I have been unable to do the thing I set out to do when I risked my life to compile those notebooks. That was to reunite mothers and babies – my one wish, all the time I worked for that hateful programme.'

TWENTY-EIGHT

KRISTEL

Trento, 2005

As Kristel and Lorenzo were leaving the care home, Kristel's phone bleeped and she saw that a text had arrived. She glanced down at it as she got into the car. It was from Joachim. He must have tried to call while she'd been talking to Margarete. He had texted her afterwards.

> *Leaving for Singapore tomorrow afternoon. It would be good to see you before I go if you can get back.*

Kristel stared at it in disbelief. What she'd resigned herself to, what she'd almost willed to happen, was now actually happening. She searched her heart, but there were no pangs of regret that he was leaving so soon.

She put the phone back in her bag. She couldn't call him now, not in the car with Lorenzo there.

Lorenzo drove her back to the hotel and pulled up in the forecourt.

'You haven't forgotten, have you?' he asked.

'Forgotten?'

'You said you would come to my place for supper this evening. I could take you straight there if you like?'

'Oh! Of course. I'm so sorry. I've been thinking about Margarete. I would love to come. I've just got one phone call to make.'

'OK. I'll wait in the car,' he said.

She hurried up to her room and dialled Joachim's number.

'Kristel, did you get my text?'

'Yes. I'll get up early and drive to Munich in the morning,' she said.

'Only if you want to. It's a very long way.'

'Joachim, of course I want to! I can't let you go without saying goodbye.' She felt she owed it to him and to their relationship to say goodbye.

'All right, if you're quite sure. I'll need to leave the flat at 3 o'clock, though.'

'It will only take me four hours or so. I'll be there by lunchtime,' she said. 'See you then.'

She ended the call, sat down on the bed and put her head in her hands. Her mind was racing. Everything was happening so quickly, and she couldn't work out how she felt about it, her emotions were in such a turmoil now, having heard his voice. But she put those thoughts aside and pulled herself together. She didn't want to let Lorenzo or his family down.

She went out to the car and Lorenzo was still there, the engine running, listening to a jazz station on the radio. He looked so calm and at ease with himself. She envied him that.

'OK? All set?' he asked, smiling into her eyes.

'Yes. I'm looking forward to meeting your parents,' she said, although in truth she felt a little nervous.

'And they you!' he replied, accelerating out of the driveway.

Lorenzo's parents lived in an apartment up in the hills on the edge of the town. It was dark outside, but the twinkling lights in the valley were visible from the front windows and Kristel got the sense of a fabulous, expansive view stretched out beneath them.

'Welcome, Kristel, we are so pleased to meet you!' Lorenzo's father, Pepe, greeted them in the hallway. He was a large man, with a friendly, welcoming face and a warm smile. He took her coat and beckoned for her to come into the kitchen.

Lorenzo's mother, Francesca, stood at the stove in an apron, stirring something in a saucepan. 'Welcome, Kristel,' she smiled. 'Thank you so much for visiting us. We love meeting Lorenzo's friends!'

Francesca looked frail, her skin was pale, but Kristel saw immediately that she was putting a brave face on her illness, trying to make everything as normal as she could. Kristel's heart immediately warmed to these down-to-earth, hospitable people.

'Sit down, sit down,' Francesca said, waving towards the table. 'Make yourself at home. Lorenzo will pour you some wine. The food will be ready in just a moment.'

'Thank you,' Kristel said, taking a seat at the table.

Lorenzo poured her a generous glass of red from a carafe. Kristel looked round her at the kitchen. It was warm and comfortable and a little old-fashioned, with a red-tiled floor and a tiled chimneypiece which housed the stove. There were many quirky, colourful paintings on the wall.

'Those are mine,' Francesca said, seeing her looking at them. 'My little hobby!'

'Hobby! She sells them in a shop in the town,' Pepe said, beaming with pride. 'Makes good money out of them too.'

'They are wonderful,' Kristel said, admiring the colourful still lifes and the studies of Trento landscapes and watercolours of the mountains.

'I haven't done much lately,' Francesca admitted. 'Lorenzo has told you about my recent troubles, no doubt?'

She brought two large bowls of pasta and ragout to the table and Pepe put a saucer of grated Parmesan cheese next to them.

'Yes, he did. I was so sorry to hear about it. I hope you are feeling better now?'

'I am. I have good days and bad days, though. Today is a good day,' Francesca said, smiling, and Kristel could see the genuine pleasure she was finding in cooking for her family and entertaining Kristel. With a pang, Kristel thought of her own mother and how she had never allowed herself to enjoy the simple pleasures of motherhood like this.

Conversation flowed easily, and the time raced by. After the meal was over, and they were sipping a digestif of grappa, Kristel looked up at the clock on the mantelpiece and saw that it was past ten o'clock.

'I really should be getting back to the hotel,' she said, with regret. 'I have an early start tomorrow.'

'Early start?' Lorenzo looked curious.

'Yes. I have to drive back to Munich in the morning. I'll be back here the following day though.'

'Oh? Something to do with work?' he asked.

She shook her head. 'I have to say goodbye to a friend, actually. He's going to work in Singapore, leaving tomorrow afternoon.'

Lorenzo didn't ask any more questions, but she could see from the look in his eyes that he would have liked to.

They left soon after that. Francesca and Pepe both held Kristel's hands warmly, kissing her on each cheek, and asked her to come back as soon as she could.

'I've so enjoyed this evening. It's wonderful to meet Lorenzo's friends,' Francesca said, and Kristel could see from the way her eyes shone that the evening had meant a lot to her.

In the car, Lorenzo asked in a voice that was studiedly casual, 'So, this friend who's off to Singapore... Is it someone special?'

'He was,' she said, deciding at last to tell him about the state of things with Joachim. 'In fact, we were engaged until shortly before I came to Trento. But I think it's over now. He's going to work in Singapore for a couple of years. Things haven't been great between us for a while.'

Lorenzo visibly relaxed. 'I'm sorry to pry,' he said. 'It's just that... well, I was hoping... that you didn't have anyone special back home.'

'And what about you?' she asked.

'I'm free, if you're interested?' he said, grinning.

Kristel laughed at the directness of his question. She realised that although it was said in a light-hearted manner, he was actually serious, and his question demanded an answer. At that moment, they pulled into the forecourt of the hotel.

Lorenzo looked at her enquiringly. 'Well?'

'I'm interested, Lorenzo,' she said. 'I'm very interested. Shall we talk about it when I get back?'

'I can't wait,' he said, leaning over and kissing her chastely on the cheek. 'Come back soon.'

Her heart was full of trepidation for what she would have to face in Munich with Joachim, but Lorenzo's words and his enquiry had sent a flicker of joy and anticipation through her.

Kristel got up early and set off for Munich before dawn. She watched the sunrise driving over the Brenner Pass, marvelling at the beauty of the golden dawn breaking over the mountains. She was dreading her encounter with Joachim, but she knew that there were things they both needed to say before he left. She didn't want him to leave with things between them in limbo as they were. She wanted them both to be able to move on without regret.

When she arrived at the flat on Marienplatz, Joachim's suitcases were packed and ready in the living room. The place looked pristine and smelled of pine cleaning fluid.

'I've packed up your things,' he said stiffly. 'They are in boxes in the bedroom. It would be good if you could make arrangements to have them removed before the end of the month, I have a new tenant coming in on the first.'

'Of course,' Kristel said.

'Would you like a drink?' Joachim asked, putting on the kettle.

'Tea would be lovely,' she replied.

'Thank you for coming,' he said. 'It's a really long way but I'm glad you did. There are things we need to talk about.'

'Yes, you're right,' she said, watching him put teabags into mugs and pour boiling water on them.

He put a cup in front of her and she sat up on one of the bar stools. He came and sat beside her.

'I've been thinking a lot about us since you went away,' he said. 'We've had a wonderful time together, Kristel, but we have to admit that things haven't been so great between us for a while now. Perhaps it would be best to acknowledge that and to have a clean break... now that I'm going away.'

Watching Joachim's face as he spoke, Kristel felt a pang of regret for all the good times they'd had together, for everything that might have been. But she knew he was right, and she was glad that he was brave enough to acknowledge the truth.

'I agree with you, Joachim,' she said. 'I really hope we can say goodbye on good terms, though.'

'I hope so too. I will always have fond memories of our time together,' he said.

'Me too.' She took a sip of tea and stood up. There didn't seem to be anything else to say and she noticed that Joachim kept looking at his watch. 'I'll leave you to get ready, then,' she said.

He put his arms around her and they hugged for a brief

moment and then she drew away and walked towards the door. She didn't want to hang around waiting for him to leave, mulling over the decision. It was made now, and she wanted to get out of there and on with the rest of her life.

Getting into her car that was parked on one of the back-streets behind Marienplatz, Kristel felt her heart lift. A great weight had lifted from her shoulders. She felt free for the first time in months.

She drove through the city centre and headed south towards the autobahn. On the slipway, she noticed a sign for Füssen and her heart skipped a beat. She had an idea. Why not head down that way and go and see Schloss Schwanburg for herself? Within seconds, she had made her mind up and she was heading south in the direction of Füssen. She turned up the radio and sang along to some West Coast rock.

It took three hours to drive to Füssen – there were hold-ups on the autobahn – and when Kristel arrived, she checked into a hotel in the centre of town. It was too late to attempt to visit the castle by then.

She'd been thinking about Lorenzo all the time she'd been driving, and she couldn't wait to speak to him. As soon as she got into her hotel room, she dialled his number and he answered straight away.

'Kristel. How's Munich?'

'I'm not in Munich actually. I'm in Füssen. I was thinking about paying a visit to the castle tomorrow morning before heading back to Trento.'

'What? Schloss Schwanburg?' He sounded surprised.

'Yes. Why not? It's sort of on the way back...'

He fell silent then and she could tell he was thinking carefully.

'Why don't I drive up to join you and we could go together?' he asked at last. 'I could bring Margarete with me...'

'Margarete?' Suddenly the visit was taking on a whole new

meaning. 'That's not a bad idea. But is she up to a journey? It's a very long way.'

'I could bring her in the care home minivan, as long as Ginetta is all right with it.'

'That sounds a great idea,' Kristel said. 'I just hope that Holge Schwartz isn't the caretaker there anymore!'

It was almost two o'clock the following day and Kristel was waiting impatiently outside the hotel in Füssen, shading her eyes with her hand and scanning the road for any sign of the minibus from Our Lady of Mercy.

That morning, she'd got up early and driven to the castle. The paint was peeling on the iron gates on the entrance from the main road and they'd stood open, so she'd taken a chance and driven up the winding, potholed road. It had snowed in the night and the surface was slippery, the forest either side of the road was dusted with snow, but Kristel was used to driving on ice and it didn't daunt her. In places, undergrowth was encroaching onto the road and she'd had to skirt carefully around it, but finally she had emerged through the gatehouse and stopped in the courtyard.

A builder's van had been parked up in front of the main entrance with ladders on the top, so there was a good chance somebody was about. Kristel had got out of the car. It was a lot shabbier than she'd expected, although Margarete had said it had already deteriorated when she'd last visited in the 1950s. Chills had gone through her at the thought of everything that had happened here during the war. Looking around her at the austere walls of the castle and the gatehouse, she had felt she already knew the place from Margarete's story.

Kristel had gone up to the entrance and pulled the rusting bell-pull beside the big wooden double doors. The bell had echoed inside, and she had heard footsteps on the flagstones, then the door was opened.

The man standing there was clearly not Holge Schwartz, who would have been older than Margarete. It was a middle-aged man with grey hair and glasses, dressed in blue overalls.

'I was expecting an electrician,' he had said, smiling. 'But I don't think that's you, is it?'

'No. I was hoping to take a look inside. Is there anyone I can ask?'

The man had shaken his head. 'The caretaker left a long time ago. We're just here to do a few emergency repairs, but when the winter's over, they're going to start on the renovations.'

'Renovations?' Kristel had asked.

'Yes. It's going to be converted into a conference centre. Now the old Count has gone, his family have sold it on. I need to get on, but did you say you wanted to have a look around?'

'Yes. I'm a journalist. I'm doing a story about what happened here during the war. It was a maternity home for the Lebensborn programme.'

'Really?' The man's eyes had widened. 'I don't know much about that, but I do know that those Nazis had some odd ideas.'

He had pulled the door back and Kristel stepped inside the vaulted hall. Again, it was just as Margarete had described, with high ceilings and a wide oak staircase rising up to a galleried hallway above.

'Look, I don't want to waste your time now,' Kristel said, 'but would it be all right if I came back later on today with a couple of others? There's an old lady who worked here during the war and her carer. It would be really useful if they could come along with me.'

The man shrugged. 'I don't see why not. It's not going to be like this for much longer, everything's going to be ripped out and replaced. So, if you want to see it how it is now...'

'All right, I'll let them know. They will take a few hours to get here, so shall we say early afternoon?'

She'd called Lorenzo straight away and he'd told her that Ginetta was happy for him to drive Margarete up there. Margarete herself was looking forward to the trip.

Now the minibus appeared round a bend in the road and Kristel waved. Lorenzo brought the vehicle to a stop beside her, and she got into the passenger seat.

'I'm so pleased you made it,' she said and turned round to greet Margarete, who was sitting in the back, wrapped up in woollen scarves and a red coat with a fur collar. She was smiling.

'I can't wait to see the castle again,' she said. 'But I've got so many mixed feelings. It's the last place I was with Tomas, but so many terrible things happened there too. I'm grateful to you both for making this happen.'

Kristel directed Lorenzo along the road beside the lake, through the castle entrance and up the winding drive. They hardly spoke on that short journey, Kristel was deep in thought about the upcoming visit to the castle and she guessed that the others were too. After some tricky moments on the ice, they finally arrived in the courtyard and Lorenzo parked the minibus beside the builder's van.

It took a while to manoeuvre Margarete out of the back and into her wheelchair. Lorenzo had also brought her Zimmer frame. He'd explained to Kristel that Margarete was able to walk but only a few steps at a time and was very slow on her feet. Lorenzo pushed the wheelchair up to the castle entrance and Kristel pulled the bell. When the builder opened the door, Lorenzo lifted Margarete's wheelchair up the steps and into the great castle hall.

Kristel noticed that Margarete's face was wet with tears. Her heart ached for her. It must be an incredibly emotional moment, she realised, for Margarete to be back here at Schloss Schwanburg. She took Margarete's hand and squeezed it.

Margarete fumbled with a handkerchief and dabbed her eyes. Then she said, 'Would you take me along that passage, please? That's where Doctor Finkel's office was, and where mine was too.'

Lorenzo pushed the wheelchair and Kristel walked beside it, holding Margarete's hand. They reached a door on the left side of the passage.

'This is it,' Margarete said, her voice tremulous. Kristel noticed there was fear in her eyes too.

The door handle was stiff, and Kristel had to put her hip to the door and shove for it to open. She pushed it wide enough open for the wheelchair to go through. Once inside, Kristel stared around her. The room was just as Margarete had described, with shelves full of books on one side, a desk on the other and a sink with a cupboard underneath it in the corner.

'Holge must have kept it like this,' Margarete said, 'though I expect all the records will have gone. He would have burned them that day everyone was leaving. They knew that the Allies were only a few miles away and were about to overrun the place.'

Kristel went to the desk and pulled the drawers open one by one. They were all empty, with only weevils and sawdust inside. The cupboard under the sink was empty too.

They left Doctor Finkel's room and went into the room next door, which was laid out in the same way, although a little smaller.

Margarete looked around her. 'This is where I did it,' she said. 'Copied out all those details. I was terrified of discovery at the time, but if I'd known it would all come to nothing, I might not have taken the risk. At the time, it felt as though I was doing something important.'

'It was important,' Kristel insisted. 'To have kept that one notebook was a feat of bravery.'

They left her office and carried on through the neglected rooms – the dining room with a huge trestle table dominating the space, and beyond that, down a tiled passage, was the kitchen, complete with ranges, still and cold, scrubbed wooden tables and many cupboards and shelves, which now stood empty.

They completed the tour of the ground floor and returned to the hallway, reaching the bottom of the great staircase. Margarete looked wistfully up the stairs.

'I would like to show you the nursery and delivery suite, but I don't think I could climb the stairs.'

'Why don't you take a look, Kristel?' Lorenzo suggested. 'I can wait here with Margarete.'

Kristel agreed and climbed the stairs with trepidation. Despite the passage of years, there was an atmosphere about the place that was chilling. The castle had never shaken off its Nazi past, probably because so little had changed in the building since those days. She could almost see the SS officers climbing these stairs, young girls on their arms, Holge Schwartz lurking in the corridors and Doctor Finkel strutting about with his clipboard.

She reached the top, turned right and walked to the end of the corridor, just as Margarete had described, pushing open a creaking door, there was the nursery. Five empty cots stood on each side of the room, with rusting metal bars. She felt shivers go through her; she was back there, in the 1940s, experiencing Margarete's story once again.

She pushed open a door at the side and went into a smaller room with armchairs ranged around the walls. This must be the nursing room, where Hedda would have sat to feed her baby for the last time before her failed attempt to leave the castle with her. Kristel thought about sitting down on one of the chairs, then decided against it. They looked filthy, with years of accumulated dust and cobwebs on the frayed cushions. There was mould too, a big brown piece growing out of the wall beside the window.

With a shudder, she left the room and crossed the nursery to the delivery room. There was the austere bed in the middle of the room. Kristel pictured the antiquated birthing stirrups that would have once dangled there. This place was the most chilling of all; she could almost hear the screams of the teenage mothers giving birth without pain relief. Under Doctor Finkel and Nurse Ekert's sadistic Nazi regime. She didn't linger here, but went straight downstairs, where Margarete and Lorenzo were still waiting in the hallway.

'What was it like?' Lorenzo asked.

'Horrible,' she said with a shudder. 'Nothing has been moved since 1945 by the looks of things.'

Then Kristel had an idea. If nothing had been moved in the nursery, perhaps that might apply to other parts of the castle too.

'Let's take a look in the cellars,' she said. 'I noticed a staircase at the end of that passageway.'

They retraced their steps down the long passage, past Doctor Finkel and Margarete's old offices, Lorenzo pushing the wheelchair once again. At the end, a stone spiral staircase led down to the cellars.

'Do you want to wait here with Lorenzo?' Kristel asked Margarete. To her surprise, Margarete shook her head.

'No. This time I want to come with you.'

Lorenzo helped her to get out of the wheelchair and then, with Kristel holding one arm and Lorenzo the other, they walked slowly down the steps. The place smelled of damp and the walls were dripping with moisture. It took a long time to get to the bottom. Each step was clearly an enormous effort for Margarete and once or twice she almost slipped. Once they reached the bottom, she guided them along the underground passage one step at a time until they reached a room right at the end. The door had obviously been kicked in – it was hanging off its hinges.

'That would have been the Allied soldiers. They must have come down here to arrest the remaining SS officers, shortly after I left,' Margarete said. 'This was the room where the officer held me at gunpoint. They were probably all cowering in here when the Allies arrived.'

Inside the office stood an old wooden desk, covered in dust and cobwebs and a broken chair. Her heart pounding with anticipation, Kristel pulled the desk drawers out one by one but each time she was disappointed. There was nothing in these drawers except dirt and mould.

'I'm sorry, Margarete, there's nothing here,' she said.

'Let's search the place thoroughly, shall we?' Lorenzo said. 'It's the only chance we'll have.'

He began running his hands over the damp walls, poking his fingers into the crevices.

'I'm looking to see if anything has been stuffed into the walls,' he explained and Kristel joined in. On the back wall was a ventilation shaft, similar to the one Margarete had climbed up in order to escape.

'I'll look in here,' Kristel said, heaving herself up into the shaft. She could see rays of light from the castle grounds filtering down from the top of the shaft, but where she knelt was in darkness. She felt all around and was about to give up and jump down again when her hands came upon a channel or a frame that went all around the shaft, lined with an iron bar. Perhaps there had once been a shutter or a window there. She ran her hand around it and in one corner felt something blocking it. She prised it out and held it up to the light. Her heart beat even faster. It was an exercise book without a cover. It had been rolled up and shoved into the groove in the shaft.

With shaking hands, Kristel clambered back into the room with the book and dusted herself down.

'Look what I found,' she said, holding the book out to Margarete.

Margarete gasped and took it from Kristel with trembling hands. Slowly and carefully, she unrolled it and peered at the faded ink, her eyes wide with shock. It was covered in mould, but the two columns of Margarete's faded handwriting could still just about be made out.

'It's the second notebook,' Margarete said through tears of joy, her voice incredulous. 'That SS officer must have hidden it up there just before the Allies came. He must have known it was incriminating. How can I ever thank you, Kristel?'

TWENTY-NINE

KRISTEL

Trento, 2005

Progress was slow, but once they were back in Trento, Lorenzo managed to track down pre-war editions of *The Great Gatsby* and *Death in Venice* from an online bookseller in Germany. Once the books had arrived, Margarete began to decode the names and addresses of the adoptive parents of the Lebensborn babies, then match them to the list of children in her first notebook. It took her a long time – her eyesight was failing and she had to use thick glasses and a magnifying glass – but she stuck at her task relentlessly. Kristel could see how determined she was to make the discovery of the second notebook count.

As soon as each complete set of details was ready, Kristel would send them through to the production team in Munich. They would then begin the process of tracking down the parents and children she had listed. It was far from easy. Most people would have moved or changed their names, and many may have died. After some discussion, the production team decided that they wouldn't automatically put parents and children in touch with each other. Instead, when the research was complete, they planned to put an appeal out on TV and let people come forward if they wanted to. If both parties were willing, they would put them in touch. That way, they wouldn't be invading anyone's privacy.

Michel, Kristel's producer, was delighted with the results.

'It's taken a while, Kristel, but I knew if I left you to it down in Trento, something brilliant would emerge. And I was right! I'm scheduling a programme in the next month or so to tell the world about the notebooks and about Margarete Weiss's part in all this. And I'd like you to present it.'

Out of curiosity, and to help speed things up, Kristel went daily to Our Lady of Mercy to help Margarete with her decoding. Margarete explained to Kristel how her system worked and then they would each take an entry in turn to decode. About a week into the work, Kristel came across a name that looked familiar to her: Hedda Jenner.

She stared at it, knowing that this was the girl Margarete had been telling her about. The girl Margarete had tried to help and had failed.

It was tricky, but with a lot of concentration, Kristel went on to decode the name and address where Hedda's baby girl had been sent. She couldn't breathe and her hand shook. She stared down at the address in Dammkarstrasse, Mittenwald.

Shock coursed through her. It was the address of her own adoptive grandparents.

She had to go back and check that she was correct several times. She stared down at the words on the page for a long time in disbelief, recalling her visit to the village and to the big old house, and the story the housekeeper had told her about her SS grandparents and her mother's unhappy childhood there.

Lorenzo happened to be in the office that day and he came and put his arms around her shoulders. They'd grown very close since her return from Munich, although neither had talked about it or tried to label it.

'What's the matter?' he asked gently. 'You look as though you've seen a ghost.'

She looked up at him. 'This is my mother's parents' address. I can hardly believe it, Lorenzo.'

'So, does that mean...'

'Yes. It means that Hedda was my grandmother. And my mother was once called Evelina.'

Kristel was dumbstruck that the woman Margarete knew as Hedda was likely to be her grandmother. But then she remembered the final details of Hedda's story and her initial euphoria evaporated. Margarete had told her that Hedda had taken her own life when she'd come back from Schloss Schwanburg so there was no chance of her being alive and of reuniting Greta with her long-lost mother.

Kristel showed the results of her decoding to Margarete. 'That is my grandparents' address,' she said, pointing to the address in Mittenwald. 'Hedda Jenner was my grandmother.' Her voice was shaking, she could hardly contain her emotions; there was sadness there, but excitement too.

'Oh, Kristel!' Margarete was stunned. 'You never told me that your mother was in Lebensborn! Is that how you came to be interested in the subject?'

'Yes,' she admitted. 'At first, I wanted answers for myself, but the more I discovered, the more questions there were to be answered. And the more I realised that this work could potentially be of benefit to many others too.'

'You know, when I first saw you,' Margarete said, 'you looked so familiar to me. I thought it was because you had blonde hair and blue eyes and that you looked so much like all the girls who came to Schloss Schwanburg. I never realised it was Hedda you looked like but now I can see her look in your eyes. How extraordinary! But what a sad, sad story.'

'It is. It's such a tragedy that Hedda died. I'll never get to meet her now, but at least I have some sort of explanation about my mother's past.'

'Are you going to tell your mother?'

'Yes. Yes, I think I need to. But it will take a lot of courage.'

That evening, Kristel talked it over with Lorenzo. They were having dinner together in a tiny cellar bistro in one of the medieval backstreets of Trento. Since they'd been back in Trento, they had eaten together every evening. Afterwards, they'd walked back to her hotel, their arms entwined, and they had kissed goodnight tenderly and lovingly. Each time he had left her at the door to her room and returned to his parents' apartment.

'We have all the time in the world, Kristel,' he said. 'Let's not rush into this.'

She knew he was right. There was no point rushing into bed together, especially since her split from Joachim was so recent. It was wonderful, getting to know Lorenzo in a slow, leisurely way. He was like no one she had ever known before and every day she learned something new about him, something that deepened and strengthened her love for him, for she already knew it was love.

He was as stunned as Kristel at her news about Hedda.

'It makes everything you've done here – this quest – all the more worthwhile,' he said, kissing her hand and looking tenderly into her eyes.

'Yes. It's so sad that she died, though. I've sent her details through to the researchers on the programme. I've asked them to let me know if they find any details of her death. Obviously, she would have died in Munich, sometime in early 1944, so they should be able to track down a death certificate. Although so many people were dying at that time, in air raids and on the battlefronts, perhaps not all deaths were properly certified.'

'I hope they are able to find some confirmation. It would be good to know for sure, to have some closure,' Lorenzo said.

'I'm going to find out as much about Hedda as I can,' Kristel vowed. 'It's amazing that she grew up and lived in Munich. I've lived there my whole life too. She must have known the same places I know. There are so many parallels.'

'And what about your mother? Are you going to tell her what you've discovered?'

Kristel sighed. 'I really want to, but I'm worried about how she will take it.'

'It must be hard, but don't you think she has a right to know?' he asked gently.

'Yes, I suppose she does. She doesn't have any plans to come to Europe for a while, and I can't really afford either the time or the money to go to America right now, so I suppose I will have to break the news over the phone. I just hope she doesn't hang up on me.'

'You're very brave, Kristel,' Lorenzo said, smiling into her eyes.

'I will call her when I get back to the hotel,' Kristel said emphatically. Talking about it with Lorenzo had given her courage.

Later that evening, back in her room, still feeling buoyed by the goodbye kiss with Lorenzo, she picked up her mobile phone and called her mother's number. Greta picked up straight away, but sounded surprised to hear from her.

'I've got something I want to talk about. Have you got a few minutes?' Kristel asked.

'Yes. It's the middle of the afternoon here and I have a free period. Fire away.'

Kristel took a deep breath and told her about her visit to Mittenwald the previous year. She described what the house-keeper had told her about Greta's father.

'Some of the things she said made me convinced that you

were adopted,' she finished. 'And when I started to look into adoptions during the war, I discovered the Lebensborn programme.'

She heard a sharp intake of breath from Greta on the other end of the line, but her mother didn't interrupt her, and she didn't hang up either, and that spurred Kristel on.

'I've been looking into it for the news network, Mutti. We've already done one programme about it, which was very successful. Since then, I've been interviewing a lady who was a nurse for the Lebensborn programme, but who tried to help people by noting down the names and addresses of the babies and their adoptive parents. And, Mutti...' Kristel paused, and she could sense her mother holding her breath, 'I think I've found out who your mother was. This lady, Margarete Weiss, knew her. Her birth name was Hedda Jenner.'

There was a long silence from Greta, but finally, when Kristel was wondering whether she had hung up, she spoke, in a voice cracking with emotion.

'This is unbelievable. How can you be sure about that, Kristel?'

'I'm not completely, but I think I am.' She paused and took a deep breath before breaking the next, monumental news. 'I'm afraid I was also told that Hedda had died, towards the end of the war, but I'm trying to find her death certificate at the moment.'

'Oh,' Greta said, sounding deflated. 'That's very sad.'

'It is... Did you know that you were Lebensborn?' Kristel asked after another pause. She was a little worried about how Greta might respond to this direct question. There had always been distance between them and she realised that her mother might clam up at that point.

'I'd suspected I was adopted from a very early age. I was so different from my parents. Polar opposites. When I was a child, I found some letters in my parents' belongings which referred to

me as being adopted. But I didn't know anything about Lebensborn until much later. I pleaded with my mother and father to
tell me where I'd come from, who my real parents were, but
they flatly refused to tell me anything. They just said I was part
of the SS family and that I should be content with that.

'The housekeeper you spoke to was right about my father.
He was one of the town officials in Mittenwald and they did
many terrible, cruel things in the town. I was ashamed to be
associated with him. I was glad that I wasn't his blood child.
That was the only thing that gave me some sort of hope for the
future. I comforted myself that in all likelihood my real parents
had been good people.

'When the Allies took over after the war, my parents went
through a de-Nazification programme. Somehow – and I've
never quite worked out how – they managed to avoid being
hanged or sent to prison for their crimes. I was so ashamed of
them. When I got the chance to go to university, I never went
back to see them.

'When my mother died though, I returned to the house and
did a thorough search through her paperwork. I discovered a
Lebensborn adoption certificate in her desk drawer. It stated
that I was born at Schloss Schwanburg in Bavaria under the
guardianship of the Lebensborn programme. There was no
mention of my mother or my father's name on the certificate.

'I had no knowledge of Lebensborn or what it was, so I did
some research. I was appalled and ashamed at what I found out.
I convinced myself that I must come from evil SS stock and that
I wasn't fit to be a mother. These thoughts went round and
round in my mind and took root there. I told Frank that I
couldn't be a wife or a mother any longer, that evil blood ran in
my veins. He tried to change my mind and to get me to stay, but
I wouldn't listen to him. I know I broke his heart when I left. I
broke my own too.'

'And mine,' said Kristel. 'I'll never forget that day.'

'I know. I'm so sorry, Kristel, but I was convinced that I was doing you a favour by leaving you and distancing myself from you. I really thought I wasn't fit to be a mother. For the rest of my life, I've been convinced that I have these evil Nazi genes. That's why I purposely kept out of your life.

'But Frank and I had an agreement. He would keep in touch with me and send me news and photos of you whenever he could, and he kept that promise to the end of his life.'

Kristel could hear the sadness in her mother's voice.

'I wish you'd told me all this before, Mutti,' Kristel said, her eyes filling with tears at the thought of all the years they had lost.

'I was too ashamed, Kristel. Far too ashamed. I thought you would reject me. And I wouldn't have blamed you. I felt I wasn't worthy of any human relationships, which is why I've been alone all these years. I'm so sorry. I've been such a coward, I know.'

'Of course you're not a coward but I'm glad I know the truth now. And I'm glad we've had this chat. We still have time to make up for all those lost years.'

THIRTY

HEDDA

Munich, 2005

Hedda was babysitting Leon when Kristel Meyer's second news report came on the television. She'd looked after him many times over the past month. He knew her well now and her heart sang to see his little face light up when he saw her. He would hold his chubby arms out to be picked up by her and would gurgle with pleasure when she took him into her arms.

She was glad to be able to help poor Inge a little. She knew the young woman was fragile and found it hard to cope. Her partner was a drunk and constantly out of work. He was of little help to her. Over the weeks, Inge had confided in Hedda about her childhood. She'd had little chance, the daughter of two alcoholics, both of whom had died when she was a child. She'd been in and out of foster homes since the age of ten. As a teenager, she'd dipped out of school and had got into drugs and bad company. Her story reminded Hedda a little of some of the people in her aunt's apartment block.

She thought about Ursula and Edward wistfully sometimes. Their apartment block had been razed to the ground in an air raid in 1944 and there had been few survivors. When she'd returned to Munich after Hari's death, she had found their graves. She would go there to put flowers on them from time to time. It made her especially sad to think that her young cousins had never had the chance to grow up, to have families of their own and to live normal lives. There was so much death and destruction unleashed by the Nazis. Hedda herself felt she had been singled out for even more than most, but she knew she wasn't alone in her suffering.

After the first time Inge had left Leon with Hedda, she often asked Hedda to look after him for an hour or two. When she came to collect him, they would sit and chat over a coffee. Hedda never offered Inge anything stronger. In fact, since she'd been looking after Leon, she had given up her regular tipples of Schnapps herself. She'd already noticed that her weight had dropped a few kilograms, she was feeling healthier, and more energised and her cheeks had more colour in them.

As well as listening to Inge's story, Hedda had found herself confiding in Inge in return. She'd never told anyone about her experiences at the hands of the Lebensborn programme before. Especially not Hari. She wondered now if their marriage might have survived if she had been able to tell him about her lost baby daughter. But Inge was curious as to why, when Hedda said she had a daughter, she never had any family come to visit her and had no grandchildren of her own. In the end, Hedda had decided to tell her the truth, and through telling it to someone else for the first time in her life, she felt a great weight lift from her shoulders.

She also told Inge about Kristel Meyer's news report and how she had wanted to call up the network and tell her story. She described how she'd even picked the phone up and dialled the number but had not had the courage to see it through.

'You should do it,' Inge urged. 'What do you have to lose?

You might find something out. At the very least you would be able to tell your story to the world.'

'I'm not sure I want to...' Hedda mused.

'Oh, you definitely should,' Inge said fiercely. 'It's an important story, it should be told.'

Inge was there having a chat and a coffee when the second Lebensborn report was aired on *Nachricht* 24.

'I hope you don't mind if I put this programme on,' Hedda asked her. 'I saw in the newspaper that they were doing another report on Lebensborn and I really want to watch it.'

'Of course. I'd like to see it too, if you don't mind me staying for a while?'

Hedda looked over at Inge and smiled at her. She'd grown quite fond of this strange, tense girl with her bleached hair and hard, pinched face. She knew that Inge had a determined heart, a will to survive and do her best by Leon, despite her terrible circumstances, and Hedda admired that in her. 'I'd love you to stay.'

The signature tune faded, and Kristel Meyer came on the screen and began her report.

'Since we last spoke about Lebensborn a few weeks ago,' she said, 'we have been inundated with calls from people who have been affected by the programme one way or another – either as a parent or as a child – who have been desperately searching for their relatives. Often, although more information has been emerging about the programme in recent years, their efforts have been thwarted because the Nazis destroyed so many records at the end of the war. They did so in an effort to prevent them falling into Allied hands, so the truth of this cruel programme might never be known.

'But one woman bravely came forward, who herself made courageous efforts to defy the Nazis and to preserve those records for future generations. Margarete Weiss was a nurse in the Lebensborn programme. She worked at Schloss Schwanburg in southern Bavaria, a maternity home where many Lebensborn babies were born. At great personal risk to herself, Margarete made notes in a code that she developed herself, of mothers and babies, and of the adoptive parents those babies were sent to. We have started work decoding those records, having only discovered Margarete's second notebook very recently.

'If you think you or a member of your family might be in Margarete's notebook, please do come forward and we should be able to help you and provide you with more information. The lines are open now and our researchers are waiting for your call.

'In the meantime, here's my interview with Margarete, who will tell you in her own words what life was like working in the Lebensborn programme.'

Hedda watched, her mouth open, as Margarete came on the screen and began to talk, slowly and deliberately, about her life and work at Schloss Schwanburg.

Hedda was amazed to see Margarete on screen. She looked so old now, her beautiful face was a little drawn and thin and her hair was grey. She was seated in a wing-backed chair in what looked like a care home.

'I knew her!' Hedda exclaimed to Inge.

'Really? How incredible.'

'Yes. She tried to help me. I told you about her.'

'That's Margarete? The kind nurse you spoke about?'

'Yes.' Hedda realised her eyes were welling with tears. 'She must be ninety-odd now. That's her, Inge – in that photo I showed you on the mantlepiece.'

Inge peered at the photograph of the two of them in the garden with baby Evelina. 'I can see the resemblance now you mention it.'

When the interview with Margarete had finished, Kristel came back on the screen. 'So, if you have a connection with the

Lebensborn programme, if you are looking for answers and want us to help you, particularly if you were born or gave birth at Schloss Schwanburg, please do give us a call. Our lines are open now and we are waiting to hear from you. And now my report is coming to a close, I will be helping out on the lines myself so I'm looking forward to taking your call.'

The number flashed on the screen again and then the main presenter was back to wrap up the programme.

Hedda saw that Inge had pulled a pen and pad out of her bag and was scribbling something.

'I've made a note of the number for you,' she said. 'You are going to call in now, aren't you? You really must.'

Hedda looked at her and the fire of determination in her eyes. Inge was right: what did she have to lose? She had lost everything back then, hadn't she? Evelina was still in her mind so much, though. She often wondered where she was and even if she was still alive.

'All right. I will do it now before I change my mind,' she said. 'But you'll have to hold Leon.'

He had fallen asleep in her arms, and she handed him carefully over to Inge so as not to wake him. Then she stood up and, her nerves jangling in her stomach, went over to the sideboard and lifted the receiver. Inge slid the piece of paper with the number in front of her and she dialled it with ease. She had virtually memorised it, she had been on the point of dialling it so many times before.

It didn't ring for long, then there was a click and an operator answered. Haltingly, Hedda told her a little about herself and the voice said, 'I will put you straight through to Kristel Meyer. I'm sure she would be interested in your story. Please hold the line.'

The line went dead and Hedda waited, her heart pounding. Had she been cut off? If she had, she wasn't sure she'd have the courage to call again. It was only a couple of minutes, but it felt like hours when at last, a familiar voice came on the line.

'This is Kristel Meyer at *Nachricht* 24. This is the Lebensborn helpline. How can I help you?'

Hedda opened her mouth to speak and she was so nervous she thought the words would never come. She had to swallow twice and when the words eventually did come, her voice sounded hoarse.

'My name is Hedda. I was Hedda Jenner. I gave birth aged eighteen at Schloss Schwanburg in Bavaria in September 1943. I had a beautiful baby girl, and I was forced to give her up. I've thought about her every day since, and I would dearly love to know what happened to her.'

There was a stunned silence at the other end of the line and Hedda thought something must have happened to the call, but in a few moments, Kristel cleared her throat and Hedda heard her saying, in a choked voice, 'Hedda? Hedda Jenner? I can hardly believe it! I think you are my grandmother!'

EPILOGUE

KRISTEL

Munich, 2005

Kristel stood waiting in the arrivals hall in Munich airport. She kept standing on tiptoe, trying to see over the heads of emerging passengers. The arrivals board showed that Greta's plane had landed. She would be coming through those sliding doors very soon.

Kristel was standing between Hedda and Lorenzo and happiness oozed from every pore in her body. She couldn't stop smiling. Each time she turned her head and looked into Lorenzo's eyes, she was overcome with love for him. It was a month since they'd first made love and her heart was overflowing. She knew, in the depths of her being that she wanted to be with him for the rest of her life and she knew that he felt the same way about her too.

Hedda stood on the other side of Kristel, their arms linking. Since the first time they'd met, a couple of weeks before, they had spent a lot of time together and had got to know one another quite well. Hedda had told Kristel her extraordinary story. Kristel had been humbled by her grandmother's steadfastness and courage in the face of so much tragedy.

She had been to visit Hedda's flat in Munich and Hedda had shown her some photographs from when she was young. Kristel had gasped, seeing the similarities between Greta and Hedda and also with herself. They had spent an afternoon poring over some old sepia photographs of Hedda's mother and sister and her father. Hedda had shed tears when she spoke about them and told Kristel how they'd lost their lives in a bombing raid.

'I only have these photos because my aunt had them. Everything in our house was completely destroyed.'

'And what about my grandfather?' Kristel had asked when the time felt right. 'Sebastian?'

Hedda had shaken her head. 'I never heard from him again, not after he left the castle that day, nor did I want to, but I did read after the war that his entire unit had been wiped out by the Red Army in Belarus so it is doubtful that he survived the war.'

'Did you regret your relationship with him?' Kristel couldn't help asking.

After some thought, Hedda had replied, 'No. Together we gave life to a beautiful baby girl. But, beyond that, I know he was indoctrinated by Nazi propaganda when he joined the army. Early on, after I lost my family, he was kind to me. He picked me up and he was the only reason I managed to carry on. So, there are good memories along with the bad.'

Kristel's one regret over the past few weeks was that, despite encouragement, Margarete had been unwilling to speak about her own daughter, and Kristel was no nearer finding out what had happened to her. And Margarete hadn't wanted to speak about her time in Norway or about when she returned to Germany to work in the 'Germanisation' facility either.

But Kristel had made a promise to visit Margarete whenever she was in Trento, which was going to be often – at least until

Lorenzo found a job in Munich and came to live with her. Her fervent hope was that, one day soon, Margarete would feel able to tell her about what had happened to her after she left Schloss Schwanburg in 1944. In the meantime, Margarete's notebooks were helping dozens of people become reunited with their birth families. Kristel knew that Margarete was overwhelmed with emotion at the thought that the risks she had taken during her time at Schloss Schwanburg hadn't been for nothing.

Kristel spotted an elegant blonde head and a fashionable red leather jacket heading towards them through the crowd and her heart missed a beat. She slid her arm out of Lorenzo's and waved madly.

'Mutti! Mutti! We are over here!'

Greta gave a quick wave and shouldered her way towards them. Then, putting her bag down, she embraced Kristel more warmly than she'd ever done before and kissed her on the cheek. Kristel didn't know if it was her tears or Greta's that made their cheeks wet.

'This is Lorenzo, Mutti,' she said and Lorenzo shook Greta's hand and mouthed a quick 'hello' because they all knew that an even more important introduction had to be made. 'And this is Hedda, Mutti. Hedda Jenner. Your mother.'

The two women looked into each other's eyes for a second, then fell into each other's arms, both of them sobbing. As they hugged and Kristel watched them through tears of her own, it was almost as if the intervening years had fallen away. The overwhelming love instantly apparent between them must have been there all the time, waiting in abeyance, throughout those long, cruel years of separation, for the time when they might be reunited.

A LETTER FROM ANN

I want to say a huge thank you for choosing to read *The Orphan List*. If you enjoyed it and would like to keep up to date with my latest releases, please sign up at the following link. Your email address will not be shared and you may unsubscribe at any time.

www.bookouture.com/ann-bennett

I hope you loved *The Orphan List* and if you did, I'd be very grateful if you could write a review. I'd love to hear what you think and it makes such a difference and helps new readers to discover my books for the first time.

I love hearing from readers – you can get in touch through social media or my website.

Thanks,

Ann

facebook.com/annbennettauthor

x.com/annbennett71

ACKNOWLEDGEMENTS

I'd like to thank my friend, Fiona Conoley, for recommending the book, *Wolfram, The Boy Who Went to War*, from which I got the first seeds of an idea for this story. I'd also like to thank my husband, Nick, for all his support, especially for coming with me to Munich and Füssen to visit Schloss Neuschwanstein and Schloss Hohenschwangau, inspirations for the fictional Schloss Schwanburg in the book. I learned so much on that trip, especially from our visit to the National Socialist – Dokumentationszentrum museum, and from a fascinating, if freezing, walking tour around Munich to see the buildings and spaces made infamous by the Nazis, organised by Radius Tours GmbH and their brilliant guide, Josh.

PUBLISHING TEAM

Turning a manuscript into a book requires the efforts of many people. The publishing team at Bookouture would like to acknowledge everyone who contributed to this publication.

Audio
Alba Proko
Sinead O'Connor
Melissa Tran

Commercial
Lauren Morrissette
Hannah Richmond
Imogen Allport

Cover design
Debbie Clement

Data and analysis
Mark Alder
Mohamed Bussuri

Editorial
Lydia Vassar-Smith
Lizzie Brien

Printed in Great Britain
by Amazon

46578607R00192